DEADLY TRAP

Off The Grid: FBI Series

BARBARA FREETHY

BARBARA
FREETHY
—BOOKS—

Fog City Publishing

PRAISE FOR BARBARA FREETHY

"Barbara Freethy's first book PERILOUS TRUST in her OFF THE GRID series is an emotional, action packed, crime drama that keeps you on the edge of your seat...I'm exhausted after reading this but in a good way. 5 Stars!" — *Booklovers Anonymous*

"A fabulous, page-turning combination of romance and intrigue. Fans of Nora Roberts and Elizabeth Lowell will love this book." — *NYT Bestselling Author Kristin Hannah on Golden Lies*

"PERILOUS TRUST is a non-stop thriller that seamlessly melds jaw-dropping suspense with sizzling romance. Readers will be breathless in anticipation as this fast-paced and enthralling love story goes in unforeseeable directions." — *USA Today HEA Blog*

"Powerful and absorbing...sheer hold-your-breath suspense." — *NYT Bestselling Author Karen Robards on Don't Say A Word*

"I loved this story from start to finish. Right from the start of PERILOUS TRUST, the tension sets in. Goodness, my heart was starting to beat a little fast by the end of the prologue! I found myself staying up late finishing this book, and that is something I don't normally do." — *My Book Filled Life Blog*

"Freethy hits the ground running as she kicks off another winning romantic suspense series...Freethy is at her prime with a superb combo of engaging characters and gripping plot." — *Publishers' Weekly on Silent Run*

PRAISE FOR BARBARA FREETHY

"Grab a drink, find a comfortable reading nook, and get immersed in this fast paced, realistic, romantic thriller! 5 STARS!" *Perrin – Goodreads on Elusive Promise*

"Words cannot explain how phenomenal this book was. The characters are so believable and relatable. The twists and turns keep you on the edge of your seat and flying through the pages. This is one book you should be desperate to read." *Caroline - Goodreads on Ruthless Cross*

"Barbara Freethy is a master storyteller with a gift for spinning tales about ordinary people in extraordinary situations and drawing readers into their lives." — *Romance Reviews Today*

"Freethy (Silent Fall) has a gift for creating complex, appealing characters and emotionally involving, often suspenseful, sometimes magical stories." — *Library Journal on Suddenly One Summer*

Freethy hits the ground running as she kicks off another winning romantic suspense series...Freethy is at her prime with a superb combo of engaging characters and gripping plot." — *Publishers' Weekly on Silent Run*

"If you love nail-biting suspense and heartbreaking emotion, Silent Run belongs on the top of your to-be-bought list. I could not turn the pages fast enough." — *NYT Bestselling Author Mariah Stewart*

DEADLY TRAP

FBI agent Nick Caruso races to Rome to rescue his grandmother from imminent danger, only to collide head-on with Isabella Rossi—a woman with whom he once shared a disastrous date. Isabella, a secretive journalist, adds friction to their uneasy partnership as they delve into the murky world of smuggling and stolen art to safeguard their grandmothers.

From Rome's historic streets to boutique art galleries and opulent villas, DEADLY TRAP is a pulse-pounding romantic suspense novel that seamlessly blends Italy's allure with high-stakes crime, testing love and loyalty amidst deception and peril.

Will they expose the criminals in time, or will the deadly trap claim them all?

ALSO BY BARBARA FREETHY

OFF THE GRID: FBI SERIES

PERILOUS TRUST

RECKLESS WHISPER

DESPERATE PLAY

ELUSIVE PROMISE

DANGEROUS CHOICE

RUTHLESS CROSS

CRITICAL DOUBT

FEARLESS PURSUIT

DARING DECEPTION

RISKY BARGAIN

PERFECT TARGET

FATAL BETRAYAL

DEADLY TRAP

LETHAL GAME

Did you read the Lightning Strikes Series?

Lightning Strikes Trilogy

BEAUTIFUL STORM

LIGHTNING LINGERS

SUMMER RAIN

For a complete list of books, visit Barbara's Website!

DEADLY TRAP

———

For more information on Barbara Freethy's books, visit her website:
www.barbarafreethy.com

PROLOGUE

Family pride was something Anna Caruso hadn't felt in a long time, mostly because her family was small now and scattered across several continents. But standing in one of the exhibition rooms at the Museo dei Capolavori in Rome and watching a group of visitors linger in front of her father-in-law's painting with awe in their eyes, sent a wave of heartwarming satisfaction through her.

Anna wasn't one to dwell on the past or the future, especially not at eighty-one years of age. She preferred to live in the present, but this exhibition had brought the past, the present, and the future together, and the niggling doubts she'd had about donating the painting to the exhibition had been erased by the flood of positive remarks she'd heard over the past two days. So many visitors had wondered why they hadn't heard about Tomas Caruso before. They'd marveled at his talent and thought it was a shame he had not been recognized in his own time.

That was her father-in-law's fault. Tomas had been a brilliant artist, but also a perfectionist. Nothing was ever good enough for him to show, which was partly why she'd worried that putting his work up now was some sort of betrayal. But that was foolish.

Tomas had been dead for fifty-plus years. It was past time for him to have his artistic brilliance recognized.

"I thought I'd find you in here," Gloria Rossi said, coming up next to her.

She smiled at her long-time friend. They'd met at twenty-one, sixty years ago, as American art students spending a summer studying in Rome. Back then, she'd been blonde while Gloria had had dark-brown hair. Now her hair was white, and Gloria's was silver. Their youthful bodies had disappeared ages ago, and the two men they'd married had both passed on.

Gloria's husband Paolo had died eight years ago, while her Marcus had been gone for a year. She pushed back the familiar stabbing sadness that came with memories of her tall, strong husband, who had loved her for over fifty years.

"I can't seem to leave," she said.

Gloria gave her a smile of understanding. "I've been sneaking in here whenever I can, too."

Gloria also worked as a docent at the museum. Their love of art still drove their lives even after so many years, not that either of them had ever been accomplished enough to put a painting on the wall of a museum. But Gloria had donated her mother-in-law's work, and Lucinda Rossi's painting hung next to the one by Tomas. It seemed fitting. Lucinda and Tomas had been the closest of friends and had both died too young.

"Their paintings have been well-received," Gloria said. "Did you read the review of the exhibition in the paper? Tomas's painting was featured. You should be proud."

"I am," she said, but she couldn't hide the worry in her voice. "I just hope I didn't make a mistake. Tomas wanted his painting hidden away, and Marcus was so protective of his father's art."

"You need to stop feeling guilty, Anna. You did what you thought was right, and you'll never know what they would have thought, so you can only think about how you feel."

"I feel proud," she admitted.

"So do I." Gloria returned her gaze to the wall. "Their paintings are so focused, one a beautiful tree with a colorful bird building its nest. The other a series of steps leading into the light at one end and the darkness at another. They seem simple and yet profound."

"Signoras?"

She turned her head as Enrique, the security guard, told them it was time to go. He needed to lock up and turn on the alarm system.

They'd already kept him waiting, so she gave him an apologetic smile and quickly headed to the door, with Gloria on her heels.

The exhibition room was on the second floor of the two-story building, and the hallway lights had already been dimmed, but they knew the museum so well, from the vast rooms on the first floor to the smaller exhibition rooms on the second floor, that they had no problem making their way to the employees' lounge, which was also located upstairs.

"I think we should treat ourselves to dinner and a good bottle of wine," Gloria said.

"Like we do every night?" she asked with a laugh. Their love of art was only equaled by their love of wine.

"Well, we don't eat out every night. Let's go to Valentino's."

"Sounds good to me. But I do want to call Nick at some point tonight. Don't let me forget."

Gloria raised a questioning brow. "Is everything okay with your grandson?"

"I think so, but I left him a message about the exhibition several days ago, and he never called me back. He's probably just busy at work, but I worry about him when he's out of touch, which seems more often these days. I wish he hadn't gone into the FBI, especially since he rarely seems to be at a desk. He's always in the field, doing God knows what. I would have liked to get his blessing on putting the painting in the exhibition. But I couldn't wait for him to get back to me."

"I doubt he'd have a problem with it," Gloria said. "I'm sure he would have told you to do what you think is best."

"I suppose so. I also worry that he might still be angry about us setting up him and Isabella a few months ago."

Gloria waved a dismissive hand in the air. "That's silly. It was just a dinner."

"But they didn't hit it off, and I don't understand why. They'd be perfect for each other."

"I agree, but they're both stubborn. Isabella has a fire burning inside her," Gloria said. "But I want her to have more than a career. I understand that being a journalist is important, but her job won't keep her warm at night. Of course, she tells me I don't know what it's like to be a young woman today. I can't say she's wrong, but I have lived a long life, and I know how important love is. I worry that growing up without a father, and with a grandfather who ignored her, has colored her thinking of men."

"I worry about Nick, too. He's thirty-three and spends half his life undercover, pretending to be someone else. One day he might discover the sacrifice he's making is just too big."

"Maybe we should try to get them together again," Gloria said.

"Perhaps this summer," she agreed, as they entered the lounge. "We'll have a big party for our birthdays in July and they won't be able to say no."

"Excellent idea," Gloria said, as they headed to their lockers.

After retrieving their belongings, they headed out of the lounge. They'd no sooner stepped into the hallway when they heard a shockingly loud crash that echoed through the building. It seemed to have come from the back of the museum by the delivery dock. They froze, glancing at each other as they heard thundering footsteps coming up the stairs at the other end of the hall.

She debated whether they should go back into the lounge and hide, but the lock on the door wouldn't hold anyone off, and they would be sitting ducks. She grabbed Gloria's hand, and they ran in the opposite direction. If they could get down the other stairwell, they might escape through the front door.

As gunshots rang out, coming from the area of the exhibition they'd just left, she sped up. She could hear Gloria's labored breathing, but neither one of them slowed down, even though their aging bodies weren't primed for sprinting. But fear drove them forward.

Unfortunately, they didn't seem to be getting away from the danger. Male voices rang out, seeming to come from almost every direction. She didn't know how many men had broken into the museum, but it had to be at least three.

"We can't get away," Gloria said in panic.

She agreed. "We need to hide." As the voices drew closer, she pulled Gloria behind a tall statue of a Roman warrior, hoping he would protect them. "Don't even breathe," she said, as they crouched down, holding their breath, squeezing as tightly together as they could, thankful for the dark shadows.

Two men came purposefully down the hall. As they passed in front of the statue, she could hear them talking. One word jumped out of all the rest—her last name—*Caruso*.

She must have gasped, because Gloria's fingers tightened around hers in a harsh warning.

"*L'hai sentito?*" one man asked. "*Qualcuno è qui.*"

He'd heard her gasp. He knew someone was nearby. Before his partner could answer, another voice rang out from further down the hallway. A third man was yelling at them to hurry. They had to leave now.

The men hesitated one more second and then moved away.

As they left, she peeked out from behind the statue and saw two men dressed in black pants and coats, with hoods over their heads and black gloves on their hands. One was holding a semi-automatic weapon. The other had a painting in his hand. She couldn't see what it was, but there were many valuable pieces of art in the museum. It could be anything.

But remembering how the man had said her name, she had

the terrible feeling the painting she'd just seen was the one she'd donated.

"Are they gone?" Gloria whispered.

"I hope so," she murmured.

"What do you think they wanted, Anna?"

"I heard them say Caruso." A knot of fear grew in her throat.

"I heard that, too. And one said he'll be happy; he's been waiting a long time."

"I didn't hear that, but my blood was roaring through my veins. Did you hear a name? Who's he?"

"I don't know. I couldn't catch anything else."

"I have a terrible feeling this is my fault."

"Tomas's painting can't be the reason this happened."

"What if it is?" she whispered, meeting Gloria's eyes. "Oh, God, what have I done?"

CHAPTER ONE

"You're a fake, a liar. I never should have trusted you."

The betrayal-filled accusation ran around in the head of FBI Agent Nick Caruso, along with the image of a shocked female, with pain in her eyes, a person he'd had to betray during an undercover operation. She hadn't been wrong. But he'd done what was necessary, as he always did. Still, it weighed on him.

Staring at his sleekly styled brown hair and heavily bearded face in the mirror, he saw a stranger. The expensive suit and tie that had been his uniform for the last three months only rein-forced that feeling. He felt more than ready to say goodbye to Elliot Wilmington, financial investments manager, a man who cooked the books at work and lived in a penthouse apartment at night.

While his living situation for this assignment had put him into the privileged world of the rich and famous, he still felt dirty from the immorality and criminality that had been his constant companions since he'd gone undercover to unravel a money-laundering operation.

Picking up his razor, he ruthlessly attacked his beard, then stripped off his clothes and jumped into the shower. An hour later, he was clean-shaven and wearing black jeans and a crew-neck blue sweater. But as he dried his hair, the man in the mirror still felt like a stranger. He was more himself, he supposed, but he wasn't sure who that was anymore. Too many assignments, too many months of being someone else, had taken a toll on him.

Turning away from his image, he headed into the living room of his two-bedroom apartment. It wasn't anything spectacular, but it was home—sort of. He'd moved to LA eight months ago, and for most of that time, he'd lived in other places, but he was here now.

He walked through the double glass doors leading to the deck, which was the main reason he'd rented the apartment. He had a great view of the Pacific Ocean and the Santa Monica beach.

It was after four on a Wednesday afternoon, and the sun was dropping low in the sky on this late March day but there were still plenty of people on the beach below, some even wading into the cold water. He took a deep breath and let it out. Tomorrow, he'd go for a bike ride or maybe a run, get rid of the restless feeling he couldn't seem to shake, but today he needed to think about food. His refrigerator and cupboards were bare, and he was hungry. He needed to either pick up groceries or get some fast food.

As he reentered his apartment, the sound of his doorbell startled him. He walked over to the intercom and uttered a wary, "Yes?"

"It's Flynn and Andi. Let us in," Flynn said.

He buzzed in the head of his special task force, Flynn MacKenzie and fellow agent, Andi Hart, surprised they were here. He'd planned on catching up with everyone tomorrow at the office. Something important must have come up. Maybe a new assignment.

Pushing aside his feeling of exhaustion, he put on his game face and opened the door.

Flynn and Andi stepped off the elevator and made their way

down the hall. Flynn, as usual, looked more like a surfer than the head of an elite task force, his blond hair long and wind-blown, and his attire faded jeans and a graphic T-shirt. Andi, with her dark hair and eyes, was much more put-together in gray slacks and a light-pink sweater. They were both carrying grocery bags, and he knew what this impromptu visit was about.

"You didn't have to do this." He took the bag from Andi and waved them into his apartment. "I was about to go out and get groceries."

"It's a tradition," Flynn said, as he moved toward the kitchen and set his bag on the counter. "Especially after a long under-cover assignment."

"We got a little of everything," Andi put in. "By the way, you look good, Nick. More like your old self. Are you going to miss your expensive wardrobe?"

"Not even a little bit," he replied as Flynn pulled out steaks and put them in the fridge along with the makings for a salad. "You guys went all out."

"We even bought cookie dough ice cream," Andi added as she reached into the bag he was holding and held up a carton with a cheerful smile. "Just in case you were tired of eating fancy desserts at five-star restaurants."

He smiled as he set down the bag. "I must say I've been dreaming about a burger and fries and not one with truffles, something greasy and bad for me."

"Such a sad life you've been living," she said dryly as she put the ice cream in the freezer. "On my last undercover assignment, I had to work as a waitress in the worst diner in town."

Andi was right. It hadn't been the worst assignment in terms of living conditions, but some things he'd had to watch and take part in had turned his stomach, and it took a lot for that to happen these days. But he didn't need to get into that. "I really appreciate this," he said instead.

"No problem," Flynn replied. "You helped us deliver a big

win. Many people will go to jail, and that's because of your work."

He shrugged. "It wasn't just me."

"You were on the inside, and that's always the riskiest place to be," Flynn said, a serious note in his voice.

"So, what's next?" he asked, eager to change the subject.

Flynn grinned. "For you—a break."

He wasn't sure how he felt about that. Too much time on his hands had never been good for him, either. "I'll be good to go on Monday."

"I want you to take at least a week," Flynn said. "You've been running nonstop since you joined the team eight months ago, and you haven't even finished decorating this place."

"It looks fine." He had never been that interested in putting up pictures or having anything more than a basic living space. "I don't spend much time here, anyway."

"I could help you," Andi offered. "I'm not great at decorating, but I'm better than you."

"That's a nice offer, but I don't need help."

"I used to be like you." Andi gave him a knowing look. "Someone who refused to ever admit I needed help."

He frowned. "If I needed help, I would ask for it."

"All right," she said with a resigned smile. "Enjoy your time off."

He walked them to the door. "Thanks again for the groceries."

"I don't want to see your face for a week," Flynn told him, pausing in the doorway. "I mean it, Nick. You're a skilled agent, but right now you're a tired agent. Catch your breath, do something fun, maybe go on a date, and come back when you're ready. Because we both know you need time."

"Fine, I'll have some fun," he said.

Andi laughed. "You sound like you're being forced to go to the dentist."

"I'm just tired."

"Which is why you need some time off," Flynn said. "We'll talk next week."

"Got it. And thanks again."

After they left, he closed the door behind him and let out a sigh. Flynn was right. He was exhausted, and even having to pretend he wasn't while they were standing in his kitchen had taken more energy than he had right now. He walked back to the kitchen to finish putting away the groceries.

As he did so, he brushed by a pile of mail on the counter and knocked half of it onto the floor. He let out another sigh and then squatted down to gather it up. All his bills were on auto-pay, and one of his team members had gone by his apartment every few days to make sure everything was in order, so it was mostly junk mail.

But one card caught his eye. He pulled it out as he stood up and dropped the rest of the mail on the counter. He slit open the envelope, reading the engraved words with a growing sense of disbelief. His parents were celebrating their thirty-fifth wedding anniversary with a vow renewal and reception at the Excelsior Hotel in Milan, the weekend after next, and the honor of his presence was requested.

"What the hell?" He shook his head in bewilderment. His parents, James and Danielle Caruso, had almost divorced at least three times. They were passionate, narcissistic, incredibly talented people who had cheated on each other off and on throughout their marriage. And now they were going to have a vow renewal?

It made no sense. Although maybe it made sense, because they both enjoyed being the center of attention, especially his father, a renowned orchestra conductor, who felt like he should be in absolute command of every group he was in. His mother was slightly better. As a talented violinist, she was used to being part of an ensemble, but she still liked a good solo.

He looked back at the envelope, realizing it had arrived two weeks earlier, so it wasn't as last minute as he thought, but still a phone call or a personal note would have been appreciated, if not from his parents, at least from his grandmother.

He set down the invite. He'd send his regrets tomorrow. He couldn't imagine that they would care, since they hadn't cared enough to call and tell him about it. And while he had been out of touch, his unit had been monitoring his personal calls and text messages, alerting him to anyone who needed to hear from him. His parents had never tried to get in touch with him.

They were even bigger fakes than he was.

His phone suddenly rang, and for a moment, he thought it would be ironic if it was one of his parents, but the name running across his screen belonged to his grandmother, Anna Caruso.

"Nonna," he said with genuine pleasure. "I hope you're not calling to tell me I should go to my parents' vow renewal, because I cannot believe they are going through with that pretense."

"Oh, no, Nick," she said. "I wasn't calling about that."

He tensed at the tone of her voice. "What's wrong?"

"I'm in trouble."

"What happened?"

"The museum was robbed today. Gloria and I were there when the thieves came in. Enrique, the security guard, was shot. He's in surgery. They don't know if he's going to make it." The words tumbled out of her mouth fast and furiously.

"My God," he said, shocked by her words. "Are you all right, Nonna?" He couldn't imagine his eighty-one-year-old grandmother having to deal with such an intense situation. Another reason she should have quit volunteering at the museum years ago. But she was the kind of woman who had to be busy, even if it was just a volunteer position. And she had always been an art fan.

"I'm all right," she said. "I wasn't hurt, but I think the robbery was my fault."

"How is that possible?"

"I know you've been working, but I left you a message a few days ago that I was going to put a family painting in an exhibition at the museum."

He vaguely remembered hearing about that message. He'd been tying up the operation, and it hadn't sounded like anything he needed to respond to immediately. "I'm sorry. I've been working a case, and I've been out of touch. Get back to why you think the robbery was your fault."

"I don't know if you remember hearing stories about your great-grandfather's painting..."

"Only that Tomas didn't want his work shown," he murmured.

"Yes, that's true, but Tomas died fifty years ago, and the exhibition was for local artists, and I thought he should be recognized for his talent. It felt wrong to exclude him. He was such a force in the art scene in the sixties. He owned a gallery. He gave art classes. And he was an incredible artist."

His grandmother was rambling. "Okay, so you put one of his paintings in the exhibition, and..."

"It was stolen, Nick. So was Gloria's family painting. There are so many more priceless paintings and artifacts in the museum, but the thieves stole three paintings from only that exhibition, all by local and unknown artists. That's all they wanted."

Now he was more confused. "That doesn't make sense."

"It doesn't," she agreed. "I thought Tomas was just a perfectionist, and that's why he didn't want to show his work, but now I'm wondering if there was another reason the painting was hidden away all these years."

"Like what?"

"I don't know, but the thieves mentioned our last name when they were leaving. I distinctly heard them say Caruso. They came for that painting, Nick. And now it's gone. Enrique is fighting for his life, and if he dies, it will be my fault."

"There were other paintings taken," he said, hating the heavy guilt in her voice. "You just said Gloria's family painting was stolen, too, so it wasn't just the one belonging to Tomas. This isn't all on you." He paused, thinking about what else she'd said. "Where were you that you were close enough to hear the thieves talking?"

"We were trying to get away, but we had to hide behind a statue, and two men came right down the hall next to us. I was so scared. I let out a gasp when one said my name. I think they heard me, but there was another man at the other end of the hall, and he yelled that they had to go."

"Damn," he muttered.

"And there's more, Nick. Gloria said she heard one of them say, 'He'll be happy. He's been waiting a long time.' I don't know who they were talking about, but it sounded like someone wanted those three specific paintings."

"It sounds like it." He felt sick at the thought of his grandmother being in danger. "Are you and Gloria at the house?" Gloria had moved in with his grandmother after his grandfather died, which he was very happy about now.

"Yes. We just got back. The state police interviewed us and then the Carabinieri T.P.C., who handle art crimes. They don't believe we are in danger, because no one saw us."

"What exactly did you see?"

"Two men. But I only saw them from the back. They were wearing all black and had hoods over their heads and gloves on their hands. I couldn't see jewelry or hair color or anything. One of them was carrying a painting, and the other had one of those big guns."

His stomach churned. His grandmother could have been killed. And she'd mentioned that the thieves might have heard her gasp, which was disturbing. It might not be that difficult for the robbery crew to figure out who was in the building, and that could put her and Gloria in danger. He had a lot of questions about the break-in, the security, and the alarm system, but he didn't want to add to his grandmother's distress.

"Maybe you should go next door and stay with Giovanni," he suggested, referring to his grandmother's longtime neighbor.

"It's after one in the morning. I don't want to wake him up. We'll be all right. Won't we, Nick?"

Her concerned question tore at his heart. "You should be. But I'm coming to Rome, Nonna. I'll get on the first flight I can find."

"Are you sure? What about your job?"

"I just wrapped up an investigation. I can get away for a few days."

"It would be nice if you were here. I'm not sure what to do next. But I have to get that painting back."

"The only thing you have to do is stay in the house and keep the doors locked. Don't go anywhere until I get there. I know you're in for the night, but I'm talking about tomorrow, too."

"I understand."

"I'll text you when I know what time I'll be getting in."

"You're a good grandson. *Ti voglio bene.*"

"I love you, too, Nonna." She was the only person he'd ever said those words to and meant them. She was the only family he'd ever been able to count on, and he was going to make damn sure she was all right.

———

Eighteen hours later, around four o'clock on Thursday afternoon, Italy time, Nick raised his window shade as the plane made its final descent into Rome. He'd slept a few hours, but he'd spent the rest of the time feeling impatient and wishing for the flight to be over as a million questions ran through his head. He'd tried to do some research on the plane, not remembering a lot about his great-grandfather Tomas, but he'd found little information about him beyond the basics. He'd been an artist, a teacher, and the owner of an art supply store, until he'd died at sixty.

He didn't really care about getting Tomas's painting back. He just wanted to make sure his grandmother was safe from whatever was going on. There might be other paintings she had taken out of the vault or other items belonging to his grandfather, and he needed to know where they were and how important they might be. He wished he'd asked more about the other two paintings that had been stolen, but there would be time to go through all that. First, he just had to get there.

As the cityscape of Rome came into view, he felt a sense of homecoming at the sight of the terracotta roofs, the majestic monuments, and the meandering Tiber River, all of which evoked memories of days spent exploring the cobblestone streets and busy markets, mingling with the ever-present crush of tourists, and the local street performers. He could almost smell the roasted garlic from the restaurants and feel the sun on his head.

He'd only spent summers in Rome growing up, but it had always felt like the closest place to home, and that was because of his grandparents. His parents had dragged him all over the world, and when they weren't touring, they were living in New York City, San Francisco or LA, but none of those places had ever felt like where he wanted to be. They certainly hadn't been as warm or as comforting or as welcoming as his grandmother's house in Rome.

His grandparents had always made time for him, and his summers in Italy had been the highlights of his childhood, his grandmother cooking for him, his grandfather regaling him with exciting stories from his job as a police officer. It was Marcus Caruso who had made him want to do something in the world that would make a difference. It had taken him a while to get to that job, but he was there now, and that was because of his grandfather.

He hadn't been to Rome since his grandfather's funeral last year. He should have come back before now to check on his grandmother, but he'd kept putting it off, telling himself he'd find some time after the next job, but he'd never taken that time, and he was glad now that Flynn had insisted he take a break. Even if Flynn hadn't given him the green light, he would have jumped on the plane, because Anna Caruso was the one person in his life who had never let him down, and now he needed to be there for her.

After the plane landed, he turned on his phone, relieved not to see panicked messages from his grandmother. He texted her he would be at the house within an hour. She replied immediately that she couldn't wait to see him, which brought forth a sense of relief that she was all right.

He hadn't checked any luggage, so he made a quick exit from the plane, grabbed a taxi in front of the airport, and made his way to Trastevere, the neighborhood where his grandmother lived.

It was almost five by the time the cab turned down her block, and the setting sun cast a warm glow over the cobblestone street. When he stepped out of the taxi, he caught the scent of freshly baked bread from the bakery at the end of the block. His stomach rumbled in appreciation and memory of the savory and sweet pastries that he'd feasted on so many mornings in his youth. He would have to go tomorrow, or, hopefully, his grandmother would have some pastries sitting on her kitchen table.

He grabbed his overnight bag after paying the driver, and then looked up and down the street. The homes surrounding his grandmother's house were three-story buildings, several of which had been converted from single-family homes to multi-family units. That had been the case with his grandmother's friend, Gloria Rossi.

After her husband had died eight years earlier, she'd sold the home to a developer who had turned it into four apartments. The top apartment was where Gloria had lived until several months ago when she had moved in with his grandmother after his grandfather had died.

As he walked up to the building, he could see signs of age,

the faded façade, adorned with ivy that was out of control, the chipping paint on the ornate iron balcony railings, and several long cracks in the plaster. Maybe it was time to talk to his grandmother about what she might do with the building. Even with Gloria living there, it was probably too big and too expensive.

But whenever he'd brought up the idea of selling it to a developer and doing what Gloria had done with her palazzo, his grandmother had turned him down, insisting that she would never sell the family home. She would keep it until she died, and then it would go to his father and eventually to him.

He doubted he would ever become the owner. His father had little interest in the property unless it was what profit it might bring in. He'd sell it in a heartbeat. And that was probably fine. He couldn't imagine himself living here, either. His life was in the States.

The large front door swung open with a loud creak, and Anna Caruso appeared, relief etched in every line of her face. Her hair was white, her olive skin still tan from her love of sitting in the sunshine, but there were more lines around her eyes and mouth now. She looked tired, but even with everything going on, she was still stylishly dressed in a pair of black slacks and a light-blue sweater to match her eyes.

"Oh, Nick," she said as she rushed down the steps to give him a hug. "It is so good to see you."

She'd always given him the best love-filled hugs, and today was no exception. In fact, he felt like she lingered even longer, as if she needed the support of their embrace. Finally, she stepped back and said what she always said every time he arrived after a long absence. "You look too skinny, *Amore mio*."

He smiled. "I'm hoping you have some pastries from Dalinda's."

"I always do." Her expression changed as a car came down the street.

He turned his head to see the vehicle stop in front of a house two buildings away from them.

"Oh, it's just Lorenzo," she said, relief in her voice, as she gave a wave to the man who exited his car.

"Who's Lorenzo?"

"My neighbor's father. He's a delightful man." She paused again as another car came down the street. This one was moving slowly, and as her uneasiness increased, so did his.

"Let's go inside." He urged her into the house, keeping his body between her and the street as they went through the front door. As he closed the door, he saw the car disappear down the street. It was probably no one, but clearly his grandmother was still on edge, and so was he. Until he knew more about what was going on, he would not let down his guard.

The entry showed similar signs of age on the weathered wood floors. And the old chandelier hanging over the round glass table in the middle of the foyer was missing several shards of glass. But the tapestries on the walls were still bright and colorful, warming up the room.

"Nick," his grandmother said, drawing his attention back to her. "There's something I should tell you."

He didn't like the nervous tone in her voice. "What's that? Has something else happened?"

"Not exactly."

Before she could say another word, two women walked out of the adjacent living room. He recognized Gloria immediately with her silver hair and friendly smile. He smiled back and then saw the younger woman standing behind her.

The irritatingly smart brown eyes and the dark-brown hair that fell in waves around a beautiful face belonged to Gloria's granddaughter, Isabella Rossi, possibly the sexiest and most annoying woman he'd ever met.

Unlike her grandmother, who wore a conservative knit dress, Isabella was in black jeans with high-heeled boots and a dark-red sweater that clung to her curves. She was as pretty as a picture. If only her personality were as sweet.

He'd heard about her for years but had only met her in

person for the first time three months ago, when his grandmother and Gloria had insisted that the two of them meet since Isabella had just moved to Los Angeles.

His grandmother had told him more than a few times that he and Isabella would like each other. He'd told her he didn't need her to set him up on a date, but she'd insisted that he make sure the granddaughter of her oldest friend was doing all right. He'd asked her to dinner. It had been a disaster and one of the worst dates he'd ever been on. He was sure Isabella felt the same.

"Hello, Nick," Isabella said, not a hint of warmth in her brown eyes.

"Isabella," he said shortly.

A tense silence followed their very brief exchange. "Who wants something to drink?" his grandmother asked with forced cheerfulness.

"We all do, I think," Gloria said quickly. "I'll help you with the drinks, Anna. You two...talk."

As the two older women disappeared, he really hoped that this whole scenario wasn't part of some elaborate scheme to get him and Isabella together again. But there was no way his grandmother and Gloria would go that far.

"When did you get here?" he asked.

"About five minutes before you." She folded her arms across her chest as she gave him a wintry look.

"Do you know what's going on?"

"Only the basics. They were in the museum last night when it was robbed. The security guard, who is a dear friend of theirs, was shot and is apparently in critical condition. There were several paintings taken, two of which belonged to our families. What do you know?"

He wished he could say he knew more than she did, but he didn't. "That's the story I got. I'm surprised you arrived before me. I took the first flight out of LA. I didn't see you on it."

"I was in New York when my grandmother called."

"You're not living in LA anymore?"

"I am. I was supposed to be at a bachelorette party this weekend, but I came here when I heard what happened." She cleared her throat. "This is awkward."

He shrugged. "I can deal."

"So can I," she said quickly. "We don't have to like each other, Nick, but we both care about our grandmothers, so let's focus on how we can help them."

"What else would we focus on?"

Her lips tightened. "You're going to make this hard, aren't you?"

"There's nothing to make hard or easy. Our one and only date was out of respect for our grandmothers. That's it. The end."

She stared back at him, and he felt a little more heated than he should with her dark eyes clinging to his.

"I wish it was the end," she muttered. Then she turned on her heel and walked back into the living room.

CHAPTER TWO

Isabella took several deep breaths as she walked into the salon, a grand room furnished with antiques and a massive stone fireplace that she really wished wasn't generating a blazing fire, because she'd started sweating the minute Nick had walked into the house. She did not like that feeling at all. It was just anger, she told herself.

The man was a cocky know-it-all who had far too high an opinion of himself. She'd met his type more than a few times. She knew exactly who he was. She just wished he wasn't so attractive. Or that her body seemed to have a different response to him than her brain did. But she wasn't going to let him get into her head. She would concentrate on her grandmother and Anna and try to ignore Nick as much as possible. Although she doubted that would be easy since the man seemed to take up a lot of space.

Hearing voices, she turned and forced a tight smile onto her face as her grandmother, Anna, and Nick entered the room. Her grandmother was carrying a plate of pastries and cookies, while Nick carried a heavier tray containing a pitcher of lemonade and four glasses.

They settled in on the two long sofas that faced each other

across an ornate coffee table. Nick poured the lemonade while her grandmother handed her the plate of treats. She took a cookie because it had been a long trip for her, too. Maybe not as long as Nick's trek from Los Angeles, but she'd gotten little sleep, and she needed sugar to keep her going.

Nick seemed as ravenous as she was, downing a chocolate croissant in three quick bites. "This is even better than I remember," he told Anna.

She gave him a loving smile. "You always loved your pastries, Nick."

Isabella wondered why his love of pastry didn't show on his very fit frame. But then again, he lived in LA, the land of healthy choices and toned bodies. She'd been living in Los Angeles for six months, and while she worked out, she still didn't feel in as good of shape as she should. In her defense, she worked a lot. Although Nick seemed to work a lot, too. But he was a man. Men could drop pounds just by skipping a meal. It was so unfair.

"Okay, tell us what happened," Nick said as he wiped his mouth with a napkin.

Her grandmother and Anna exchanged a look, and then Anna began to talk, which was normally the way the two women operated. Her grandmother was just as strong as Anna, but when the two of them were together, it was usually Anna who led the conversation.

As Anna recounted the events at the museum, Isabella grew more concerned. She could picture them hiding in the shadow of a statue, praying they wouldn't be shot, and that image brought forth the realization that she could have lost her grandmother yesterday, which was an unspeakably horrible thought. Her grandmother had saved her life when she was sixteen, and she couldn't stand the thought of losing her.

"You both must have been terrified," she said when Anna took a breath.

"So scared," Anna admitted. "Especially when I heard my

name. But we're all right, and we're sorry that you both had to leave your jobs and your lives to come here."

"You don't have to apologize," she said. "I'm just grateful you weren't hurt. I assume you spoke to the police yesterday."

"Inspector Vincenzo from the Polizia di Stato, and then Captain Lavezzo from the Carabinieri T.P.C.," Anna replied. "Captain Lavezzo said his team would investigate the theft, as their unit is dedicated to protecting cultural heritage. They specialize in robberies like this."

"Well, not exactly like this," Gloria interrupted. "Captain Lavezzo was very curious as to why the three paintings were the only ones taken when there were many items of greater value in the museum. Of course, we couldn't tell him why. He didn't seem confident that we'd get the paintings back, either."

"Who painted the third one?" she asked.

"Frederico Germain," her grandmother answered. "He was a friend of Lucinda's. He ran the art school that Anna and I attended when we first came to Rome as college students. And Lucinda taught there as well."

"Is he still alive?" Nick asked.

"No, he died years ago," her grandmother replied. "Louisa Del Vecchio donated the painting to the exhibition. She's Frederico's granddaughter, and she runs the school now. But I don't believe Frederico's painting was any more valuable than the ones by Tomas or Lucinda. He was talented, but he wasn't particularly commercial or successful."

"It doesn't make sense," Anna agreed. "The worst thing is that the paintings that we were entrusted to protect are gone now."

"I don't think that's the worst part," Nick said dryly. "But I understand why you're upset about it."

"Because Marcus put his father's painting in a vault a long time ago, and I should have left it there," Anna said. "I just thought it was such a shame no one would ever see his talent, and it had been so long. I didn't think it would matter. I was wrong."

"This is not just on you, Anna," Gloria said, reassuring her friend. "I put Lucinda's painting in the exhibit as well. And it had also been tucked away for a long time."

"Where was Lucinda's painting, Grandma?" she asked curiously.

"It was unframed, a loose canvas rolled up and tucked among the paintings your mother did when she was a young girl. I think Sylvie might have taken it to study at some point. I found it hidden deep in a closet when I moved out of my apartment." Gloria gave her a questioning look. "Is that important?"

"It might be," she replied. "You mentioned that one thief said something about someone waiting to get their hands on these paintings for a long time. If both paintings were with you and Anna all these years, I wonder why no one tried to get them before. Tomas's painting was in a vault, but it sounds like Lucinda's was in your house at some point, and then here, Grandma. I just wonder why no one would have looked for either painting in the homes of their descendants."

"We had a break-in a long time ago," Anna said slowly. "It was a few months after Tomas died. Vandals tore up our home. Marcus thought it was a team of thieves working the neighborhood, because several other houses were broken into as well, including Gloria's."

"That's right. I'd forgotten about that," Gloria said. "It was such a difficult time after Tomas and Lucinda died that while the break-in was disturbing, it was just another awful moment in a terrible year. I was so worried about Paolo's emotional state after losing his mother that I was just glad nothing of value had been taken from our home."

"Wait a second," Nick interrupted, drawing everyone's attention to him. "Lucinda and Tomas died at the same time?"

"They died together," her grandmother confirmed. "In a fire at Tomas's house. They often painted together in the evenings.

It was late when they finished, so Lucinda stayed in the guest room. Apparently, one of them had been smoking and dropped some hot ashes onto the sofa and started a fire."

"I don't think I ever heard how Lucinda died," Isabella said as she considered that part of the story.

"It happened long before you were born," her grandmother replied.

"I remember hearing Tomas died in a fire, but not that anyone was with him," Nick muttered. "Was there something going on between him and Lucinda?"

"No, of course not," her grandmother said firmly. "They were dear friends, but Lucinda was married. She would not have cheated on her husband. She was not that kind of woman. She was passionate and loyal."

"But she was staying at the home of a man who wasn't her husband," Isabella interjected. "And I can't imagine that didn't create gossip."

Her grandmother waved a dismissive hand. "They were artists. Tomas ran classes out of his home studio. There were often other artists there, and they would paint for hours on end. Lucinda's husband, Eduardo, understood that she had to express herself through art, and he trusted her and Tomas. They had been friends for years." She paused. "Eduardo also traveled a great deal, so much so that he and Lucinda gave up their house and lived with us that last year. That was another reason Lucinda needed a place to paint."

"That makes sense," she said, but she still thought it was a bit odd.

"Eduardo was out of town when the fire occurred," her grandmother continued. "He was devastated when he returned. His sorrow at Lucinda's funeral broke my heart. And my husband, Paolo, was so upset; he wouldn't even talk about his mother after she was gone. Neither he nor Eduardo would speak her name. I thought it was wrong, but if I had said anything, it would have caused an upset."

She wasn't surprised to hear that. Her grandfather, Paolo, had been a hard man—harsh, strict, unforgiving, and even a little cruel. She'd always felt like her grandmother had been beaten down by him, not that her grandmother would agree. But she'd seen firsthand how he'd treated Gloria and her own mother, not to mention herself.

"So," Nick said. "To recap, Tomas and Lucinda were painting buddies, best friends, and died together in a fire that destroyed Tomas's house."

"Yes, the house was completely gone by the time they put the fire out," her grandmother confirmed.

"But Tomas's painting didn't burn in that fire," Nick said, looking to his grandmother for an answer.

"No. Tomas gave his painting to Marcus before he died. He said something about too many people coming through his house and studio, and he wanted Marcus to put it away somewhere and keep it safe. Actually, I thought there were two paintings, but I only found one in the vault."

"And Lucinda's painting wasn't destroyed," Nick continued. "Because it was in her house, or your house, Gloria. The same house that was vandalized shortly after the fire."

Her grandmother sat up a little straighter. "Do you think someone was looking for the paintings right after they died?"

"I do," she put in. "And that the fire might not have been accidental."

"Oh," her grandmother said, surprise running through her eyes. "Really?"

"We need to know more about how they died," she said.

"No," Nick said, shaking his head. "Tomas and Lucinda died a long time ago. We need to focus on what's going on now, who broke into the museum, and whether the authorities have any leads on the thieves."

"The past could be tied to the present," she argued.

"Our priority is to make sure our grandmothers are safe." His gaze moved to his grandmother. "I want you both out of this. It's a good time for a vacation."

"We can't just leave," Anna protested.

"Why not?" he challenged.

"Because we can't let these thieves drive us out of our home," she answered.

"It doesn't have to be for long," Nick argued. "Hopefully, the Carabinieri will find the thieves and retrieve the paintings in short time."

"They may not care that much," Anna argued. "The paintings weren't valuable."

"They were valuable enough to steal."

"If we leave and don't put pressure on the Carabinieri to find the paintings, they'll be gone forever. I can't let that happen," Anna said. "I owe it to my husband, to his father, to all the Carusos. I have to fight."

Isabella was beginning to see where Nick got his stubbornness.

"Anna is right. We're staying put," her grandmother said. "I care about getting Lucinda's work back, too."

Nick sent her a pointed look, but she didn't want to join his side, to have some man come in and order them around.

"Anna and I don't need anyone else to fight our battles," her grandmother continued. "Nor do we want to put either of you in danger. So, we've already decided that we'll make dinner for you. We'll have a lovely evening, and then you two can go home tomorrow."

"I'm not leaving until I know what's going on," Nick said, not a trace of doubt in his voice.

"Neither am I," she declared.

"Why don't we discuss it over a meal?" Anna suggested. "You both must be hungry. We'll make dinner."

"I'm not changing my mind, Nonna," Nick said. "If you're not leaving, neither am I. Isabella, of course, is free to leave."

Her gaze narrowed in irritation. "If you're staying, I'm staying."

"Well, it looks like we're all staying for now," her grandmother said. "We should start cooking, Anna."

"I can help," she offered.

Her grandmother smiled for the first time since she'd arrived. "You are good at a lot of things, Isabella, but cooking is not one of them."

"I can cook," she said defensively.

"No. You rest." Her grandmother got to her feet, followed by Anna. "We can handle the cooking."

As they left the room, Nick turned to her. "We need to work together to get them to leave, Isabella. You should have told them to go."

"You heard what they said."

"They don't know what they're up against."

"Neither do you."

His lips tightened. "I can find out more easily than any of you can. I have resources."

"I hope you do. Then we can all be done with this as fast as possible. Until then, I'm going to help with dinner."

"I thought you couldn't cook," he said as they both stood up.

"I'm not as bad as my grandmother thinks. I noticed you didn't offer to help. But then, you wouldn't, would you? I'm sure you're used to being waited on."

"You really have no idea who I am, Isabella."

"Oh, I think I do, Nick," she said confidently.

He shook his head. "You don't know me."

"I know you don't care if you're late to meet someone. That you take calls in the middle of a date, and when someone goes to use the restroom, you bail without a word."

To his very small credit, he winced at her words.

"I had a job I had to get to. I left you money for dinner and a ride home. I texted you an apology."

"Such a gentleman," she drawled sarcastically.

"I shouldn't have met you that night. I should have cancelled, but I thought I could slip away for dinner. It didn't work out. I am sorry that I left without a word. But you were taking forever, Isabella, and I had to leave."

She'd taken forever in the restroom because she was pissed off that she was stuck having a meal with a man who was treating her with a complete lack of respect, just like her last boyfriend. She'd lingered, debating whether she wanted to leave before dessert, but when she'd gotten back to the table, she'd discovered that Nick had beaten her to the punch.

After hearing about the amazing Nick Caruso for years, she'd been incredibly disappointed by the actual man, but she was used to men disappointing her. And that night had been an awful night for her, too. But she'd put her personal problems aside to meet Nick because it was important to her grandmother.

"We don't need to do this," she said. "You don't like me. I don't like you. Let's just leave it at that."

CHAPTER THREE

As Isabella left the living room, the doorbell rang. She hesitated, then walked to the window next to the door and peeked through the curtain. There was a man standing on the porch wearing a dark-blue uniform. He had jet-black hair, a tall, thin frame and appeared to be in his fifties or sixties.

"Who's here?" Nick asked.

"A police officer." She dropped the curtain, then opened the door. "Hello? Can I help you?"

The man's jaw dropped as his gaze ran across her face. "You look just like Sylvie," he said in bemusement.

Her muscles tightened at his unexpected words. "Sylvie is my mother. I'm Isabella Rossi."

"Ah, *Sì*. Her daughter." The man shook his head again, as if he couldn't quite believe his eyes. "I apologize for staring. Sylvie and I were friends when we were young. You look very much like the girl I remember." His lips tightened. "I was very sorry to hear about the trouble she got into, but I am happy that she has come back to Italia—to Firenze."

She frowned at that reminder and quickly changed the subject. "How can I help you?"

Before he could answer, her grandmother and Anna came

into the entry.

"Stefano," her grandmother said with delight. "Is that really you?"

"*Sí*," he replied as her grandmother grabbed his hand and pulled him into the house. She gave him a kiss on each cheek. "It's lovely to see you. It's been a long time."

"Since Marcus's funeral," he said with a sad nod. "I've been meaning to stop by for a while. I'm sorry I haven't made the time."

"Well, it's good to see you now." Gloria's expression turned serious. "Would I be correct in assuming you're not just here to say hello?"

"I heard about what happened at the museum yesterday," he admitted. "I wanted to make sure you were all right."

"That's so sweet of you. Anna and I are fine." Gloria stepped back so Anna and Stefano could exchange a hug.

"Did you meet my grandson?" Anna asked.

"Not yet. I was surprised when I looked at Isabella and saw Sylvie in her eyes." Stefano turned to Nick. "I should have introduced myself. I'm Stefano Gangi. I'm a family friend and an inspector with the state police. Your grandfather, Marcus, was one of my mentors."

"Mine, too," Nick said. "What can you tell us about the investigation?"

"It is in the hands of Capitano Lavezzo at the Carabinieri T.P.C. I have heard that the security system was disengaged when the thieves entered the building, so there was no video evidence. The back door by the loading dock was the point of entrance. Because no alarms went off, it was some time before the police were alerted by someone walking in the street who said he heard gunshots in the museum."

"What about exterior cameras on the building?"

"Turned off," Stefano replied, a grim look in his gaze. "It is my understanding that the only eyewitness was the guard, but no one has spoken to him yet, as he is currently sedated." Stefano looked back at Anna and Gloria. "I was told neither of you could identify anyone."

"We were hiding," her grandmother replied. "We heard the men mutter a few sentences. One said Caruso and that someone would be happy to get the art, that they had been waiting a long time."

"I wasn't aware that you heard them speak. Could you recognize that voice if you heard it again?" Stefano asked.

"Oh, I don't think so," her grandmother replied.

"And you didn't see anything else?" Stefano pressed. "Often, when witnesses have time to think a minor detail will come back into their mind, like the type of clothing, the color of hair, or a particular shoe brand. Has that happened?"

"Not for me." Her grandmother looked at Anna. "You saw more than I did."

"Which was very little," Anna said. "There were two men. I only saw them from the back, and they were dressed completely in black: pants, coat, hood, and shoes. Even their hands were covered with black gloves. There was nothing identifiable about either of them. I wish there was. I want them to be caught. I want them to be punished for what they did to Enrique, and I also want to get our paintings back."

"I understand," Stefano said with a nod. "Do you have any other paintings from your relatives here in the house?"

"No," Anna said.

"Do you think we're in danger, Stefano?" her grandmother asked.

"I wouldn't think so. You didn't see anyone, and you don't have any other paintings. I believe the thieves got what they wanted. I can't see why they'd come after you."

"That's a relief," her grandmother said.

"However, I would like you to call me if you have any other worries or if you remember something later that might be helpful." He pulled out a card and handed it to Gloria. "Here is my number."

"Thank you, Stefano," Gloria said. "We appreciate your concern."

"I always felt like you were family." He paused. "Did Sylvie tell you we spoke a few days ago?"

"No. I didn't realize you two kept in touch."

"We hadn't talked in thirty years, but a mutual friend told me that Sylvie had come back and was working at a gallery. She gave me Sylvie's number, so I called her. She was quite surprised to hear from me, but we had a pleasant conversation. We're going to meet up soon."

"That would be nice," her grandmother said. "The two of you were such good friends, and I think Sylvie could use some of her old friends as she starts over."

"I should go," Stefano said. "Please, be careful."

"Let us know if you hear anything more about the investigation," her grandmother said.

"I will do that."

As Gloria closed the door behind Stefano, Nick said, "Were you both telling the truth about not having any more paintings?"

His question surprised Isabella, but to her amazement, guilt entered her grandmother's eyes.

"Really, Grandma?" she asked. "I thought you just found one loose canvas."

"That's true," Gloria said quickly. "But I did find a sketch book. They're rough drawings. I'm sure no one would care about them. It's not another painting. I wasn't lying."

"What about you, Nonna?" Nick asked.

"I believe there is another painting by Tomas somewhere, but it's not here or in the vault," Anna answered. "I'm not sure where it is. But I always thought Tomas had given Marcus two paintings to take care of. When I was getting the painting from the bank, I found some letters between Tomas and a woman referred to only by the initial J. She mentioned something about his gift to her. I wondered if he might have given her the painting. But I don't know who she is."

Isabella's mind raced with possibilities. Her job as a journalist was all about following leads, unraveling threads of information, and finding the truth. She hadn't heard any leads until just now. "I want to see the sketchbook and the letters."

"So do I," Nick said. "Is there anything else the two of them left behind?"

"Tomas had a few personal items," Anna said. "They're in the vault as well. We can go to the bank tomorrow."

"All right." Nick paused. "Were either of you surprised that Stefano showed up here asking questions?"

"Why would we be surprised?" Gloria asked in wonder. "Stefano grew up with Sylvie. Paolo and I were friends with his parents."

"And Marcus mentored him when he first joined the police," Anna said. "I remember how happy he was when Stefano became a police officer. Stefano had been rather wild as a younger man. It was good to see him get himself together. Why are you suspicious of him?"

"He seemed very interested in what you witnessed and whether there was other art in your possession."

"He wants to make sure we're safe," Anna said.

"I hope so," Nick said. "But going forward, let's eliminate any doubt about whether you could recognize a voice. You saw nothing and you know nothing."

"You're scaring me a little, Nick," his grandmother said with a worried glint in her eyes.

"I think you should be careful, even around people you've known a long time. Everyone wears a mask. Everyone has their own agenda."

There was a harshness to his words that made Isabella think he was talking about much more than the immediate situation. But she had enough to figure out without wondering about a man she didn't even like.

"You're so cynical, Nick," Anna said with a sad sigh.

"I prefer realistic."

"In his last year, your grandfather had the same look in his eyes that you have in yours now, a disillusioned weariness," she added. "I don't enjoy seeing it in you."

"Well, I am tired, so I'm sorry if I didn't sugarcoat my words the way I should have, Nonna, but I stand by them. Stefano might be the greatest guy in the world, but the only people you should talk to about this situation are in this room."

"I understand."

"I do, too," Gloria said. "But I believe Stefano came here because he was worried, and for no other reason. That said, we'll be careful. Now, we should get back to cooking."

As their grandmothers returned to the kitchen, Isabella turned to Nick. "You really think Stefano had an ulterior motive?"

"I don't know. Did your mother ever talk about him?"

"No. She mentioned a boy she'd loved when she was young, but I don't know if it was him. Although, he said he was her best friend, so if it wasn't him, then he probably knew who it was."

"Maybe you could ask your mother."

She immediately shook her head. "My mother isn't relevant to this situation. I don't need to talk to her."

"Isn't relevant?" he challenged. "She's Gloria's daughter. Why isn't she here if she's living in Florence?"

"My mother isn't the person you call in a crisis. That's why she's not here, and we don't need to involve her in anything." She let out a breath. "My grandmother said that I can have the attic room. I'm going to unpack before dinner."

"What's the deal with you and your mom?" he asked curiously.

"It's not your business."

"Do you ever answer a question?"

"You had plenty of time to ask me questions when we went to dinner, but you weren't interested then, and I'm not interested in answering now."

"I had a lot on my mind that night, but I was rude to you,

Isabella, and I'm sorry about that. However, you have to admit you were hating on me the second I sat down."

"Because you were thirty minutes late, and I'd spent a solid half hour enduring looks of pity and questions about whether my date was going to show up. When you arrived, you didn't even apologize."

"I'm sure I said I was sorry."

"Your exact words were 'I thought we were getting a table outside.' But I couldn't get a table on the patio unless you were there, so I had to stay inside."

"Are you sure I didn't say sorry first?"

"Absolutely one-hundred-percent positive."

"Your memory might be blurry. You'd had a fair amount to drink before I got there."

"Because I was waiting so long," she said with extreme annoyance and also some guilt that she had drunk too much during that painful half hour. "I had a lot on my mind, too. But I stuck it out. You're the one who ultimately bailed on me without a word. I've been ghosted before, but not while the date was actually going on."

"I had a work emergency."

"So you said. I'm sure there wouldn't have been an emergency if you wanted to be on the date. You shouldn't have invited me to dinner if you didn't want to go."

"My grandmother wanted us to meet."

"So what? You either do it with enthusiasm or don't do it at all."

He gave her a thoughtful look. "Were you enthusiastic? I don't remember seeing even one smile on your face."

"Because you were late."

"You really have a problem with people being late," he said dryly.

"I have a problem with people who think their time is more important than mine." She waved her hand in the air. "And this conversation is going nowhere. You will never admit you were wrong."

"I will."

"Not with any genuine feeling."

"I was wrong, Isabella. I should have cancelled the date because there were too many things going on, and I wasn't able to get there on time or to stay, and I couldn't explain why. That wasn't fair to you."

She stared at him in amazement, shocked he had actually apologized, and that he sounded sincere. "Okay," she said finally.

"Just okay?"

"I don't know what else you want me to say, Nick."

"You could apologize, too. You jumped down my throat on everything I said, even after we got over the part of me being late."

He might have a point, but she really didn't want to admit that.

"I got the feeling you weren't just seeing my face when you were telling me off, either," he added. "It felt like there was more going on."

She licked her lips. "I probably should have canceled, too," she admitted. "But I didn't want to disappoint my grandmother. I also didn't want to keep hearing about how I should meet you."

"Same for me. I guess we have one thing in common: not wanting to disappoint our grandmothers. Maybe we can build on that."

"Build what?"

"Why don't we start with a truce? Being at war with each other won't make this situation better."

"Fine. We'll call a truce. For our grandmothers."

He held out his hand. "Shake?"

She reluctantly put her hand into his, and as his warm fingers closed around hers, a wave of heat ran through her body, and she let go as fast as she could. But it probably wasn't fast enough.

CHAPTER FOUR

Nick was happy to call a halt to the war with Isabella. And as she walked up the stairs, he found himself admiring the sexy sway of her body. She was a fiery, stubborn, like-to-win-at-all-costs kind of woman, but she was sure as hell attractive.

Maybe he should have kept the war going, because he could feel something else simmering between them, and that could not possibly end well. He needed to keep his guard up because this woman was related to his grandmother's best friend in the entire world, and he could never hurt Isabella without hurting his grandmother.

Putting Isabella out of his mind, he took out his phone and punched in Flynn's number. It was Thursday morning in LA, and he should already be at work.

"No, you can't come to work today," Flynn said, bypassing hello. "I told you to take time off, Nick."

"That's good, because I won't be in today. I'm in Rome."

"Seriously? Well, good. An Italian vacation sounds fun."

"It's not a vacation. My grandmother witnessed a robbery at the museum where she volunteers. A painting she put into an exhibition was also stolen. It was one of only a few pieces targeted, which is odd because the artist was my great-grandfather, whose work had no particular value."

"Well, that's not what I was expecting you to say. How can I help?"

"I may need a contact in the art world. I'm going to speak to a Captain Lavezzo at the Carabinieri T.P.C. tomorrow, but I'm not sure how forthcoming he'll be. You worked art crimes, right? Did you ever deal with him?"

"Not him, but I consulted on a case with that unit. They were territorial, but I could understand that because I was invading their territory. That said, everyone was professional, and we all had the same goal: to recover stolen art."

"Good. I'm going to call him in the morning. Do you have any thoughts about why three paintings by unknown artists would be stolen from a museum while pieces of greater value were ignored?" Flynn had more than just experience working art crimes with the FBI. His father had been an art gallery owner and a very successful art thief, who, as far as Nick knew, was still running from the law.

"I would say the paintings do have value. It's just not obvious what that value is. But it's there. What can you tell me about the art itself?"

"Honestly, nothing. I don't even know what the painting was about or what the style was. I need to ask my grandmother about that. But I know that the painting was hidden away fifty-something years ago at my great-grandfather's request and that he and one of the other artists whose work was stolen died together in a fire."

"That sounds intriguing. But why don't you ask me what you really want to know?"

Trust Flynn to get to the point. "Are you still in touch with your father?"

"I'm not. I haven't seen Sam Beringer since he disappeared on me a few years ago after saving my life."

He'd forgotten that Flynn had changed his name to avoid

being connected to his father. "Sorry. I shouldn't have asked. I'm sure he's not your favorite subject."

"He's not. But I've made peace with his life choices. I would start digging into the lives of the artists whose works were stolen."

"They're all dead now. It won't be easy to find information."

"Someone isn't dead. Someone who knows the value of their work. Someone who was willing to steal it."

"And perhaps kill a guard in the process," he murmured. "That's the part that worries me the most, that my grandmother and her friend were hiding in the building when it happened. If someone figures out they were there, it may not matter that they can't identify the thieves."

"Maybe you should get your grandmother to go on vacation with you."

"I already suggested she leave town, but she's digging her heels in."

"Sounds like a family trait," Flynn said lightly.

"Probably," he admitted.

"I'll make a few calls for you, see if I can get someone who's up to speed on Italian art crimes. They might be able to help you figure out why the paintings were targeted." Flynn paused. "One thing I've learned about art crimes is that both the artists and the thieves who steal from them don't always act out of logic. Art is about passion, sometimes about obsession. You can't expect to add two plus two and get four. It's never that simple."

"Got it. Any help you can give me would be appreciated. I'm less interested in getting the painting back than protecting my grandmother, but I'm not sure I can do one without the other."

"I doubt you can. After you make sure your grandmother is all right, why don't you take a real vacation? I'm serious, Nick. You've done great work for me, but I think you're burned out, even if you don't want to admit it."

"I'll think about it." He blew out a breath as he ended the call. Flynn wasn't wrong. He was burned out. It wasn't just working for Flynn's team that had brought on the feeling of intense exhaustion, it was the five years before, the endless jobs, one after another.

But he couldn't take a break now, not until he was certain his grandmother and Gloria were safe.

As the smell of garlic and onions drifted down the hall, his stomach rumbled, and he followed that delicious fragrance to the kitchen. He found his grandmother at the stove, wearing her favorite apron while three different pots were bubbling on the stove. The scene evoked many wonderful memories in his mind and brought forth a feeling being at home.

"It's almost ready," his grandmother said as she stirred the sauce. "Gloria went upstairs to help Isabella get settled. They'll both be on the third floor. You can have your old room down the hall from mine."

"Sounds good." He grabbed an olive off an antipasto tray she'd put together on the table. "Do you enjoy living with Gloria?"

"Oh, yes. We each have an entire floor to ourselves, not that we need the space. We eat our meals and watch television together, and we always enjoy each other's company. We're so close, we're like sisters."

"You two have known each other for a long time."

"Sixty-one years. I can hardly believe it's been that long since we met as twenty-one-year-old women who came to Rome to study art for the summer. We had no idea what we were getting into, but we wanted an adventure."

"Did you get it?"

"A thousand times over. I only wish your grandfather was still here to share in that adventure. I miss him, Nick."

He nodded, her words touching a part of his heart that he rarely used. "I miss him, too."

"It's hard to be without him. But it has been better since Gloria moved in. It's nice not to be alone, especially at night." She paused. "I'm glad you came. I know I interrupted your very busy life, but it is good to see you. I wasn't sure when that would happen again."

"It's good to see you, too. But were you thinking we might see each other again at my parents' vow renewal next week?" he asked pointedly. "You should have given me a heads-up, Nonna."

She sent him a guilty look. "I know. But Danielle told me that your father would call you about it, and I didn't think I should get in the middle."

"He didn't call me. I just got an invitation like everyone else. Not even a personal note."

"Since you're already here in Rome, you could stay until next weekend and then go to Milan to be there for them."

"No," he said flatly.

"You should think about it. Your parents love you. I'm sure they want you to be there."

"I can't watch them act like they're living out some great love story. I've had a front-row seat to their marriage, and it hasn't been awesome."

"They've had their problems, but they love each other. They wouldn't have stayed together all these years if they didn't."

"If their relationship is love, I don't want any part of it."

Her lips turned down in a frown. "Love can be wonderful, Nick. I hate to see you turn your back on such an important emotion to have in your life."

"I'm not turning my back, but my expectations are not high. Anyway, we don't need to talk about it."

"Well, if you don't want to talk to me about it, maybe you should talk to your parents."

"If they really wanted me there, they would have called. But that's not the way our family operates. They have their lives; I have mine. And I suspect there's a hidden agenda behind this ceremony. Maybe it's a way to get some extra publicity for an upcoming concert or something." He popped another olive into his mouth. "Let's get back to the problem at hand. Did Papa ever tell you why the paintings had to go in the vault?"

"Only what I said before that Tomas wanted his work to be protected and away from the eyes of all the artists who came in and out of his studio when he taught classes there."

"I wonder why he wanted his work hidden away. Tomas was an artist. Why wouldn't he want his work to be shown to the world? Isn't that why he painted?"

"It might have had something to do with being a perfectionist. If it wasn't perfect, he didn't want to show it."

"If it wasn't perfect, why did he give it to his son for safekeeping? It sounds like he wanted to protect it, hide it, maybe. For what reason?" His mind raced around the puzzle taking shape in his head. "Was there something in the painting? Was it even his painting?"

"What? You think he stole it?" she asked in shock. "Your great-grandfather was not a thief."

"I'm just considering all the possibilities. Tomas knew someone wanted that painting or both of his paintings. That's why he gave his work to Papa and told him to keep it safe. Then he dies in a fire where his entire studio is destroyed. That seems like an enormous coincidence."

She gave him a troubled look. "When you put it together like that, it does. I never thought of it that way. The fire was an accident. It was a tragedy, but it wasn't a mystery."

"Maybe it wasn't an accident. Perhaps it was purposefully set to destroy Tomas and his work. Lucinda might have been in the wrong place at the wrong time. Or she also had something that someone wanted. Her painting is gone now, too."

"But she didn't hide her painting. It was just loose in Sylvie's things. It wasn't framed or anything."

"Which would have made it more difficult to find. Both of your houses were burglarized. I can't believe Papa didn't think that was odd after just losing his father in a fire."

"Marcus was distraught when Tomas died. He wasn't thinking clearly."

"I wish I could have seen the painting," he muttered.

"You can see a picture," she said, taking out her phone. "I took several photos at the exhibition." She opened her photo app and handed him her phone. "The first one is Tomas's painting and the second one is Lucinda's."

He enlarged the photo so he could see the painting better. He had never been that interested in art and knew little about it. Tomas's painting was a bright swirl of colors of a tree heavy with leaves, with a bird building a nest. The rest of the painting was a blurred wash of sunset colors, pinks, purples, and oranges.

"It looks better when you see the actual painting," his grandmother said. "The brush strokes really make the scene come alive."

He nodded as he moved to Lucinda's painting. She'd focused her perspective on stairs that went up one way, then turned to the right, each step a mix of browns, lined and weathered. There was a light at the top right corner that gave an almost eerie look at the stairs. The rest of the painting was black. "This feels a little darker."

"I thought so, too. But they're both good, don't you think?"

"Honestly, Nonna, I have no idea." He flipped to the next picture. "What's this one?" She leaned over to take a look. "That one is by a woman named Lisette."

"It's much busier than the other two, looking at a park carnival scene."

"There wasn't a theme to the exhibit. Each artist just had to have been born in Rome."

"What about the other painting that was stolen? Do you have that one on your camera?"

"Yes, I took photos of all twelve paintings. Keep going," she said. "It should come up. Frederico's painting features geometric colored shapes and patterned tiles."

He flipped through several more pictures until he got to that one. As she'd said, Frederico's painting was a combination of shapes and colors that didn't really make sense to him. They could have been floor tiles or ceiling tiles or just shapes, but like the other two, the edges of the painting were blurry. He had no idea if it was good or not, but someone else might. "Do you mind if I send these to my phone?"

"Of course not."

He texted himself the series of photos so he could pass them along to other experts. Then he handed back her phone.

"It was a nice exhibition," she said, as she put her phone on the counter. "The paintings were all well-received, even though the artists were unknown."

"I'll take your word for it. I think the love of art skipped my generation."

"Your father's, too. Although James replaced art with music, so I can't say he hasn't contributed to the culture of the world, just differently."

Her words made him wonder what he'd contributed. Certainly not any kind of art. But he hoped he'd made the world a little safer.

"Your work is important, too," his grandmother said, always able to read him better than anyone else.

"I know."

"I hope you do."

He cleared his throat at her pointed gaze and changed the subject. "I'd like to see Tomas's letters."

"We can go to the bank tomorrow. I don't know that the letters will be that helpful. They don't mention the woman by name. And she might not be alive anymore Tomas would be over a hundred now, if he had lived."

"Maybe she was younger than him."

"I suppose that's possible." Setting down her spoon, she said, "Now, about Isabella—"

He immediately held up his hand. "Let's not talk about Isabella."

"You never told me what happened. Gloria said Isabella has been vague as well. But it's clear there's tension between you two."

"We didn't have a great date. I wasn't my best self that night, and I don't think she was, either."

"What does that mean?"

"It means you should leave it alone, Nonna. We're here to help you and Gloria. Let's just focus on that."

His grandmother gave a reluctant nod. "All right. I won't ask you any more questions, but Isabella is a lovely woman, and maybe you should give her another chance."

"Even if I wanted to, she wouldn't take it. Now, what can I do to help you with dinner?"

———

"Can I help you, Isabella?" Gloria asked.

"I'm done. I only brought a few things," Isabella replied as she finished hanging up her clothes in the closet while her grandmother took a seat on the twin bed in her very small room, which apparently was usually a junk room. There was a sewing machine in one corner with piles of fabric next to it as well a basket of yarn and a few knitting projects that had been started but not finished. There was also a chaise lounge by the window with a nice view of the river, so that was a plus. And the bed she could deal with. She didn't plan on being here that long.

"I hope you'll be comfortable," her grandmother said. "This mattress is rather hard. Maybe you should take my room."

Her grandmother had always been generous, a trait she had not seen replicated by anyone else in her family, including herself. "I'll be fine. Don't worry about me."

"I really appreciate you coming, Isabella. You didn't have to."

"I wanted to. I had to," she amended, meeting her grandmother's gaze. "You came to the States when I needed you."

"That was different. You were sixteen years old, and your mother had just gone to jail."

"Well, you're eighty-one years old, and you witnessed a terrifying robbery, so both were terrible circumstances."

"I was a little shaken after the robbery, but I'm feeling better now. I can pull it together."

She knew her grandmother believed that, but she could see the frailty in her grandmother's frame, the slight tremor in her hands. She hoped that wasn't the beginning of something more serious and was just nerves. "You don't have to handle it alone."

"I have Anna. I'm not alone."

She was actually a little envious of her grandmother's long-term friendship with Anna. She'd never had a friend like that, someone who knew everything about her, and she knew everything about them. But that was on her as much as it was on anyone else. When friends opened up to her, she backed away, knowing she wouldn't be able to reciprocate.

"Anna is amazing," she said. "But I still want to help."

"But if I'm in danger, then you are in danger, too, simply because you're here, and I don't want that."

"I don't think you're in danger, but we need to find out more about Lucinda's painting. Where is the sketch book you mentioned?"

"It's in the attic. I'll get it for you tomorrow. The lighting isn't very good, and it will be dark up there now. You must be tired with the time change and the trip, anyway."

"A little," she admitted as she sat down on the edge of the chaise lounge. "But I'll bounce back after a meal."

"You always bounce back," her grandmother said, her smile fading with her next words. "We should talk about your mother and why you are barely speaking to each other."

"We text occasionally. It's no different now than it has been the last several years."

"She said you didn't even comment when she told you she was moving to Firenze. And never responded when she sent you photos of her place or mentioned she was excited about reconnecting with old friends."

"You mean old boyfriends. I don't want to hear her talk about any more men in her life. They always turn out to be losers, and she never listens to me." She paused. "Although now that I've met Stefano, I realize she was probably talking about reconnecting with him."

"But they're not dating each other, just catching up. And I think that will be good for her. Sylvie's life fell apart when she went to the States. Maybe she can get it back."

"I'm not confident she can. She makes terrible decisions, Grandma, and she can't be swayed. When she wants something or someone, she convinces herself that's the best idea in the world. I can't let myself get bogged down in her life anymore. It's too much. I'm sorry if you think I'm being harsh, but that's just the way it is."

"I understand. But I'm going to stay hopeful."

"Did you tell her about the robbery?"

"No. She's just getting settled. I didn't want to upset her. I didn't want her to feel like she had to come here. I didn't actually want you to feel that way, either."

"I'm glad you told me, and I'm very happy to be here. I will always come when you call."

"You're so sweet, Isabella. Not that you let many people see that side of yourself."

"Sweet doesn't go well with hard-edged journalist."

"You're more than just a hard-edged journalist, and before we go downstairs, I want to ask you about Nick."

"What about him?" she asked warily.

"You didn't tell me what happened when you had dinner. You were cryptic and sounded quite annoyed about the whole thing."

"Nick and I didn't hit it off. But it's not a big deal. We're fine."

"You didn't seem fine when he arrived, and neither did he. You were both stressed out when you saw each other. I don't know why you don't like him. He's such a good person."

"We met at a bad time." As much as she wanted to tell her grandmother what a jerk Nick had been, she knew it would only make her feel bad. "Don't worry about it, Grandma."

"I'm not worried, just disappointed. I was hoping you'd hit it off. Maybe you'll get to know him better now and change your mind."

"You have enough on your plate without trying to be a matchmaker."

"I want you to find love, Isabella. You didn't have good examples growing up, but there is something wonderful about finding the right partner."

She had to bite her tongue, because she didn't believe her grandmother had found the right partner, even though she'd stayed married to him for a long time. But there was no point in dredging up that history. "I will figure it out on my own. I'm more interested in Lucinda's love life."

Her grandmother gave her a pointed look. "I told you that Lucinda and Tomas were not having an affair. There is no love story there."

"But if she was sleeping at his house when her husband was out of town, there would have been gossip and rumors. I can't believe no one thought it looked bad. Knowing how Grandfather treated my mother when she got pregnant without being married, I can't believe he wasn't judging his own mother."

"Paolo spoke to her about it. He was concerned that she was hurting her reputation, but she insisted she and Tomas were friends, artists, and they shared a common purpose. She assured Paolo she wasn't doing anything wrong. And she wasn't interested in what he had to say, either. Lucinda had a mind of her own. I think Paolo asked his father to step in, but Eduardo was always busy with work, and as long as Lucinda was happy and not bothering him, he didn't seem troubled by her relationship with Tomas."

"Did you ever talk to her about it?"

"Oh, no. It wasn't my place. I was trying to be a good daughter-in-law, and I didn't want to get in the middle."

She could say that her grandmother never wanted to get in the middle, even when she should, but she wouldn't let those words come out. Because no matter how little she'd done before, Gloria had come to help her when she needed her the most, and maybe she shouldn't be like her grandfather and judge everyone so harshly.

"Anyway, Lucinda and Tomas are long gone," Gloria said. "It doesn't matter anymore."

"But their story could be important to what is happening now. They died together in a fire and their paintings were stolen at the same time. That doesn't feel like a coincidence. We need to find out everything we can about their relationship."

"I don't know, Isabella. I want to protect our family legacy, not destroy it. The Rossi family took me in when I married Paolo. Lucinda treated me like a daughter, and I loved her. She was the artist I had imagined myself to be, but never was. She lived out her dreams. I gave mine up. I don't regret that because I had a husband and a daughter and then a beautiful granddaughter. But I always admired her. And I wouldn't want to tarnish her reputation. I know you feel distanced from the family, but I still have a sister-in-law, a brother-in-law, nieces and nephews and grand-nieces and grand-nephews. They wouldn't want me to hurt the family."

The mention of all those family members who had never been part of her life only made her feel sad and bitter. It also made her wonder where they were now. Why hadn't any of them come rushing to see if her grandmother was all right? "Have you spoken to any of our extended family members about the robbery?"

"I spoke to Victor, my nephew, yesterday. His parents have been in ill health, so he didn't want to trouble them with the news. He was concerned and worried about me. He's been in Paris the last few days. He said he'll be back tomorrow, and he'll stop by with his daughter, Joelle. She would be your second cousin. Joelle is a jewelry designer and is very creative. When I saw her at Christmas, she asked me about Lucinda's work, wondering if I had any of her art tucked away somewhere. That got me thinking, and that's when I looked through the things I'd brought from my apartment and stuck in the attic."

"Did you tell her you found the painting?"

"I left her a message last week, but she was out of town with her father. She called me a few days ago and said she couldn't wait to see it when she got home."

"So, she knew you put it in the exhibition?"

"Yes, she was delighted. So was Victor. They believed it was a nice tribute to Lucinda's talent. I feel even worse now that the painting is gone because Joelle may never get to see it."

She hadn't thought she was interested in meeting any of the extended family until now. It seemed somewhat coincidental that Joelle would have suddenly become interested in Lucinda's work, although the woman was an artist. Maybe she had just been looking for inspiration.

"We should go downstairs," her grandmother added as she got to her feet. "Dinner must be nearly ready. Anna is making a feast. I hope you're hungry."

"I am," she said as she stood up. But as they went downstairs, she felt hungrier for information than for food.

She'd come to Rome thinking her grandmother had gotten caught up in a random robbery, but now it felt personal, which was an odd feeling. She'd grown up hating the Rossi family for not accepting her or her mother, but now she wanted to know more about every one of them.

CHAPTER FIVE

Nick woke up Friday morning, feeling markedly better than he had the night before, when, after a delicious but very heavy dinner, he'd slept twelve straight hours. He'd needed the rest, but now he was ready to get to work.

After a long, hot shower, he changed into dark jeans and a blue polo shirt. Then he walked downstairs to the kitchen. There wasn't anyone around, but there was coffee in the pot and pastries on the table, so he filled a mug, grabbed a croissant, and sat down to eat.

As he ate, he checked his phone and saw a message from Flynn, suggesting he contact Francesca Ribaldi, an art historian in Rome, who he had worked with when he was assigned to art crimes several years earlier. She might be able to figure out the value of the paintings and why they had been targeted.

He immediately punched in the number that Flynn had given him, but after several rings, it went to voicemail. He left a quick message using Flynn's name and asked Francesca to call him back. As he set down the phone, Isabella entered the kitchen.

She looked refreshed as well, her dark hair loose around her shoulders, her brown eyes alert, and her skin practically glowing.

She was dressed in jeans with a cream-colored sweater over a white tank top. She hesitated when she saw him at the table, but then she moved forward, carrying an oversized pad in one hand.

"What do you have there?" he asked.

"Lucinda's sketch book. My grandmother pulled it out of the attic a few minutes ago." Isabella opened to the first page, and he could see a fairly detailed pencil sketch.

"That looks better than a rough drawing," he said.

"It's very good," she murmured, her gaze perusing the page. "It also feels vaguely familiar. I want to say I've seen this before, but I don't know where." She turned the page and looked at the next sketch. "This one is rough," she said, giving him a quick look at a sketch that seemed to be part of a face but hadn't been completed.

Isabella moved through several more pages without comment, and he sipped his coffee, wondering how the sketches could help them. They belonged to Isabella's great-grandmother, but they weren't paintings; they weren't valuable. And they already knew Lucinda was an artist. Maybe Isabella was just interested in the work because Lucinda was her great-grandmother.

"Do you know much about Lucinda?" he asked.

"No."

"Your grandmother didn't tell you about her, or maybe your mother?"

"My mother told me Lucinda inspired her to become an artist, but my mother was born after Lucinda died, so she never met her. I don't know how or when my mother got this sketch book. Grandma said my mother probably dug it out of their attic when she was a girl. Same with the loose canvas. She said my mother was always drawing, so she encouraged her to study Lucinda's work, what little of it was left."

He'd never met her mother, but his grandmother had told him that Sylvie and her husband had gotten into trouble with some fraudulent scheme that sent them both to jail. He'd never asked for more detail, but now, having met Isabella, he was curious.

"Your mother went to prison, right?" he asked.

She stiffened. "I'm sure you already know the answer to that is yes."

"But I don't know more than that. How old were you? How long was she in jail? What did she do?"

Isabella gave him an irritated look, and he thought she'd refuse to answer, but after a moment, she said, "I was sixteen when she was convicted. She was in jail for a little over two years. And the charges were part of a long, complicated story."

"What happened to you when she went to prison? Did you live with your dad?"

"My biological father was never in my life. My stepfather also went to prison. I would have been sent to foster care if Gloria hadn't come and rented an apartment in my school district so I could stay in school. The house we'd been living in was taken back by the bank. With Gloria there, I was able to finish out my junior year. Then she brought me back here for the summer, where I had the not-so-delightful experience of spending time with my grandfather, who didn't want me here at all. I was a symbol of his daughter's sinful ways," she said, a bitter edge to her voice.

"That sucks. My summers with my grandparents were a great break from life with my parents."

"Well, I couldn't wait to leave. At the end of the summer, my grandmother took me back to Chicago, where we were living, and stayed with me until I graduated. She did that against Paolo's wishes. It might have been one of the few times she stood up to him." Isabella paused, her brown-eyed gaze reflective. "She saved me, and I can never thank her enough for that. I don't know what would have happened to me if she hadn't been willing to stay with me."

"What did you do after high school?"

"I went to college in New York, and my grandmother moved back here. Paolo died two months after she arrived, and my grandmother blamed herself for not being here when he first started getting sick. Not that he told her. He was such a proud, arrogant man. She'd made her choice to stay with me, so he froze her out."

Nick could imagine Paolo doing that. He hadn't spent a lot of time with the man beyond being in the same room when there was a dinner or a party. "Paolo always seemed cold and rigid to me. I don't remember him smiling much. He was such a contrast to your grandmother."

"I don't know how the two of them got together or why they stayed together, except that my grandmother is religious, and she took her vows seriously. She'd married for life, which probably ruined her life. Not that she'd admit that."

Isabella had told her story in harsh, icy tones, but he could see the emotions brimming in her eyes. No wonder she had built such a defensive wall around herself. She'd done that to survive, and he felt a rush of sympathy for what she'd had to deal with as a teenager. "I'm sorry you had to go through all that."

"Me, too. But I've moved on."

He wondered if that was true. "Are you close to your mother now?"

"Not at all. When she got out of prison, I was living in New York, and she was in Chicago. I would sometimes see her on school holidays, but I was so angry with her I didn't try very hard to make that happen. As I got older, I thought about attempting to mend our relationship, but then she got involved with another man, and I just didn't see the point. I've texted with her a few times a year, but that's about it. I love her and sometimes I hate her." She bit down on her lip. "I shouldn't have said that out loud. My grandmother would be sad to hear me say that."

"Well, Gloria isn't here, and I like honesty."

She gave him a skeptical look. "A guy who spends his life undercover likes honesty?"

"Maybe that's why I do. It's a rare commodity from what I've seen."

"It is rare. Most people have hidden agendas. I've learned not to take anything at face value." She cleared her throat. "Speaking of parents, where are yours? Why aren't they here checking on Anna?"

"They're on tour. She said she spoke to my father, who didn't really care that the painting was gone, which is no surprise. He cares about little that doesn't involve him or my mother or music."

"It doesn't sound like you care much for your parents," she commented, interest gathering in her eyes.

He shrugged. "I don't think much about them anymore. They haven't been in my life for a long time."

"Why? Were they abusive?"

"No. They were fine. They just didn't care very much. I was an accident. I was raised by nannies, and when I got older, they dropped me off here in the summers while they traveled. Those were some of my happiest days. I might have struck out in the parent department, but the grandparents were great."

"What about your mother's parents?"

"They were divorced and lived in different places, so I saw little of them."

"Hmm," she said, her gaze speculative as it met his. "I thought we had absolutely nothing in common except our love for our grandmothers, but maybe there's a little more."

"You're quick to judge, Isabella."

"I am. I'm afraid I get that from my grandfather, which pisses me off."

He smiled. "And you don't look for the best in people."

"You're right. I look for the worst, so I won't be surprised. What about you?"

"To be honest, I don't know anymore."

Something clicked between them again, some innate understanding, some odd connection that sent a tingle down his spine.
Isabella seemed to feel it, too. She stiffened and then turned her
attention to the sketchbook.

As she went back to studying the drawings, he couldn't help
studying her. She was a beautiful woman with a lot of sharp
edges, an aggressively defensive attitude, and some serious
baggage. But now that he knew more about her, he had a better
sense of why she might feel she needed to defend herself, to
always be in control.

"This is weird," she said suddenly, breaking into his thoughts.

"What is?"

"This drawing has a number on it, buried in the scratches on
a piece of wood." She turned the sketch around so he could see
it. "The number two. I wonder what it means."

"I don't know if I would have noticed it if you hadn't pointed
it out."

"My mother made me look at a lot of art over the years. She
used to tell me that artists often leave Easter eggs in their work,
little signs of something that you wouldn't notice unless you
looked long enough."

"So the number two is an Easter egg?"

"I don't know," she murmured as their grandmothers came
into the room.

"What don't you know?" Gloria asked.

"I was just looking at this sketch and noticed a number two
on the piece of wood. The way it's drawn, you can barely see it."

Anna and Gloria peered at the sketchbook. "I think that's a
stair," Gloria said. "Maybe the beginning of Lucinda's staircase
painting, the one that was stolen."

"I see the number," Anna said. "That's odd. I don't think it
was on the final painting."

He took out his phone and brought up the painting,
enlarging the bottom stair. "I see nothing in this photo, but I
can't see every detail."

"She must have just been experimenting with something in this sketch. I thought I was on to something," Isabella said with a sigh.

Isabella was working hard to find some sort of clue, but she was wasting her time trying to decipher an old sketchbook. It was his turn to step up to the plate. "We should focus on the actual robbery. I'd like to speak to Captain Lavezzo. Did he give you a number, Nonna?"

"He did," Anna replied. "It's in my bag. I'll get it."

He finished his coffee as he waited for her to return while Isabella and Gloria continued to study Lucinda's sketches. His grandmother returned a moment later and handed him a card.

He took out his phone and called the number. A woman answered, and he asked to speak to Captain Lavezzo. She replied he was unavailable, but she could take a message.

"I'm Nick Caruso, Anna Caruso's grandson," he said. "She was a witness to the robbery at the Museo dei Capolavori Romani. I'd like to speak to him about the investigation. I'm happy to come to his office to do that. Besides being Anna's grandson, I'm also an FBI agent and would love to offer him any resources that I can."

"Un momento," she said, putting him on hold. A few minutes later, she returned. "He can meet with you at noon today, if that is convenient."

"That's perfect." He jotted down the address she gave him and then ended the call. He met his grandmother's questioning gaze. "Captain Lavezzo will meet with us at noon." Glancing at his watch, he realized it was just past ten, so they had some time. "Maybe we can go down to the bank vault now and get the letters and whatever else is there before my meeting."

"Our meeting," his grandmother said. "I should be there. I'm the witness."

"I can handle it on my own. You already told him what you witnessed. I'm more interested in what they're doing to find the thieves. I can speak to him as one law enforcement official to another." His grandmother didn't look convinced. "I do this all the time, Nonna."

"In America," she said. "This is Italy."

"I'm aware. I will be respectful. Trust me."

"I do trust you."

"Well, I think I should go, too," Isabella put in. "To represent my grandmother's interests."

"That's sweet of you," Gloria said. "But Victor and Joelle are coming by at noon, and I would like you to meet them, Isabella."

He was thrilled that Gloria had given Isabella a pressing reason to stay here, because he wanted to meet with the Carabinieri officer on his own.

"All right," Isabella said somewhat reluctantly.

He got to his feet. "Are you ready to go now, Nonna? How far away is the bank? Do we need to get a cab, or can we walk?"

"It's a few miles. I have my car in the garage. We can take that."

"Great."

She collected her things and then they walked out the back door, through the yard, and into the garage. The bright yellow two-door Fiat 500 boasted several dents on the back bumper, and he gave his grandmother a pointed look. "What happened here?"

"Someone backed into me. It was very disturbing. There are so many careless drivers now. I don't drive much anymore."

He could see by the glint in her eye he was only getting part of that story. But as long as she'd decided to stop driving, he would let it go.

The car was so small, he felt like he was stuffing himself into a toy vehicle, but the engine started, and that was all that mattered.

"It's nice to have you here taking care of things, Nick," she said as he pulled out of the garage. "Sometimes you remind me of Marcus. He was always so protective of me. I miss that." She gave him a somewhat teary smile. "But I tell myself I was lucky to have had him for over fifty years. I really can't complain. I had a good man."

"You did."

"Tomas was a good man, too. I know you and Isabella think he had an inappropriate relationship with Lucinda, but I don't believe that's true. He was very moral. And I'm sure that the letters he exchanged with this other woman occurred after his wife died. She passed away about six years before Tomas."

"Are there any dates on the letters?"

"I didn't read them that closely, but I remember seeing just a day and a month, no year."

"So you don't know when they were written or how they survived the fire at his home?"

"No, I don't," she admitted. "I wasn't aware of their existence until I retrieved the painting. Marcus never mentioned the letters. I wish he was here now so I could ask him more questions."

"I wish he was here, too," he said heavily.

"I want the painting back, but I don't want to hurt the family, Nick. Am I wrong to show you the letters? Am I wrong to try to find out why the painting was taken? What if..." Her voice trailed away.

He stopped at a light and gave her a searching look. "What if...what?"

"What if Tomas did something bad? What if Marcus covered it up for him?"

He was surprised by her questions. Not so much the first one, but definitely the second. "Do you think that's a possibility?"

"I don't know, but after what happened to the painting, I'm wondering if I should let everything else stay locked away where it's been for so long. Maybe the truth will hurt someone in the family—me, you, everyone..."

"I'm not afraid of the truth, Nonna. I'm more afraid of what we don't know. That's where the danger lies. That's why we need to find out everything we can."

CHAPTER SIX

"What are you doing, Isabella?" her grandmother asked as Isabella opened her laptop computer on the kitchen table.

"A little research. And I want to check my emails. But would you like me to help with lunch?" Her grandmother had already started working on an antipasto and a pasta dish for Victor and Joelle's visit. When people came over, Gloria Rossi was always ready to feed them.

"I have everything under control. How is work going these days? Was the move to LA a good one?"

"It was. I needed a fresh start."

"Not just from the job, but from Joel, right?"

"From everything," she said vaguely.

"I know Joel hurt you, because one minute you were sending me photos and texts saying you were having the time of your life, and then it was over."

"Someone always gets hurt when there's a breakup." She opened her email and skimmed the list of messages.

"Did you do the hurting, or did he?"

She looked up at her grandmother. "What do you think?"

Gloria gave her a look of disappointment. "I'm sorry. Maybe you need to look for a different kind of man."

She had to smile at that. "Probably. But I'm happy to be on my own right now. Having a boyfriend isn't a priority. I'm more interested in building my career and creating a new life for myself in LA."

"There hasn't been anyone in Los Angeles who has drawn your interest?"

"Not really." She sent her grandmother a warning look as she saw the gleam reenter her eyes. "Don't even say it, Grandma."

"You don't know what I'm thinking."

"I'm sure I do. And your sauce is boiling."

Her grandmother quickly turned back to the stove.

Isabella opened up her search engine, ready to do what she always did when she caught a lead—research. Thinking about the robbery had made her wonder if there had been any other museum break-ins in the last year. After a few minutes of searching, she found an article about a break-in at an art gallery in Firenze six months earlier. Only one painting by David Leoni had been taken.

"Do you know a painter by the name of David Leoni?" she asked.

"Yes. Why?" her grandmother asked as she turned to look at her.

"His painting was stolen from an art gallery in Firenze six months ago. It was the only piece taken. Is he famous?"

"He's had some modest success. I met him years ago at Tomas's studio."

Her pulse jumped at her grandmother's words. "Seriously?"

"Yes. He was a very young man then, probably eighteen or nineteen. I remember Tomas telling me David was his protegee. He thought he could help him harness his talent into something amazing."

"And his painting was stolen six months ago, the only one taken out of the gallery. That doesn't seem like a coincidence. Is he still alive?"

"I have no idea."

Isabella opened a new tab and typed in David Leoni, but a million hits came back. The name was too common. She narrowed her search to artist, theft, and the name of the gallery and then discovered a public page about him, which showed his birthdate and his date of death, which was eighteen months ago.

"It looks like he died a little over a year and a half ago."

"That's sad. He was younger than me. How did he die?"

"It doesn't say. But I've just started looking; I'll find more," she said confidently.

"I'm sure you will," her grandmother said, a gleam of admiration in her eyes. "Because you don't quit, Isabella."

"I don't."

"Sometimes that makes me worry."

"Why? Not giving up is a good thing."

"It can be. Unless whatever you're working on becomes an obsession, a reason to overlook other parts of your life."

"You have a one-track mind when it comes to my life," she said with annoyance. "Love, love, love."

"Or lack thereof."

"I date, Grandma. I just haven't found someone I want to think about more than I want to think about my job. Maybe it will happen one day. Maybe it won't. I'm not concerned about it, and you shouldn't be, either."

As she finished speaking, she was startled by a loud crash in the backyard. Her grandmother jumped, too, fear entering her eyes.

"What was that?" her grandmother asked.

She stood up. "It sounded like it came from the backyard."

"Don't go out there. The last time I heard a crash, it was followed by men with guns."

"Let's go upstairs." She grabbed her grandmother's hand, not sure if she was making the right move to go up the stairs instead of toward the front door, but if someone was outside, she thought staying in the house was the best move.

They hurried up the stairs, her grandmother breathing

heavily by the time they made it to the third floor. At the landing, she glanced out the window which overlooked the backyard. She couldn't see everything, but she could see a shadow moving by the shed in the garden.

"Is someone out there?" her grandmother asked.

"I'm not sure. I saw a shadow, but now it's gone." They stood still for several long minutes, but there was no other sound. "I think it's okay for me to go downstairs and check it out now."

"No," her grandmother said, squeezing her hand. "Maybe we should call the Polizia."

"It could be nothing. And I left my phone downstairs."

"Mine is there, too."

As she was debating what to do, the doorbell suddenly pealed, and they jumped again.

"A thief wouldn't ring the bell," her grandmother said. "It's probably a neighbor checking on us. Or maybe it's Victor and Joelle. They might be early."

"An hour early?"

"I don't know," her grandmother said as the bell rang once more. "But I don't think it's a thief."

"Okay. I'll check it out." She jogged down the stairs, her grandmother following more slowly. She peered through the window next to the door and saw an older man and a woman about her age standing on the porch. "Is Joelle a redhead?" she asked.

"Yes. At least, she was the last time I saw her," her grandmother said as she came down the last flight of steps.

"It's them." She opened the door as her grandmother came up next to her.

"Sorry, we're early," Victor said. "If it's not convenient, we can go get a coffee and come back."

"Don't be silly. I'm happy to see you both," her grandmother replied, moving past her to hug and kiss her nephew and then his daughter.

"We weren't sure you were here," Joelle said. "When you didn't answer right away."

"I was upstairs," her grandmother replied. "This is Isabella, Sylvie's daughter."

Surprise flashed in Joelle's green eyes. "Isabella? I never thought we'd meet." Joelle stepped forward to give her a kiss on each cheek.

"I would have known you were Sylvie's just by looking at you," Victor said as he welcomed her. "You look very much like her."

"It's nice to meet you both. Please come in."

As they stepped into the house, she looked around the street. It was empty. No one in sight. She closed and locked the door as her grandmother escorted Victor and Joelle into the living room. Then she went through the kitchen and laundry room to the back door. The dead bolt was still in place, which was a good sign. She turned the bolt and opened the door, her gaze sweeping the small garden and patio area, landing on the shed in the corner.

The door to the shed was wide open and two watering cans that were next to the shed were lying on one side. She debated for one more second and then walked down the stairs and into the yard. She didn't think anyone was still there, but she had to make sure.

When she got to the doorway, she peered through the dim light. It was a small space with mostly gardening supplies and some random boxes. One of those boxes had been upended, the contents spilling onto the floor, and those contents appeared to be Christmas decorations. Had the boxes been knocked over by an animal? It was possible, but it seemed more likely that someone had been in the shed.

She backed out of the small building and pulled the door closed. Then she hurried into the house and turned the dead bolt. She leaned against the door, debating what to do. She could call the police. But what would she say? If there had been someone in the shed, they were gone now. And nothing had been taken. Maybe she was seeing a problem that wasn't there. Or maybe Nick was right, and the danger wasn't over.

As she debated her options, she heard laughter wafting through the house.

Her grandmother was enjoying a visit with her relatives. They were okay for now. She'd wait until Victor and Joelle were gone and then discuss what might have happened with her grandmother, as well as Nick and Anna, when they returned.

———

Nick watched as the bank employee opened a large locker door and then left them alone in the vault to review the contents. In the gaping space of the locker, which had apparently been large enough to hold a painting, there were also two cardboard boxes with lids.

"This one is Tomas's," his grandmother said, taking out the top box and putting it on the counter next to him.

"What about the other one?"

"It has our personal papers—Marcus's and mine. He said it was safer to keep them here than at the house."

"Let's look through that, too."

She frowned but pulled out the box. "I guess there's no harm in that."

He pulled the lid off of Tomas's box first. A rubber band held together three letters. There was a velvet pouch next to that stack, which he picked up first, sliding out a thick ring with an interesting design on it. "What's this?"

"Tomas's ring, I assume, since it was in this box. I don't remember seeing him wear it, however."

He turned it around several times, studying the lines. "Do you know what this design represents? It looks like there is a letter *P* in the middle of it."

"I have no idea."

"And you never saw it when Tomas was alive?"

"Not that I recall, but I spent little time with Tomas. He was a busy man, and I had a baby to worry about during the last years of Tomas's life. Frankly, I never saw this box before last week. Marcus was responsible for putting things here or taking them out."

He was surprised by that. "Did Papa purposefully keep you away from here? Did you feel he was secretive in some way?"

"No, of course not. We were always honest with each other."

There was something in her eyes that gave him pause. "What aren't you telling me, Nonna?"

She hesitated, then said, "He never tried to keep me away from here. But right before he died, he was stressed out about something. And when we were running errands one day, he said he wanted to put some things in the vault, and he came inside while I waited in the car. It just took him a minute."

"What was he stressed out about?"

"I don't know. He was retired. Everything was wonderful with us, with the family. But there was something on his mind he didn't want to talk about, and he kept getting calls at odd times of the day and night. He told me someone he knew was having a hard time, and he was trying to help them out. I didn't ask for details. He loved being a mentor. I'm sure it was nothing, but when you asked if he was being secretive, it popped into my head."

He considered her words. "Papa's car accident," he said. "He skidded in the rain, right? Or was there another car involved?"

"No. It was just a wet road. The Polizia investigated the accident thoroughly. He was one of them. Hundreds came to his funeral."

"I remember," he muttered. Of course his grandfather's crash had just been an accident. His grandfather had been eighty years old and retired. He hadn't worked as a police officer for more than a decade. He wasn't involved in anything, and there was no mystery. Maybe he was stressed out about someone's problems, but that might have nothing to do with anything. He needed to focus on Tomas and not on his grandfather.

Although that thought reminded him that both his grandfather and great-grandfather had died under somewhat unusual conditions. A fire and a solo car crash. Did they both just have bad luck?

"Shall we take the boxes home with us?" his grandmother asked. "We can look through them there."

"That's a good idea." He closed the lid on Tomas's box and picked up both boxes as his grandmother closed the door to the now empty safe deposit box and followed him out of the vault.

He stashed the boxes in the back seat of the car, then squeezed himself behind the wheel. As he pulled away from the bank, he noticed a car coming up fast behind them.

His pulse jumped as he looked into the rearview mirror and saw a man in a black hoodie with dark glasses over his eyes. He hit the gas, but the car stayed right on his tail as he swerved through traffic.

"Nick, why are you going so fast and in the wrong direction?" his grandmother asked, bracing her hand on the door.

"Someone is following us."

"What?" She turned to glance over her shoulder. "It's a man wearing a black sweatshirt with a hood like the thieves I saw in the museum. Do you think it's one of them?"

"I don't know."

"Why would he be following us?"

"Maybe he's not, but he's been on my bumper for the last three turns."

"What are you going to do?"

"Drive to Lavezzo's office—Piazza San Ignazio. Do you know how to get there?" He didn't want to slow down to put the address into his phone.

"Yes. Turn right at the next light." For the next several minutes, he followed her directions, keeping an eye on the traffic and the car behind him. It had dropped back slightly now. Maybe he'd realized he'd been caught tailing them.

When he pulled up in front of the Palazzo Raguzzini, where the headquarters of the Carabinieri was located, the car sped past him. He made a mental note of the license plate number before it disappeared, then grabbed his phone to jot it down.

"He's gone now," he said, seeing his grandmother's tight grip on the armrest. "We're okay."

"Maybe he wasn't following us. Otherwise, he would have stopped when we did, right?"

"Possibly." He didn't want to upset his grandmother, but he was absolutely certain the car had been following them, and that was disturbing. Whatever was going on was definitely not over.

CHAPTER SEVEN

After parking the car, Nick escorted his grandmother into the eighteenth-century building that housed the headquarters of the Carabinieri T.P.C. He'd forgotten how beautiful and old the buildings of Rome were, a far cry from the law enforcement offices he frequented. After getting through security, they made their way upstairs to meet with Captain Lavezzo.

Antonio Lavezzo had a corner office with windows overlooking the piazza. He appeared to be in his fifties with light brown hair and sharp green eyes. After Nick introduced himself as an FBI agent and Anna Caruso's grandson, they sat down in the chairs in front of the captain's desk.

"How are you feeling today, Signora?" Captain Lavezzo asked.

"I'm still shaken, even more so after what just happened."

Lavezzo straightened, interest gathering in his eyes. "What happened?"

"We were followed here by a man wearing all black with a hood and dark glasses," Nick replied. "I got the license plate number."

"I'll take that." Lavezzo picked up a pen and jotted down the numbers that Nick read off his phone. "I will look into this as soon as we are done speaking."

"We'd appreciate that. How's the investigation going? Has the security guard been able to give you any information?"

"Unfortunately, he could not identify the thieves, and the security system was hacked, turning off the alarms and the cameras."

"Will Enrique be all right?" his grandmother interrupted.

"Yes. His condition is serious, but he is expected to recover."

"I'm so glad," she said with relief.

"What about the paintings that were stolen?" he asked. "Any idea why they would have been targeted over other more valuable works?"

"That is the most puzzling part of this theft. Obviously, someone was willing to kill to get them, so they have value, but it's not apparent to us what that value is. I've spoken to several art experts, and no one has come up with an answer. None of these artists were well- known, and all three passed away years ago. But it is early days. We hope to find more leads as we continue our investigation. It can take weeks, months, sometimes years, to track down stolen paintings."

"We may not have that kind of time. I'm concerned about my grandmother's safety. They may think she can identify them."

"But I can't," his grandmother put in.

"When did you notice the car following you?" the captain asked. "Was it when you left your house?"

"No. We went to the bank before coming here," he replied. "The car picked us up after that."

"But he drove away once you arrived here? And he allowed you a view of his license plate by driving right past you?"

"Yes, and that was odd. He clearly didn't care that I could read his license plate."

"What is the name and location of the bank?" Captain Lavezzo asked, picking up his pen again.

He gave him the bank name and address and then said, "Perhaps there's a camera around the bank that might pick up the car. It was a blue Toyota Yaris."

"Why don't you give me your number, and I will let you know what I find out? In the meantime, perhaps it would be wise to take your grandmother out of Rome, maybe back to the States."

"We've been talking about that, haven't we, Nonna?"

"Yes, and I don't need you two making decisions for me. I've been doing that longer than you've both been alive," she said sharply.

Captain Lavezzo nodded. "My apologies. I simply wish to keep you safe, Signora."

"Finding the thieves who stole my father-in-law's painting is the best way to do that, Captain," she said.

"I will do everything I can to make sure the stolen paintings are returned to their rightful owners."

"I'd like to help you do that," he said. "I have resources I can offer."

"I appreciate that, but my team has a great deal of expertise in these matters, especially where it concerns Italian artists and their art."

"Of course. Let me know if you change your mind."

"Certainly. And now I will return to work," Lavezzo said as he rose. "Thank you for coming in."

He had more questions he wanted to ask, but he could see that Captain Lavezzo was not interested in collaborating with him, so he simply muttered his goodbye along with his grandmother.

"Do you think he's going to find the paintings?" his grandmother asked as they headed downstairs.

"I hope so, Nonna." But as they left the building and headed home, finding the paintings was the least of his worries. Things weren't adding up, and that had his nerves on edge. He needed to figure out what was going on before anything else happened.

———

It was both awkward and entertaining getting to know her extended family members, Isabella thought, as she and Joelle took their coffees into the living room after a very filling lunch while her grandmother showed Victor around the house.

Victor had turned out to be a charming, sophisticated man, who traveled extensively, and loved to talk about those travels, as well as wine and food. Joelle was not as smooth as her father. She was more arty, flamboyant, and also very sarcastic.

Joelle had asked a lot of questions about Lucinda's art and the robbery and exactly where Gloria had been and what she'd heard. Her grandmother hadn't seemed uncomfortable with the questions, although she'd stayed a little vague on the details. Perhaps Nick's warning about not trusting anyone but the four of them had stuck in her head.

She had to admit that she liked Victor and Joelle more than she'd thought she would. She'd had a chip on her shoulder her entire life when it came to family. Because her grandfather had kept her away from the family during her summer in Rome, she'd assumed that no one wanted to meet her, but perhaps that wasn't true.

Even now, she could see Joelle eyeing her with blatant curiosity.

"What?" she asked as she sipped her coffee.

"I'm just wondering what it's like to be a journalist," Joelle said. "Do you travel all over the world? Do you interview world leaders? Do you report on grisly crimes?"

"I've traveled the US, interviewed congressmen and senators and reported on some grisly crimes," she said with a smile, appreciating the fact that someone was actually interested in her and not just that she was Sylvie's daughter or Gloria's grand-daughter. "But I haven't gone international. Maybe one day."

"Well, you're here in Rome now. And it sounds like you have a personal story to chase."

"It's turning out like that. I just came to make sure my grandmother was all right, but I've become very interested in Lucinda's life."

"Our great-grandmother was a fascinating woman. She spent time with men who weren't her husband. She was adventurous and artistic. She hung out with artists and smoked cigarettes and drank lots of wine."

She laughed at the look of envy in Joelle's eyes. "How do you know all that?"

"My grandmother used to talk to me about Lucinda. She said her mother was fire, a bright flame that never dimmed, which is weirdly ironic since she died in a fire. But while she was alive, she lived. Lucinda chased her dreams. She's always inspired me."

"She's beginning to inspire me, too."

"Well, you're already doing amazing things, so clearly you didn't need the inspiration."

"Tell me about your life as a jewelry designer. Do you work with celebrities?"

"A few. I'm still growing my clientele. But I love designing personal items for people. It's my specialty. I've also been going to some fashion shows in Berlin, Paris, and London, and I've been able to find clients there, both fashion designers and celebrities."

"That sounds more exciting than Lucinda's life."

"It's starting to be," Joelle said with a laugh. "But I'm not there yet. I want to be great. I want to be famous. I probably shouldn't say that out loud, but you're family. I wish I had met you before now, Isabella. I was always intrigued by the daughter of the black sheep we weren't allowed to discuss. I swear your grandfather made your mother sound like a...well, I don't want to say the word he used, but it wasn't good."

"He thought she was a terrible person for getting pregnant without being married."

"That certainly wasn't a crime, and Sylvie got a beautiful daughter out of it, so it all worked out, didn't it?"

Clearly, Joelle was not one to judge, which made Isabella like her even more. "Do you have a shop here in Rome or do you work out of your house? I'd love to see your jewelry."

"I work mostly out of my apartment, but I sell my work in various stores and at art and jewelry shows. I would love to show it to you. How long will you be in Rome?"

"I'm not sure. I might have to wait until all this is resolved before I can look at your jewelry, though, but definitely before I leave."

"That would be lovely. I heard your mother moved to Firenze. Will you be seeing her on this trip?"

"I'm not sure yet."

"I'm surprised she's not here checking in on Gloria."

She shrugged. "She's busy getting settled in."

"So, what do you think about this robbery? Is there a mystery behind Lucinda's painting? Because I don't understand why anyone would break into a museum to steal it."

"I have no idea. Maybe it just got caught up in the heist."

"Heist is such a sexy word. It sounds so James Bondish."

She smiled. "It does, but from what my grandmother described, the robbery was terrifying, not at all sexy."

"I shouldn't be making light of it. I'm glad she's all right. Gloria is so kind and loving. I just wish she'd told me about Lucinda's painting earlier. I'm sad I may never get to see it. She doesn't have any idea who stole it? She saw nothing when they were in hiding?"

"No," Isabella confirmed, wondering why Joelle kept asking her the same question in a slightly different way, as if Joelle thought she was hiding something from her.

"It just seems like she'd have some idea, that she would have heard some story about the painting over the years," Joelle persisted.

"Did your father ever hear anything?" she asked.

"Only rumors that Lucinda and Tomas were having an affair."

"My grandmother says that wasn't true."

"True or not, staying overnight with a single man who wasn't her husband would have been quite scandalous during that time period. Lucinda was a modern woman living in a very traditional era. The stories she probably could have told us, if only she hadn't died so young."

"I don't think we would have heard them regardless of when she died. She was a lot older."

"I know. I just find Lucinda to be the most fascinating person in the family, and now I'm even more intrigued because of the theft of the one and only painting she had left. Let's exchange numbers so we can set up a time to meet, and if you find out anything about our wild great-grandmother, I would love to know."

"Of course," she said as she rattled off her number. She still felt a bit bemused by Joelle's outgoing and friendly nature.

"I'll text you right now," Joelle said as she typed out a note and sent it.

She smiled at the greeting. *Hey Cuz, it's me, Joelle.* "I've never had a cousin before," she said.

"Well, you have one now."

"I like that."

"Me, too," Joelle agreed.

They both turned toward the doorway at the sound of voices. At first, she thought it was Victor and her grandmother, but it was Nick and Anna who walked into the living room.

"Who is this handsome man?" Joelle murmured as she got to her feet.

"Nick," she said as she stood up.

"Joelle?" Anna asked, a smile lighting up her eyes. "My goodness. You are all grown up now."

"I have been for a while, Signora Caruso."

"Oh, you know you can call me Anna," she said as she kissed Joelle on each cheek. "I don't know if you ever met Nick, my grandson."

"Definitely not. I would remember if I had," Joelle said, flashing her dazzling smile at Nick. She took his hand and pulled him in for the same warm greeting she'd exchanged with Anna.

Isabella frowned, not sure why it bothered her that Joelle had just kissed Nick. She certainly didn't want to kiss him. Well, maybe in a purely objective way, she was slightly curious, only because he was very attractive, but his personality was not at all appealing.

Nick seemed to enjoy the attention, but she got the feeling he was also distracted, and not by Joelle.

She wondered what had happened at the bank. Anna, too, showed stress behind her smile. But she didn't want to ask in front of Joelle, who had already shown a propensity to ask a lot of questions.

Fortunately, Gloria and Victor returned, and after more introductions, Victor said they needed to leave, as he had an afternoon meeting to attend.

Joelle seemed disappointed to be going, and Isabella had a feeling that was because she was now interested in getting to know Nick, but her father was urging her toward the door.

"I hope we can all get together again," Joelle said. "Maybe the three of us can get a drink. What do you say, Nick? Isabella?"

"Sounds good to me," Nick said.

Like she wanted to be a third wheel on that date. But as Joelle turned an inquiring eye in her direction, she simply said, "Sure. We'll make a plan."

"I'm going to hold you to that. I'll text you later."

As Gloria walked them to the door, Anna sat down rather heavily on the sofa, while Nick abruptly left the room.

"Everything okay, Anna?" she asked.

"Oh, Isabella, I don't think so," she replied.

Her stomach turned over at Anna's words. "Did you find something at the vault?"

Before Anna could answer, Nick and Gloria returned. Nick was holding two boxes in his hands, which he set down on the coffee table.

"What's in the boxes?" she asked.

"The letters Tomas exchanged with someone with the initial J and a ring," Nick replied, as he and her grandmother sat down. "That's what we know so far, but we haven't looked at the rest."

"Let's do that now," she said, eager to see both.

He held up a hand. "In a minute. We need to talk first."

"We do," Anna agreed.

"Has something happened?" Gloria asked worriedly.

"Someone followed us from the bank to the offices of the Carabinieri," Nick said. "I couldn't see the driver's face, but he was wearing a black sweatshirt with a hood and dark glasses."

"Like the men in the museum," Gloria breathed.

"Yes. He sped away when we got to the Carabinieri head-quarters," Nick said. "But I got a license plate number and Captain Lavezzo will try to find out who he is. That said, Captain Lavezzo suggested everyone would be safer away from Rome, and I agree. I don't like that someone followed us. They may think you two heard or saw more than you did, or that you have another painting that they want. I don't know the reason, only that this isn't over."

"We can stay in the house. It's safe here," Anna began, then paused as Gloria let out a heavy sigh. "Do you want to go, Gloria?"

"I don't want to leave, but I'm not sure the house is safe. Isabella and I heard a crash in the backyard earlier."

"What? Why didn't you say that before?" Nick turned an accusing gaze in her direction.

"You just sat down. I haven't had a chance to say anything," she returned. "We were in the kitchen when we heard a crash in the yard. We went upstairs and when I looked out the window, I saw a shadow, but that's all. A few minutes later, the doorbell rang, and it was Victor and Joelle. After they came in, I went into the yard, and I saw the door to the shed was open and a box of Christmas decorations was knocked over. I don't know if it was a person or an animal."

"That's it," Nick said. "I need to get you all out of here. Where do you want to go? I will pay for your tickets. I think you should leave Italy. In fact, why don't you go to LA and stay at my place? I have two bedrooms. You can decorate while you're there; I don't have much on the walls. Isabella can show you around, make sure you're comfortable."

Remembering how scared and winded her grandmother had been when she'd rushed her up the stairs, she knew Nick was right, as much as she didn't want to admit it. "It's a good idea," she said, turning to her grandmother. "You and Anna haven't been to the States in a long time, have you?"

"No." Gloria looked at her longtime friend. "What do you think, Anna?"

"I want to get our paintings back. I'm afraid if we leave, that won't happen."

"I'll do everything I can to make that happen," Nick said. "But it will be easier to pursue that goal if I'm not worrying about you."

"But I'll be worrying about you. I don't want you to get hurt, Nick."

"I can take care of myself. This is what I do, Nonna. And I'm good at it."

Anna let out a sigh of resignation. "All right. I'll go to Los Angeles if Gloria will go, too."

Her grandmother slowly nodded. "That's probably best."

"Good," Nick said with relief. "I have a team there who can watch out for you. And Isabella will get you whatever you need."

"No," she said, bringing their gazes to her. "Anna and Grandma should go to LA, but I'm staying here. I want to find the paintings, too."

"I don't need your help," he said.

"I don't need yours, either. I'm not leaving. You'll have to deal with that." She frowned at her grandmother, who was exchanging a small smile with Anna. "What are you so amused about?"

"Just thinking this might not be the worst idea," her grandmother replied. "You and Nick can get to know each other better."

"That's not what this is about," she said firmly.

"You'll take care of her, Nick, won't you?" her grandmother asked.

"I'll try, but I can't promise anything. She'd be safer in LA."

"It's not your call," she interrupted. "I can take care of myself. I've been doing it most of my life. You don't have to worry about me, Grandma."

"If I was twenty years younger, I'd fight you both," her grandmother said. "But today was exhausting and I don't have the energy. Just remember that working together will get you further than going it on your own." She got to her feet. "Let's go look up flights, Anna."

"I want you on the first flight out," Nick said. "And first class only. No coach seats. I want you to be comfortable."

As they left the room, he turned to her. "I understand why you want to stay, but there's real danger here, Isabella. I didn't want to say that in front of our grandmothers, but this isn't a story you're chasing. These are people who shot and almost killed a security guard. And after what happened earlier with the tail and maybe someone in the shed here, I don't think they're done."

"I'm aware of the risks, Nick, but I can be helpful. We won't find those paintings unless we know more about the people who painted them. You're not interested in that, but I am. We can each play to our strengths. You can deal with law enforcement, and I'll do research. We might make a better team than you think."

He blew out a frustrated breath. "Your stubbornness could get you hurt, or worse."

"So could yours. You're taking the same risks I am."

"I'm a trained agent. This is what I do. Why would you want to risk your life for some old painting anyway?" he challenged.

"And don't you have a job you love, one you want to get back to? What are you really going to accomplish here?"

His questions gave her pause. She did have a job she would need to get back to, but not immediately, and today she'd been introduced to her family, and she wanted to know more about them. "I want to help get Lucinda's painting back," she said. "But it's more than that. Today when I met Joelle and Victor, I realized that I have a family I don't even know, a history that's never been allowed to be mine. For the first time in my life, I felt like a Rossi, but I don't know what that means because I don't know my history."

"You could find a history you don't like."

"I could. But I still want to look."

"That's not a good reason to put your life in danger."

"What's your reason? You could go back and leave this to the Carabinieri to solve. If your grandmother isn't here, she's no longer in danger."

"I don't think she'll go if I don't stay. She's so guilty about losing that painting. I have to make it right for her." He paused. "I can't make you leave, but I still don't believe you staying here is a good idea."

"Then you can tell me 'I told you so.'"

"Not if you're dead," he said darkly.

A shiver ran down her spine. "Well, I'm going to try to not let that happen. And then I'll tell you, 'I told you so.'"

"I hope you do."

CHAPTER EIGHT

The rest of Friday passed in a blur for Isabella as she helped her grandmother and Anna pack their bags. She arranged for a car service to pick them up in Los Angeles and another service to deliver food. Nick had told her he had some food that his friends had dropped off after he'd finished his undercover assignment, but his refrigerator and pantry could use a refresh, as he'd barely been living there the past few months. Fortunately, he had a colleague at work with a key to his apartment to help facilitate the delivery.

She wasn't looking forward to spending time alone with Nick, but she was feeling better about getting her grandmother to a safe location. She'd seen how breathless, pale, and anxious her grandmother had been when she'd rushed her up the stairs earlier. She had been through too much the last few days. She was eighty-one years old. She needed to rest and breathe more easily and just be free of all this. And Anna needed the same.

A little before eight, Nick drove Anna and Gloria to the airport for their late-night flight while she cleaned up the kitchen after a hastily eaten dinner. After they left, it felt strange to be in the big house alone. Every creak seemed magnified. She told herself not to let her imagination run away with her. She'd be fine for an hour, and Nick would be back soon.

Nick had wanted her to come with them, thinking they should all stay together, but there hadn't been room in Anna's compact car with their bags, and he hadn't wanted to get anyone else to take them to the airport. She'd agreed with that. She could handle herself. She'd been alone a lot growing up. Her mother had often worked at night to make ends meet and had left her on her own when she was as young as ten years old.

Back then, she'd pushed a table against the door when she got nervous. Once she had hidden under the bed for almost an hour until whoever had been playing with the door handle of their apartment had left. She'd told her mother she didn't like to stay there by herself, but it was that or starving, so she'd had to be brave. In the end, she'd been okay. No one had ever gotten in.

Instead, the danger to their lives had come from a friendly man who she'd initially liked very much, her stepfather, Gary. Unfortunately, that good beginning had ended badly.

So many good things ended up exploding in her face. She blamed most of them on her mother, but her last career explosion was all on her. And this trip to Rome had come at a good time because she was in the doghouse with her boss. She'd had a feeling he'd been on the verge of firing her when she'd told him she had to go to Rome to save her grandmother. Instead, he'd said he hoped the break would be good for her and that she'd come back with a better attitude. She would try to do that because she had been a little in the wrong, even though she hated to admit that.

Once the dishwasher was loaded and running, she wandered into the living room and sat down on the couch. She hadn't looked in the boxes that Nick had brought back from the bank, and she was eager to read the letters.

But first, she opened the velvet pouch and took out a large, heavy male ring. It was silver and black with a design of lines and swirls around the letter *P*. That didn't match Tomas's initial or the initial J of the person he'd been writing. *What did the P signify?*

She turned it over and over in her hand as the light caught it from different angles. It felt like there was something more to the design, but she couldn't figure it out. Setting the ring down, she pulled out the stack of three letters. The first one was in an envelope with no return address. It had been delivered to Tomas Caruso at an address in Rome, which she assumed was where he used to live.

Opening the envelope, she pulled out a single sheet and saw a date at the top, but no year. She quickly realized the letter was written in Italian. She could speak some Italian, but not a lot. When she was with her grandmother, they'd always spoken English.

She pulled out her phone and typed the letter into a translation app. Fortunately, the note was not very long, only two paragraphs.

The translation read:

25 March

Tomas,

I hope this letter finds you well. I received your note and your very special gift. I promise to keep it safe. I know how much it means to you. As you said, both of our hearts are tied up in it. Thinking about everything that happened this past year makes me want to cry. But I must hold the tears back so that no one will know how much it meant to work with you.

I am a different person and a better artist now, having met you and become a part of the group. I am inspired and filled with a sense of righteousness that I did not know I could feel. I lived such a small life until I met you, until I saw a bigger world, one that I could make a difference in.

I know I left without a proper goodbye, but I had to go, and you know why. I still think of you often and hope you are all well and that you are happy. One day perhaps we will meet again. That is my secret wish.

With love, J

Isabella's heart was beating fast as she set down the letter, a dozen different thoughts running through her head. The gift that Tomas had sent to J could have been anything. It didn't precisely say it was a painting, but *J* had talked about working with Tomas and their hearts being tied up in that gift, so it could have been art.

Their relationship seemed very personal, very intense, which made her eagerly reach for the next letter, which was also from J, delivered to the same address in Rome with no return address. Clearly, J had not been interested in giving away her location.

She put the words from the second note into the translation app.

14 April

Tomas,

I am worried about you. I have heard whispers that loyalty is wavering, things are unraveling. I have wanted to reach out but know it is better to have no communication with you. However, I could not resist. My stomach is in knots. Please be careful who you trust. It's possible someone close to you could have their own secrets, their own desires. Stay well.

With love, J

Now, Isabella was worrying about Tomas, too. She didn't know exactly when he had died. She needed to find out when, not that she had a year on this note, but she had a month, and if Tomas had died in May or June, that could be telling. Maybe the fire hadn't been just an accident.

She grabbed the last letter from the stack and saw it had been sent back as undeliverable. The address read: J.J., CP #2310, 50123 Firenze, Italia. The return address was the house she was in right now. The envelope had been opened, but she didn't know who had done that. It could have been Tomas or perhaps his son, Marcus or his daughter-in-law, Anna.

Opening the envelope, she pulled out the letter. The handwriting was very different, more masculine with harder strokes. She typed in the Italian words again, impatient to read the translation as she could already see that this letter was from Tomas to the mysterious *J*.

She wondered if *J.J.* were really their initials, or if he'd simply repeated the *J* so as not to say a last name. Their correspondence so far had been carefully worded.

The translation popped up.

16 June

My dearest J,

You were right to warn me. Everything is going wrong. There is a traitor in our midst. Now I am worried about you. Please be careful with your gift. No one should ever know you have it. I am sorry now that I sent it to you. I only wanted it to bring you joy. Now I worry it will bring you danger.

I fear our dreams were too big. I thought we had more power. I believed we were all thinking as one person, but evil is finding us through the shuttered light of our art. I hope we have done enough, but I fear we have not. It all may come crashing down.

I have sent my creation to my son. He asked me questions I couldn't answer, but I know he will keep it safe. I pray you are well and that you are happy. Please let me know. Even though we are apart, you are still my inspiration, my muse, my reason to be a better man. With all my love, Tomas.

Isabella let out a breath. Tomas's powerful and emotional words touching her deeply. This was a man in love but also a man who was afraid his world was ending. And he'd been right, because he'd died in a mysterious fire that now seemed to have been deliberately set.

She wondered why the letter had come back. Had he put the wrong address or had the mysterious *J* moved away? If the letter had been written in the same year, then three months had passed between her letter and his. *What had happened in those three months?*

It was sad to think that the woman had never read his heartfelt words.

She read through the translation once more. Tomas had

written in cryptic, sometimes poetic language, and while the translation could be slightly off, the gist of what he'd written came through. He'd been involved with some kind of group. It sounded like *J* had been a part of it at one time. She'd warned him not to trust the people around him. He'd responded that there was a traitor in their midst. *Everything was unraveling.* But what was everything? What on earth had Tomas been involved in? *Evil was finding them through the shuttered light of their art.* That was quite a phrase. And Tomas feared they hadn't done enough, but she had no idea what he was talking about.

Her phone buzzed with an incoming message from Nick. He'd dropped off their grandmothers and was on his way home. She texted back a thumbs-up. She wasn't thrilled they would have to work together, but she wanted to talk to him about what she'd learned.

They needed to find this *J* or at least figure out who she was. She'd clearly left Tomas and the group before his death. Even if she wasn't still alive, maybe one of her descendants knew her story, knew where her gift from Tomas was. It felt like that gift was important. They'd referenced keeping it safe more than once.

She just didn't understand why the paintings that had been stolen were important.

Was it the art itself—the technique or subject, or was it the artists who'd painted them? Or was it something else entirely?

Learning more about Tomas and Lucinda would be helpful, too. She felt excited to dive in, but there wasn't a lot she could do late on a Friday night. While the internet would be helpful, she'd probably find more information at a local library or by talking to people at museums or art galleries. She needed to get into the art scene, find some older artists who might have some idea what was going on with this group of artists back in the sixties.

She almost wished they hadn't sent Anna and her grand-mother to LA. While Nick might speak more Italian than she did, they would still be seen as outsiders and would have to work harder to build trust. But their grandmothers would be safer in California. She would simply have to find other ways to get information. She felt even more determined now that she'd realized how deeply personal the robbery was to her family.

It was odd how connected she and Nick were with their grandmothers and their great-grandparents, Tomas and Lucinda. Whatever had happened fifty years ago and whatever was happening now was tied to both of them. That seemed so odd.

After their disastrous date, she hadn't thought she'd ever see Nick again. Nor had she wanted to. But having learned more about him, she didn't feel quite so negatively as she had before. Although she had a feeling he'd try to take over as soon as he got back, and she did not intend to let that happen. He wasn't going to call all the shots.

She put the letters and ring back in the box and was about to open the other box, not sure what she would find since neither Anna nor Nick had mentioned what was inside, when the lights in the house suddenly went out. The curtain of blinding darkness sent a jolt of fear through her. It wasn't rainy or windy. *Why would the lights just go out?*

Grabbing her phone, she turned on the flashlight, just as she heard someone at the front door. They weren't knocking or ringing the bell, but they were trying to get in. She grabbed both boxes, jumped to her feet, and ran out of the living room and up the stairs as the front door shook from someone pounding on it.

Her heart was in her throat as she raced up to the third floor. She stashed the boxes in the linen closet, burying them behind a pile of towels, then dashed into her grandmother's bedroom and locked the door. Her hand was shaking so badly that she dropped her phone before she could call for help. It went spinning across the floor, the light now under the bed, leaving the rest of the room shrouded in darkness. She heard men's voices in the house. There were at least two of them. And they weren't being quiet. Maybe they didn't think anyone was home. That could work to her advantage.

She jumped again as she heard a loud crash, as if some piece of furniture had been knocked over. And then there was another shout and heavy footsteps coming up the stairs.

She didn't have time to get her phone. She needed to find a weapon. If someone came into the room, maybe she could take them by surprise, because she didn't think hiding in the closet would work. It sounded like they were searching the house. And they would look everywhere.

Moving to the dresser, she grabbed a solid and heavy ceramic vase and then ran behind the door. It was a long shot, but she didn't know what else to do. She just knew she wasn't going down without a fight.

CHAPTER NINE

When Nick pulled up in front of his grandmother's house, he was shocked to see the house completely dark, with beams of light flashing through the living room windows. The front door was also wide open. He pulled into the drive, cut the lights, and jumped out of the car, wishing he'd been able to bring his gun to Italy. But even without a weapon, he had to do something. Isabella was inside. And she was probably in trouble.

He stayed in the shadows as he went around to the back of the house, his grandmother's keys in his hand. When he got to the back door, he could see damage to the door, but it was still locked. Apparently, the burglars had given up and gone around the front. He hit the SOS button on his phone to call for help and then slid a key into the lock and opened the door as quietly as he could. As he moved into the house, he could hear someone in the living room. It sounded like they were tearing things apart.

He took a long knife out of the kitchen drawer, then moved down the hall, thankful that he was so familiar with this house, he knew exactly where to go.

He had no idea where Isabella was. Someone was walking around upstairs. He hoped to God she was hiding, and that she hadn't been hurt. When he got to the living room, he saw a man wearing dark clothes and a beanie with a headlight on it, shedding light on what was a destructive scene. He'd broken the glass in the cabinet and was in the process of pulling it away from the wall.

He moved forward, hoping to catch the thief off guard, but as he did, shards of broken glass crunched beneath his feet, and the man whirled around, a gun in his hand.

With a split-second advantage, he jumped on him, knocking the gun away with his left hand as he used his right hand to stab the blade into the guy's arm.

The man screamed in pain and shoved Nick away, yelling in Italian as he ran from the room.

Nick chased after him, but as the burglar fled through the front door, he heard a scream from upstairs that sent him straight to the staircase.

He pulled out his phone, turning on the flashlight, then took the stairs two at a time. When he got to Gloria's room, he found Isabella battling a stronger and taller attacker, who was wearing the same dark clothing and headlight beanie as the man who'd just left.

This guy was bleeding from a gash on his head, but his hands were wrapped around Isabella's neck as he pressed her back against the wall.

As she struggled and kicked out her legs in terrified panic, Nick ran forward, stabbing the man in the back.

The man roared with intense pain as he swung around to face him, the back of his right hand connecting with Nick's face.

The phone flew out of his left hand as he staggered backward.

Isabella slid to the ground, gasping for air.

He recovered his balance, going on the attack one more as he jabbed the knife into the man's stomach, but the thrust wasn't deep enough to slow his attacker down.

They wrestled for control of the knife, the light and shadows adding more challenge to the fight.

"Run," he yelled, needing Isabella to get out of the room.

She moved, but she didn't head to the door. He didn't know what the hell she was doing until she jumped on the bed and grabbed the lamp off the nightstand. Realizing her intention, he shoved the man away from him, and she hit the attacker over the head.

The man crumbled to his knees, then fell face forward to the ground as he lost consciousness.

"Did I kill him?" Isabella asked breathlessly as she held the base of the lamp in her hands, pieces of ceramic tile and glass littered across the bed.

"No. You just knocked him out."

She got off the bed, dropping the lamp onto the mattress. He picked his phone up from the floor and then turned the light on Isabella. Her brown hair was wild and tangled, her eyes lit up with a mix of emotions. "Are you alright?" he asked.

She nodded, putting her hand to her throat, where bruises were already forming. "You came just in time." Her lips trembled at that thought.

As sirens rang through the air, he felt a wave of relief. "Finally."

"Did you call them?" she asked. "I was going to, but I was shaking when I heard that guy coming up the stairs. I dropped my phone." She got down on her knees and peered under the bed as he provided light to help her search. "Got it," she said as she grabbed her phone and stood up.

"Why don't you go downstairs and tell the police where we are? I'm going to keep my eye on this guy. He might be the best clue we have."

"There was another man. I heard two people."

"He took off. I was going to go after him, but I heard you yell."

"I tried to knock this man out when he came into the room,

but the vase just caught the edge of his face and then he tried to strangle me." She touched her throat again. "I couldn't breathe. Everything was going blurry. I thought I was done."

He could see the fear catching up with her adrenaline. "You're okay now."

"I know. I just thought I might not be. I'll go downstairs."

As she left, the man stirred, and he flashed the light back on him. His eyes were still closed, the mask on his face was half off, revealing a short beard. He appeared to be in his thirties and was dressed all in black: jeans, sweatshirt, and beanie. This one wasn't wearing the black gloves he'd seen on the other guy. In fact, his fingers were heavily tattooed. Hopefully, once the police identified him, they'd have a good lead.

Isabella entered the room with two armed officers, whose flashlights brightened the room. They quickly handcuffed the man on the ground, who had struggled as soon as he regained consciousness. The police got him onto his feet and took him down the stairs while he and Isabella followed.

When they got to the entry, two more officers were entering the house. One helped take the prisoner out to the car, while the other introduced himself as Inspector Ferrara and motioned them into the living room. As their lights swept across the room, Isabella gasped at the destruction.

"Oh, my God. I can't believe they tore apart the furniture like this," she said.

"It appears they were looking for something," the inspector commented. "Do you know what?"

"Probably a painting," he replied. "This is my grandmother's home, Anna Caruso. She witnessed a robbery at the Museo dei Capolavori Romani on Thursday. Her family painting was one of the ones stolen."

"My grandmother lives here as well," Isabella put in. "Gloria Rossi. Her family painting was also stolen."

"Your names please?" he asked.

"Nick Caruso, Isabella Rossi," he replied. "You need to

contact Captain Lavezzo at the Carabinieri T.P.C. He's working on the museum robbery, and this break-in will be tied to that."

The officer nodded. "Please wait here."

"Our grandmothers would be so upset to see this," Isabella murmured. "Thank God they weren't here."

"You shouldn't have been here, either. I shouldn't have left you here alone."

"I would have been fine if I hadn't dropped the damn phone. The police would have been here sooner. I should have done better."

He had a feeling Isabella would always feel like she could have done better. She had high expectations for everyone, including herself. "You shouldn't have had to deal with this alone."

"Stop beating yourself up, Nick. It was my choice to stay. And there was no room in the car, anyway. It was either letting them get to the airport on their own or me staying here."

She had a point, but there had been other options. He could have sent her to the neighbor's house. But there was no point in going over all the things he could have done. "You must have been terrified when they cut the electricity."

"I was sitting on the couch looking at the letters you brought back from the bank. When the lights went out, I heard someone at the door. I took the boxes upstairs, hid them in the linen closet, and then ran into my grandmother's room. I locked the door, but he kicked it open. I grabbed the vase and tried to take him by surprise. It didn't really work."

He was impressed with her quick thinking and her courage. "It was a good idea."

"I don't know if they would have cared about the boxes from the bank. They were probably looking for a painting." Her gaze moved to the cabinet. "Did they think it was hidden behind that? The guy who got away, he didn't get anything, did he?"

"There was nothing in his hands but a gun."

"A gun?" she echoed. "How did you get past that?"

"I took him by surprise with the knife I grabbed in the kitchen." He swept his light around the room. "The gun went flying out of his hand when I jumped him. I didn't see where it went. And I didn't have time to look for it when I heard you scream." He walked toward the cabinet and spotted the weapon under a side table.

He moved the table but left the gun on the ground in case the police could pull prints off it. But their best lead was the guy they'd taken into custody. Hopefully, this whole thing would be over soon.

A moment later, the lights went on, which brought both relief and an even brighter reminder of what had just happened.

When Inspector Ferrara and another officer returned, he pointed out the gun under the table so they could collect it.

"Captain Lavezzo will be here soon," Inspector Ferrara said. "He wishes to speak to both of you about what happened. In the meantime, we will take photographs of the scene and collect any other evidence we might find." His gaze narrowed on Isabella's face. "I would like to take pictures of the injuries you suffered. We can do it now, or perhaps you should go to the hospital to be examined?"

"No. I don't need to be examined. I'm all right," she said. "The photos are fine." She lifted her hair as he took photographs of the bruises on her neck.

Seeing her injuries more clearly sent another rush of anger through him. She should never have had to go through this. He needed to get her out of this situation as fast as possible, but he couldn't order her to leave. She wouldn't respond well to that. He had to make her see how much danger she was in and how she might not be so lucky the next time. Although, he hoped there wouldn't be a next time.

When he'd finished taking photos of Isabella, the inspector said, "The front door is damaged. You'll need to board up the entrance. Do you have anything in which to do that?"

"I have no idea, but I'll figure something out," he replied.

"Two officers will remain outside until Captain Lavezzo arrives to take your statement."

"Thanks," he said.

Once the inspector and his partner had taken photos of the living room, Isabella put a cushion back on the couch and sat down. Her face was extremely pale now, the bruises standing out on her neck. She'd been brave and strong, helping to take down a man far bigger than either of them. But he sensed she was feeling the letdown and the pain of being almost choked to death.

"I'll get you some water," he said.

"No," she said sharply, then licked her lips. "I mean—I'm okay for now. I don't need any water."

He sensed that she also didn't want to be alone.

"What are we going to do about the door?" she asked.

"My grandfather used to keep some wood in the shed. Maybe there's still some there."

"Do you think they're going to come back?"

"I don't believe so, but I don't know."

Her gaze clung to his. "They didn't get what they were looking for."

"It's probably not here. We'll find out more when Lavezzo talks to the guy who attacked you. Having him in custody could be the break we need. If he can connect us to whoever is ordering these break-ins, we'll be closer to getting the paintings back and putting the thieves in jail."

"If he talks. He seemed very mean, very cruel. His eyes were stone-cold, completely unemotional. I think he would have killed me and not thought a second about it."

He could hear the bemusement and confusion in her voice, which was completely understandable. He doubted she'd ever been in such a dire situation before. "Tomorrow morning, I'm taking you to the airport. You can go back to LA and stay with our grandmothers until this is over."

She immediately shook her head, the fight returning to her eyes. "I'm not running away."

"It's not running away. It's being smart and knowing when to retreat."

"Are you leaving?"

"No, but that's different."

"Because you're a man."

"Because I'm a trained FBI agent, and you are not."

"I think it's better if we stick together. It worked well tonight. You had my back, and I had yours," she reminded him.

"Your grandmother would kill me if anything happened to you."

"And Anna would kill me if you got hurt because you were here alone."

"She would not blame you, Isabella."

She held up a weary hand. "Please stop trying to make me leave, Nick. I'm in this now, and I'm seeing it through to the end."

"You have no idea how bad that end could be. You survived tonight. Who knows what might happen the next time?"

She swallowed hard, then winced. "Maybe I'll change my mind at some point, but not now. If you're staying, I'm staying."

"I hope you won't regret that decision."

"Me, too."

———

Isabella took a deep breath as Captain Lavezzo entered the room. She wasn't feeling nearly as brave nor as courageous as her recent words to Nick. In fact, there was a part of her that wanted to run to the airport and get out of Italy. But a bigger part of her wanted to stay and find out what was going on. There was a story right in front of her, a dangerous story tied to her family, and she needed to unravel it.

She got to her feet, forcing the shaky feeling aside. She

needed to put herself on the same level as Nick and Captain Lavezzo, who were already discussing everything that had happened. While she hadn't yet met the captain, it was clear Nick was telling him who she was and what had happened.

He gave her a sharp look as she joined them, his gaze moving to her neck. "I understand you were attacked, Signorina Rossi. Do you need medical attention?"

"No. I'm all right," she said, trying to stand upright on her wobbly legs.

Nick must have read her mind. "Why don't we sit down?" he suggested, urging her toward the sofa.

She resumed her seat, while Nick sat next to her, and Lavezzo moved to the opposite side of the coffee table, perching on the edge of the couch. He was dressed in regular clothes today, which made sense since it was late on a Friday night.

"Do you know anything about the men who broke in here?" she asked.

"Not yet. The injured male is receiving medical attention. He has no identification on him, but we should be able to find out who he is in short order. Inspector Ferrara told me what happened, but I'd like to hear it from you as well, Signorina. You were sitting in this room when the men came in the house?"

"Yes. The lights went out. Then I heard someone at the front door, I ran up the stairs and hid in my grandmother's bedroom. One guy came up the stairs; the other one stayed down here." She waved her hand around the destruction in the room, noting for the first time that the heavy drapes on the window had been yanked down and were hanging off the rod. "They must have thought there was another painting in the house. They moved big furniture. This wasn't random."

"I don't believe it was. Do you know if there's another painting here?"

"None that were painted by Tomas Caruso or Lucinda Rossi," she replied.

"But perhaps something was hidden away," Lavezzo pressed.

"It certainly seems like someone believes that."

"The two of you should go to a hotel tonight. Or better yet, get on a plane and go home. There's nothing for you to do here."

"We're considering our options," Nick said. "I'm very interested in what you can learn from the man at the hospital."

"As am I. This could be a significant break." Captain Lavezzo paused as another man entered the room, then quickly got to his feet as Stefano moved toward them with great concern in his eyes.

"Inspector Gangi," Lavezzo said. "What are you doing here?"

"Capitano Lavezzo," Stefano returned as the two men gave each other a somewhat assessing look. Clearly, they knew each other, but there seemed to be a wariness between them. "I am a friend of the family," he added, before turning to them. "Please tell me your grandmothers are not hurt."

"They're not here," Nick replied. "They've left Italy."

"Oh, that is good," Stefano said with relief. "Where did they go?"

"It doesn't matter," Nick said. "They're safe."

"Excellent. I understand that one burglar was caught. Has he been identified?" he asked, turning to Captain Lavezzo.

"Not yet. But we will know who he is soon."

"If there is anything I can do to help, please let me know," Stefano said.

"We've got this, Inspector," Lavezzo returned. "Perhaps you can convince these two to go back to the States, where they will be safe."

"I have already suggested that," Stefano said. "It would be wise."

"We'll think about it," Nick said.

"Very well." Captain Lavezzo gave them a resigned nod. "I'll be in touch."

"I'll walk you out."

As Nick walked the captain to the front door, Stefano sat

down next to her with concern in his gaze. "There are bruises on your neck," he said in a somber voice.

"You should see the other guy," she tried to joke.

"I understand he was injured. But I'm sorry for what he did to you. Do you need to go to the hospital?"

"No. I'll be fine."

Stefano gave her a thoughtful look. "I know that Signor Caruso is an FBI agent, but he is not in the US, and his ability to protect you will be limited here. He doesn't have a weapon, does he?"

She thought that was an odd question for him to ask. "All I know is that he grabbed a knife from the kitchen and stabbed the man who was choking me. So, he's the reason I'm alive."

"That was fortunate. Next time..."

"We'll be better prepared," she finished. "If we stay. As Nick said, we haven't decided. We were shocked anyone would come to the house. Our grandmothers saw nothing during the robbery, and there is no art here worth anything."

"Are you sure? Your grandmothers may have a painting they're not aware they have. I know Gloria just moved in several months ago. Perhaps there was something in her things from her many years in her previous home."

"There's not," she said flatly. Nick's earlier warning that they shouldn't trust anyone but each other rang through her head. Stefano was a police officer who had been mentored by Anna's husband. It was unlikely he was doing anything but trying to help them, but sometimes his questions seemed odd. Maybe it was just the Italian way of investigating a crime.

Nick returned to the room a moment later and said, "Stefano, do you mind waiting here with Isabella while I look in the shed for some plywood to put over the front door?"

"It would be my pleasure."

"Great. I'll be back shortly."

"You don't have to babysit me," she told him. "You're not in uniform, so I assume you weren't working tonight."

"No, but I had asked my coworkers to notify me if any calls came in from this house."

"So, you were worried even before this?"

"Yes," he confirmed with a serious nod. "I didn't like the circumstances your grandmothers found themselves in, but like you, I did not expect this to happen. I'm glad they weren't here." He paused. "Have you spoken to your mother about this?"

"No. Have you?"

He sat up a little straighter, then shook his head. "We spoke before this all this happened. It was the first time in thirty years."

"That's a long time."

"And yet it seems like barely a day has passed. The years in between faded to nothing. I'm planning to go to Firenze when she is more settled and then we can catch up in person."

"You said you were childhood friends. Were you more than friends?"

A smile crossed his lips, a reflective gleam entering his eyes. "When we were young, we imagined ourselves in love with each other."

"Really? So you were boyfriend-girlfriend?"

"I would say so, but your mother didn't like labels. She was a free spirit, and she had her eyes on a life that was not here. She wanted to live in America, to be an artist like her grandmother, to be away from her father, who could be very stern with her."

"She told me she couldn't wait to go away to college. Were you together when she left? Were you hurt when she left Italy?"

"I was very sad. She took a piece of my heart with her."

"Did you ever think about going to the States to see her?"

"I did. We wrote often the first year she was gone, but that slowed down, and eventually I heard she was seeing someone and having a great time, so I knew it was truly over." He paused. "I've always had a soft spot in my heart for her. She was my first love. But I was disappointed to hear that she has made some big mistakes in her life."

"She doesn't always make the best decisions."

"Are the two of you close?"

"Not really," she said with a shrug.

"Why is that?"

"Too long of a story."

"My apologies. It is not my business." He paused as they heard hammering. "It sounds like Nick found some wood." He got to his feet. "I'll help him with that. Take care of yourself, Isabella."

"I always do," she muttered as he left the room.

She waited a few minutes, hearing more hammering, and then a conversation between Nick and Stefano. She probably should listen to what they were talking about. Forcing herself to her feet, she walked into the entryway. But now she heard only hammering and Nick was on the other side of a massive piece of plywood, so she headed up the stairs instead.

After retrieving the boxes from the linen closet, she walked into her grandmother's bedroom. Seeing the broken lamp and vase, the messy bed, the blood on the floor, and the wall she'd been pressed against while fighting for her life sent an overwhelming number of emotions through her. The boxes slipped from her hands just as Nick came through the door.

"Isabella?" he questioned.

She couldn't respond. Her whole body was shaking, and tears were welling up in her eyes. She blinked them back. She wouldn't cry. She never cried.

"Hey," he said softly as he approached her.

She looked into his eyes, biting down on her lip as she tried to keep it together.

"You're okay," he said as he wrapped his arms around her body.

She tensed, trying not to sink into the comfort of his embrace, but she couldn't stop herself. He brought her in close, her head resting against his shoulder, and she slid her arms around him, feeling like he was the only reason she was still on her feet.

A few sobs slipped through her tight lips, but she fought hard to silence them.

"You can cry," Nick whispered.

"I don't want to be weak." She tried to take in as much warmth as she could so that maybe her body would stop shaking.

"Isabella. Look at me."

She didn't want to look at him because she didn't want him to read anything in her expression, but he was waiting, and slowly she lifted her gaze to his.

"You're not weak. You're incredibly brave. Annoying but also courageous," he added with a smile.

"You're super annoying, too," she said, because it was easier to say that than anything else. "But you saved my life tonight."

"You saved mine as well."

"So, we're even."

"You like to keep score, don't you?"

"How else do I know if I'm winning?"

He grinned. "Good point. Yeah, we're even."

As they gazed at each other, something shifted inside of her. She felt a tingle that had nothing to do with fear or the cold, and everything to do with the heat running between them.

Nick suddenly let go of her and stepped back, giving her an odd look that she couldn't read at all. "Let's get out of here," he said.

"Good idea." She looked down at the floor where she'd dropped the boxes. One lid had flown off, but everything was still intact.

"We'll take these downstairs to the kitchen. The thieves didn't get in there," Nick added. "It looks normal."

She could use a little normal right now, so she grabbed one box while Nick grabbed the other and they headed down to the kitchen.

CHAPTER TEN

While Isabella sat down at the kitchen table, Nick busied himself filling the teapot and rifling through his grandmother's selection of herbal teas, thinking tea would calm everything down. "I see chamomile and jasmine," he said. "What would you like?" He deliberately didn't look at her, because he was feeling rattled since he'd put his arms around her in the bedroom. He'd actually liked seeing the vulnerability behind her hard edges. Maybe he'd liked it a little too much.

"Chamomile sounds good, although I'm not much of a tea drinker."

"I'm not, either, except in this house." He turned on the stove and then finally faced her. "My grandmother thought tea was the answer to every mood. If you were happy, you celebrated with tea. If you were sad, tea would comfort you, and if you were stressed out, it would help you relax."

"Were you a moody kid?"

"I wouldn't say moody, but sometimes I had a chip on my shoulder. My grandfather would knock it off as soon as I arrived for the summer. And I'd have a good three months before I picked it up again."

"Why the chip on your shoulder?"

"My parents." He crossed his arms as he leaned against the counter and waited for the water to boil. "They dragged me all over the world, whether or not I wanted to go. I was always having to change schools, start over, and when I got old enough, they'd send me here for the summer so I was completely out of their hair."

"That doesn't sound fun."

"It was the opposite of fun, unless I was here. Then I had people who actually gave a crap about me and wanted to talk to me, to hear what I thought. My grandfather was the greatest guy. I don't know if you ever met him."

"One time. I liked Marcus. He was much warmer than my grandfather. He had a great smile, and he was funny, too."

"He was. He had a sharp mind and was very passionate about giving back to the community. He was all about protecting the people in his neighborhood. Everyone was family to him. He took their well-being seriously."

"Is he the reason you became an FBI agent?"

"He was part of it. I didn't start out in law enforcement, though."

Surprise ran through her gaze. "You didn't? What did you do?"

"Finance. I liked numbers, so I went into financial investments after college."

She shook her head in disbelief. "I would not have guessed that. How did you go from finance to FBI?"

He didn't answer right away as the kettle whistled. Instead, he poured hot water into two mugs, dropped in the tea bags, and took both to the table. Then he sat down across from her. "I went from finance to the FBI through a money laundering operation I discovered at work. I basically became a whistleblower, and then the bureau recruited me. I enjoyed doing something more than helping make other people rich, so it was a good move."

"My grandmother says you work undercover a lot."

"I do. I've spent a great deal of time being other people."

"What's that like?"

"It's...hard." He surprised himself by the honesty of his statement.

"Being someone else? Having to lie? What's the most diffi-cult part?" she asked curiously.

He thought for a moment. "None of it is easy. When I start a job, I go in under a fake name and backstory. I build a new iden-tity and get close to whoever I need to get close to. I have to gain trust in order to be accepted and often I have to betray that trust in the end. Some investigations go on for months, which means I have to stay in that life for a long time. That can be tricky. When you're acting in a certain way for a long time, you can lose sight of who you really are." He cleared his throat, feeling like he was exposing far too much. "But it's worth it in the end. I've been able to take down horrific people and large criminal operations."

"That part must be rewarding."

"It is, but it's not as black and white as it sounds. There are many people I meet along the way who fall into gray areas, and they often end up as collateral damage."

"But that's their choice, right? If they get hurt, it's because of their decisions, not yours."

"Right," he said, appreciating her words.

"You sound a little tired, Nick."

"I am. My boss told me to take a vacation right before my grandmother called me. I fought that idea, because even though I knew I needed a break, I always feel better when I'm working."

"Me, too. My job is the one area of my life where I feel confi-dent, where I'm really good and on top of my game. Well, most of the time."

He raised a questioning eyebrow. "That sounds like a story."

"That's the problem. I became the story instead of being an objective observer. That is never supposed to happen."

"What did you do?"

"I kind of told a congressman that he was a corrupt asshole and that I was going to nail his ass to the wall."

"You kind of told him that?" he asked with a laugh. "Or you explicitly told him that?"

"I wasn't wrong," she defended. "But my boss had me turn over my notes to another reporter and suggested I take a vacation."

"And what did you say to him?"

"I bit my tongue."

"Really? You can actually not say what you're thinking or feeling?"

"Occasionally," she said, making a face at him. "I like my job and I should have just nailed the congressman to the wall without insulting him first. I won't make that mistake again." She took a sip of her tea. "Anyway, it was a good time to come to Italy for me, too. But it hasn't been much of a vacation so far, which doesn't matter. I'm not very good at relaxing."

He was starting to realize just how much they had in common, which was a little disturbing, so he turned his attention to the boxes from the bank. "So, did you read the letters?"

"Yes. Two were from *J* to Tomas. In the first letter, she talked about getting a gift and keeping it hidden away. In the second one, she was trying to warn him that someone might be about to betray him."

"Really? How would they do that?"

"She wasn't specific. Tomas wrote her back, but his letter was never delivered. It was returned to sender. It was, however, opened, so someone read it. Maybe Tomas."

"Or both of my grandparents," he said. "My grandmother seemed to know what was in the letters."

"In Tomas's note, he sounds like he's a man in love. He's worried about J and having sent her his gift. He wonders if that was a mistake. He talks about how he thought everyone was on the same page, but they weren't. He's anxious. You can read the translations. I have them on my phone. Unless you read Italian? How fluent are you?"

"I used to be fluent, but it's been a long time since I spent summers here, so my knowledge has faded."

"You can read the translations then."

"I'll do that later. Did you see the ring?"

"Yes. It's beautiful. I wonder why there is a letter *P* on it. It doesn't match anyone's initial that we know of."

"No, it doesn't."

She tapped her finger on the second box. "I didn't look in this one yet."

"My grandmother said it's filled with their personal papers."

"Let's see." She pulled off the lid, revealing a stack of papers. She picked up Anna and Marcus's birth certificates and found more of the same nature, with a marriage certificate, a school diploma, and baptismal and communion records for his father, James Caruso. Isabella put everything she pulled out of the box on the table between them so that he could look through them as well.

"It looks like what my grandmother said," he muttered. "Personal papers, nothing that's tied to the paintings."

"This is interesting." Isabella handed him a driver's license with the name Juliette Sabatini on it.

The woman had short black hair and big, dark eyes, a melancholy expression on her face. The license had expired many years ago. Judging by the date of birth, Juliette would be eighty-three years old if she were still alive.

"I don't know who this is," he said, staring at the woman's face. "And I have no idea why my grandfather would have put it in his box."

"The woman's address is in Firenze, and her name starts with a J," Isabella pointed out.

He frowned. "True, but this wasn't with Tomas's letters."

"Maybe it got misplaced."

"I can ask my grandmother if she knows who Juliette is. But she won't land for several more hours, so it will have to wait."

"Maybe we can find something about her online." Isabella got up to retrieve her computer from the counter where she'd put it earlier.

He watched as she quickly typed the name into search, her face a picture of intensity and determination. Isabella certainly didn't let the grass grow under her feet. A short time ago, she'd almost been choked to death. She'd been terrified and unsteady and almost falling apart, but now she was in fighting mode. She might get knocked down, but she didn't stay down.

He'd worked with a lot of tough, courageous women in his line of work, but they'd all been trained to face danger. Isabella had not, but she certainly had guts and a strong survival instinct. Although, he had a feeling her headlong rush toward any lead also had the potential to land her in trouble. He would have to make sure that didn't happen.

"I'm not finding anything," she muttered.

"You just started."

"I didn't say I was giving up. I just said nothing is jumping out at me."

As he took another sip of tea, he felt the weariness of not just tonight but the last several months seep back in. He probably should have gone for an energy drink instead of sleep-inducing tea.

Isabella let out a sigh as she rubbed her eyes. He glanced at the clock on the wall. It was only eleven, but it felt much later. "I think we should call it a night, Isabella. We can follow up on this tomorrow."

"I can keep going."

"You can, but at some point, you'll have to close your eyes. I know you don't want to."

She lifted her gaze from the computer to look at him. "I'm not worried about closing my eyes."

He stared back at her, seeing the defiance burning bright.

She was terrified of being seen as weak. He tried a different approach. "I need you to be fresh tomorrow. I have a meeting set up with an art historian."

"You do? When did that happen?"

"I got her name from one of my associates. When he was working art crimes for the FBI, he used her as a resource. I sent her a text earlier, and she responded when I was on my way home from the airport. We can meet her at eleven a.m. tomorrow."

"Great. Maybe she'll be able to tell us why Tomas and Lucinda's paintings are important."

"That's what I'm hoping. What do you say we call it a night?"

"I guess." Reluctance filled her gaze, but she closed her computer and got to her feet. "I am tired. I think it was the tea."

"I'll turn off the lights if you want to go upstairs."

"Okay, thanks."

After she left, he rechecked the back door and then turned out the lights in the kitchen and the rest of the downstairs before moving up to the second floor.

He entered his bedroom, which still felt like his teenaged haven. His grandmother hadn't changed much in the room, although she'd replaced the bedspread, but there were still some movie posters from his youth and an old guitar that his grandfather had encouraged him to play. He'd refused to do that because he didn't want to get involved in any part of music. That was his parents' world, not his.

Marcus used to tell him he'd had some talent as a boy, and he'd probably inherited that from his mother or his father. He'd also suggested that maybe Nick would understand his parents better if he entered their world. Of course, as a teenager, he'd said no to all those suggestions. His life would never be a part of their world.

Sitting down on the bed, he kicked off his shoes, then stretched out and stared at the ceiling. He'd been a stubborn kid. He was a stubborn man, too, but being back in Italy, surrounded by his family's heritage, he wondered if he hadn't been a little narrow-minded. Maybe not about his parents, but about the rest of the family. He'd spent time with two of his cousins, but that was it. Now, he was intrigued by the bigger family, by a great-grandfather he knew nothing about.

Isabella was intrigued by her family as well, maybe even bordering on obsessed. Some of that obsession tonight probably came from not wanting to think about almost dying. She compartmentalized her feelings by diving immediately into something else.

He'd done the same thing many times. Frowning, he told himself they were not at all alike, but that thought was beginning to feel wrong because they shared a lot of similarities. Not that it mattered. Nothing was going to happen between them.

Closing his eyes, he tried to turn off his brain, but his mind wasn't cooperating. It kept circulating unanswered questions around and around in his head, creating more tension, more frustration, and a worry that if he didn't figure things out fast, he and Isabella would never get ahead of what might be coming next.

When he heard footsteps above him, his eyes flew open. Isabella wasn't sleeping, either.

After another ten minutes of hearing her pace, he rolled out of bed and went up the stairs, seeing the light under the door. He knocked. "Isabella?"

She opened the door a moment later, wearing a T-shirt over a pair of pajama bottoms, her hair a beautiful, wavy mess, her eyes troubled, annoyed, and wary at the same time.

"What?" she asked.

"I can't sleep."

"Well, drink some more tea."

"Is that what you're going to do, because you're not sleeping, either. I could hear you pacing from my room. Are you worried someone will come back tonight?"

"No. Yes. Maybe." She tucked her hair behind her ears. "I don't know."

"I think we're safe for tonight."

"But you don't know that."

"That's true," he agreed. "Can I come in?"

"Why?"

"Because we could both use the company." He moved past her before she could kick him out and sat down on the chaise lounge across from the bed. "I remember this. It used to be downstairs. My grandmother loved to read in it. I wonder why she moved it up here."

Isabella shrugged and sat down on her bed. "Who knows? I think this is a junk room/sewing room," she said, tipping her head to the sewing machine in the corner and a box of fabrics.

"Do you sew?"

"Not even a little bit. Do you?"

"Less than that. My grandmother once tried to show me how to sew on a button, but I was not a good student."

"My grandmother tried to show me how to hem my jeans the summer I lived here. I was terrible at it. But I did like that she tried to teach me something. She really is a sweet person. Submissive and too weak, but also sweet."

"What's your mom like?"

"I don't want to talk about her."

"Then let's talk about something else."

"Like what?"

"Whatever you want." He settled back against the pillow on the lounger. "Why don't you turn the light off and get in bed, and we'll just talk until we get tired?"

"Just talk?" she challenged.

He met her gaze. "You want to do something else?"

"No. I want to be clear that I don't want to do something else."

"Then we'll talk."

"I thought we were supposed to be sleeping."

"Well, I'm hoping you'll bore me into sleep," he said with a laugh.

She made a face at him and then turned off the light and got into bed. "I think you'll be the one boring me. Like any typical man, you probably have lots of stories you want to tell me about how great you are."

"You have a low opinion of men."

"Guilty," she admitted.

"Where does that come from?"

She didn't answer right away, then said, "A therapist told me once it comes from my absent father. But I could throw in my grandfather, my stepfather, another one of my mom's boyfriends, and then the last idiot I dated."

"Who was the last idiot?" he asked, thinking it was a lot easier to talk to her with the darkness surrounding them.

"A lawyer. It turns out he had a lot of *girlfriends* besides me."

"That sucks."

"What bothered me most was that I should have seen it earlier. I can read people pretty well, but he was fun and charming, and my friends kept telling me I was too picky."

"You probably are picky."

"Not picky enough, apparently. What about you? Do you date a lot? Are you selective?"

"No, and no. I like to go out, but I don't do it a lot because I'm usually working."

"Do you date when you're undercover?"

"Only if it's part of the job for me to get close to someone."

"What do they call that—the honey trap?"

"You must watch spy movies."

"A few. Do you break hearts when you're living your fake life?"

"I try not to, but sometimes it happens."

"What about in your regular life?"

He thought about that for a minute. "I've moved around so much that my regular life hasn't involved romantic relationships in a while." He decided they'd talked enough about his love life. "How did you become a reporter?"

"I wanted to be a journalist from the time I was young. And once I set my mind on something, I don't stop until I get what I want."

"I believe that. But what made you want to be a journalist?"

"When I was a kid, I loved watching reporters on TV. It seemed exciting to be out in the field, covering a car chase, or a kidnapping, or a corrupt politician. I liked the idea of being able to put a spotlight on something important, to stop someone from getting away with something."

She paused, then added, "It's ironic that it was a reporter digging into my stepfather's company who figured out he was a fraud. I probably should have hated that person because she started the ball rolling on an investigation that sent my mom to jail. But when the story broke, I thought, *yes*, someone else finally sees this guy the way I do. While I liked him in the beginning, I saw the shady side of him long before my mother did. She believed everything he told her. And she did everything he wanted her to do, including signing papers, giving him money, and never asking a question. I guess that was what was really at the heart of my desire to be a reporter. My mother never asked questions and ended up in trouble. I wanted to ask every question so I could see exactly what was happening around me."

"Why aren't you close to your mom now? Are you still angry with her?"

She let out a sigh. "I'm not sure how I feel about her anymore. I've had a hard time loving her the way I used to when I was small, when it was just the two of us, before Gary, my stepfather, came into our lives. Even after she went to prison for him, she didn't seem to blame him for anything. That was hard to stomach."

"I can see that. Did you ever talk to her about that?"

"I sort of tried, but I was really mad when she first got out. I was living away at college, and I didn't want to be a part of her life. I barely spoke to her when she called, and I refused all invitations to go back and see her. Eventually, as time passed, I relented, and we started talking again. But by the time I graduated, she was involved with another man I didn't like, and I just didn't want to go down that road again. So I put the distance back between us."

"That makes sense. What do you think about her moving to Florence?"

" Grandma thinks it will be good for her to be in Italy and in the art world again. I have no idea if that's true or if it's another bad decision."

"Would your mother know something about Lucinda's painting? It was with her belongings. You might need to talk to her about that."

"Let's leave that as a last resort," she said with a yawn. "Tell me something random about yourself."

"Random, huh?" He paused for a moment. "I like to fish."

"You do not," she said with disbelief. "That seems way too slow for someone who moves as fast as you do."

"That's why I like it, not that I do it very much. My grandfather used to take me to Lake Bracciano when I was a kid. We'd spent half the day on the lake catching black bass. Sometimes we'd be lucky if we caught any, though. I like to fish, but I'm not very good at it, and I don't think my grandfather was, either."

"That's a nice memory to have."

A memory that now made him feel sad because he'd never see his grandfather again. He pushed away that painful thought. "Tell me something random about you."

"I'm a good singer."

"Like in the shower or on a stage?"

She laughed for the first time since he'd known her, a sweet, melodic sound that made him want to make her laugh again. It seemed like she needed some lightness in her life.

"I'm terrific in the shower, and not bad on the stage," she continued. "I actually sang with the glee club in high school.

Until my mom went to jail, and then there were too many eyes on me."

And just like that, the darkness was back in her voice.

"What's your favorite kind of book?" he asked. "I'm guessing since you're a writer, you're probably a reader."

"True crime, suspense, thrillers, history. I love non-fiction. Oh, and biographies, too."

As she continued to talk about her favorite books, he found his eyes growing heavy. He finally felt relaxed.

When she asked him to talk about his favorite books, he had to tell her he wasn't big on reading, but he had watched a great documentary a few weeks earlier. He was just getting into the story when he heard her breathing change. He paused. "Isabella?"

She didn't answer. He had finally bored her to sleep. He smiled to himself and closed his eyes, feeling like he could sleep now, too.

CHAPTER ELEVEN

Isabella woke up Saturday morning, feeling more rested than she would have imagined. A quick glance across the room revealed an empty lounger. Nick was gone. She had a feeling she'd fallen asleep in the middle of something he was saying, but it wasn't because he'd been boring. She'd just finally felt safe enough to sleep, and she had him to thank for that. If he hadn't pushed his way into her room and insisted on talking, she probably would have gone over and over that moment when the breath was being squeezed out of her.

Rolling out of bed, she went into the hall bathroom and took a shower. Then she put on dark-jeans and a pink pullover sweater before making her way downstairs. When she eventually got down to the bottom floor, the smell of bacon drew her immediately into the kitchen. Nick stood at the stove, flipping a piece of bacon in a sizzling frying pan. She could see eggs in another pan, scrambled with bright red tomatoes and green leafy spinach.

"What is all this?" she asked in amazement.

"I'm making us breakfast."

"It looks great. Do I smell coffee, too?"

He tipped his head to the coffeemaker. "It might be a little strong."

"I like it strong."

"I figured that," he said with a dry smile.

She felt a little uncomfortable with that smile, with the feeling of intimacy between them. That was a ridiculous thought. They hadn't slept together. Well, not in the same bed, anyway. They hadn't even kissed, but she was feeling an emotional connection to him. Talking to him last night had been easy. And having him in her room had made her feel safe.

She was sure he'd come upstairs because he knew she was too on edge to relax. But he hadn't made a big deal out of it. He hadn't made her feel weak.

As he reached over her to grab two plates from the cupboard, she felt a tingle and a rush of warmth race through her body. It wasn't just an emotional connection she was feeling, it was also a physical attraction, which she'd never thought she'd feel after their first terrible date. But all that seemed far too complicated for the situation they were in.

Filling a mug, she pushed aside her feelings, which was what she always did when it was time to work. She was ready to dive back in and was looking forward to talking to the art historian, but first she would eat.

She took a seat at the table as Nick set down two heaping plates.

"I have to admit, this looks impressive," she said. "I guess someone taught you to cook."

"Anna made sure I helped in the kitchen when I was here. She regretted never making my father learn to cook, and she didn't want to make that mistake with me."

She smiled at that. "My grandmother tried, too, but I was pretty bad at it. And I never got much better." She scooped up a forkful of eggs and vegetables and found it as delicious as it looked. For several moments, they ate in comfortable silence.

"Do you want more bacon?" Nick asked as she cleaned up her plate. "There's another piece on the stove."

"You can have it. I'm stuffed."

"I'm good."

"I haven't had fried bacon in a long time. I usually make it in the microwave."

"I also do that, but my grandmother thought microwaving was one of the seven deadly sins, so since we are here in her kitchen, I thought I'd use her favorite frying pan."

"You really love her, don't you? I can hear it in your voice."

"I do. Speaking of my grandmother, she texted me they arrived safe and sound. The car service met them at the airport. The kitchen was stocked with food. And she's horrified that I have little to no décor in my house. Apparently, she and Gloria are going to do something about that after they've had a long rest."

"So, you can cook, but you can't decorate," she teased.

"I can decorate. I just haven't cared enough to do it."

"Did you tell her what happened here?"

"I told her there was a break-in, but we were all right, nothing was taken, and that the police had a man in custody. I played down the danger. At some point, we'll have to let them know about the destruction in the living room, but maybe when we have some good news to deliver."

She nodded in agreement. "They don't need to be worrying about us."

"I asked her if she had heard of Juliette Sabatini. She didn't recognize the name. She said she hadn't seen the license in the box, but she also hadn't really looked through it."

"I can keep researching Juliette today. Oh, and there's something I forgot to mention to you. I was looking up art robberies online yesterday, and there was a robbery six months ago at a gallery in Florence where only one painting was taken. It was by an artist named David Leoni. My grandmother told me that David was one of Tomas's students. That he would have been in his late teens when Tomas died. I think there might be a connection between that robbery and the museum robbery, because once again Tomas is the common denominator."

His eyes lit up. "That's very interesting. We should pass that on to Captain Lavezzo. What else did you learn about David Leoni?"

"Not much. I didn't have enough time before Victor and Joelle arrived. Then you and Anna came back, and we had to pack them up and get them out of the house. Anyway, I'll put him on the list to look into. Maybe the art historian will be familiar with him. My grandmother said she thought David had more success than Tomas or Lucinda."

"It feels like someone is collecting paintings from everyone that Tomas painted with or taught," Nick said. "That can't be a coincidence."

"I agree. There is a mention of a group in the letters. That group may be the key to everything."

Nick grabbed his phone as it buzzed. "It's Captain Lavezzo."

"Could you put it on speaker?"

He nodded, then answered the call. "Captain Lavezzo? What have you learned?"

"We identified the man who attacked you. His name is Gio Carmine," Lavezzo said. "He has a long record of assault, burglary, and other crimes. He was released from prison last month."

"Who's he working for?"

"He claims he doesn't know. He was hired on the internet, employer unknown. He was paid in cryptocurrency, and we are trying to trace the transaction."

Nick frowned at that piece of information. "What about his partner?"

"He met the guy last night an hour before they went to your house. All he had was a first name—Sal."

"He has to know more than that."

"I don't believe he does. Everything he told us checked out. He's a gun for hire, and whoever hired him has hidden their tracks. He also said they were told to look for a painting signed by Tomas Caruso and that it could be hidden anywhere in the house. They should rip everything apart to find it."

"What about the gun that was left behind?"

"No prints. We're still trying to track it or match it to other crimes. I also have some information on the vehicle that tailed you and your grandmother. The car was rented at the airport by Jennifer Lawson, an American venture capitalist. She left her car with a valet at the Bellarmine Hotel in Trevi when she checked in. She attended a conference there yesterday, and we confirmed she was giving a talk when you were followed. She hadn't checked to see if her car was still parked somewhere on the property, because she wasn't using it today."

"Someone at the valet gave her keys away."

"That was my assumption, however one of my team members went to the hotel this morning and saw the parking attendants leaving keys in cars that were double-parked on the street a block away from the hotel entrance. Because there is a conference going on this weekend, there were more cars than usual."

"So, our thief helped himself to a car, and we have no way of tracking him."

Isabella heard the frustration in Nick's voice, which was completely understandable. Every time they got a lead, it evaporated.

"We will continue investigating," Captain Lavezzo said. "How is Signorina Rossi?"

"She's right here," he said. "Isabella?"

"I'm doing all right," she said. "But I want to make sure this man is charged with trying to kill me."

"He will be. You don't have to worry. He will go back to prison for a long time. That said, I hope you two have reconsidered staying at the house. Without knowing the employer of the man in our custody, I can't promise you won't be in danger again. Clearly, he or she has money to hire whoever he needs to do whatever he wants."

"I understand. Nick and I are considering all our options. Is there anything else?"

"Not at this time."

"Thanks for the update," Nick said.

"That wasn't very helpful," she muttered as Nick ended the call.

"No. It wasn't, and I don't like when things are too perfect."

"What do you mean?"

"There's no such thing as the perfect crime, but so far, every thread has been perfectly snipped. Security cameras and alarms at the museum were conveniently disabled. No eyewitnesses to the robbery, a burglary here that leaves no evidence, no finger-prints on a weapon, no link to anyone besides an elusive contact on the web."

"Maybe we just haven't found the loose thread yet." She paused, seeing the speculation in his eyes. "Or?"

"Or someone on the inside is working against a resolution."

"Are you suggesting that Captain Lavezzo is not trying to find the thieves? Why? What would be his motive? That's his job, right?"

"It is his job. But there's something about him that bothers me. Stefano, too. He seems to show up a lot."

"Stefano is a family friend."

"Who is very interested in the robbery and the paintings."

"That's true," she admitted. "Stefano told me he asked to be alerted if any calls came in from this house. But that's because he's concerned about our grandparents. It's difficult to see why either Stefano or Captain Lavezzo would have a motive not to solve this crime."

"You're right. We have no evidence they aren't doing exactly what they're supposed to be doing. I'm just frustrated that we keep running into walls. And I want to do more to help. If we were in the US, I could get a team of people on this. But here, I'm an outsider. I'm lucky Lavezzo is talking to me at all.

Anyway, we'll just keep looking into things on our own until we have more information."

"I'm glad to hear you say that because I was expecting you to suggest taking me to the airport and putting me on a plane again."

"I'm not against that idea, Isabella."

She was sorry she'd brought it up. "I want to talk to the art historian and dig into David Leoni and this Juliette woman. While I could do some of that from California, I feel like I'm going to need to speak to people here in Rome, and that would be better done in person. But I'm not stupid, Nick. I know there's danger. Leaving is on the table, but not right this second."

"Fair enough," he said, meeting her gaze. "We'll see how the day goes."

CHAPTER TWELVE

As Nick drove through Trastevere, he appreciated the deep blue sky and bright sunshine, which helped lighten the dark shadows he'd been living under. After crossing the bridge over the Tiber River, he made his way through the historic district of Rome, where narrow medieval cobblestone streets melded into busy, more modern thoroughfares.

"I forgot how beautiful Rome is," Isabella muttered as he stopped at a light.

"When were you here last?"

"I came back for a long weekend about four years ago, but I just spent time with my grandmother. I didn't do any sightseeing."

"You haven't seen your grandmother in four years?" he asked with surprise. "I got the feeling you were close."

"We are close. We video chat regularly, and she met me in Paris two years ago. She's been asking me to come back to Rome, but my memories of this country are complicated."

"Because of your grandfather?"

"Yes. But when I met my cousins yesterday, I realized that not everyone in the family felt the same way about me as my grandfather did. They just never had the chance to get to know me, and I didn't have the opportunity to get to know them. The summer I spent here as a teenager would have been more fun if I had spent time with Joelle, with people my age, if I could have seen that the family didn't hate me for being a child of sin."

"That sounds dramatic," he teased.

"No. Those were my grandfather's exact words. That's the way he saw me."

His smile faded as he heard the pain in her voice. "He was wrong, and you know that."

"I do. But knowing it and feeling it are different things."

"I don't understand how he could have been so cruel to you. Or how Gloria let him say things like that."

"Well, he didn't say them when she was in the room, and when I tried to talk to her about it, she just made excuses for him. She said he was traditional and old-fashioned and very religious. None of that mattered to me. All I could feel was the sting of his glare and his harsh words. I couldn't wait to get out of there."

"I'm beginning to understand why Italy is a complicated place for you," he said as he drove through the intersection. "I guess he's the reason your mother never wanted to come back."

"He was a big part of it. And she had given him far more reasons to hate her than I ever did. She hadn't just gotten pregnant; she'd also gone to jail."

"That couldn't have sat well with him."

"It didn't. But I think it just reinforced his opinion that she was no good, and I probably wasn't, either." She drew in a breath and let it out. "Let's talk about something else. Tell me about the historian we're going to meet."

"I don't know anything about her except that my boss, Flynn MacKenzie, worked with her on art crimes. He said she'd be an excellent resource. Hopefully, it will be a productive meeting."

"It feels good just to get out of the house. Although, I wonder how safe the house will be if we're not in it."

"It wasn't particularly safe when we were in it. Or rather, you were in it."

"I was probably a surprise. They watched you leave and thought we'd all gone. Maybe we should search the house more thoroughly when we get back. What if the painting is there?"

"My grandmother said she is absolutely certain that there is no other painting by Tomas or Lucinda in her house."

"I'm sure she's right, but I might still look around when we get back." She paused, waving her hand toward the neighborhood. "This is a nice area. Art historians must make some money in Italy, if she can afford to live here."

"I have no idea, but there's a lot of art and a lot of history here so maybe art historians are in demand."

"Probably. Being here reminds me how modern everything is where we live. And not just modern but also boring."

"I don't know about boring. Los Angeles has its own vibe: the film and music industry, the great weather, the beaches..."

"I do like the weather."

"Have you made friends in LA?"

"Not yet. But that takes time."

"It does," he agreed. "When I was growing up and moving around with my parents, it always felt like it took a year in any new city to be comfortable, to really know people. And then it was usually time to leave and start over again."

"Some might say that was an exciting childhood."

"Some like my parents would agree with you. But it wasn't their childhood; it was mine." He paused as he maneuvered into a tight parking spot just down the street from Francesca's building. "We're here."

They got out of the car and walked down the street. He pushed the button for 3B, and a woman answered in Italian, asking who was there.

"Nick Caruso and Isabella Rossi," he replied.

"*Sí*. Top floor."

The door buzzed, and they made their way up four flights of steep, stone stairs, which were typical for buildings in Rome.

"That was a workout," Isabella muttered breathlessly as they reached the top floor. "Why don't Italians like elevators?"

"They prefer stairs to work off all the pasta," he said lightly, drawing a smile.

"Good point."

"And even with renovations, it's difficult to get elevators into these buildings." He was about to knock on the door when it opened, revealing an attractive blonde wearing tight jeans and a blue V-neck sweater that matched the blue in her eyes. She appeared to be in her late-thirties. "Francesca Ribaldi?" he asked, surprised that the art historian wasn't someone older and more buttoned-up.

"Yes. Come in." She waved them to her apartment, which was far more modern than the outside of the building, with a white and gray color scheme that included plush carpeting, high-end furniture, and impressive sculptures in the vast living room that looked out over the city. The walls were covered with paintings, which appeared to be old and probably very expensive. Some were lit by small lights placed under the frames.

"Your place is beautiful," Isabella commented, pausing by one painting, which appeared to be a scene from ancient Rome. "Whose work is this?"

"Fernando Albano, a not-so-well-known Italian painter from the seventeen hundreds, but someone whose work I very much like. His colors and brush strokes were bold for that time period. He was a visionary, and I like artists that paint more than anyone else can see," Francesca said. "Would you like something to drink before we talk?"

"No, thanks," he said as Isabella shook her head, and they sat down in the living room.

He couldn't imagine living on so much white furniture. He'd be afraid to eat or drink anything. But there wasn't even a hint of a smudge on the white sofa.

"Flynn told me about your situation," Francesca said. "The robbery at the museum and the paintings that were stolen. I believe two belonged to your great-grandparents."

"Tomas was my great-grandfather," he confirmed. "And Lucinda was Isabella's great-grandmother. We understand they painted together, that Tomas also taught other artists, and that there was a group that met regularly at his studio in the sixties. But they weren't particularly successful artists. They didn't sell any work as far as we know. I'm not sure they even had any showings. So why would someone want to steal their works of art after all this time?"

"I don't know, but my guess is that the theft of these paintings is personal. Perhaps a private collector, an art dealer, a jealous artist or lover."

He frowned. "But there was another painting taken as well by Frederico Germain. It seems doubtful one person would have been jealous of all three of them."

"Maybe four," Isabella interjected. "There was a painting by an artist named David Leoni that was stolen from a gallery in Florence six months ago. David Leoni was also a student of Tomas Caruso."

"I hadn't heard about David Leoni's work being stolen," Francesca said. "So, you believe these four paintings were all taken by the same person?"

"Yes," Isabella said. "But it wasn't one person at the museum. There were at least three."

"Someone is running a crew," he added.

Francesca nodded. "That confirms what a friend at the Carabinieri told me. She said that the thieves at the museum were dressed all in black, including black gloves. I found that interesting because in the sixties, the same time period in which your relatives were painting, there was a crew of thieves known as *La Mano Nera*—The Black Hand."

"Really?" Isabella asked, sitting up straighter as interest fired up her eyes. "Is that because they wore black gloves?"

"Yes. During the Cold War, there were a great number of art thefts in Italy. Many were purported to be done by thieves dressed all in black, wearing black gloves. The crew was started by a master thief with the name Roberto Falconeri. He and his brother, Bruno, stole and smuggled art out of the country to private collectors and criminal organizations. Roberto Falconeri burned his hands in a fire, so it was believed that he wore gloves to prevent the scars from being used to identify him. When he grew his one-man operation into a criminal enterprise, he insisted everyone wear black gloves."

"Was Falconeri caught and prosecuted for his crimes?" he asked.

"No. After the Carabinieri was created in 1969 to stem the flow of stolen art and culture out of the country, the crew dropped out of sight. I'm not sure they ever operated again, or if they did, they changed their clothing and made sure there was no tie to *La Mano Nera*."

"That's fascinating," Isabella said. "But if the police knew who Falconeri was, why couldn't they find him?"

"Bruno Falconeri was killed in 1970. He was shot in the head, and his killer was never found. Roberto disappeared after that. I don't believe he was ever located."

"Would Roberto be alive today?" Isabella asked.

"I doubt it, but if he was, he'd be in his late nineties by now."

"What about kids? Maybe one of them has recreated their family's criminal enterprise."

"Roberto had no children. Bruno had a daughter, but she died in her teens. It could be another relative or a former associate who might still be alive today."

"Wouldn't Captain Lavezzo at the Carabinieri know about this group called *La Mano Nera*?" Isabella asked. "It sounds like they were a legendary crew of thieves."

"He would know about them," Francesca confirmed. "But as I said, there have been no thefts tied to them in the last fifty years."

"But the paintings stolen this week were all at least fifty years old," he murmured. "Let's bring it back to the present. Frederico Germain was the other artist whose painting was stolen. What do you know about him?"

"He started the Istituto d'Arte Roma, a school for budding artists not far from here. He was probably a better teacher than an artist, but he had some success early in his life. As he grew older, he became an alcoholic and one day he burned his paintings in a drunken rage. I was actually surprised to hear there was a painting left to be stolen."

"Do you think he knew Tomas or Lucinda?"

"I would think so." Francesca paused, her expression changing slightly as if she were debating whether she wanted to say something.

"What?" he asked.

"Have you ever heard of Sam Beringer?"

He nodded, his body tensing at her question. "I have. Why?"

"There was speculation he might have been involved with Falconeri. They were both very good at stealing. Some might have said they were rivals. Others might have said partners."

"Who's Sam Beringer?" Isabella asked. "I haven't heard that name before."

"He's a renowned art thief," he told her. "And he's the father of my boss, Flynn MacKenzie."

Her eyebrows shot up in surprise. "Seriously? Your FBI agent boss has a father who's an art thief?"

"Yes. They work on opposite sides of the law."

"If Sam Beringer was involved in The Black Hand, maybe your boss has information that could help us."

"Flynn doesn't know where his father is. That's a dead end."

"But—"

"Trust me," he said, cutting Isabella off. He turned to Francesca. "There's one more thing I wanted to ask you." He reached into his pocket and pulled out the ring. "Do you recognize this ring or the design?"

She took it out of his hand and studied it for a moment. "No, but I don't study jewelry. You should talk to a jeweler about it. Did it belong to Tomas?"

"I believe so. It was tucked away in a safe deposit box, so it makes me think it's important."

"I can't help you on that, but I will continue to look into the art, and I'll let you know if I find anything."

"I'm happy to pay you for your time."

"That's not necessary. I like to do my part to bring stolen art back to its rightful owners, so I will try to make that happen."

"Thank you. We'll let you enjoy the rest of your Saturday."

"It was lovely to meet you," she said as they all stood up. "I hope I have more answers when we speak again."

They said their goodbyes and then headed downstairs. When they got to the lobby, Isabella paused, giving him an annoyed look, "I can't believe your father's boss is an international art thief, and you don't want to use the connection. I get that it's a little complicated—"

"More than a little. Flynn runs my unit."

"I understand that, but—"

"There's no but," he interrupted again. "And you, of all people, should understand why Flynn would want nothing to do with his father. Your mother participated in criminal activity, and you don't want anything to do with her. You don't even want to talk to her about the painting she had in her possession for a very long time. So don't you think you're being a little hypocritical demanding that I ask my boss to just get over his complex relationship with his criminal father in order to help us?"

She frowned as he made his point. "You're right, Nick. I don't want to talk to my mother, and I guess I can understand why Flynn wants nothing to do with his father. I just have a hard time not following a lead that's right in front of me."

"Flynn doesn't know where his father is. He's made a point not to know. So, he wouldn't be able to help us even if I asked."

"Okay." She tucked her hair behind her ears, then quickly

kicked into fighting mode once more. "We'll find another way to get information. I know we need to go to the school to talk to Louisa Del Vecchio about Frederico's painting. But why don't I call Joelle first? My cousin is a jewelry designer. She might know if the design on the ring has any meaning."

"It's worth a shot. But the ring may not be as important as the paintings."

"It feels like they're connected, and we're not getting very far on the art, so we might as well try the ring," she said as she sent Joelle a text. "Hopefully, she gets back to us quickly. We can either meet her before we go to the school or after. Wait a second, she's writing back." She paused as she read the text. "She's showing her jewelry in a booth at Campo 'de Fiori today with another designer if we want to come by. She'll be there for another hour."

"Then we'll go there first."

CHAPTER THIRTEEN

Campo 'de Fiori was a popular square in the historic district, with outdoor cafes running around the edges and an open-air market in the middle of the plaza. One half was dedicated to food and produce, while the other half was filled with artisan booths. She'd come here with her grandmother several times when she was a teenager, and she'd loved it. They'd have lunch and then get gelato at one of her grandmother's favorite stands. It had been a nice escape from her grandmother's house, which felt so quiet and somber, especially when her grandfather, Paolo, was around. Gloria's personality had certainly been stifled by her husband's insistence on neat and clean. Now that she was living with Anna, it was like she was back in a world of color.

Of course, she didn't want to be happy that her grandfather had died. That was wrong. Even if they hadn't had a good relationship, her grandmother had loved him, so there must have been something about him that was good; she'd just never seen it.

Shoving those old, dark memories out of her head, she turned to Nick. "Did you come here when you were a kid?"

"Lots of times. It hasn't changed all that much."

"No, it hasn't. I had some happy memories here."

He smiled. "I'm glad there were some good memories from your one summer in Rome. I was thinking there weren't any."

"I guess the bad ones stuck with me." She spied a flash of red hair. "I think I see Joelle."

"Yeah, there she is," he said, an odd note in his voice.

She gave him a thoughtful look. "You don't sound very excited."

"Joelle is very...touchy."

Isabella laughed at his awkward words. "She liked you. I would think you'd be used to women being touchy."

"I think she likes all men," he said dryly.

"You might be right. But Joelle was nice to me and wanted to know me, which was a shocker. I have never met anyone in my family, besides my grandmother, who was interested in who I was or what I thought."

"I understand, and I can handle whatever she dishes out."

"I'm sure you can." She was actually amused by Nick's reaction to how flirty Joelle had been. And maybe even a little pleased that he wasn't all that excited to see her cousin again, although she really didn't want to look at that feeling too closely.

Joelle wore a colorful figure-hugging dress, her red hair pulled back in a loose bun. She was helping a young woman try on some earrings while her partner, an older blonde woman, was finishing a sale.

She waited until Joelle's customer moved away before stepping forward.

Joelle greeted them with a huge smile. "Isabella. Nick." She came around the display table to give them both a hug and a kiss on each cheek, and Isabella couldn't help but notice that Nick got a much longer embrace than she did. But he had a smile on his face, which reminded her he was a man who lived undercover, who knew how to be what someone wanted him to be. And Joelle wanted him to be interested, which he now appeared to be.

"So this is your work," he said, waving his hand at the display table. "Impressive."

"Thank you," she said as she moved back around the table. "These are my more modest pieces. I was telling Isabella yesterday that my focus right now is high-end personalized designs, but until that takes off, here I am, hawking my earrings and necklaces like I've been doing the last eight years."

There was a tinge of irritation in Joelle's voice, despite her pleasant smile. She clearly was a woman with far more ambition than this. Isabella could appreciate that. She wanted to get to the top of her field, too, something else she had in common with her second cousin.

"So, show me this ring you found," Joelle said. "Whose did you say it was?"

"It was in my great-grandfather's things," Nick replied as he showed her the ring.

Joelle took it out of his hand and spun it around, the silver glittering in the sunlight. "It's a beautiful design."

"Have you seen it before? Do you have any idea what the *P* might mean?" she asked.

Joelle shrugged. "No idea. You're talking about Tomas Caruso, right? It's not his initial." She chewed on her bottom lip. "The swirling lines of the design around the letter remind me of some of Lucinda's drawings."

"Do you have some of Lucinda's drawings?" she asked in surprise. "I didn't think there was anything left."

"Lucinda always made a special birthday card for my grand-mother, Lucinda's daughter. She saved the cards and when I got interested in art, she showed them to me."

"Does your grandmother still have them?"

"Possibly. I can ask her."

"That would be great. And the sooner the better."

"Oh, wait a second. I have a date tonight. It will have to be tomorrow," Joelle said with an apologetic smile. "I'm sorry."

"That's fine," she said, even though she hated to wait even a second to find another clue. On the other hand, it was doubtful some old birthday cards would reveal that much.

"Maybe we could all meet for brunch tomorrow," Joelle suggested, including Nick in her smile. "We can get better acquainted."

"That sounds good," she said. "I'm not sure exactly what we're doing tomorrow, but I'll text you later and we can confirm a time and a place."

"Perfect." As Joelle handed the ring back to Nick, she added, "You should ask your mother about this ring, Isabella. It's my understanding Sylvie studied Lucinda's work. She had her sketches, too, I believe. Do you have those?"

"I do. But there's nothing like this in the book."

"But some of her other work is there? I'd love to see that. Maybe you could bring it to brunch."

She hesitated, then said, "Sure."

"Great. I better get back to business," she said as a group of young women descended on the booth. "I'll text you later."

She nodded as they stepped away from the booth and continued down the path to a less- crowded area. Pausing, she turned to Nick. "I know what you're thinking. I shouldn't have told Joelle I have Lucinda's sketchbook or agreed to show it to her."

"You do know what I'm thinking," he said with a gleam in his eyes.

"But she's my cousin, and Lucinda is her great-grandmother, too. I didn't see how I could say no."

"You don't seem to have a problem saying no to me," he said dryly.

"That's different. Anyway, should we go to the school now?"

"Why don't we get some lunch first? I'm hungry."

Despite the lovely breakfast he'd made for her, she was feeling hungry, too, maybe because the smell of garlic was every-where. "I used to go to a pizza place around here with my grand-mother. I don't remember the name. And it's probably not even still around. But they had bright, red-checkered tablecloths, and I remember thinking I felt like I was in an Italian movie when we ate there. It was probably decorated for tourists to think just that."

"Maybe that's it," he said, pointing to the right. "I see red tablecloths. Let's check it out."

They moved through the booths to the far end of the square, where her memory came to life. "This is definitely it," she said. "I also remember it was right across from that gelato place where we went after we ate pizza."

"Food looks good," he said as a waiter passed by with a pizza. "I'm in."

"Me, too."

A moment later, the hostess took them to a table surrounded by potted plants that faced the square. The menu was delivered immediately, along with some glasses of water.

"Do you want pizza?" she asked. "There are other options."

"I like pizza. Why don't we share? Unless you don't think we can agree on pizza toppings?"

"I really don't argue about everything, Nick."

"I'll have to take your word for that. What do you like on your pizza?"

"Everything," she said. "See, I can be flexible."

He smiled. "So, anchovies, sausage, olives, peppers, ham, pineapple...all good for you?"

"Well, maybe not all together. And maybe not anchovies."

"But everything else?"

"You are so annoying and so cocky," she said, seeing the teasing light in his eyes.

"I thought you liked everything."

"Okay, I love sausage, pepperoni, bell peppers, olives, and onions. That would be my choice. Not that I couldn't eat the other things you mentioned, but let's go with that, since I'm assuming you are ultra-flexible."

He set down his menu. "I am, and that sounds good." He

turned to the waiter hovering nearby and ordered the pizza along with a beer for him, while she opted to stick with water.

As the waiter left, she looked around and gave a little sigh of unexpected pleasure. "This is a charming square, isn't it?"

"Even more so on a perfect day like this one. It's like we're in a picture postcard."

"It does feel that way. When was the last time you were in Rome?" she asked curiously.

"A year ago, for my grandfather's funeral. It was a quick trip. I could only take two days, so I didn't do much beyond sit with my grandmother and try to comfort her. That was difficult. I meant to come back sooner, but I couldn't seem to work it into the schedule."

"Well, you're here now."

"I just wish the circumstances were different."

She nodded in agreement. "So, do you know a lot of your extended family members? You spent a lot of summers here. I imagine you must have seen your relatives."

"I had some second cousins around my age who showed me around the city, especially when we were older teenagers. We had more fun than we should have."

"Do they still live here? Do you ever see them?"

"I haven't seen either in a while. One of them moved to London, the other to New York. I saw the one in New York when I was assigned there several years ago. He had just gotten married and had a kid on the way, so we mostly met for a beer or pickup basketball. No more wild days for us."

"So, the FBI agent has a wild past?" she asked.

"I've had my moments. What about the dedicated journalist committed to saving the world? Any wild stories you'll tell your grandchildren?"

"No. I never thought I could be wild. My mother owned that space. I had to be responsible, steady, and in control. I'm also not sure my goal is that big. I'd be satisfied with saving a few people, maybe not the world."

"Oh, come on. I think you want to save everyone. Why not own it?"

"Because it makes me sound egotistical."

"Saving the world isn't selfish. It's admirable."

"That's true. Okay, I will admit that I tend to live by the mantra *go big or go home*. I don't believe you're any different."

"I used to think bigger than I do now. I've come to realize it's impossible to save everyone. And not everyone wants to be saved. Sometimes just making a difference in one person's life is enough," he said, a somber tone entering his voice.

"It sounds like you lost someone," she commented.

"More than one," he admitted.

"How do you live with that?"

He shrugged. "You just live, because there's no way to change it."

"You must have had some nightmares over the years."

"I rarely sleep until I'm exhausted. Then I don't dream."

"I wish I could say that. I dream too much. I crave being able to turn my brain off and just be still, no thoughts, no worries."

"Have you ever tried meditation?"

"I have, and I spend the whole time telling myself to stop thinking, which is pretty much thinking."

He smiled. "It's a practice. You can't just do it once."

"Okay, Yogi, are you an expert meditator?"

"I've found it helpful in my line of work. I can't afford to let emotions get in the way of my job, so I've learned how to manage my breathing, stay calm, look for a way out or a way in, whatever the case may be."

"Does it work?"

"Not always, but most of the time." He paused as the waiter dropped off his beer.

"That's sacrilege, you know." She tipped her head at his beer. "You're in Italy. You should be drinking wine."

"Don't tell anyone," he said with a grin. "And you're not much better than me. You're drinking water."

"I want to stay alert, and wine can make me tired. I also don't drink that much, despite what you may think after our disastrous date in LA."

"We've moved past that, haven't we?"

"Yes. But I have to say I'm still surprised we ended up here together. I would never have thought we'd even see each other again after that awkward dinner."

"Life is filled with unexpected twists."

"That might be the truest thing you've ever said." She paused, knowing she was treading into dangerous territory, but she couldn't stop herself. "Tell me more about your boss and his father."

A frown crossed his lips. "There's not much to say, Isabella. Sam left Flynn and his mother when Flynn was a kid. Apparently, Sam was on the verge of going to jail. He disappeared instead of facing the music and being there for his family."

"Did Flynn go into the FBI to protect his father or to find him?"

"I think it was more about righting his father's wrongs. It's like what you just said about your mother. You couldn't be wild, because she owned that space. Flynn couldn't be bad or a criminal, because his father owned that space. He had to be the opposite. He had to be better than good." Nick paused. "But Flynn never told me that; I'm just guessing."

"It makes sense."

"I know they didn't see each other for decades until a few years ago, when Flynn was working on a murder investigation tied into the art world. His father unexpectedly showed up to help him. Sam apparently saved his son's life. But he disappeared again in the aftermath, and Flynn hasn't seen him since."

"Interesting that Sam took the risk of helping his son. He doesn't sound all bad. I wish we could find Sam and ask him about *La Mano Nera*."

"I already told you that Flynn doesn't know where his father is. After the incident several years ago, there were a lot of eyes on Flynn's actions regarding his father. I suspect that both Sam and Flynn made sure there was no contact between them after that. It would have been dangerous for both of them." He paused. "That said, I will ask Flynn about the group. He worked art crimes and he sent me to Francesca, so he may know something about *La Mano Nera*."

"It's worth asking. I'm also going to research *La Mano Nera* and the Falconeri family when we get back to the house."

"You like to research, don't you?"

"It's what I do all the time. I'm pretty good at it."

"I'll bet you are. I could see your eyes light up when Francesca mentioned the crew. You were immediately hooked just by the name. But..." His smile faded. "While the name might make them sound fascinating and historically interesting, that doesn't mean they weren't just evil criminals."

"I know. I'm sure they were criminals and probably did terrible things. I just hope that finding out more about them will get us another step closer to figuring out who stole our family paintings. I'm surprised that Captain Lavezzo didn't mention them to us. Surely, if he's an expert on art crimes, the black gloves would have made him think of them."

"I'm sure there are many things the captain didn't share with us."

At his disgruntled tone, she couldn't help but poke at him a little. "I thought you said you could get more information from him than I could because you're FBI. What happened?"

"Clearly, he wasn't interested in collaborating, which isn't that surprising. Agencies can be very territorial, especially those outside of the US. But I had hoped he would be different."

"Well, this is why you need me."

"How so? He's not going to tell you more than he'll tell me."

"No. But we can bounce ideas off each other."

He smiled. "I'm a little surprised you would think two heads are better than one, Isabella. You seem like someone who likes to work alone."

"I'm someone who often has to work alone, but I'm not against having a partner, as long as they're not a complete idiot."

He laughed. "So, I'm not an idiot?"

"Well, the jury is still out," she returned, enjoying their back and forth probably more than she should be. Fortunately, the pizza was arriving, and she was instantly distracted. "This looks amazing."

Nick was too busy putting slices on a plate to answer.

To her surprise, he handed her the plate, and then filled one for himself.

It was a small gesture, but it touched her heart. She'd thought Nick was an egotistical ass when she'd met him, but he'd stayed with her last night, talking her down from the ledge she was on. He'd made her breakfast, and now he'd handed her the first slice of pizza. She had misjudged him. He was more generous than she would have imagined, more kind. And it was a little unsettling to realize how wrong she'd been. It was also disturbing to feel the strange sensation of butterflies in her stomach every time he smiled at her.

"Something wrong?" Nick asked, his gaze narrowing. "You're not eating."

"Just letting it cool," she said hastily as she picked up her slice and took a bite. She needed to focus on food and not on Nick. That became very easy, because the pizza was absolutely delicious, an explosion of flavor, and even better than she remembered.

"So, after this, we should go to the school," Nick said as he finished his first slice of pizza and grabbed another.

"I agree. I'm kind of excited to see the school where our grandmothers first met. Although it seems oddly coincidental that our investigation into the past should take us there. It's like so many things are intertwined that I wouldn't have thought went together."

"Like you and me?" he asked with a grin.

There went the damn butterflies again. And she couldn't help but smile back. "The perfect example. But I was thinking about the relationship between our families and how all these artists are connected. The art world in the sixties seems very small."

"Maybe the passion for art always makes that world small," he said. "It is interesting that our grandmothers went to that school."

"And my mother, too. I think Lucinda might have taught there as well. That's a lot of generations of Rossi women."

"Did you ever have any interest in art?"

"When I was really young, I thought it was fun to paint, but that's probably because it was something my mother and I did together. She used to sit by the window and paint, and I'd be on the floor at the coffee table, doing the same." She paused. "Funny, I haven't thought about those days in a long time."

"When did your mother stop painting?"

"It was probably a gradual thing. She had to work a lot because we had little money, so time and energy to paint were in short supply. My grandfather told me once that my mother could have been so much more if she hadn't had me. I was the dream killer."

His gaze narrowed as he frowned. "You didn't kill her dreams, Isabella. I'm sure your mom didn't think of you that way. Paolo was just a crusty, bitter, and angry man. He should never have said such a cruel thing to you. If he was alive, I'd kick his ass."

"I don't think our grandmothers would let you. But I appreciate the thought."

"Your mom was young when she got pregnant. And she was alone. She should have been treated with more compassion."

"I agree. And she tried to be a good mother for the early part of my life. She would even tell you she married my stepfather because she wanted me to have more opportunities. Unfortunately, that's not what happened. She'd made another mistake, and it was an even worse one. Anyway, we don't have to talk about her."

"That might become more difficult if we keep going down the road we're on," he said, a serious note in his voice. "I don't know what we'll find when we dig further into the pasts of our respective families, Isabella. Maybe it will all be good, but there's a chance it could be bad, and you're just starting to like your family after meeting Joelle. Are you sure you want to take that risk?"

"I can't stop now. Not just because I want to find the paintings or figure out why they were taken. Someone tried to kill me last night, and I want that person to pay."

"He's already in custody. He'll go to prison for what he did."

"He will, but not the person who sent him. And I want to get him, too."

"Or her. We don't know if we're dealing with a man or a woman."

"That's true. Everyone is a suspect."

"Everyone, including people you might like very much."

"It's not Joelle," she said, reading his pointed gaze. "Why would you even think that?"

"I didn't say her name. You did."

She didn't like that he was right—again.

"She's a little much," he said. "A little too interested in..."

"Getting to know me?" she asked. "You think she's using me. That she's not being genuine?"

"I honestly don't know. But she showed up yesterday. She's super friendly, eager to meet, has a background in art, even if it's focused toward jewelry, and she asks a lot of questions."

"But Joelle is my age. She wouldn't have been waiting a long time to get her hands on the paintings. And she's not a criminal mastermind. She's an ambitious jewelry designer."

"How ambitious?"

She frowned again. "Very. But ambition isn't a crime. I'm ambitious, too. So are you."

"Just remember what you said a minute ago—everyone is a suspect."

"I won't forget that. But I still don't think Joelle is involved in any of this."

CHAPTER FOURTEEN

Isabella was happy when they arrived at the Istituto d'Arte Roma a little after three. She wanted to stop thinking about Joelle having a hidden agenda and focus on the school that tied so many people together. As they walked up to the two-story U-shaped building set on the edge of the Tiber River, they found the front doors to the school wide open, with a sign for a Plein-Air session from one o'clock to four o'clock in the courtyard.

"What's this?" she murmured, pausing by the sign.

"I think that's referring to painting in the open air," Nick replied. "And this is good for us. The school is open, and hopefully Louisa Del Vecchio is here."

She followed him up the stairs and into the building. The admissions office was closed, but she could see doors open to the right of them, so they headed in that direction. Along the way, she couldn't help but notice the amazing amount of student artwork plastered on the walls. Every available inch was covered with drawings, paintings, sketches, even some framed floral paintings that mixed paint with dried flowers. Some of it was good, a lot of it was messy, but it was all creative. Generations of budding artists had passed through this school, reminding her again that three generations of Rossi women had walked these hallways. And now it was her turn. It was Nick's turn, too. He was also tied to this school through Anna.

"It's strange to be in a place where our grandmothers met so many years ago," she said. "They were only twenty-one and very far from home."

"Probably why they forged such a strong friendship. They found home in each other."

"They did." She felt oddly emotional at his words. It was probably just being in this place where there was so much history. She'd lived her entire life with no family history, and now it was all around her. It was a lot to take in. And time to get outside.

Moving through the open doors, they found themselves in a courtyard, which was surrounded by the school on three sides, while the open side faced a patch of thick trees and a stone wall overlooking the river and the hillside beyond, where a majestic and very old castle added even more appeal to the view.

"This is inspiring," she murmured. She didn't feel like painting, but she felt like writing it all down. She'd never been a journal keeper, which probably surprised some people because she loved to write. But she didn't like to write about herself or her thoughts. This scene she could write. She could bring it to life with words. But she wasn't here to write about the scene, and she needed to get her head back in the game.

"I wonder if that's Louisa," Nick said, interrupting her reverie. He tipped his head to a woman dressed in white jeans and a bright red sweater; her silver hair pulled back in a long braid that fell halfway down her back. She appeared to be in her fifties or sixties.

"Let's find out," she said.

They walked across the courtyard, hovering nearby until the woman finished her conversation.

When she turned around, she gave them a curious look. "Ciao," she said.

"Are you Louisa Del Vecchio?" she asked.

"*Sí*. And you are?"

"Isabella Rossi." She waved her hand in Nick's direction. "And this is Nick Caruso."

"Rossi?" Louisa echoed, surprise in her gaze. "Are you Sylvie's daughter?"

She was shocked by the question. "You knew my mother?"

"We were students here when my grandfather ran the school. You look so much like her." Louisa shook her head in bemusement. "I feel like I've gone back in time. Sylvie was one of my good friends. She was a wild child, so beautiful and passionate and extremely talented. Of course, it ran in the family. Her grandmother, Lucinda Rossi was brilliant, too. My grandfather, Frederico, told me that Lucinda used to teach an evening class here that was so popular, it was standing room only." She paused. "I'm sorry. I'm rambling."

"It's fine. It's nice to know more about my mother and great-grandmother. Did you ever meet Lucinda?"

"No. I just knew of her through what my grandfather told me about her. He was quite enamored. I think he might have had a crush on her." Louisa paused. "How is Sylvie?"

"She's well."

"I'm glad. I remember when she left Rome to study in the States," Louisa said. "She was determined to see more of the world. She felt certain it would inspire her art. I was impressed that she would leave her darling boyfriend behind. Stefano was heartbroken when she left. But he loved her so much, he had to let her go."

"You knew Stefano, too?"

"Yes. He didn't attend classes here, but we often went to the same weekend parties. I actually saw him several weeks ago when he came to an open house. One of his nieces is applying to the school. I couldn't believe he was an inspector with the Polizia. He also used to be wild. He told me that Sylvie is moving to Firenze."

"Yes," she said, not really wanting to talk about her mother.

"Anyway, I know you're busy, but Nick and I wanted to speak to you about the robbery at the museum last week. Your grandfather's painting was stolen along with paintings by my great-grandmother, Lucinda Rossi, and Nick's great-grandfather, Tomas Caruso."

"Tomas Caruso," Louisa repeated, her gaze moving to Nick. "Sorry. I hadn't put your last name with Tomas." She cleared her throat, turning back to Isabella. "I was shocked by that robbery. I was going to visit the exhibition on Thursday. Unfortunately, I was out of town when it first opened. I couldn't wait to see Frederico's painting on display. When I heard it was stolen, I couldn't believe it." She shook her head in bewilderment. "I don't understand what happened."

"Neither do we. Was Frederico's work valuable? Were there buyers who wanted to purchase his paintings over the years?"

"He made some sales when he was a younger man, but my grandfather died over twenty years ago, and he hadn't painted for a decade before that. He was quite mad at the end of his life, demented from years of alcohol abuse and his frustration with his own talent. He burned most of his work a few days before he drank himself to death. Luckily, I had taken a painting out of his home years before that night and tucked it away. I wanted to make sure my children and grandchildren could appreciate his talent. Of course, he wasn't just an artist, he was also a teacher, and some might say he left a bigger mark on the students who came through this school."

"So you took his painting years ago?" Nick asked. "How long would you say?"

"I can't remember. He went through many dark periods, threatening to destroy everything, and that's when I decided to slip it out of his house and tuck it away. Why? Is that important?"

"We're just trying to figure out where all these paintings were before they were stolen," Nick said. "We know that Lucinda, Tomas, and Frederico knew each other. What we don't know is why their paintings were stolen together in what appeared to be a targeted robbery. Do you have any ideas?"

"I don't. They were definitely friends at one time, but that changed at some point."

"What do you mean?" she asked.

Before Louisa could answer, another woman interrupted their conversation, a woman who was Louisa's identical twin right down to the white jeans. Only her sweater was purple instead of red. But she had the same hair, the same face.

"Ciao," she said. "Is something wrong? You all look so serious."

"This is my sister, Victoria," Louisa said. "Isabella Rossi and Nick Caruso, descendants of Lucinda Rossi and Tomas Caruso."

"Ah, *Sí*," Victoria said, giving them a thoughtful look. "Then you are related to Sylvie Rossi, too?"

"Sylvie is my mother."

"I can see her in your face," Victoria said with a nod.

"They're asking about the relationship between Frederico, Lucinda, and Tomas, because their paintings were stolen together a few days ago," Louisa told her sister.

"That was terrible news," Victoria said.

"I know Frederico had a falling out with Tomas and Lucinda," Louisa continued. "But I don't remember why. Do you, Victoria?"

"Our grandfather came to hate so many people in his later years," Victoria murmured. "It's impossible to say. But it is funny that you're asking. A little over a year ago, I got the same question from an inspector with the Polizia."

She was shocked by Victoria's words. "Stefano Gangi?" she asked. "Was that the inspector's name?"

"No." Victoria gave Nick a thoughtful look. "His name was Marcus Caruso. Is he related to you?"

"My grandfather," Nick replied, his lips tightening at Victoria's words. "What did he ask you exactly?"

"He wanted to know about Frederico's relationship with

Tomas and Lucinda."

"Why?" Nick asked.

"He didn't say. He also asked if I had any of Frederico's paintings at the school, which I did not. I didn't actually realize that anyone in the family had any of his work until Louisa mentioned last week that she had one of his paintings and was going to put it in the local exhibition."

"You never knew Louisa had the painting?" she challenged, surprised that Louisa wouldn't have shared that with her twin.

"I told her a long time ago," Louisa interrupted. "Victoria just forgot, which she does a lot."

"I really don't think you mentioned it," Victoria returning, giving her sister an annoyed look.

"What else did my grandfather ask you?" Nick said, bringing their attention back to him.

Victoria thought for a moment. "He asked if I had ever heard my grandfather mention a woman named Juliette. I don't remember the last name, but he did give me one. Anyway, he seemed disappointed that I didn't know who she was, and that I couldn't show him any of Frederico's paintings."

"You never mentioned any of this to me," Louisa said to her sister.

"I didn't think it was that important, and we were dealing with so many other issues at the time. The roof was leaking. The heating was becoming a problem. Attendance was down. The school was falling apart, and I didn't know where we were going to get the money to fix anything. Everything was coming to a head, and you were in Fiji, vacationing with your husband."

"For a week," Louisa said defensively. "And then I came back to help you deal with everything, as I continue to do."

"Well, by that time, I had forgotten all about my conversation with Signor Caruso." Victoria paused. "Actually, I hadn't forgotten, I just didn't want to bring it up, Louisa. I thought you might want to find out more, and I didn't. Frederico was dead, and, frankly, if he had done something wrong a long time ago, I didn't want to know about it or for anyone else to know about it."

"Was my grandfather accusing Frederico of something?" Nick asked.

"He didn't come right out and say that, but he mentioned something about a criminal organization tied to stolen art. I told him my grandfather would have never been involved in anything like that. He had very high moral standards when it came to art, and no patience for artists who took shortcuts."

"That's true," Louisa agreed. "When he was old and dying, Frederico used to rant to me about people who didn't appreciate art for what it was, and how he'd believed it was up to him to protect it, to be the caretaker. But it was difficult when so many people were stealing things and using art to fund their criminal activities. He didn't make a lot of sense, but I know he wouldn't have gotten involved in anything illegal."

Isabella wondered about that. Why would Nick's grandfather have come to this school investigating people who had been dead for a very long time? He had to have been on to something. But what?

"Your grandfather also asked me if Frederico had spoken about the fire that took Tomas and Lucinda's lives," Victoria added.

"Had he?" Nick asked.

"My grandfather mentioned their names often, and he would get upset about how they died too young. He wished he could have stopped that from happening. But he never said anything specifically to me about the fire. Louisa?"

Louisa shook her head. "No, nothing specific. Just rambling comments that never made sense. He got mixed up on time and people's names. He really wasn't well for most of the second half of his life." She paused as her watch buzzed. "That's my timer. I need to wrap this session up. I'm sorry we couldn't be more helpful. Please let us know if there's anything else we can do."

"We will," she said.

"We're both usually here at the school," Victoria added. "And we would love to get our grandfather's painting back."

"Grazie," she said as Louisa called for attention to announce the session was ending, and Victoria moved away to speak to one of the artists.

"Let's walk out this way," Nick said, heading through the courtyard and the trees to the river.

He stopped by the waist-high wall, looking out at the water, his profile hard but not particularly unreadable.

"Are you thinking about your grandfather? About why he was here asking questions about Tomas's death?" she enquired.

"Yes." He turned to face her. "Why would he come here with questions last year, so long after his father had died? And so close to when he died?"

"And he wanted information on Juliette, too," she reminded him. "He wouldn't have waited fifty years to look for her. That ID must have come to him more recently than when Tomas died. Maybe it was what triggered his questions."

"But where would he have gotten it?"

"I don't know."

Nick let out a sigh as he ran a hand through his hair in frustration. "None of this is adding up in a good way. My grandfather's questions, his trip to the school, the ID in the box...and then he dies in a solo car crash. A man who never drove over the speed limit a day in his life allegedly loses control of his vehicle in the rain and drives into a tree at a high rate of speed."

"Allegedly?" she queried. "What are you saying, Nick?"

He stared back at her, a grim look in his eyes. "I think my grandfather was killed. And I believe Tomas and Lucinda were killed, too. That the fire was purposefully set and not an accident. It's my guess both events are tied together."

Her stomach turned over. "But why would any of them be killed?" she asked, a chill running down her spine.

"I don't know, but I'm going to find out, Isabella. I won't rest until I do."

CHAPTER FIFTEEN

Nick's determined words rang through her head as they made their way back to the car. She wasn't sure what to say. The situation had just gotten a thousand times more personal for him.

She couldn't imagine why his grandfather would have suddenly been investigating the deaths of Tomas and Lucinda as recently as a year ago. And if Marcus was investigating, he had to have gotten some new piece of information, which also seemed unbelievable because it had been fifty years. What had happened to make Marcus ask questions? There had to have been a trigger.

And the consequence of Marcus's questions seemed to be a tragic accident that didn't look suspicious on the face of it, but putting everything that had happened before that and was happening now definitely raised questions.

Nick wasn't a man who jumped to conclusions. In fact, he was usually warning her not to make a big leap, but he'd put pieces of information together in a way that led to murder.

That thought raised goosebumps on her arms, reminding her she could have been killed last night, and Nick could have died, too.

What the hell was going on? Why was someone after their families?

The questions ran around in her head as Nick drove back to

the house. She wanted to talk things out with him, but he seemed completely lost in his head. He probably just needed a minute to process what they'd learned so far, to consider whether he was putting clues together in the wrong way.

But if his instincts were right, and if Marcus was murdered, then the stakes had been raised. For Nick, it wouldn't just be about getting the paintings back or making sure their grandmothers were safe; it would be about avenging his grandfather's death, the man who had inspired him and mentored him. He would never quit until he found the truth.

She just didn't want the truth to kill him, the way it had killed Lucinda, Tomas, and Marcus.

She also didn't want it to kill her.

But they were in this together, and she wouldn't bail now.

When they arrived at the house, she was happy to see that it was still standing, but also surprised to see a woman at the front door holding a large basket.

"Who's that?" she asked as Nick slowed down to turn into the driveway.

"I don't know." He stopped the car before opening the garage door. "Let me check it out."

He was out of the car before she could say she wasn't staying behind. But it didn't matter. She didn't believe the fifty-something woman who was now walking toward them was dangerous. She was wearing a teal knit dress with very high heels and her short, angled blonde hair framed a very pretty face. Not that evil couldn't be dressed up, but her gut said there was no danger here, so she got out of the car and walked across the grass.

"Ciao," the woman said, following up her greeting with a quick spate of Italian that included the names of their grandmothers.

"Sorry," Nick said. "My Italian isn't that good. Who are you?"

"Pardon. I'm Catherine Vigonas, the curator of the Museo dei Capolavori Romani. I came to check on Anna and Gloria."

She lifted the basket in her hands. "I brought them fruit and sweets."

"That's very nice," Nick said. "I can take that from you. I'm Nick Caruso, Anna's grandson."

"Oh, the infamous Nick," Catherine said with a gleam in her blue eyes. "The FBI agent. Your grandmother is very proud of you. And Gloria raves about her very smart granddaughter, who is setting the world on fire as a reporter," she added, giving Isabella a smile. "I assume that's you."

"It is. I'm Isabella Rossi."

"It's wonderful to meet you both, but I am sorry for the situation. How are Anna and Gloria feeling now? I spoke to them Wednesday night after the robbery, and I've been meaning to follow up, but I've been tied up with the Carabinieri and getting our security system back in place so that we can reopen."

"They're feeling better," Nick said. "But they're not here."

"Will they be back soon? Are they well? I heard that there was a break-in here last night, but they were not home when it occurred. I hope they are somewhere safe."

"They are, and they're doing all right. I'll let them know you stopped by," Nick said. "Perhaps you'd like to hang on to the basket. I'm not sure when they'll return."

"Oh, well, if you're staying here, why don't you keep it? Unless you're also leaving? I know you both live in California now."

"We'll be here for a while," Nick said vaguely.

"Then, please, enjoy the basket."

"Have the Carabinieri told you anything about suspects?" Isabella asked. "Do you have any idea why those three paintings were targeted?"

"I do not. It was quite shocking. There are many more valuable pieces in the museum; it's puzzling."

"Who came up with the idea for the exhibition?" Nick asked.

"Several of us were discussing how we could do more to feature lesser-known Italian artists and thought perhaps we would start with older generations whose work the public might not know about but would appreciate. We started with the sixties and seventies. We had many visitors the first two days. It was more successful than we imagined."

"How did you come up with the list of artists to invite?" she asked.

"We had input from people in the art community. Many of our local artists went to the school that Frederico Germain created in the fifties. He was a local legend," Catherine replied. "I was thrilled to get his painting. Your grandmothers brought the work of Lucinda Rossi and Tomas Caruso to my attention, and I was happy to display them as well. Now, I feel terrible they're gone. Anna was beside herself with guilt when I spoke to her after the robbery. I understand the painting has great sentimental value to your family, Signor Caruso."

"My grandmother would definitely like to get it back," Nick replied. "Do you have any idea how the security systems and cameras were turned off?"

"I don't believe I can speak about that. You should talk to Captain Lavezzo. I'm sure he'd appreciate your help. Please tell your grandmothers I'm thinking of them and while I'd love to have them back whenever they want to return, I will understand if they'd prefer not to do so for a while. I just need to know, as I will have to get additional volunteers. They are my most dedicated docents. They are always willing to show visitors around the museum and everyone loves them."

"We'll let them know," she said.

"Grazie," Catherine said. Then she walked down to the sidewalk and got into a silver Mercedes before driving away.

"Do you want to hold this basket while I pull the car into the garage?" Nick asked.

"Sure." She took the basket from his hands and waited as he got into the car, opened the garage with the remote and pulled inside. Then she followed the car into the garage so they could enter the house from the backyard. The lock showed signs of someone trying to break in, but she believed those marks had come from the day before, because the lock was still intact.

Nick opened the door, and they walked into the kitchen. Everything was quiet, still.

She set the basket on the table and followed Nick down the hall. They didn't speak as they made their way through the house, checking for problems. Her body tensed with each closed door, each unexpected creak of a board beneath their feet. When she finally realized everything was as they'd left it, she let out a breath of relief.

"No one was here," she said as they returned to the kitchen, which seemed to be their happy place. "That's a small win."

"Yes," he agreed, taking a seat at the table.

She looked through the basket, which was filled with fruits, a bottle of wine, and assorted cookies and pastries. "This is very generous. Do you want something?"

"I'm still full from the pizza."

"Me, too." She sat down across from him. "What did you think of Catherine?"

"Not sure. I thought she tripped herself up when she said she came to check on our grandmothers but then mentioned she knew about the burglary and that they weren't here at the time of the break-in. Why come by today with this offering?"

"Maybe she believed they were back now."

"If she knew they weren't here last night, then she talked to the police, and the police knew they left the country because I told both Stefano and Lavezzo that."

"True," she said slowly. "But it's possible they didn't tell her they were out of the country. Let's say she knew they weren't here. Why would she come by?"

"To see if it was true that they were gone. Perhaps to check whether we were still in town, if the house was occupied."

"You're suggesting that the curator of the museum that was robbed was in on the robbery there and the break-in here, Nick? Do you really believe that?"

Nick frowned and ran a hand through his hair. "I don't know."

"But your gut is setting off alarm bells."

"That seems to happen a lot these days. Maybe it's Italy. This country is throwing me off."

"It doesn't hurt to look at everything through suspicious eyes. We don't want to be surprised."

"So far, we've been nothing but surprised. We have to find a way to get out in front instead of playing catch up."

"I agree. But first, maybe we should talk more about Marcus and his accident."

"There's nothing to talk about," he said shortly. "We need more information. Without it, we're just going around in circles."

"Why don't you talk to Stefano? He worked with Marcus. He said your grandfather was a mentor to him. Perhaps Marcus talked to him about whatever he was looking into?"

"That's a thought. My grandmother told me that my grandfather was getting a lot of calls in the weeks before he died, that he seemed stressed out about something, and he said he needed to help someone. She just didn't know who. She thought it was a friend and most of his friends were from his days as a police officer, but he'd been retired for at least a decade before he showed up at that school last year asking questions. That's partly why I can't wrap my head around what he was doing. It couldn't have been official police business."

"But he told Victoria he was with the police department. He made it sound like he was on official business," she reminded him.

"That's true," he muttered. "But he probably just wanted to use his former position to get answers."

"I think Stefano is your best bet. He left his card." She got up and walked over to the counter where her grandmother had put Stefano's card next to her address book, which she was still more comfortable using than her phone contact list. She handed it to Nick. "I know you don't trust him, but it's worth a call."

"I'll call him. At the very least, he can tell me about the crash that took my grandfather's life," he said heavily.

She gave him a long, thoughtful look. "Are you okay, Nick?"

He met her gaze. "I'll be fine."

"Meaning you're not right now."

He shrugged. "Meaning you don't have to worry about me. What are you going to do now?"

She was going to say she'd get on the call with him, but it looked like he wanted to do this on his own. Since it had to do with his grandfather, whom he adored, she decided to give him space. "I thought I'd look in the attic, just to see if there's anything else tucked away that might be helpful."

"I'll join you in a bit."

She nodded, then said, "We're going to figure it out, Nick."

He met her gaze. "I hope so, Isabella, but I have a terrible feeling my grandfather thought the exact same thing, and then he was dead."

———

Isabella's face paled at his words, and Nick mentally kicked himself for sounding so harsh. Not that what he'd said wasn't true. But Isabella had just survived a brutal attack and probably didn't need a reminder of the danger they were in.

"Sorry," he muttered.

"You don't have to apologize for speaking the truth. But we're going to make sure we don't meet the same fate, right?"

"There's no guarantee."

"I never thought there was." She put a hand as he opened his mouth. "Don't tell me again to leave. It's a waste of your breath and my time. I'm going upstairs to look around the attic. Let me know what you find out from Stefano."

After Isabella left the kitchen, he took several deep, calming breaths, knowing he was far too worked up and personally invested, and that was a dangerous combination. He needed to look at the situation without letting his family connections color his thinking. But he had to admit that learning about his grandfather's visit to the school, his questions about Juliette, and the fire had rattled him. Thinking about the way his grandfather had died had only shaken him up more. He'd never thought it was anything but an accident. Now, he was almost a hundred percent convinced it was not. And he blamed himself for not having questioned the solo car crash when it happened.

Maybe if his grandfather hadn't been eighty years old and retired, he would have done that. But he'd just assumed that the storm and the wet roads had combined with his grandfather's aging eyesight and slower reflexes to result in an accident. Clearly, his grandfather had been a lot sharper than he'd given him credit for.

He didn't trust Stefano, but he punched in his number, anyway. He had to find out whatever he could. And Isabella was right. If his grandfather had spoken to anyone in the police department, it was probably someone he'd mentored, felt close to, and that was Stefano.

"Inspector Gangi," Stefano answered in a crisp voice.

"It's Nick Caruso."

"How I can be of service?"

"I have a few questions." He decided to start with an art question and then work his way to his grandfather. "Have you heard of a group called *La Mano Nera*?"

"*Sí*. They were responsible for multiple art thefts in the sixties."

"It's my understanding that the crew always wore black gloves, which fits the description of the men at the museum."

"I'm sure Capitano Lavezzo made a note of that similarity, but the group disappeared a long time ago. It's doubtful they're back now. If anything, it is someone who is copying them."

"What do you know about the crew, the leaders?"

"Well, let me think about that." He paused for a moment, then said. "I believe the crew was run by a thief named Roberto Falconeri. His brother was also involved, but I don't remember his name off the top of my head. I think they both passed away years ago."

"What about their families, their descendants?"

"I don't know. I can look into it. But I'm curious why you're asking me about it and not Captain Lavezzo."

"You seem to be more interested in helping us. Captain Lavezzo has not been forthcoming."

"He likes to run his operations without outside input," Stefano said, suggesting he'd experienced a similar lack of cooperation from Captain Lavezzo. "But I'm certain he will conduct a thorough investigation and will do his best to recover the paintings."

"I hope so, but if you can find out anything about that investigation or a possible tie to *La Mano Nera*, I'd appreciate hearing about it."

"Certainly. Is there anything else?"

"Yes. My other question is about my grandfather's accident. Is there a police file on it? Would you be willing to share that with me?"

Stefano hesitated. "Why are you asking about your grandfather's accident?"

"I want to know what happened that night."

"I can tell you what happened. It rained heavily. The streets were quite wet and puddled. Marcus braked suddenly and skidded off the road into a tree. He was sadly killed on impact."

"There were no other vehicles involved?"

"No. It was late in the evening, and he was on a road outside of Rome that was not well-traveled. A passerby reported the accident but said he did not see it happen. He called for help, but it was too late. I wasn't working that night, but I went down there as soon as I heard the news. Everyone in the department was devastated. Your grandfather was one of the best police officers to ever serve this country. We all respected him a great deal. I can assure you that if there had been any evidence that the crash was not an accident, we would have left no stone unturned to find out what happened."

There was nothing but passionate sincerity in Stefano's voice, and it made him feel marginally better. But he wasn't completely convinced. If the department had had knowledge of what Marcus was looking into, maybe they would have viewed the crash differently, just as he was doing now. Everything looked different when the context changed.

"I'm curious," he said. "Had you spoken to my grandfather in the weeks before he died?"

"Actually, I did. We ran into each other at Mass one Sunday and talked for a while afterward. He said he was enjoying retirement, that he and Anna were talking about taking a cruise."

"Did he mention anything about his father's death?"

"His father's death?" Stefano echoed. "No. Wasn't Marcus's father killed in a fire years ago? Why would that be on his mind?"

"I'm not sure. My grandmother said he was stressed about something in the weeks before he died."

"He didn't mention his father to me."

"What about a friend with problems? Maybe another police officer."

"No. I'm sorry. We didn't discuss anything serious, and Marcus didn't appear stressed in any way." Stefano paused. "Why are you so worried about your grandfather now? Perhaps I could be of more help if you tell me what you're concerned about."

"I'm just caught up in the past because of the stolen paintings," he said, not wanting to share what Victoria had told him.

"That's understandable. Have you decided if you and Signorina Rossi will be staying in Rome?"

"Not yet."

"I hope Signorina Rossi is feeling better after the attack last night."

"She's doing well," he said, reminded of just how well Isabella was doing. She hadn't mentioned the attack once. She hadn't acted like someone who should be taken care of or coddled. Instead, she'd been resolute. She really was a gutsy woman. Beautiful, too. As the errant thought entered his mind, he pushed it away. He didn't need to think about how pretty she was and how much he was starting to like her. He had enough problems. "Thanks for your help," he said.

"I don't think I helped you at all, but I would very much like to. Please feel free to call me any time."

"Thanks." He ended the call, then punched in another number on his phone.

Flynn answered on the first ring. "Ciao," he said cheerfully. "How is Rome?"

"More exciting than I was hoping for. Did I wake you up?"

"Are you kidding? It's almost seven, practically lunchtime. By the way, Andi checked on your grandmother last night and said she and her friend were tired but in good spirits."

"I appreciate that."

"I'll check in with her again later this morning. In the meantime, I just read your earlier text, asking for information on Inspector Gangi and Captain Lavezzo. Any reason you need information on Italian law enforcement?"

"Inspector Gangi appears to be a friend of the family, but he keeps showing up, and I'm not sure what I think about him. Captain Lavezzo has been polite but not forthcoming. Just wondering about his background. It might help me figure out a way to better work with him."

"Captain Lavezzo probably just doesn't want to work with anyone from the bureau."

"That could be it. I also met with Francesca Ribaldi today. She told me about a robbery crew in the sixties who called themselves *La Mano Nera*. Ever heard of them?"

"I have," Flynn said, the lightness from his voice immediately gone. "Did she also tell you my father was suspected of being one of its members?"

"She did. Is that true?"

"I don't believe so. My father worked alone. He wasn't a team player. But I have no evidence to prove whether he was involved or not." Flynn paused. "I don't know where my father is or how to get in touch with him, if those were going to be your next questions. But Francesca might. Her stepmother, Lydia, dated my father, after he left my mother, and before Lydia married Francesca's father."

"I had no idea. Francesca didn't mention that she could get in touch with your father."

"Maybe she can't. I don't know. But if you want to ask her, go for it. Just don't tell me about it. The conversations you have with Francesca are between the two of you."

"Understood. Is Lydia involved in the art world?"

"Yes. Lydia and Francesca's father, George Ribaldi, are collectors. Both come from wealthy families, who have long been art patrons, which is how my father first met Lydia. I think he was facilitating a purchase for her."

"A purchase of stolen art?"

"I couldn't say. He worked both sides. Was Francesca able to help you figure out why your great-grandfather's painting was worth stealing?"

"She was as confused as everyone else, but she's looking into it." He paused. "The stakes have gotten higher since yesterday, Flynn."

"What happened?"

"Two men broke into the house while I was dropping my grandmother and her friend off at the airport. Isabella was here alone, and she was almost choked to death by one of the intruders. I subdued him, and he's in custody, but he hasn't proved to be helpful. He was hired on the web, employer unknown. Captain Lavezzo believes he can trace the money, but so far he has shown no evidence that he can get results."

"Is Isabella all right?"

"She's hanging in there. I tried to get her to leave, but she's determined to find out what's going on. I need to get some answers fast."

"You need to get her out of Rome. Maybe yourself, too. Why not let the authorities handle this?"

"Because it's getting more personal. I received some information earlier today that my grandfather's death last year might not have been an accident. It's possible that both my grandfather and great-grandfather were murdered, and despite the decades in between, I think their deaths might be connected."

"That's disturbing. What else can I do to help?"

"I need you to run a search on a Juliette Sabatini. I have an expired ID that I can scan and send to you." He looked around for Isabella's bag, but she must have taken it upstairs, and she'd put the ID in there earlier, in case someone broke into the house again. "I'll send it when we're done talking."

"All right. What does she have to do with all this?"

"I'm not sure. But I found her ID in my grandfather's belongings, and he was asking about her before he died."

"I'll contact you with what I find out."

"Thanks." Before he went upstairs to get the ID, he made one more call to Francesca. "It's Nick Caruso," he said when she answered. "You didn't mention that your stepmother was friends with Sam Beringer."

"You spoke to Flynn."

"I did."

"I probably shouldn't have mentioned Sam, but I think he could be a valuable resource. I didn't say more because I didn't know if Flynn would want me to."

"Flynn said whatever we talk about stays between us. He'd not involved."

"I understand."

"Any idea where I can find Sam? Is he in Italy?"

"I had heard that he might be," she said. "I'll try to see if I can facilitate a meeting."

"I would appreciate that. It's important, Francesca. There's more at stake than stolen art."

"What does that mean?"

"It means I need information fast."

"I'll be in touch. But if you do speak to Sam, you need to remember that he almost always has a hidden agenda. If he wants to talk to you, it's because he's looking for information, too. Don't mistake his charm and humor for complete honesty and sincerity."

"It sounds like you have some experience with him."

"I'm sure Flynn told you Sam was involved with my step-mother. She still has a soft spot in her heart for him, and he for her. I've met him on occasion and he's quite likeable. But that said, you should never trust him."

"I'll keep that in mind. Thanks for your help."

"I can't promise he'll agree to talk to you, but since you're connected to Flynn, it's possible he'll consider any favor to you a favor to his son."

"I just want to make sure we keep Flynn out of this."

"I'll let you know."

As she ended the call, he got to his feet, happy that he'd started a few more wheels in motion. Hopefully, Flynn would be able to tell him more about Juliette Sabatini, and if Francesca could get him a meet with Sam, he might be on his way to solving this whole damn thing.

A sudden crash jolted his heart. He ran toward the stairs, taking them two at a time. He found Isabella in the attic with dirt smudged across one cheek, a pile of books all around her. But she was alone. "What happened?" he asked.

"I grabbed a book off a shelf, and they all came tumbling down." She gave him an apologetic look. "Did I scare you? Sorry about that."

"I'm just glad you're all right."

She stood up and dusted herself off. "I am. Did you talk to Stefano?"

"Yes. He told me that my grandfather's accident was just that —an accident. He was on a rain-slicked highway. He hit the brakes, probably hydroplaned and skidded into a tree. He also said my grandfather had not mentioned any problems to him when he spoke to him a few weeks before his accident."

"Do you believe him?"

"Honestly, I don't know. If I hadn't heard my grandfather was asking questions at the school about Juliette, I'd probably think about it all differently. In fact, I didn't even consider it wasn't an accident until I heard that. Maybe I'm jumping to the wrong conclusion, but I still need to figure out why my grandfather was asking about Juliette."

"Did you tell Stefano about your grandfather's visit to the school?"

"No. He seemed sincere in wanting to help us, but I still don't want to tell him too much. I also spoke to Flynn, who told me that Francesca's mother had a fling with his father, Sam Beringer, and if anyone might facilitate a meeting with his dad, it would probably be her."

Surprise ran through her eyes. "That's interesting. Why didn't Francesca tell us that?"

"She told me she wasn't sure how Flynn would feel about her bringing his father into our conversation. But I just spoke to her as well, and she agreed to see if she can facilitate a meeting with Sam."

"You've made some progress. I'm impressed."

He shrugged. "It doesn't seem like enough, but it's something. Flynn is also going to run Juliette Sabatini through our systems. I need her ID. Do you have your bag?"

"It's right behind you."

He turned around. Seeing the ID sitting in the open pocket, he took it out and then scanned it through an app on his phone.

Then he sent the scan to Flynn. When that was done, he put the ID back in her bag and said, "Did you find anything up here?"

"Nothing of substance. There are definitely no paintings up here."

"Then maybe you should call it a day."

"I will, but I need to clean this up first. My grandmother will not want to see this mess when she comes home. A place for everything, and everything in its place. Her favorite expression."

He smiled. "I heard something similar from my grandmother."

"It's funny how they're so alike and we're so different."

He wondered if that was true. He was starting to understand what drove her, and it wasn't all that different from what drove him. "Maybe we're more alike than you think."

"I don't know. You're much more detached and able to compartmentalize than I am. Although, you have been jumping to conclusions today, which is more my thing. I'm usually more impatient than you to get to an answer."

"Or to get a date started," he teased.

"You were late. That wasn't on me. And I think we're done talking about that night." She paused, giving him a speculative look. "It's probably easier to joke about the worst date of all time than to talk about what's really on your mind."

She was starting to know him a little too well. "I have a lot on my mind that I'm still trying to unpack and put into the right compartment," he admitted.

"I know how much you care about your grandfather, and that this latest information has upset you. You don't always have to be the calm, cool FBI agent. You can talk to me."

As her gaze clung to his, he realized that he wasn't feeling anything close to cool and calm. But it wasn't thoughts about his grandfather that were shaking him now. It was Isabella, her beautiful, earnest brown eyes, her silky hair glistening in the light from the single bulb hanging from the ceiling, and the tantalizing smudge of dirt at the corner of her mouth, her soft, very kissable mouth.

He was suddenly obsessed with that smudge. He found himself clenching his fists to prevent himself from wiping it off with his finger or maybe with his mouth.

"Nick?" she questioned. "What are you thinking?"

"You don't want to know," he said tensely.

The air crackled between them as he felt a strong, impossible to resist, pull in her direction. He had to fight that pull. *Or did he?*

Isabella sucked in a quick intake of breath, desire flashing in her eyes, as she read the intent in his gaze, and he knew he wasn't the only one feeling the attraction. What had started out as intense dislike now felt like the complete opposite emotion. The sparks that had been simmering between them since they'd arrived in Italy were no longer from anger but from want, from need.

He could feel her body moving toward his, or maybe he was the one moving. *Who could tell?*

All he knew was that suddenly his mouth was on hers, her breasts against his chest, her arms sliding around his waist.

The kiss was more than he'd imagined filled with searing heat and intense emotion. One kiss led to a second and a third. He couldn't seem to stop. He wanted to keep tasting her, touching her. He wanted to take her breath away, to lose himself in her, to escape from everything that wasn't her. And she seemed to be right there with him, until she wasn't.

She pulled away so abruptly he almost lost his balance. They stared at each other, their breathing ragged and fast.

Her eyes were lit up, her cheeks flushed from their heat, her mouth pink from their kisses.

Her body was saying yes to everything, but he could see her mind overriding her feelings, and he felt more disappointed than he would have imagined.

"We can't do that again, Nick," she murmured.

"Why not?"

Indecision ran through her eyes. "Because we shouldn't."

"I'm not good at *shouldn't.*"

She licked her lips, which made him only want to kiss her again. But she took a step back.

"I'm not good at shouldn't, either," she said. "But there's too much going on. And this—whatever this is—will only complicate things. You know that, Nick. You just want to make out with me because you don't want to think about your grandfather or anything else. That's it, isn't it?" There was a slightly desperate edge to her voice as if she needed him to agree with her, needed to believe that's all it was.

"That's not the reason," he said quietly. "That's not it at all. I kissed you, because I wanted to, and because it felt like you wanted the same thing."

"It wasn't a bad kiss," she admitted. "That's kind of the problem."

"I get it. The timing isn't right."

Relief ran through her gaze. "It's not. We need to focus. And if we keep kissing, that won't happen."

He gave her a small smile. "You're right about that. I have a feeling you could make me lose my mind."

"I have the same feeling about you. So, we'll call this a moment of temporary insanity."

"A really good moment," he said. "And if you want to go a little crazy again sometime, I'm open to it. But I won't be the one to initiate it. If you want another kiss, you'll have to ask me for it."

"Then it won't happen," she said firmly.

"I guess we'll see."

CHAPTER SIXTEEN

Nick was so annoying, Isabella thought, as he left the attic, having gotten the last word. He was also a really good kisser. Although she still wasn't sure how that had happened. One minute they were talking and the next they were kissing, and it had taken all her resolve to take herself out of his arms.

She wasn't quite certain exactly why she'd stopped, because she'd been as into him as he'd been into her. Maybe that was the reason. She'd felt like she was getting swept away, giving into desire, losing control, and it had scared her. Not because they might have had sex on the attic floor, but because she was feeling too many things for him that went beyond the physical, and that made her nervous.

She'd done the right thing. She'd backed away, and she wasn't going to ask him for another kiss, even though her lips were still tingling from the last one. She knew better than to let a man get her off course. Her mother had shown her numerous times how bad of an idea that was.

Turning her attention to the books, she picked them up and stacked them against the wall. Most were romance or fiction novels, but one with a red leather cover jumped out. It was a journal, and when she opened the first page, the name and the writing made her catch her breath. It was her mother's journal. A knot of emotion formed in her throat. She didn't need to look at this book. Her mother wasn't involved in anything. This journal wouldn't help her solve the mystery of the paintings. *Or would it?* Her mother knew art. She'd studied Lucinda. She'd gone to the school run by Frederico. She'd been friends with Stefano. Maybe this book was exactly what she needed to read.

She sat down on the ground and leaned against the wall as she turned the page to the first entry.

Her mother's familiar handwriting tugged at her heart. She'd gotten a lot of letters from her mom while she was in jail and was very familiar with the slightly crooked scrawl and the way her mom wrote short sentences that weren't always explicitly clear. Her mom had a mind that loved to jump around from thought to thought, which was probably one reason why she rarely thought things through.

Her gaze ran down the page. The words were in Italian, which made sense since her mother had written it when she was a teenager. But a name jumped out that she immediately recognized: Stefano.

Taking out her phone, she spoke the words into the translation app and then read the English translation.

I might be in love with Stefano. Or maybe I'm in love with him because he's in love with me. He makes me feel so warm, and I like the way he kisses, the way he takes care of me. But when Stefano talks about the future, I just can't see him in mine. I don't want to stay here in this house or this neighborhood or even this country. I want to go to the States, to where my mom was born. I want to go to college there and meet new people, and I can't let Stefano stop me. But he is so sweet. What should I do?

Now she knew Stefano hadn't been lying about being good friends with her mother. It was slightly ironic to read about her

mother putting herself first before a boy. That had changed
when she'd gotten to the US.

Or maybe it had changed when she'd had a baby, when she'd
been more desperate to have someone care for her.

Flipping through the pages, she searched for other familiar
names, not wanting to take the time to translate every page. And
then she found one—Lucinda.

Her heart sped up. She spoke the words in one very long
paragraph and then hit translate. It came back a moment later.

*I'm not as good an artist as Lucinda. My art teacher says I should
find my own voice and not worry about being able to paint like someone
else, but my art just falls flat. And my grades are terrible. I told Jeff I
needed to stay in tonight and paint for extra credit, and he said that was
the worst idea. He thinks I should have more fun, experience life, so I'll
have something to paint about. I just need to live a little more. And he's
so cute. How can I say no?*

Isabella swallowed hard at the mention of Jeff. That was her
biological father's name, the one her mother had a passionate
romance with during her final year in college, only to end up
pregnant, alone, and raising a child.

She couldn't help but think it was typical of her mother to
turn away from her art and her studies because a cute boy had
wanted her to go out that night. That was more the woman she
knew than the girl who'd left Stefano behind to chase her own
dreams. She wished her mother had kept that sense of indepen-
dence when she'd come to the US, but once there, she'd become
a follower.

She closed the book and got to her feet. That was a long
enough trip into the past. And it wasn't her mother's history
that was important now; it was Lucinda's past. At some point,
she might have to talk to her mother about that, but she was
hoping they could figure things out before that had to happen.

She tidied up the rest of the books then stashed the journal
in her bag as she left the attic.

There was no sign of Nick on the third or second floor, so

she made her way down to the living room, where he was sweeping up broken glass. She felt guilty that she hadn't put cleaning up this room ahead of looking for clues in the attic, but she hadn't wanted to be reminded of the night before. She'd also avoided her grandmother's bedroom, although that needed to be cleaned up, too, especially the blood on the floor.

"Can I help?" she asked, putting her bag on the coffee table.

"I've got this." He used a dustpan to scoop up the glass and then dumped it into the garbage.

Her phone vibrated with an incoming text, and she pulled it out of her pocket. "It's Joelle," she said. "She forgot she has another engagement tomorrow, and she can't meet us for brunch. But she's still looking into the ring, and she'll get back to us on that, and we'll set up another time to meet." She wrote a quick message saying thanks, and she hoped to see her again soon.

Then it was Nick's turn to check his phone as it buzzed.

"Who's texting you?" she asked, seeing his expression grow tense. "What's happening?"

"We have a meeting with Sam Beringer."

Excitement ran through her. Maybe they would finally get some answers. "When and where?"

"Church of Saint Angelo at eight p.m. tonight. Upon arrival, we go to the confessional on the right side of the church and open the door closest to the altar. Once inside, tap on the window."

"That sounds dramatic."

"And risky." He lifted his gaze from the phone to meet hers.

She read the look in his eyes and shook her head. "No way. I'm not staying here, Nick. This place is more dangerous than a church."

He frowned. "That's a fair point."

"I don't think Francesca would set us up for something bad, do you?"

"I would hope not."

"Then I'm going. It sounds like Sam Beringer doesn't want anyone to see him, including us. I grew up Catholic. I've been in a confessional. You can't see the priest through the window. Although, I could smell the wine on Father Michael's breath."

"I know. I'm not a stranger to the confessional," he said. "My mother used to make me go all the time."

"Really? Were you an altar boy?"

"No. We didn't stay in one place long enough for that, and my father wasn't interested in religion." His gaze turned reflective. "It's strange, but confession and Mass were two of the few things I did with my mother alone."

"Do you go to church now?"

"I haven't been in a while. You?"

"I went at Christmas. Not confession, just Mass. I can't remember the last time I uttered the words, '*Father, I Have Sinned*'."

"Well, we won't be talking about our sins. We need to find out if Sam Beringer can tell us anything about *La Mano Nera*."

"If he was part of it, why would he?"

"I'm thinking he wasn't part of it, and that's why he's willing to meet. Although, it's possible that when he heard I work with Flynn, he might just want to send his son a message through me."

"Would he have to do that with so much mysterious drama?"

"Considering he's avoided the police for several decades, I would say yes."

She glanced at her watch. "It's six now. We have some time. I'll help you finish up here, and then we should probably go into my grandmother's bedroom. I know there was blood on the floor. I certainly don't want her to come back and see that."

"Agreed. Why don't you finish this room? And I'll work on that."

She knew exactly why he'd offered, and her first instinct was to tell him she could handle seeing that blood and cleaning it up, but she couldn't get the words out.

He handed her the broom. "Don't worry, Isabella. I won't tell anyone that the sight of blood makes you sick."

"You don't know that I feel that way."

"Yes, I do."

"You're a know-it-all, Nick."

"I don't know everything, but I'm starting to know you, Isabella. And I think you're starting to know me."

A shiver ran down her spine as they gazed into each other's eyes. But this time, he was the one to turn away, and she felt far more disappointed than she should.

———

The church of Saint Angelo was small and hundreds of years old. It was located at the top of a hill, with probably five-hundred steps from the sidewalk to the church. The Italians had been very good at turning a trip to Mass into a trek. She was barely at the midpoint when she started to feel breathless. She needed to get back on the elliptical. She'd gotten out of shape only chasing stories through the Internet.

Finally, they reached the top.

"Need a minute?" Nick asked with a smug smile.

"I really hate the fact that you're not at all winded."

"I run a lot."

"Even when you're on a job?" she asked as she took a minute to catch her breath.

"If I can. It's how I keep the stress at a manageable level." He looked at his watch. "Five minutes to eight. We should go into the church."

"I'm ready." She hated that she'd slowed them down even a little. They walked across a flat area to another shorter flight of steps. The front door of the church was open. A small sign said the building would close at nine.

As they stepped through heavy wooden doors, she felt almost immediately transported back in time with the stone floors, the narrow wooden pews, and an altar that would seem very small by American standards.

There was a woman lighting a candle near the altar, with another woman kneeling in prayer in the second row. She was working a rosary through her fingers, her lips parted in silent prayer. The air felt musty, and the lighting was dim. In her mind, she could see generations of Italians praying together in this very small church at the top of a very steep hill.

She felt more connected to her religion here than she had in a very long time. The more modern churches she'd grown up in had felt nothing like this. They'd been larger and, in some ways, more majestic, but this felt humbling and very real.

Nick took her hand, startling her with a new feeling of heat and connectedness, but it soon became clear he'd only done that so he wouldn't have to speak. He led her across the church to the confessional on the right side. There were three doors to the confessional. The priest would enter through the middle door, with parishioners entering on each side. She'd been to confession during busy times where there would be a line for each door, but today there was no one there, and no way to tell if anyone was inside.

Nick opened the door to the left of the center compartment as instructed, and she squeezed into the small space with him. It was about the size of a phone booth or a small closet, a tight fit for two people, but she wasn't letting him do this alone.

He knelt down in front of a small window while she stood behind him, her body pressed against his back, creating all sorts of very non-spiritual thoughts, which she tried to erase from her mind.

Nick tapped on the window. A moment later, it opened. Sometimes there was a light on in the middle compartment, but there was no light today, although she could see the shadow of a figure.

"We've come as instructed," Nick said, when the man on the

other side of the window remained silent. "I'm Nick Caruso. Behind me is Isabella Rossi."

"I thought I would be speaking only to you," the man said, a very faint British accent to his voice.

"Isabella's great-grandmother was Lucinda Rossi, and my great-grandfather was Tomas Caruso. We're both trying to find out why their paintings were stolen last week. There's speculation that *La Mano Nera* has come back to life, a group you might be familiar with."

"You sound very much like another FBI agent I know. Direct. To the Point. No small talk." The man paused. "How is he?"

Nick hesitated, then said, "He's good."

"Happy? Married?"

"Yes, to both."

"But no children?"

"Not yet." He waited a moment, then said. "Can you help us?"

"I wasn't in *La Mano Nera*, but I am familiar with the group. I was a very young man when they were operating in the sixties and early seventies. I had no respect for them. Despite their pristine black gloves, they were messy. They made mistakes. Costly errors."

"I thought they were very successful," she interjected.

"Not as much as you might believe."

"Do you know anything about the art of our ancestors?" she pressed. "A reason why someone would steal their work? They were talented artists, but they weren't very successful."

"I met Lucinda and Tomas," he said.

She sucked in a breath at his answer. "You did?"

"I was twenty years old. I went to Tomas's studio on a few occasions under the guise of being an artist myself. But I was more interested in meeting the artists, some of whom were connected to private collectors, museums, and galleries. Tomas's store and his studio were an important part of the art scene in

Rome." He paused. "Are you sure you want to know more about them? Sometimes, the truth is not what you want it to be."

"We want to know the truth. We don't care what it is," Nick said firmly.

"Very well. Lucinda Rossi and Tomas Caruso were not well-known artists because they weren't real artists."

"What does that mean?" she challenged. "You might not have thought they were good, but art is subjective."

She didn't know why she felt the need to defend Lucinda, but she did.

"They weren't artists," the man said. "They were forgers. They didn't create art; they copied it. And from that perspective, they were very, very good."

"You're lying," she said, shocked by his words.

Silence followed her statement.

"Aren't you?" she asked.

CHAPTER SEVENTEEN

Nick was as stunned by Sam's statement as Isabella. "How do you know they were forgers?" he challenged.

"Because I made the mistake of stealing a painting that turned out to be a fake. My customer was not happy, and I barely escaped with my life. I was determined to find out who had painted such a brilliant piece of work that I could have been fooled, because I was very good. Someone told me there was a group of students working at a studio run by Tomas Caruso, and some of them might be working on forgeries. I went to the studio under the pretense of being an artist, and I became friends with some of the younger ones, most notably David Leoni."

"That's another guy who had a painting stolen," Isabella murmured.

"I didn't realize that."

"Let's get back to the group," Nick said. "What did David Leoni tell you?"

"After many cocktails one evening, he said that Lucinda was a brilliant forger, that she could copy any painting and no one would know, and that he was learning a lot from her. I asked him why he would want to do that, and he had a one-word response

—money. He needed money to live so he could support his own art. Over the next few weeks, I tried to get closer to Lucinda, but she was guarded. I didn't have success getting her to open up to me. David also clammed up, probably regretting what he'd already said. There was a change in the workshops after that. Some were closed to only private, smaller groups of students, and I couldn't get into them. I didn't want to spend my life chasing them. I had other things to do, so I moved on. About a month later, I heard Lucinda and Tomas died in a mysterious fire."

"All you have is some drunk guy's theory about Lucinda," Isabella said, a heated note of anger in her voice as she defended her great-grandmother. "That's not worth much."

"You can believe me or not. It makes no difference. I heard you wanted information about your relatives. Because you are connected to someone I care about, I came—at some risk of personal jeopardy, I might add."

"Your personal jeopardy doesn't matter to me," Isabella retorted. "You're a thief."

As her anger increased, Nick knew he had to keep the peace. He didn't want Isabella to run Sam off, not when they needed information.

"Let's talk about *La Mano Nera*," he said. "You weren't a part of it, but you knew of it. Is it possible there are members of the group operating today?"

"I wouldn't have thought so. But from what I heard about this recent robbery, perhaps someone is imitating their use of the black gloves."

"What do you know about the man who started the group, Roberto Falconeri?" Nick asked.

"Roberto was an artist, but when he was twenty-two, his hands were burned in a fire. He couldn't paint after that. He became bitter, angry, and desperate for money. His older brother, Bruno, ran an auto shop, but that was his front for many illegitimate businesses. When Roberto couldn't work at his craft anymore, he went to work with his brother. They didn't start out stealing priceless paintings, but when Roberto was offered a job at a museum, Bruno saw an opportunity to smuggle art to private collectors. Roberto could be the inside man. A year later, two paintings were stolen from that museum and never recovered. The Falconeri brothers had gotten a taste of success, and that was just the beginning. Over the next several years, they were responsible for many thefts in Rome and also a few in Florence."

"It sounds like Bruno was in charge," he said. "And not Roberto."

"They were partners. Roberto was much more intelligent, and he knew the art world. He had connections everywhere. He was able to build a crew of thieves and gain access to museums and galleries. Bruno was the seller. During the robberies, Roberto donned black gloves so that no one could use his scars to identify him. Everyone working with him did the same. After one robbery, an inspector dubbed the crew *La Mano Nera*, The Black Hand, based on a witness description. From there, they grew bolder and more successful, until they stole a fake and sold it. Just as I had done. But my mistake was mine alone, and I was a small player back then. The entire crew of *La Mano Nera* suffered because of that counterfeit painting. Their other buyers became nervous. They no longer trusted the crew. There were rumors it wasn't the first time they'd sold a counterfeit copy, and it was suggested that they had hired forgers to copy the paintings so they could keep the originals for themselves and resell them. If a buyer received stolen goods, they had no recourse to get their money back if the painting was fake. They couldn't contact the police. What would they say?"

Nick didn't bother to answer that question because he had a more important one to ask. "Were the Falconeri brothers working with Lucinda? Was she copying what they stole?"

"I don't know, but my guess is yes."

"What about Tomas Caruso?" Isabella asked. "Was he also a forger?"

"I have no idea. But Tomas and Lucinda were close. It was rumored they were lovers. Since they died together in Tomas's house in the middle of the night, I believe that was true."

"Do you know anything about that fire?" Nick asked.

"Only that it was deemed an accident. However, it seemed suspicious to me. Unfortunately, when you play with fire, sometimes you get burned."

"How can you be so callous?" Isabella challenged. "If it wasn't an accident, then someone killed them."

"Murder and stolen art often go together. Staying alive is difficult in that business, especially if you're creating fakes and selling them."

"But you don't know that's what my great-grandmother was doing," Isabella pointed out. "You don't have proof."

"Why were you even in Rome when you were in your twenties?" Nick asked. "I thought you lived in the UK. Weren't you married there? Didn't you have a child there?"

"I traveled around Europe as a young man. I didn't marry or have a son until long after Lucinda and Tomas died."

"What happened to Roberto and Bruno?" he asked, turning the focus back to the Falconeri brothers.

"Bruno died about six months after Tomas and Lucinda perished in the fire. He was shot in the head. I have no idea who killed him. I heard Roberto passed away a few years later while skiing in the Alps, but his death was shrouded in mystery. Some didn't believe he was actually dead. They thought he might be faking his death so as to escape prosecution of his earlier crimes. That was the last I heard of either of them until this week."

"Francesca told us Bruno had a daughter," Isabella said. "But Roberto had no children. Is that true? Was there no one left to take over the family business?"

"That's correct. Bruno's daughter died of a drug overdose shortly after her father's death. As far as I know, the crew's last job was in the early seventies, right before Bruno was killed, which might have been the reason they went out of business. Bruno ran the smuggling network. Roberto was more into the art scene, and after Bruno's death, Roberto was probably running scared. Another reason might have had to do with the creation of the Carabinieri T.P.C. in 1969. Art theft became more closely scrutinized after that. Security measures became more stringent as well. My job got tougher, too, so I moved out of Italy."

Nick thought about that. His knees were cramping from his kneeling position, but he wanted to keep Sam talking as long as he could. "Why would someone come back now, imitating *La Mano Nera* but only stealing a couple of paintings by artists who died a long time ago?"

"The paintings must have a hidden value."

"Like what?" he and Isabella asked at the same time.

"There could be a painting under a painting. That might be how Lucinda and the others moved their art. By covering up the forgeries with original work no one would care about it."

"Wouldn't you have noticed that when you were there?"

"As I said, they had private groups I couldn't penetrate. And I wished I could. I was intrigued by Lucinda. Many dismissed her as a bored wife dabbling in art to keep herself busy, taking up painting so she could spend time with Tomas, her secret lover. But she was much more than that. Her outer appearance was as fake as her paintings. She was much smarter and more talented than people thought she was."

"How do we know you're not lying about everything?" Isabella asked.

"You don't. But you want to find stolen paintings, and who better to do that than a thief?"

Sam was sharp and very smooth. There was almost a hint of humor in his voice, as if he'd found Isabella's question to be ridiculous, and maybe it was. Sam clearly knew more than they did.

"There is a party tomorrow afternoon," Sam continued. "One

you should attend. I have asked our mutual contact to get you an invitation."

Nick straightened at those words. "Who's going to be at this party?"

"Artists, collectors, dealers, rich people, and celebrities. It's a charity event at a private villa hosted by Dario Micheli, a wealthy businessman, gallery owner, and avid art collector, and his American socialite wife, Jennifer Abrams Micheli. They will be sharing their private collection and also selling off select pieces. The cost of entrance is one thousand euros a ticket. The money from the tickets and the art will go to a children's health charity. All the important people in Rome connected to the art world will be there."

"Then so will we," he said.

At his words, the window slammed shut.

"Wait a second," Isabella said quickly, leaning over Nick to tap on the window. "I have more questions."

"He's gone, Isabella. Let's get out of here."

She opened the door and moved outside. He quickly followed, and as he'd predicted, the door to the middle compartment was open and there was no one inside. There was also no one else in the church.

"How did he get out of here so fast?" Isabella asked in annoyance.

"I have no idea. But we got some information and an invitation."

"Yes. But he never actually said who he was, Nick. How do we even know that we met with Sam Beringer?"

"He knew I worked with Flynn."

"He could have been told to say that. He never actually mentioned Flynn's name."

He met her gaze. "What are you getting at?"

"Should we believe anything he told us?"

"Are you asking because you don't want to believe that Lucinda was a forger?" he challenged.

She let out a sigh as his point hit home. "Maybe. I think it would break my grandmother's heart if that were true. She admired Lucinda. My mother did, too."

"You don't need to tell either of them yet, not until we're sure, maybe not even then."

"I'll have to tell Grandma at some point." She paused. "If Lucinda was a forger and maybe even working with *La Mano Nera*, could finding the paintings actually destroy our families? If we want to protect our grandmothers, how far do we go?"

"I'm surprised you're asking me that question. I thought you wanted to go all the way to the truth, no matter what it was."

"I thought I did, too. But my goal has always been to protect my grandmother. Now I'm afraid I'm going to hurt her."

"What we don't know could be more dangerous to our grandmothers. Once we get the truth, we can decide what to do with it. But we're not there yet. We need to dig deeper into the Falconeri family. Maybe some distant relative reinstated the group." He paused. "Or Sam did."

Surprise ran across her face. "I thought you were trusting Sam."

"I would never trust a thief. I just said I believe the man we spoke to was Sam Beringer. The rest is a question mark."

"Okay. What about Francesca setting us up with Sam? How is she involved with him? Can we trust her? She didn't tell us about this big party of art people."

"No. But she told us about *La Mano Nera*. She also hooked us up with Sam. That said, it could be misdirection," he conceded. "If they wanted to send us down the wrong path."

"They're going to a lot of trouble to do that."

"Which is probably why they're not, but I consider all possibilities."

She gave him a thoughtful look, and there was a gleam of reluctant admiration in her gaze. "You might be smarter than I first thought."

He couldn't help but smile. "Wow, a compliment. I'm shocked."

"Don't let it go to your head. So where now?"

"How about the nearest bar?" she asked.

"Is there a clue at the nearest bar?"

"No, but I think there will be alcohol, and I could use a drink."

———

He found a touristy bar a few blocks away from the church. It was crowded, not surprising on a Saturday night, and there was a mix of English, Italian, and other languages creating a cacophony of sound that seemed even louder after the quiet church. He ordered a bottle of red wine while Isabella picked out a couple of appetizers.

The wine arrived first, and he was happy to take a sip. In recent years, he'd become more of a beer or whiskey drinker, but being in Italy made him want to savor a deep, smooth red. He couldn't help noticing that Isabella's first sip was half her glass. That reminded him of their disastrous date when he'd watched her down two glasses of expensive champagne that he was quite sure she'd ordered on purpose when he'd been late.

"What?" she asked, giving him a wary look.

"Nothing."

"I'm not a big drinker, Nick. I know you think I am because of the first time we met, but that night was an exception."

"You can just say I drove you to drink," he said dryly.

She smiled at his words. "That would be the easiest explanation, but not the whole truth. My career was stuttering because of my big mouth, and I was still reeling after finding out the man I'd been seeing had been cheating on me. You became the epitome of all things bad in my life. And every minute you were late increased my frustration level. I'm really not a lush."

"I'm not judging, Isabella."

"You act like you don't judge, but you do. You have this way of watching people. It makes me nervous sometimes."

Her admission surprised him. "I'm not watching you to judge you, Isabella. It's because I have trouble taking my eyes off you. You're a beautiful woman."

She flushed at his words and then reached for her glass, taking another long sip. "Okay, that time you did drive me to drink."

"You don't like compliments, do you?"

"Of course I like compliments. Who doesn't want to be told they're beautiful, but..."

"But what?" he asked with interest.

"This sudden flirting is taking me off guard. Why are you doing it?"

"I'm not flirting. I'm talking."

"In a sexy way."

"You find me sexy?"

She shook her head. "I didn't say that. Let's talk about something else, something that won't make me want to drink."

"Then I better not say what I was going to say."

She raised a questioning brow. "What were you going to say?"

"That we need to talk to someone who knows more about Lucinda than we do."

Her lips tightened as she read his gaze. "I don't think so, Nick."

"You know where this is heading, Isabella. You're not only beautiful, you're also incredibly intelligent. Your mother studied Lucinda's work when she wanted to become an artist. She had that painting in her hands for years. She must have looked at it a million times. You have to talk to her."

"Lucinda died when my mother was a toddler. She didn't know her."

"She knew her work, and that might be more important."

"I really don't want to talk to my mom, Nick."

"I get that. I do."

"Do you? Because I could suggest we talk to your parents, too. Your father might know more about Tomas and your grandfather than you do. In fact, where are your parents right now?"

He didn't like that she had turned the tables on him. "I don't know where they are this second, but they're supposed to be in Milan in a few days, so if I'm still in Italy when they arrive, and we still have questions, we can talk to them, but they weren't artists. They had nothing to do with the art world. Sylvie did. Would it really hurt to have a conversation with her? You don't have to see her. You can speak to her on the phone."

She stared back at him for a long moment. "If I decide to talk to her, it won't be on the phone. And I won't do it alone. She's a sucker for an attractive man. She'd probably tell you more than she'd tell me."

"Whatever I can do to help."

"Let's see what we find out tomorrow at the party. Then I'll consider whether we need to go to Firenze and talk to my mother." She picked up her glass and finished her wine. "I am going to need another drink. And you're paying."

CHAPTER EIGHTEEN

Sunday morning, Isabella woke up with a headache that had more to do with the prospect of seeing her mother at some point than with the two glasses of wine she'd consumed. She'd also spent a restless night trying to sleep. Every creak of the old house had set her nerves on edge, and when she wasn't thinking about someone breaking in, she was thinking about Nick, about how he'd kissed her earlier, and how he'd called her beautiful with a look in his eyes that had made her stomach do a somersault.

Despite her resolve, she was starting to like him too much. He wasn't just attractive and kissed really well; he was also smart and quick. She enjoyed a man who could keep up with her. Maybe even stay ahead of her. That made her want to try harder, be smarter, do more. She didn't know if that was just her competitive streak kicking in, or because she just wanted to change his opinion of her. Either way, he was taking up way too much space in her head, and she needed to concentrate on figuring out what happened to the paintings and how her family might have been involved in the dark side of the art world.

She still couldn't wrap her head around the idea that her great-grandmother might have been a forger. But Sam had sounded very sure of himself, and she couldn't see a motivation for him to lie. Although, that didn't mean he didn't have one. As Nick had said, Sam was a thief, and she needed to keep that in mind. Right now, she was just going to let his accusations be. The truth would eventually reveal itself—hopefully. But it seemed like the truth had been buried for a very long time, and it might take a lot of effort to uncover it.

She was up to the challenge. She just needed to get up and get going. Rolling out of bed, she headed into the bathroom and took a long, hot shower. A half hour later, she felt more energized and ready to face the day.

When she got downstairs, Nick was at the stove again. Today he was making pancakes with fresh blueberries and a dollop of whipped cream, which made her shake her head in bemusement.

Was there anything sexier than a barefoot man standing at a stove cooking breakfast? His hair was wavy and tousled, his face showing a shadow of beard, and his faded jeans and T-shirt hugged his body in all the right ways, making her yearn to see what was under those clothes. She'd thought she was all about a man in a suit, someone powerful and sophisticated, but this look worked. Her mouth was watering, and it wasn't really for pancakes, but she couldn't let him see that.

"Just in time," he said as he handed her a plate.

"This looks like dessert." She turned her gaze on the pancakes instead of his sexy grin.

"Are you turning down my special pancakes?"

"Not a chance," she said, taking her plate to the table.

She hadn't been quite sure how this morning would go. Things had gotten a little weird last night when they'd returned from the bar, the sexual tension between them going up a notch once they were back in the quiet house. But true to his word, Nick hadn't tried to kiss her again, and she'd managed not to ask him to.

Nick brought his plate to the table and also a mug of coffee for her.

He really was a considerate person. "Thanks," she said.

He gave her an expectant look as she took her first bite. "Well? Is it too sweet?"

She shook her head. "It's perfect," she mumbled, her mouth full.

"My grandmother used to make pancakes for me when I was feeling down."

"You don't seem like a person who feels down a lot," she said as she swallowed and dove back in for another bite.

"I have my moments. Not as much now as when I was a kid. Back then, I had no control over where I had to be, and it drove me crazy."

"You said your parents are going to be in Milan in a few days. Are they performing there?"

"I think so, but they're also renewing their vows."

His statement surprised her. "Really? That's nice. Are you going?"

"No. And I don't think it's nice; I believe it's a show, a gimmick."

"Why would they need a gimmick?"

"Who knows? They're all about their careers. This certainly isn't about love."

"Is that why you're not going, or do they not want you there?"

"They sent me an invitation, which I received right before I got on the plane to come here. There was no personal note, no phone call, just a request for my presence. I'm done fulfilling that request. I think renewing their vows is a joke."

"Why?" she asked, curious to know more about him, about his immediate family.

"Because they're a volatile couple who are always fighting. They've cheated on each other more than once, and they've almost gotten divorced at least three times."

Since she didn't think much of her mother, she could hardly judge him for being angry with his parents. But she wondered if he was misreading the situation. It wasn't her business, she told herself, as she focused on her breakfast. But she couldn't stop thinking about what he'd said.

"What?" Nick asked. "I can see the wheels turning in your head, Isabella. If you have something to say, just say it."

She really hated that he could read her mind. "I'm hoping that you're wrong about them. Perhaps the vow renewal is about love. They could have rediscovered their commitment to each other."

"I thought you weren't a romantic," he said dryly.

"You're right; I'm not. I don't know why I said that. It probably is a stunt."

"What else could it be? I watched them fight my entire life. My mother would cry. My father would shout. And then they'd make up and do it all over again."

"Some couples thrive on drama."

"They certainly did. My mother used to tell me they were two passionate people, and neither of them meant half of what they said. There was always love beneath it all. If that was love, I didn't want any part of it."

"Do you still feel that way?"

He shrugged. "I don't want to spend my life fighting with someone. Growing up in that environment was exhausting. I never knew if they were going to break up, if I would wake up in the morning and find one of them gone. A few times that happened. Sometimes it was my mom, sometimes my dad. That's why coming here, being with my grandparents was so stabilizing. They were the opposite of hot-tempered and overly passionate. They loved each other with kindness and generosity."

"At least you had one good example in your life. I didn't."

"What about your grandmother?"

"She would say she had a wonderful marriage, but it looked cold and rigid to me. My grandfather dominated her. She treated him like a king. He did not reciprocate as far as I could see." She took a sip of her coffee. "My mother would say she had a great marriage, too, but she picked a scam artist who got her sent to prison. I am not going to follow in either of their footsteps. I don't even know if I believe in marriage. I haven't seen very many happy couples."

"I've seen some. Several of my fellow agents are exceptionally happy with their partners, their growing families. I have to say, when I am around them, it makes me think about what I want for myself. Obviously, some relationships can work, but finding that right person seems like a long shot."

"I'll say," she muttered.

His gaze narrowed on her face. "You look tired this morning. Did you sleep last night?"

"Not much. This old house makes a lot of noises."

"Maybe we should have kept each other company again."

"That might have been even more dangerous," she said, seeing the sly look in his eyes. "We need to focus on what we're doing, not get caught up in anything else, Nick."

"Anything else could be fun and distracting."

"And complicated," she pointed out.

"True." He picked up his suddenly buzzing phone. "I have a text from Francesca. She can get us into the party tonight, but I'll need to send two thousand euros to cover our tickets."

"That's a lot of money, Nick, for what could be nothing more than a party. Is anyone really going to talk to us about stolen art?"

"No idea, but I think we should go. I can cover the tickets."

"I can pay for mine. I just hope we get our money's worth."

"It's a gamble, but no risk, no reward."

"That's usually my mantra, but I don't have a good feeling about this, Nick."

He gave her a thoughtful look. "Do you want to stay here?"

"Alone? Absolutely not. If you're going, I'm going. I'm just a little worried that we're being set up. The party could be a way to get us out of the house for a specific time period."

"That's true. But staying here won't get us to the truth."

"What time is the party?"

He glanced back at his phone. "Five to eight o'clock tonight. Oh...damn. It's black-tie."

She sighed, having brought absolutely nothing with her that would be appropriate. "Then it's good we have time to go shopping."

———

Isabella had thought Nick was sexy in jeans and a T-shirt, but in a black suit and silver tie, he was even more impressive. As her cousin Joelle had mentioned the other day, he had a definite James Bond vibe to him.

"We clean up well," Nick said as they met in the living room.

His gaze ran down her long, champagne-colored gown that fell off her shoulders and hugged her curves. She'd left her hair down but had styled it with long waves, spending a bit more time on her makeup and hair than she normally did. She didn't have any fancy jewelry, so she'd opted to leave her neck bare. Since she still had faint bruises on her neck, she also hadn't wanted to draw attention to that part of her body.

"You look good, too," she told him, realizing they'd been staring at each other for a very long minute. "Hopefully, we'll fit in."

"We will. And we paid for the tickets, so no one will throw us out."

"That's true. Let's do this." As she followed Nick to the car, she felt both excited and nervous. While she could go into any high-class event as a reporter and mix and mingle with the rich and famous to get a story, attending a high-class party as just herself was a lot scarier. It was easier when she had a job to do, which reminded her that she did actually have a job to do. She needed to look at this party like any other event she attended in pursuit of the truth.

That thought calmed her down, and she settled into the car with more confidence than she'd had a few minutes earlier. But when they pulled up in front of a magnificent villa, their Fiat sticking out like a sore thumb among the luxury sedans and pricey sportscars, her nerves returned.

"I don't belong here," she muttered, as Nick escorted her to the stairway leading up to a three-story mansion sitting on a hill above them.

"You belong anywhere you want to be," he said, taking her hand.

She wanted to pull her hand away, but how could she after he'd said something so nice? She was a little embarrassed by her clammy hands, though. "Sorry, my hands are sweating."

"Mine, too."

"And here I thought you were a better liar," she said dryly.

He gave her a smile. "Ready?"

"As I'll ever be." She squared her shoulders and lifted her chin. "I just hope we find out something."

"If not, we'll enjoy what I'm sure will be a nice spread of food and first-class cocktails. It won't be a total waste, no matter what happens."

She nodded and walked up the stairs with him. As they got closer to the entry, the villa was even more impressive, with magnificent columns framing the front door. They were greeted by a young woman who checked their names against a list on her tablet, gave them a glossy sheet listing the paintings for sale, and then waved them inside.

They joined a throng of glamorous people moving into the entry. The glittering jewels and scents of expensive perfumes were overwhelming, and she found her fingers tightening around Nick's. She soon realized they'd become part of a receiving line that led to a handsome older man and his beautiful, much younger, wife, a striking blonde dressed in a shimmering blue dress that was studded with crystals. The plunging neckline emphasized her very busty figure.

"These must be our hosts," Nick murmured.

Her tension increased as they neared the very glamorous couple. When it was finally their turn, she forced a smile on her face as they introduced themselves to Dario Micheli and his wife Jennifer Abrams Micheli.

"Caruso?" Jennifer said with a question in her gaze. "Are you related to James and Danielle Caruso?"

"Those would be my parents," Nick replied.

"Oh, my goodness. That is amazing. They are so very talented. I have seen many of their performances. I was actually a violinist when I was younger," Jennifer continued. "Your mother was my idol."

"I'm glad she inspired you."

"I would love to meet them someday. They're not with you tonight, are they?"

"No. They're on tour."

"Perhaps we can set something up for another time. We have your information on the guest list. Would it be all right if I have my assistant contact you?"

"Of course," Nick said. "I'm sure they would love to meet you."

"Not more than I would love to meet them."

"Now, now, Jennifer," Dario said. "You don't want him to think you're a stalker."

She gave Nick an apologetic look. "My husband is right. I'm sorry."

"No need to apologize. We're excited to see your art."

"Dario has a spectacular collection," Jennifer said, casting her husband an adoring glance. "He has a brilliant eye. He sees so many things I do not."

"I understand you own several galleries," Nick said.

"In Roma, Firenze, and Milano," Dario replied, pausing when a man with light brown hair and striking green eyes joined him. "This is one of my most trusted associates, Matthew Pierre. Matthew is responsible for putting together tonight's collection.

He also oversees my galleries so that I can spend more time with this beautiful woman."

"Which makes him so valuable," Jennifer crooned, giving her husband another infatuated look, which kind of made Isabella's stomach turn. Were they really that much in love? It seemed a little much.

"This is Nick Caruso and Isabella..." Dario gave her an apologetic look. "I'm sorry. I forgot your last name."

"Rossi," she supplied.

"*Sí*. My apologies, Signorina Rossi."

She gave Dario a smile, then said hello to Matthew.

"It's a pleasure to meet you," Matthew said. "I hope you'll spend some time in our gallery. We have some unique pieces that will be sold tonight."

"We will definitely check it out," Nick said.

"I am sorry to interrupt," Matthew added, giving them a regretful look. "But Capitano Lavezzo has just arrived, Dario, and he would like to speak to you. He's waiting in the study."

She stiffened at the mention of Captain Lavezzo, and all her insecurities disappeared when she realized there might actually be information here. "Are you talking to Captain Lavezzo about the robbery at your gallery in Firenze?" she questioned.

Both men looked at her in surprise.

"You heard about that?" Matthew asked.

"Yes. A painting by David Leoni was stolen. Have you been able to recover it?"

"Unfortunately, no. It is a tragedy. It was his only remaining piece of art, as far as we know. Do you know David's work?" Matthew asked. "He was a brilliant, but a rather obscure artist."

"I know he painted with my great-grandmother, Lucinda Rossi, and Nick's great-grandfather, Tomas Caruso, whose paintings were recently stolen from a museum." She didn't miss the quick look the two men exchanged, although Jennifer didn't appear to be listening; she was still staring at Nick as if she would love to get him alone somewhere, and Isabella didn't think that was just about his connection to his parents.

"I haven't heard those names in years," Dario said. "A very long time ago, when I was a teenager, I went to a workshop at Tomas's studio. He was very talented." Dario paused. "I was shocked to hear about the museum robbery. I was even more surprised to know Tomas's art was still in existence. There was a fire that destroyed most of it, or all of it, I had thought. I hope Capitano Lavezzo will find our missing paintings."

"I hope so, too. We haven't been able to get much information from him." She paused. "Do you know if David Leoni's work was connected to the paintings by Tomas and Lucinda? It seems odd they have all recently disappeared."

"It does." Dario turned to Matthew. "Do you have any ideas?"

"No. I wasn't aware there was any connection between the robberies or the paintings," Matthew said. "But I don't know art as well as you do, Dario. Why don't we speak to the capitano now and hopefully we will get more information?"

"Perhaps we should go with you," she boldly suggested.

"The capitano asked only to speak to us," Matthew said. "But we have your contact information from the guest list, so I would be happy to follow-up with you."

She didn't care for that response, but the two men were moving away.

"I didn't realize you were related to any artists," Jennifer said, her gaze still fixed on Nick. "There is so much talent in your family, Signor Caruso. What do you do?"

"Not art or music," he replied. "That artistic talent skipped my generation."

"Well, if your great-grandfather was an artist, perhaps your parents would appreciate a gift from our gallery," she said. "It's for the children—such a good cause."

"We'll take a look."

"Please do. And I'll look for you later," Jennifer promised.

"I can't believe Captain Lavezzo is here," she murmured as they moved away from Jennifer and entered the grand salon. There were two suited men wearing earpieces just inside the door. Clearly, there was plenty of security at the party. Probably far more security than there had been at the museum.

"I can't believe you asked to join their private conversation," Nick returned. "That was bold."

"When I heard Lavezzo was here, I figured it was worth a shot." By Nick's expression, he didn't seem to agree. "What? Did I move too fast?"

"Maybe. You might not have wanted to mention David Leoni right away. We don't know if Dario and Matthew are involved in any of this."

"The painting was stolen from their gallery."

"Still. It's not wise to show your hand too early."

"I didn't think it was too early. If they're completely inno-cent, then my mentioning a connection between the robberies would be helpful to them. And they might be helpful to us in return and put pressure on Captain Lavezzo. He's here at their party. They seem to have a better relationship with him than we do."

"That's a good point," he conceded. "But what if they're part of whatever is going on? Now they know we think the thefts are connected."

She frowned. He had a point, too. "I guess it was a risk. It felt right in the moment."

"We'll see what happens."

A waiter offered them glasses of champagne, and she took a quick sip of the sparkling liquid as she looked around. The grand room was immense, and its floor to ceiling windows overlooked a patio lit with fairy lights. There were tables outside, surrounding a pool, and there appeared to be a guest house in the distance. "What a place. Can you imagine living here? I read earlier that Dario was married and divorced with two children prior to marrying Jennifer three years ago. I think it's just the two of them living here now."

"Probably."

She gave him a curious look. "Did it bother you when she raved about your parents?"

He shook his head. "Not at all. I'm used to people raving about them. They're at the top of their profession."

"I bet this isn't the first time you've been to a party like this."

"Not the first, no. But they didn't take me to many parties. Having a kid along would have detracted from their glowing presence. I honestly did not care. The few times I went with them, I was bored out of my mind. Let's take a walk around and see who else is here."

"Do you think Francesca will be here?"

"I would assume so."

"What about Sam?"

"I know he used to steal from private parties, so this seems like fertile ground," he said dryly.

"But there are security guards stationed all around."

"That wouldn't stop him."

She fell into step with him, happy to see more of the villa. Besides the main salon on the ground floor, there was a smaller living room and a magnificent dining room with a table that could easily seat twenty. There were thick, rich rugs on sparkling marble floors, statues near every doorway and, of course, a plethora of beautiful paintings lit by warm lights on every wall.

There appeared to be two kitchens, both bustling with staff, so they didn't bother with those rooms, moving toward the other side of the house which had a study, a music room with a grand piano, and another room that had been set up like an art gallery, displaying the paintings on sale for charity.

It was in the gallery that she saw a woman with bright red hair, holding onto the arm of a very attractive blond man. The woman turned and let out a surprised and happy squeal, rushing forward as she dragged her date with her.

"Isabella," she said with delight. "And Nick. You both look amazing. I didn't know you were coming."

"It was a last-minute thing," she replied as she was enveloped in Joelle's embrace, her cousin's perfume surrounding her in a thick haze that lingered even after Joelle moved on to greet Nick.

Joelle's kisses with Nick seemed a bit airier than those she'd given him in the past, but that probably had to do with the fact that her date was looking at them with hawk-like dark eyes.

"This is Colin Devonshire," Joelle said, introducing the man at her side. "He's one of Dario's lawyers. Have you met Dario?"

"Yes, when we arrived," she replied.

"Isabella is my cousin," Joelle told Colin. "And this is her good friend, Nick Caruso. Colin is an art fanatic," she added, putting her hand on his arm. "And he's a very generous patron to young artists and designers." She gave Colin a flirtatious look. "He knows talent when he sees it."

"I do," Colin said, seemingly fascinated by Joelle. "Especially when the talent is wrapped up in such a beautiful woman."

"You're so sweet," Joelle told him. "Why don't you get me a cocktail? Isabella and I need to use the ladies' room."

She didn't need to use the restroom, but Joelle grabbed her hand, and she had no choice but to leave with her. Nick frowned as she moved away from him, as if the distance between them bothered him. And maybe it bothered her, too, because she felt a cold chill run through her as they left the room.

CHAPTER NINETEEN

Joelle dragged Isabella into a guest room at the end of the hall. "I am so surprised to see you, Isabella. Why are you and Nick here?"

"We wanted to talk to some people in the art world. I had no idea you were coming."

"Colin invited me, and since he's interested in sponsoring some of my expenses as I create more valuable pieces of jewelry, I couldn't say no."

"Is he your patron or your boyfriend?"

Joelle laughed. "Can't he be both? And I prefer lover. Boyfriend sounds so juvenile."

And lover sounded so sophisticated and European, Isabella thought. She also wondered if Colin's appeal wasn't his checkbook as much as anything else, although he was an attractive man. She hated to think Joelle was that shallow, but she might be.

"What about you and Nick?" Joelle asked. "He was holding your hand. I thought you were just friends."

"We are. He was just leading me through the crowd."

"Oh, come on. We're cousins. You can tell me. He's so hot. How can you just be friends with him?"

She shrugged, not sure what to say. She didn't know Joelle very well, and her feelings about Nick were too mixed up to define. "I don't know. It just is what it is."

"Sorry. I shouldn't be so curious. I just love a good love story."

"Well, it sounds like you have one of those going on."

"We'll see. I'm glad I ran into you. I was going to text you later. I talked to my father about the ring, and he said that Lucinda had one just like it. His mother took it after Lucinda died. He doesn't know if she still has it. He's going to ask her."

"It would be interesting if they both had the same ring."

"Maybe it was some kind of commitment ring for whatever their relationship was."

"Maybe." She paused, knowing that Nick would not want her to reveal too much, but if she didn't ask questions, she wouldn't get answers, so she pressed on. "You said Colin works with Dario Micheli as one of his lawyers?"

"Yes. Why?"

"There was a painting stolen from Dario's gallery in Florence six months ago. It was by an artist named David Leoni. David was a student of Tomas and Lucinda. The robbery was similar to the one that happened at the museum, where only one piece by an unknown artist was taken. I know Dario is talking to Captain Lavezzo from the Carabinieri, who's apparently here at the party, but I don't know what they're talking about."

"And you want me to ask Colin to find out," Joelle said, quickly catching on.

"Yes, but in a not-so-obvious way."

A sly smile crossed her lips. "I understand. I'll ask him if he knows if there's been any progress on that investigation, and then I'll share it with you. Because we're family."

"Thank you. I have to tell you that this concept of family helping each other is rather a foreign one to me."

"Well, you're in Italy, and you know me now, so get used to it. So, I really have to use the restroom. You don't have to wait for me. I'll call you later if we don't get a chance to talk again tonight."

"Okay, I'll see you soon."

As Joelle went into the attached bathroom, Isabella walked out of the bedroom. The noise in the hallway was deafening, with the burgeoning crowd spilling out of the nearby gallery, so she went in the other direction. Seeing an open door, she stepped onto a small patio. It wasn't the main patio with the pool but a smaller garden area with a trickling rock waterfall on one side and a trio of chairs surrounding a fire pit that was thankfully not turned on, because she was already hot.

She stood for a few moments, enjoying the cool breeze and the sound of water rushing over the rocks. It was very calming, and she would just take a minute and then look for Nick. She was about to go back into the party when she heard voices coming from beyond a thicket of bushes. Someone sounded angry. She moved closer to the bushes and peeked through the branches to see who was so upset. She was stunned to see Captain Lavezzo talking to Catherine Vigonas, the museum curator.

Lavezzo wore a black suit with a maroon tie while Catherine had on a black gown, a stark contrast to her blonde hair, which was in a sophisticated updo, a few loose tendrils falling over one ear. They were speaking in Italian, and she could only make out a few words here and there, but it was impossible not to notice the body language.

Catherine waved her hand in the air, clearly upset about something. Lavezzo put a calming hand on her shoulder, and she knocked it away. He said something else, anger simmering in his tone. Catherine stiffened and took a step backward, her body language hostile. Isabella could feel the tension between them.

Catherine said something about him helping her, but Isabella didn't understand the rest or his rapid reply. Whatever he'd told her seemed to comfort her a little. She let out a sigh, but then stiffened as Matthew Pierre and Dario Micheli approached them.

The four of them exchanged polite greetings. Which seemed odd. Hadn't Matthew and Dario just been speaking to Captain Lavezzo in the study?

Catherine didn't seem interested in talking to the other men. She muttered something and quickly excused herself. The three men conversed in low tones for a moment, and then Dario and Matthew went in one direction while Captain Lavezzo went in another.

She cursed herself for not knowing more Italian. She really wished she could have understood what they were saying. And, of course, this conversation had to happen the one time that she and Nick were not together. He might have been able to under-stand more of it.

A few things were clear, however. Catherine Vigonas and Captain Lavezzo knew each other. They'd been arguing and then appeared to be on the same page. It was possible they were talking about the robbery at the museum. Maybe Catherine had been angry at the lack of progress Lavezzo was making. But it had seemed more personal than professional, especially when Lavezzo had put his hand on Catherine's shoulder, and she'd jumped.

And then there were the men. She didn't know why Dario and Matthew were suddenly in this private part of the yard, where they had come from or where they were going, but they seemed to know Catherine. That wasn't surprising. They were all in the art world. And when Catherine left, the men had spoken only a few sentences to Lavezzo. So, they had undoubtedly had a longer conversation within before this meet-up. Not that the meet-up was probably even planned. They'd all just run into each other.

But that didn't seem quite right, either. There was a huge party going on. Why were any of them in this seemingly private part of the yard?

Frustrated, she headed back into the house. Maybe she could catch up to Catherine and talk to her, get a clue as to why she was upset with Lavezzo. But first, she needed to find Nick. As much as she hated to admit it, they were better when they worked together.

———

Nick wandered around the pool area, wondering where Isabella had gone. He hadn't seen her anywhere in the house and when Joelle returned to the gallery, she'd been alone. That made him nervous. Isabella was fine, he told himself, wanting to believe that. He just needed to make sure.

He moved toward the pool house. The door was locked, and the lights were off, with no sign of anyone inside, so he turned back toward the main house. The floor-to-ceiling windows revealed throngs of people in every brightly lit room on the first floor of the villa, while the balconies above on the second and third floors were completely dark.

"You won't find your answers out here," he heard someone say, a British accent in his voice.

He turned to see an older man smoking a cigarette a few feet away. His hair was blond, his eyes a sparkling blue, and he had a familiar expression on his face.

"What are you doing here, Sam? Casing the party?" he asked.

"Just like the good old days," Sam said with a laugh. "I look too much like my son, don't I?"

"There is a resemblance. And you didn't answer my question."

"I couldn't let you have all the fun, Nick."

"You insisted on meeting in a church confessional last night so I wouldn't see you, and now you're here as if you're an invited guest. Are you on the guest list?"

"Guest lists are tiresome," he replied.

"Do you find everything to be a joke?"

"Life is easier when you don't take it too seriously."

"Some things in life are serious."

"Now you sound like my son. Flynn used to laugh so much when he was a kid. It didn't take much to make that happen. He had a joyous personality. Little things made him happy."

"I doubt he was joyous or happy when he lost his father."

Even in the shadows of where they were standing, Sam's expression darkened. "That was a sad time for me, too."

"It was your choice to leave, not his. At least, that's the way I heard it."

"That's the way it happened. But life is more complicated than one decision. He was better off in the long run that I was gone."

"And you were better off being a free man. Don't you ever get tired of running?" He couldn't imagine how Sam could exist for so many years pretending to be someone else, always staying on the run, looking over his shoulder. He only did it for weeks or months at a time, and that could feel too long.

"It doesn't matter if I'm tired; it's the path I chose. My only regret is losing my son. But I'm glad he's happy, that he doesn't have the burden of my sins hanging over him."

"I wouldn't go that far. Flynn said after you disappeared the last time, he got a lot of scrutiny from the higher-ups, wondering if he let you go."

"I didn't give him the choice to let me go, but it sounds like the scrutiny went away. He still has his job, leads his team, rights the world's wrongs."

"He's a great leader, agent, and an even better friend."

"I'm not going to ask you to tell him I said hello."

"Good, because I don't think he wants to hear from you."

"I know." Sam took a long draw on his cigarette.

"Why did you agree to meet with me?" he asked. "Why did you send me here?"

"You're his friend. I can't help him, but I can help you."

"You haven't been all that helpful so far."

"You're here, aren't you? This is where everyone is. It's up to you to figure out who can help you." He paused. "Where is your beautiful friend?"

"I'm actually looking for Isabella. Have you seen her?"

"I have not, but you should keep an eye on her. She's fiery and brave, but sometimes that can draw too much attention. When someone sees a fire, they want to put it out."

Sam's words sent a shiver down his spine, and he wanted to rush toward the house in case Sam knew something he didn't. But Isabella was okay. She could handle herself. She was just working the party. And now that he had Sam, he didn't want to waste the opportunity to get more information.

"Is there something you didn't tell me last night that you want to share more?"

Sam smiled. "What's the fun in the game if you don't figure things out for yourself?"

"It's not a game to me, Sam. But if it is to you, why don't you give me a hint?"

Sam cocked his head to the right as he considered the question. "You wanted to know more about the Falconeri family."

"Who are apparently all dead."

"Perhaps not."

He raised a brow. "Explain."

"I told you Roberto had no children and Bruno's daughter died, and that was true, but there was someone else in the family, a sister. Her name was Juliette."

Nick sucked in a breath. "Juliette Sabatini?"

"Yes. But her maiden name was Falconeri. Juliette was the much younger sister of Roberto and Bruno, by about twelve years. She was an artist herself, but nowhere near as good as Roberto. She married a man who worked for her brothers."

"Why didn't you tell me this last night?"

"I had forgotten about her," Sam said.

He didn't believe that for a second. "I found a copy of Juliette's driver's license, long since expired, in my grandfather's things. But I don't know why he had it. Do you? Is Juliette still alive?"

"She died last year."

He blew out a breath of frustration. "Great. Another dead Falconeri that I can't talk to. How about giving me someone who is alive?"

Sam smiled. "I was getting to that. Juliette had a daughter. That woman is at this party."

His heart skipped a beat. "Who is her daughter?"

"She was born Katerina Sabatini, but Juliette changed her and her daughter's names when she ran away from her husband and her family years ago. Katerina became Catherine, and when she got married, her last name became Vigonas."

His heart dropped into his stomach. "The museum curator? Catherine is running a new version of *La Mano Nera*? Is that why the museum security cameras were turned off? Why would she want those paintings?"

"I don't have the answers. I don't even know if she's in charge, but she's definitely involved."

"I need to speak to her."

"Tread carefully. I suspect she has a partner, maybe someone at this party. You'll want to get her alone." He dropped his cigarette to the ground and stubbed it out. "I think your beautiful friend is looking for you."

As Sam tipped his head toward the doors leading out of the living room and onto the patio, he saw Isabella in the crowd, her gaze swinging from one person to the next, clearly searching for him.

He turned back to Sam, but the man was gone. *Damn!* He really was a ghost.

Walking forward, he met Isabella by the side of the pool. "There you are," he said with relief. "I've been looking for you."

"I've been looking for you." She grabbed his arm, a light of excitement in her eyes. "I overheard a conversation between

Catherine Vigonas and Captain Lavezzo in one of the side gardens."

"What were they saying?"

"I don't know. They were speaking fast and in Italian, but Lavezzo put his hand on her shoulder like this," she said, demonstrating the gesture. "And then she pushed him away. It felt like there was something personal between them. The body language went back and forth between comforting and angry. I wish you had been there. I'm sure you would have understood more than I did."

"I wish I'd been there, too." His brain spun with this latest piece of information. "I just ran into Sam Beringer."

"He's here? At this glittering party? I thought he stayed in the shadows."

"Well, he was in the shadows, but he was dressed like a guest. I don't believe he was invited, but that doesn't matter. He told me that Catherine Vigonas is Roberto Falconeri's niece. Her mother was Juliette Sabatini. Juliette was the younger sister of Roberto and Bruno."

Isabella's gaze widened. "Wow. That's not what I expected you to say."

"Apparently, Juliette's husband worked for her brothers, and she may have been involved as well. At some point, she ran away from her husband and her family with her young daughter and changed their names." He put up a hand as he saw the question about to hit her lips. "Juliette died a year ago."

"No," she breathed in disappointment.

"Yes. Which is about the same time my grandfather died. I can't help wondering if those two deaths are connected. He had her information in his personal papers. There has to be a link."

"It sounds like it. But Juliette might not matter anymore. If Catherine is a Falconeri, does that mean she orchestrated the robbery at her museum? Why would she do that? She could have just handed the paintings over to someone without the guard getting shot or our grandmothers witnessing anything."

Her question made him frown. "Maybe the guard wasn't supposed to get shot, and she needed the cover of a robbery."

"If she was involved in the robbery, and she's tight with Captain Lavezzo, then that says something about him."

"We need to talk to her. Let's see if we can track her down."

"This might be the break we've been looking for, Nick. But why didn't Sam tell us about her last night?"

"He said he just remembered. Honestly, I feel like we're pawns in some game he's playing. You suggested misdirection before. I'm not sure you were wrong."

"Well, it should be possible to verify Catherine's true identity. Sam would know that you have FBI resources to check that out."

"Yes, he would. Sam said he wants to help me, because it's what Flynn would want him to do. Maybe it's not a game; I don't know. But that's not important right now."

"We can try to talk to Catherine tonight, but I don't think she'll tell us anything in this crowd of people."

"I agree. We might have to wait until tomorrow. We could go to her house or the museum and try to catch her alone."

"I hate to wait even a second, though. Let's try to see what we can get from her tonight."

He was about to reply when something caught the corner of his eye.

An object was falling from the third floor of the villa. He jumped back, pushing Isabella to the side as it hit the pool next to them with a heavy splash. A woman screamed, as he stared in shock at the body floating in the pool next to them.

"Oh, my God," Isabella cried. "That's Catherine."

He jumped into the pool along with two security guys. Together, they pulled the woman out of the water and laid her on the deck, one guard administering CPR. But she wasn't responding and there was blood pouring from her head and neck. The crowd by the pool was hushed in terrified silence that would only be broken if Catherine took a breath. But her eyes remained closed, her body still.

A man came out of the crowd, claiming to be a doctor. Another woman rushed to help, saying she was a nurse. As Catherine's body was surrounded, he took Isabella's hand and pulled her away from the pool. They stood under the shadow of a large tree.

"Is she going to make it?" Isabella asked.

He looked into her eyes and shook his head. "No. She's dead."

"Oh, God, Nick! Do you think she jumped?"

"No. Someone killed her."

Isabella's eyes widened in shock and fear. "Right here? In the middle of a party."

"It looks that way." He suddenly realized what was coming. "The police will be all over this party soon. We're going to be questioned along with everyone else. You saw nothing. You heard nothing. You know nothing about her."

"But I did see something. I saw her talking to Captain Lavezzo."

"A high-ranking officer of the Carabinieri. We don't know who we can trust. He could have friends in the police department. We have to be careful. If anyone asks why you're here, simply say you love art and you wanted to support the charity. Don't talk about the museum robbery, David Leoni, Tomas and Lucinda, no one."

She met his gaze and slowly nodded. "Got it. I'll keep my mouth shut."

"You have to, Isabella. Your life might depend on it."

CHAPTER TWENTY

Isabella was exhausted and still shaken when they returned to the house a little before eleven on Sunday night. They'd spent hours at the villa. No one could leave after Catherine's shocking death. The guests had been questioned one by one by officers from the state police. They hadn't been allowed to speak to anyone, including each other, while they were waiting, and the entire party had been sequestered in the downstairs rooms while the third floor had been examined for evidence. The police had given out little information, but it seemed certain that they believed one of the guests had pushed Catherine off the third-floor balcony.

When they'd been questioned, they'd been asked if they knew Catherine. They admitted to having met her once because their grandmothers volunteered at the museum. They also had to give statements about what they had witnessed since they had been very close to the pool where Catherine had landed. However, that fact seemed to make them less interesting to the inspector questioning them. They could not have physically pushed her off the balcony and then been by the pool when she fell. It was a relief to finally be allowed to go home.

As they entered the kitchen together, she immediately

moved to the kettle and filled it with water while Nick went upstairs to take off his still-damp clothes. While the water was heating, she sat down at the table and kicked off her heels. Then she grabbed a pear out of the basket on the table, only to realize the irony of eating fruit from a basket that Catherine had delivered only the day before.

Images of Catherine's limp body floated through her head, and she felt sick to her stomach. She didn't think she'd ever forget the sound of Catherine's body hitting the water, or the sight of her blood filling the pool. How quickly Catherine's life had changed. She'd been beautiful, vibrant, alive and then she was dead.

She was still staring at the pear when Nick returned in jeans and a T-shirt. She quickly returned the fruit to the basket. "I can't eat this. Not after what just happened." She licked her lips. "When Catherine hit the pool, I didn't even realize it was a person. I thought something had fallen off the roof. But you figured it out immediately. You jumped right in. You tried to save her."

"I wish I could have saved her. But I suspect she was dead before someone threw her off the balcony. It was a bold move killing her in such a public way. On the other hand, the cover of the party provided an easy escape for the killer. He or she could get away quickly, blend into the background unnoticed, just another guest at the party."

"That's true."

"But it was a risk, and it may turn out to have been a costly one if the police can find evidence on the balcony."

"I hope they can." She paused. "But what if it was someone no one would question, like a police officer?"

"Like Captain Lavezzo?"

"Yes. But I didn't see him anywhere when we were being questioned. Did you?"

"No. He could have left the party before she was killed," he replied.

"There was probably about twenty or thirty minutes between when I saw Lavezzo and Catherine together and then found you by the pool," she murmured. "Long enough for him to have left before Catherine was killed."

"Or to kill her and get away."

She shivered again. "It's hard to wrap my head around any of this."

"I know."

"I thought Stefano might show up when the other officers arrived. He must not have been working tonight."

"I'm sure he'll surface at some point."

"Maybe we should call him, see what he knows about what happened."

"Let's save that for tomorrow." He grabbed the pear she'd just discarded. "I'm hungry," he said, at her questioning gaze. "And this pear had nothing to do with Catherine's death."

As he ate, her mind raced with theories and suspects. "I was thinking about the scene in the garden. When Dario Micheli and Matthew Pierre arrived, Catherine didn't seem interested in talking to them. But it felt like they all knew each other. There weren't any introductions, just greetings. Then Catherine quickly left."

"She probably didn't want anyone to see her with Lavezzo."

"I wondered why they were all in that part of the garden. It was very secluded. I wish I knew what the three men talked about after she left. I shouldn't have been so resistant to learning Italian from my grandmother. But I felt like an outsider when I was here in Rome, and I stubbornly clung to the idea that not learning their language was one way I could control my situation."

"That's insightful, Isabella."

"I have some self-awareness. But it often arrives too late to be helpful."

He set down the core of the pear. "You had no way of

knowing any of this would be happening now, so give yourself a break."

"What about Sam?" she asked, her mind jumping in a different direction. "Could he have killed Catherine? He gave you information about her. He disappeared into the shadows. A short time after that, she hit the pool. He gave us a lead, but now the lead is dead."

Nick gave her a thoughtful look. "That's interesting, but I don't believe there was enough time for him to get to the third floor and orchestrate her death. I was talking to him just before you came outside."

"Sam could be working with someone else. His partner, whoever that might be, could have killed Catherine. Clearly, there were multiple people involved in the museum robbery. If it was just Catherine, she wouldn't be dead." She took a breath. "What are we going to do now?"

"Keep going. We have new clues. We know Catherine was Juliette's daughter, and Juliette was the sister of Roberto and Bruno. Juliette disappeared with Catherine years ago, and her personal information ended up in my grandfather's belongings. Both Juliette and my grandfather died a year ago. It seems like too big of a coincidence for those events not to be linked."

"And Juliette could be the mysterious *J* from the letters," she reminded him. "The address for Juliette was in Firenze, but if she changed her name, and that ID expired years ago, then we don't know where she's been recently. Only where she was a very long time ago."

"We can probably find out more about her now that we have the link to Catherine. I can get my team on that."

"I like that you have a team to get on things. I'm always working by myself. Maybe your team should also look into Dario Micheli. It was his gallery that lost the Leoni painting. I wonder where he got that painting from."

"Probably a relative. Wasn't Leoni living in Firenze at some point?"

"I think so," she said.

"A lot of signs pointing in the same direction."

She could see where he was going, and she didn't like it. "Really, Nick?"

"We need to go to Florence tomorrow, Isabella. Things are moving fast. We're getting close to something."

"I feel like we're getting farther away."

"No. We're making connections. We just need more of them, and it might be good to get out of Rome for a while."

"That might be true. There is one other thing I forgot to tell you. Joelle said her grandmother had a ring like Tomas's. She might still have it. Her father is going to ask her."

"What else did Joelle have to say? I wondered why she'd whisked you away."

"She said little, just that her boyfriend, or her lover as she called him, Colin Devonshire, is one of Dario's lawyers. I asked her to talk to him about the theft of Leoni's painting at Dario's gallery."

Nick frowned. "I'm not sure that was a good idea."

"Me, either. I don't want Joelle to get hurt because she's asking questions for me, and we don't know anything about Dario. What if he's involved in all this? I'm going to text her not to say anything." She took her phone from her clutch and sent Joelle a text that she didn't need her to ask Colin about David Leoni or the robbery at the gallery. She'd explain more later. After sending the text, she put down the phone. "I hope she gets my text before she talks to him."

"I didn't see her or her lover while we were being questioned," Nick commented.

She started at his words. "I didn't see them, either. They must have been held in another room." Letting out a weary sigh, she sat back in her chair. "I have too many questions and not enough answers."

"I know that feeling."

"I also feel kind of sorry for Catherine. I don't know why."

"I'd save your compassion until we know what she did or didn't do," Nick returned. "You realize this isn't just about finding the paintings anymore, Isabella. It's about murder, and I'm not just talking about Catherine. It's about Lucinda and Tomas. Maybe my grandfather. Perhaps Juliette. The bodies are adding up and we have to figure out who's making that happen before there are any more deaths."

His words sent another chill down her spine along with a wave of frustrated hopelessness. "How are we going to do that, Nick?"

"I'm not sure, but we will figure it out. I don't just want the paintings back. I want justice. I want people to pay for what they've done. Some of them may be dead already, but not all of them."

She felt the same resolve. "I want the same thing, Nick. We'll go to Firenze tomorrow. We can visit the gallery, see if we can find the person who had David's painting before it went missing, and we can talk to my mother."

"It's the right move," he said.

"I'll talk to her about the mystery, the history, but not about her and me. So don't think you're going to be part of making some family reunion happen." She waved a warning finger in his direction. "This is business."

"Got it. I would never force you to talk to your mother. It's your choice."

"And I've made it," she said, appreciating his words. She got up to turn off the kettle and make them some tea. "I hope this works," she said a few minutes later as she took their drinks to the table. "Because after what I just saw, I don't think I'm going to sleep any better tonight than I did last night."

"Let's stay together. I'll take the lounger in your room."

She knew she should tell him no, but she didn't want to argue, and the real truth was that she didn't want to be alone.

"We're just going to sleep," Nick added. "Unless..."

It was a little difficult to resist his questioning gaze, because losing herself in Nick sounded like a much better way to spend the night than thinking about Catherine dying right in front of her. But if she was going to be with Nick, it wouldn't be because she wanted to forget something.

"We're just going to sleep," she said firmly. "And don't ask me again, because that might make me want to change my answer, and I really don't think I should."

He smiled. "Fair enough. No more questions about anything tonight. But tomorrow is a new day."

———

Nick found sleeping in the lounger in Isabella's small room to be more comfortable than his bigger bed downstairs, and that had a lot to do with her being close to him. They'd spent so much time together that being apart felt odd. Somehow, after everything that had happened, they both managed to sleep. And when he woke up Monday morning, Isabella was already out of bed, dressed, and making coffee when he got into the kitchen.

He filled a mug because he needed coffee, and he needed to see her face, and he wasn't sure which was more important.

She gave him a tense smile. "I'm not a cook, as you know, but I did make some oatmeal and there's fresh fruit to go in it, if you're interested."

He seemed to be interested in everything that had to do with her. "Sounds good," he said, taking a seat at the table.

She brought him a bowl of oatmeal with strawberries and blueberries on the top, and he dug in, knowing that he needed some fuel for the day ahead. "Did you already eat?" he asked.

"Yes, but I'm not hungry."

"You're dreading this trip, aren't you?"

"Parts of it. But I know I need to talk to my mom. So that's what I'll do."

He nodded approvingly. "I appreciate that. I suspect it won't be easy."

"It really shouldn't be that difficult," she said. "But I can't shake the feeling that it will be. Anyway, when do you want to leave?"

"As soon as I take a shower and grab a bag. You should bring some clothes, too. It's a long drive. We may need to stay overnight."

"I've got my tote bag ready to go."

"Good." He finished the last of his oatmeal and then took the bowl to the sink. He rinsed it and put it in the dishwasher.

"I'll start that while you get ready," she told him.

He paused, seeing the stress in her eyes but also her resolve. "Did you sleep last night?"

"Better than I thought. You were out when I got up, so you must have slept, too. The lounger couldn't have been that comfortable."

"It was fine. And it was nice to have you nearby."

"It did feel good not to be alone," she murmured.

A silence fell between them, as their gazes clung together. He wanted to fill that silence, but his thoughts were too chaotic and contradictory. He wasn't sure what would come out of his mouth, and this really wasn't the time to find out.

"I'll just be a few minutes," he said, then quickly left the room. He jogged up the stairs to the second floor and headed into the bathroom for a cold, bracing shower that would hopefully clear his head.

————

They left the house around ten. When they entered the garage, Isabella said, "I can drive, Nick. In fact, I'd really like to, if you're okay with giving up control for a few hours."

He hesitated, then tossed her the keys. "All right."

Surprise widened her eyes. "Really? I thought you'd insist on driving."

"You were wrong." He liked when he could throw her off

balance. "I keep telling you, Isabella, that you don't really know me."

"I'm getting to know you pretty well," she said dryly as they got in the car. "But we have a long drive ahead of us, so plenty of time to get to know each other even better."

He wasn't opposed to that. He found Isabella more and more interesting by the minute, and he wanted to know everything about her, which was a desire that made him a little uncomfortable. He wasn't used to wanting to know a woman the way he wanted to know her, which was more than physical, although he really wanted that, too. But he also liked the way her mind worked. He liked the way she challenged him.

He told himself not to get carried away. They weren't going on vacation together. They were on a mission to find the truth, to get justice, and that was the only priority.

Fifteen minutes later, he knew a little more about her. She liked to drive fast. She was impatient in the Rome traffic, and quick to mutter a curse at a poor driver. But she had complete control over the vehicle, and he was slightly more comfortable not being behind the wheel in his grandmother's ridiculously compact car, so he was happy with his decision to let her drive.

The traffic thinned once they left Rome and got on the A1 highway with two lanes in each direction. The route took them into Lazio, a region known for rolling hills, olive groves, and vineyards, and once there, Isabella seemed to relax.

"It's beautiful out here," she murmured.

He couldn't help but agree. While Rome had urban charm, the countryside was absolutely beautiful, and it felt good to get away from the city and be in nature on a bright, sunny day.

Despite Isabella's earlier comment that they'd have plenty of time to get to know each other on the trip, neither one of them was talking much. But it wasn't an awkward silence. In fact, it felt very comfortable, which was surprising.

He'd never imagined after their first awkward date that they'd be anything even close to friends or more than friends.

His mind flashed back to the feeling of her mouth against his, and he really wished he hadn't promised he wouldn't kiss her again unless she asked him to. That was probably never going to happen.

Needing to get his mind off kissing her, he pulled out his phone and checked his email, realizing he'd missed a note from Flynn that had been sent several hours ago. He read the email with increasing interest.

"What are you reading?" Isabella asked, flashing him a quick look.

"An email from Flynn. I had asked Flynn to look into Juliette Sabatini before Sam gave us more information." He scanned the email. "He came up with some of the same details. Juliette was the younger sister of Roberto and Bruno Falconeri. She was married to Rocco Sabatini when she was twenty years old, and they owned property in Rome and in Florence. Rocco was ten years older than Juliette and was an accountant. One of his clients was an importer that Flynn traced back to Henry Falconeri, the father of Roberto and Bruno. Sam had suggested that Juliette's husband was working with her brothers."

"Does he say anything else?"

"Juliette had a baby girl named Katerina. Katerina was enrolled in a Catholic school in Rome until she was eight. She left that school in 1971, the same year that Juliette and her daughter disappeared."

"That was the year after Tomas and Lucinda died."

"Yes." He kept reading. "Flynn couldn't find any information on Juliette after 1971. So he decided to look into friends of the Sabatini's. He located an American woman named Marie Bennett, who was in Juliette's wedding. Flynn figured someone had to help Juliette disappear or know what happened to her. Marie lives in San Francisco now. She's in her nineties, but her memory is sharp, and she told him she helped Juliette escape from her marriage. Juliette and Katerina became Stephanie and Catherine Mayer, and they moved to Paris after leaving Italy."

"Wow, that's impressive, Nick."

"My team is good," he said, continuing to read. "Marie didn't know what happened to Juliette or her daughter after they went to Paris. Juliette thought it was too dangerous for them to have any contact. That someone could trace her through Marie. And Marie told Flynn that Rocco had pressured her several times about whether she knew where Juliette was, but she protected her friend and never said a word." He paused. "Once Flynn got the name Stephanie Mayer and the location of Paris, he looked through public records and discovered that Juliette, AKA Stephanie, had a second child shortly after she arrived in Paris."

"Second child?" she echoed in surprise.

"It was an unnamed boy with the father unknown." His heart pounded. "If this is correct, Juliette had two children." He looked at Isabella, who met his gaze with excitement in her eyes.

"This is great, Nick. If she had two children, then there might be someone else we can talk to about all this. We just don't know who the unnamed boy is," she added. "We get so close but not all the way there."

"One step at a time."

"I'm tired of steps. I want to leap," she said in frustration.

"Me, too. But we are where we are."

"Well, at least we have more information than we did. That's something. And maybe Flynn will be able to figure out who the second child is."

"He's going to keep working on that." As he finished speaking, he saw Isabella changing lanes and heading toward an exit. "Where are you going?"

"GPS says to get off, accident ahead." She pointed to her phone, which was lying on the console between them. "Looks like we're going to see more of this region than just the highway."

He picked up her phone, seeing the estimated delay was well over thirty minutes. There were quite a few other cars getting off with them, so that quieted the sudden doubt he'd gotten when she'd left the highway.

"This isn't too bad," she said a few moments later as he put her phone back on the console. "It's actually even prettier, not that we're here to sightsee, but it's still nice to see more of the countryside."

"Have you been in this area before?"

"Not by car. My grandmother took me to Florence on the train to see Michelangelo's David and the Uffizi Gallery. It was a fun trip. I liked the train, and what I saw of Florence, which wasn't much, just the touristy areas. What about you?"

"I spent a long weekend here when I was on a college break. I went to Florence with my cousins. We mostly drank and tried to pick up cute Italian girls."

"I'm sure you were successful."

"It was a good weekend. But I was nineteen or twenty, so every weekend was good." He looked at his phone again, thinking he might do his own research, but he had very few bars on his phone and no sites were coming up. "Not much reception out here."

"Cell phone towers would mar this beautiful landscape," she said as she drove further into Tuscany. She rolled down her window, letting some warm, fresh air blow through the car. "Why don't you see if there's anything on the radio?"

He did as she suggested. There weren't a lot of choices, so he paused on the first music station he could find, only to realize it was classical. "Not this."

Isabella shot him a quick look. "Why not? It was pretty, and there doesn't seem to be much else."

"Reminds me of my parents. I can't tell you how many times I had to listen to my mother practice or watch an orchestra perform." He scanned the radio for more options and finally settled on a station playing music from the nineties. Then he rolled down his window as well, letting the music, the warm breeze, the beautiful woman now singing along with the radio ease his tension.

Isabella's voice wasn't bad. She could definitely carry a tune, but what he liked most about her was how very comfortable she was in her own skin. She didn't care that she was singing, and he wasn't. She wasn't worried whether or not she was singing off-key. She was just enjoying the moment, and he couldn't help but enjoy her.

He'd never really met anyone like her. She had a lot of sharp edges, but they were mostly there to protect herself from being hurt, and she had been hurt a lot. He could relate to some of what she'd gone through growing up. He'd had two parents, but he'd still been alone much of the time, and so had she.

She flung him a smile. "You can join in."

"I don't know the words. By the way, you were right when you told me you were a good singer."

"More like enthusiastic than good. But it's very freeing to just belt out a tune. Takes the stress away."

"I'll take your word for it," he said, squirming in his seat as he attempted to find a more comfortable position, but his long legs had nowhere to go.

"It's such a nice day, isn't it, Nick? Look at that big mansion." She pointed toward the hills rising above them and some majestic structure. "I wonder if someone lives there."

"It could be a winery."

"You're right. There's the sign." She gave him another smile as the car in front of them took the exit. "I wish we could go. It would be a lot more fun to stop at a winery, taste some wine, have some cheese, maybe a picnic."

Her words painted a shockingly tempting picture, shocking because he wasn't a man to be lazy, to have a picnic, but he also wouldn't mind rolling around on a blanket with her.

"But we can't do that," she said forcefully, as if trying to convince herself. "We're on a mission."

"We are. But when this is over, I'm taking you on a picnic."

"We'll see. I just hope this will be over before anyone else dies."

"Are you sure we're still going the right way?" he asked as the one-lane highway took them into the hills.

"I'm following the GPS. Uh-oh."

"What?"

Her face tensed as she looked into her rearview mirror.

Turning around, he saw a car bearing down fast on them.

"It came out of nowhere," she muttered, pressing down on the gas. "They're probably going to pass us, don't you think? It's a one-lane road. I can't pull over. There's no shoulder now."

His bad feeling returned. The detour could have been purposeful, a way to get them off the main highway, but that would have meant causing some sort of accident and sending a lot of people in another direction, which seemed like a stretch.

Maybe the detour had simply provided an opportunity for someone who had been following them out of Rome to jump into action, although he'd looked several times for a tail and hadn't seen one.

"They're getting closer, Nick." She pressed down harder on the gas. "I'm flooring it. I can't go any faster."

He looked back once more. A black Audi was behind them. There were two men in the front seat of the car, and they had hoodies over their heads and dark glasses covering their eyes. He couldn't see their hands or identify them in any other way, but it didn't matter who they were, only how they were going to get away.

"They're not going to pass us." His gaze shot down the road, looking for an exit, but there was nothing but a hill on one side and increasingly steeper terrain on the other.

"What should I do?" Isabella asked.

He wished to hell he was driving now because Isabella wasn't trained for this. However, she was doing a damn good job, keeping her head together and going as fast as she could. But there were turns coming up, and there was no shoulder on the right side of the road, just terrain that grew steeper with each passing minute.

"Nick?" she asked, panic entering her voice.

"Just keep going until we see a place to turn out."

"I don't see an exit coming up. I'm scared, Nick. I don't want to be killed by someone making this look like another accident."

Her words reminded him of what had happened to his grandfather, to Tomas and Lucinda. As he looked back once more, he saw one man halfway out the window on the passenger side, a gun in his hand. His curse was cut off by the blast and the shattering of glass on the back window.

"Oh, my God! They're shooting at us," Isabella said, doing her best to stay on the road. But the next shot hit the back tire, and she battled to hold on to the wheel as the tire blew out and the car skidded across the road.

He braced his hand against the dash as she tried to turn away from the skid, but there was no stopping the momentum of the car, and they flew off the side of the road, tumbling down a bush and rock-covered hill until they were turning over in body-shaking somersaults. The last thing he heard was Isabella's scream.

CHAPTER TWENTY-ONE

Nick woke up to his ears ringing and a heavy feeling on his chest. He felt pain in his back, in his shoulders, and in his legs, as he squinted, then blinked his eyes open, trying to remember what had happened. When he saw the crushed car next to him, it all came back. He rolled on to his side, knocking a heavy branch off his chest and saw the open door hanging off the car and the seatbelt that had broken when he'd been thrown from the vehicle.

He was so dazed it took him a second to realize that Isabella was still in the car. Her head was resting on the steering wheel and there was glass in her hair. She wasn't moving. And that thought drove the cobwebs out of his head.

He scrambled to his feet, stumbling through a wave of dizziness as he climbed into the car.

"Isabella," he said, fear running through him at the blood running down her face and her very pale skin color. He put two fingers on her neck and was ecstatic to feel a faint pulse. But she was barely breathing, and she was crammed against the steering wheel.

He reached for the seatbelt clasp and struggled to release it. It took a few moments to finally get it unhooked. When it snapped free, she seemed to have a little more room, but she still wasn't waking up. He reached under the front seat to push the seat back. That took almost more energy than he had, but he needed to give her more space to breathe.

Eventually, the seat moved back an inch or two and the movement made Isabella take a deeper breath.

"Isabella," he said again, brushing the blood off her face so he could see that it was coming from a cut on her forehead. The gash didn't look too deep. She'd probably been cut from the windshield glass.

Guilt and rage ran through him. He never should have let her drive. Never should have let her stay in Italy. Never should have let any of this happen. This was his fault. She had to wake up. She had to be all right. He couldn't live with any other result.

"Isabella," he said again, pressing his mouth to hers, and then saying, "Please wake up."

He was thrilled to see her eyelids fluttering. His heart turned over when she gazed back at him with her big, beautiful brown eyes.

"Nick?" she asked, confusion in her gaze.

"It's me."

"What happened?"

"We crashed."

She blinked a few times, and then mumbled, "Did you kiss me? You said you weren't going to kiss me unless I asked you to."

He smiled. "Sorry. I was trying to wake you up, like Sleeping Beauty."

She grimaced as she tried to sit up straighter.

"Don't move," he said quickly. "Where does it hurt? Tell me where the pain is before you move again."

"My head."

"What about your neck? Your back? Your legs? Can you feel your legs? Can you wiggle your toes?"

"Yes, but my knee hurts a little."

He thought it was a good sign that she was only having pain

in her knee and her head. "What about your ribs? Can you breathe?"

She took a breath and then said, "My chest feels sore, but it's not that bad. You have blood on your face, too."

"I'm okay. But I think we might have the same bad headache."

"Like knives stabbing my temple."

"That sounds about right."

"I want to get out of the car," she said. "It smells funny."

It smelled like gas, which created new worry. "Okay. I'll get out and open your door."

"Where's my bag?"

He looked around and saw it on the ground where he'd landed, along with his backpack and her phone, all of which had flown out of the car when his door had broken open.

"Let me get you out of here, and then I'll get our stuff."

Backing out of the car, he ran around to the driver's side. She'd already managed to get the door partway open, and he helped her squeeze out of the vehicle.

Once on her feet, he put his arm around her and moved her away from the vehicle in case it caught fire. Then he ran back to retrieve their things.

"I can't believe we survived," she murmured, when he returned. "Look at the car. How is it possible we're alive?"

"I don't know. We got lucky."

She turned her head toward the top of the hill. "I can't see the road. There are too many bushes."

"That's probably what buffeted our fall," he said.

"What about the men who shot at us and ran us off the road? Will they come back?"

"I think they're long gone," he reassured her, hoping that was true.

"I don't understand, Nick. Did they think we had a painting in the car? Did they just want to destroy it and didn't care if we died in the process?"

He shook his head as he gently flicked some glass out of her hair. "No, Isabella. This wasn't about getting or destroying a painting."

She gazed into his eyes. "They just wanted to kill us, didn't they?"

"Yes. Someone doesn't like the questions we're asking or the search we're on. They want to stop us."

She took a breath. "Okay. Well, no one has tried to kill me for asking questions before, so this is a first."

"And a last. As soon as we get out of here, you're going back to the States."

"What are you going to do?"

"Find and punish whoever ran us off the road and whoever ordered them to kill us."

"That's what I want to do, too."

"You can't. You're hurt. You could have died, Isabella. I don't think that has sunk in yet, but when I saw you unconscious and slumped over the steering wheel, I was afraid that you were gone."

"I'm sorry I scared you, Nick."

"You don't have to apologize. You just have to go home. I clearly cannot protect you," he said, anger in his voice now, as he mentally kicked himself once more for not having foreseen this outcome. "When you got off the highway, I had a bad feeling. I should have listened to my gut."

"There was an accident, a delay. What does that have to do with anything?" She paused, thinking for a moment. "It was a setup?"

"Maybe. Or it might have just provided a good opportunity to take us out. Either way, it was a dangerous move. We should have stayed on the main road, no matter how slow it was."

"Well, I was driving, so that's on me."

"Isabella—"

She held up her hand. "We can keep fighting about this,

Nick. But not now. Let's focus on getting out of here. It's pretty steep. I don't know if I can climb the hill."

He knew she thought she'd won, and maybe that was fine for now, because she was right, they needed to get out of here. He pulled out his phone and tried to make a call for help, but he still didn't have a signal. "Nothing," he said.

"Where's my phone?"

He pulled her phone from his pocket, but she had no reception, either. He handed her the phone, and she slipped it into the back pocket of her jeans. Then he tipped his head toward the direction they'd come from. "Let's walk that way. The road should go down and the hillside along with it."

"Okay. I can carry my bag."

She looked like she could barely stay on her feet. "I've got it." He put his backpack on and then slinging her bag over his shoulder. "Let's go."

They trudged through rocky terrain and thick brush for almost an hour, and as the sun beat down on their heads, he felt increasingly hot and even a little dizzy. His head was throbbing, and he suspected Isabella was feeling as badly as he was, maybe even worse. But she wasn't complaining. She was just moving forward. She was definitely a strong woman.

It seemed like they'd been walking forever, when the hillside finally flattened, and they could see the road. Eventually, they were able to make their way to that road, which felt like a major achievement. There were no cars around, which was good and bad. Good because the men who'd been chasing them weren't waiting for them to surface. Bad because they needed to get a ride.

He took out his phone again, relieved to see a signal. He opened up the app he used in Italy for taxi service, since some of the other rideshares weren't operating in this area. He was able to hang on to the signal long enough to get a cab, which was apparently seven minutes out. "I got us a ride. Let's wait under that tree."

Isabella nodded as she wearily followed him a little further down the road.

It was nice to have some shade as the sun had risen higher in the sky now.

"Where are we going to go?" she asked him.

"The nearest hospital."

"I don't want to go to the hospital," she said with a frown.

"You might need a stitch or two," he said as her cut continued to bleed. "And you should be checked for a concussion."

"Well, you should be checked, too. And if you're not going to be, then I say we try to get to Florence."

He was still thinking about their options when the cab arrived. There was no way he would feel comfortable not getting Isabella medical attention. He asked the driver to take them to the nearest urgent care or hospital. Then he slid into the back-seat next to her.

She wasn't fighting him now. In fact, her eyes were closed, and that bothered him. Maybe the trek from the car had taken too much out of her. He really hoped she didn't have something wrong that had been made worse by the walk. Seeing her now, he knew he'd made the right decision to go to the hospital. He needed to make sure she was all right before they went anywhere else.

It took about ten minutes to get to a small hospital. Fortunately, the waiting room was not crowded and after explaining they'd been in a car accident, they were each ushered into an exam room. He hated to be away from Isabella for even a second. While he thought the men who had tried to kill them were gone, there was no way to be sure of that. They might have seen the crashed car and their unconscious bodies and thought they were dead. The hillside had been too steep for them to climb down easily, which might have prevented them from checking on their condition.

He hoped the men thought they were dead. That might buy them some time.

While he was waiting for the doctor to come in, he stretched out on the exam table and stared at the ceiling, going over everything he knew. Someone had to have been watching the house and followed them. But they'd hung back for a long time. They'd been on the road for over an hour before the attack. Had they just been waiting for the right opportunity? What if they'd never gotten off the highway? Would they have been followed all the way to Florence?

And why? They'd uncovered very little information, but they'd made someone nervous. His mind jumped around, thinking about all the people they'd spoken to in the last few days. There were too many to count. He sighed as the frustration only made his head hurt.

He didn't know what to do next. If it was just him, he'd keep going. But it wasn't just him. Isabella was part of this, too, and she didn't want to leave Italy, and he wasn't sure he could make her go. But he also wasn't sure he could keep her safe.

The door opened, and the doctor entered.

He quickly sat up, then winced as pain ran through his head.

"Easy," the doctor said with a kind smile. "It looks like you have similar injuries to your friend."

"Is Isabella all right?"

"She will be," the doctor said, relieving him of one worry. "Let's take a look at you."

———

Isabella was done first, the cut on her head stitched and taped, and antiseptic applied to multiple scratches on her arms and face. The doctor believed she had a mild concussion and a severely bruised knee, but an X-ray hadn't revealed any greater damage. Her ribs were also bruised, but the pain medication she'd been given had already kicked in by the time she got to the waiting room. She was just grateful she wasn't in worse condition, because she could have been dead or paralyzed or suffered any number of other injuries.

She drew in a deep breath as those thoughts sent a wave of fear coursing through her. But she was okay, and she needed to be grateful, and maybe more on guard. She hadn't thought she was being careless, but maybe the prettiness of the day and the scenery and being with Nick had made her feel like nothing bad was going to happen. The evil had certainly come out of nowhere. She had been checking her mirrors during the trip, and she had not seen that car until it was roaring down the highway at a tremendous rate of speed.

She really should have let Nick drive. Maybe he would have been able to get them away. But she didn't see how. There had been nowhere to go, and his grandmother's small, economical car had been no match for the powerful vehicle intent on running them off the road.

It would have looked like another accident in a line of accidents that were probably all murders—every last one of them. That was two people in Nick's family and one person in hers. They couldn't walk away from this. They couldn't let evil win.

But convincing Nick they needed to stay together and fight this out wouldn't be easy. He felt responsible for her injuries. But he wasn't, and she needed to make him see that.

The door opened and as Nick walked out, she got to her feet, noting that the cuts on his face and arms had also been cleaned and treated. But he looked as pale and as tired as she felt.

"Well?" he asked. "What's the diagnosis?"

"Mild concussion, bruised knee, sore ribs, and some stinging cuts. What about you?"

"I've got a few aches and pains, but I'm all right."

She had a feeling he was downplaying some of those aches and pains considering he'd been thrown out of their vehicle. "I'm glad you're okay."

"Right back at you. And you can rest on the long trip home to California."

"I can't fly yet. Not with a mild concussion." She actually had no idea if that was true, but the reason had just jumped into her head, and she'd latched onto it.

"Is that true?" he asked doubtfully.

"Didn't the doctor tell you that?"

"I don't have a concussion, but I could go in there and ask him whether you can fly," he said pointedly.

"Or you can just believe me. I do want to rest, but I can do that on the train to Florence."

His lips tightened. "If anything, we should return to Rome."

"We're closer to Florence, and that house isn't exactly a safe harbor. I think we should go to Florence, get a hotel room, and then figure out what we want to do tomorrow."

"I don't know, Isabella. I appreciate your fight—I do. I'm incredibly impressed by how strong you are. But sometimes you just have to quit."

"I don't quit, Nick, and neither do you. I get that you don't want to be responsible for me, so if you don't want to stay in a hotel together, I will go to my mother's house."

His eyebrows shot up in surprise. "Seriously?"

"Well, I don't want to," she said honestly. "But I'm not running away, so if you want to part ways, then so be it. I'll stay with my mother, and I will not be your responsibility."

He stared back at her. "No."

"No?" she echoed, waiting for more. "No to what?"

"If we're both going to Florence, we're staying together. That way I can keep an eye on you."

She was relieved by his words, because she really didn't want to stay with her mother, who presented an altogether different danger. "Good. And I can keep an eye on you, too. I was just about to look up the train schedules."

"Let's sit down while we do that."

"Are you sure you're okay, Nick?"

"I will be, Isabella. Don't give me another thought."

She wished she could make that promise, but when she wasn't thinking about almost dying, she was thinking about him and the kiss that she'd woken up to. She didn't even know if it had been much of a kiss at all, but it had been enough to pull her out of the darkness. She just didn't know what else it was pulling her into, and she was afraid to find out.

CHAPTER TWENTY-TWO

They turned off their phones before leaving the hospital, because Nick was concerned they could be used for tracking. Now that they had become a target, he wanted to be even more careful. They boarded a train for Florence a little after three, and she slid into the seat by the window while Nick took the aisle.

At first, she worried they were trapped on the train, and every time the door at the end of their carriage opened, she tensed, but gradually she relaxed. And at some point, she fell asleep, not waking up until Nick told her they'd arrived.

As she opened her eyes, she realized she had her head on Nick's shoulder and was snuggled up against him.

"Sorry," she muttered.

"No need to apologize. I'm glad you got some sleep."

"I bet you didn't. You were probably determined to stay awake and alert."

"I'll take a nap later."

When the train stopped, they gathered their things and left the carriage. Nick took her hand as they walked through the busy station, and she was more than happy to have his fingers wrapped around hers. They got a cab in front of the station, and Nick gave the driver the name of a hotel. She assumed it was some place he'd stayed before, and she didn't much care. She was just looking forward to getting somewhere safe where they could regroup.

The trip from the train station to the center of town was very scenic, with a glimpse of iconic old churches, narrow medieval streets and a mix of old-world charm and more modern buildings. But driving over the Arno River on the famous Ponte Vecchio bridge was the highlight. The bridge was lined with shops selling mostly touristy items, but also jewelry and art.

The traffic grew thicker as they entered the center of the city. There were so many cars, so many people, and for a moment, she felt a little panicked. Had it been smart to come here, to this crowded city filled with strangers, two of whom could be the men who ran them off the road?

"Wouldn't they have guessed we were heading here?" she asked Nick, seeing the answer in his eyes even before he spoke.

"Probably. We've been talking a lot about David Leoni. Someone might figure we'd go to the gallery to ask more questions. Or we'd look for his family."

"That's true. But my mother also lives here. Would they go after her?"

"She hasn't been involved in anything, Isabella. I'm not sure anyone would know about her."

"Stefano knows she's in Florence. But they were in love when they were kids. I don't think he would hurt her. And we don't know if he's a part of this."

"We'll talk about everything when we're in our room."

"This is where we're staying?" she asked in surprise as the taxi stopped in front of a beautiful hotel.

"Were you expecting more or less?"

"Less," she said as he helped her out of the car. "It's luxurious. Have you stayed here before?"

"Once with my parents. And I like it for several reasons. It has a twenty-four-hour doorman, concierge, controlled access to the elevators, and room service."

She hadn't thought about food in hours, but now that he'd mentioned it, she was feeling hungry. And since her headache was returning, it might be a good idea to eat something before she took more medication.

As they approached the front desk to check in, she noted a curious look coming from the clerk, but she didn't comment on their ragged appearance.

She was surprised again when Nick used another name and pulled an ID and credit card out of his wallet that apparently matched that name. The man had some tricks up his sleeve.

When they got the key to their room, they headed to the elevator, where they had to insert the key into a card slot in front of an attendant, which made her feel better. But she was still nervous when a man got in the elevator with them. He was older, wearing a suit and glasses. He barely glanced at them, but she couldn't help but slide closer to Nick. He was quickly becoming her anchor in a very chaotic sea.

She didn't take a full breath until they entered their room and Nick turned the deadbolt. She dropped her bag on the floor and sat down on one of two queen-size beds. Nick walked over to a table by the window and took his computer out of his backpack.

He opened it and turned it on, then said, "It still works. I wasn't sure after the pummeling my backpack took."

"I hope mine does, too," she said, but she didn't have the energy to check. Instead, she got up and grabbed the room service menu before getting back onto the bed, scooting toward the pillows so her back was supported against the headboard. Her head was hurting, and she felt a little shaky. She needed to take more pain medication soon, and she wanted something in her stomach.

"What do you want to eat?" she asked, glancing at the clock. It was only five thirty, which was practically lunch time in Italy, but since she had eaten nothing all day, she needed food no matter what the meal was called.

"I could eat anything. Or maybe everything."

"Me, too. It's a good menu. Meat, pasta, fish, pizza...they have it all."

"Why don't you order a couple of entrees, and we can share? Throw in a salad and dessert, too. And charge it to the room."

"Sounds good, Mr. Jamison," she said, sending him a pointed look.

"I never know when I need to be someone else," he said with a smile.

"How many identities do you have?"

"On me?"

"Let's start there."

"Two. Bill Jamison and myself."

"You have two passports?"

He nodded. "Yes. Hopefully, using that identity will keep anyone from tracking us. But I need more than another ID," he murmured. "I need a weapon."

"You didn't come over with one?"

He shook his head. "Italy has strict rules about bringing guns into the country, even if you're in law enforcement. I would have had to go through a lot of red tape, and there wasn't time for that. I'll see if Flynn can help me out with a local contact."

"I thought we weren't using our phones."

"My computer has an encrypted text app," he replied.

While he did that, she picked up the hotel phone and called room service, probably ordering way too much food, but she was suddenly starving. When that was done, she headed into the bathroom to take a shower or maybe a bath, she thought, when she saw the large tub. She needed to relax and get her head together.

———

When Isabella closed the door to the bathroom, Nick called Flynn through his video app. It was past eight o'clock in the morning in LA, and Flynn answered almost immediately, but he was not in the office. He was outside on what appeared to be a running path.

"Did I catch you at a bad time?" he asked.

"No. I'm just doing my cooldown. What did you think of my email?"

"Great work. Now, I need another favor. I need a gun." He gave Flynn a quick wrap-up on what had happened, both to Catherine at the party and to them on the road. "I have to be better prepared for next time, because there will be another time. I can't split up from Isabella now, either. We've been together since I arrived in Rome. They know who she is. I need to keep her close so I can protect her."

"You could come back to the States, both of you."

"I can't do that yet. I know what the risks are, Flynn. What I'm doing is not sanctioned by the FBI. As far as you know, I'm just on vacation. If I get into trouble, it will be on me. If I lose my job because of this, then that's what happens. This is my family. And since someone just tried to kill me, I'm even more determined to find them."

"I understand. I'll see if I can hook you up with a local contact who doesn't work for the bureau. Anything else you need?"

"That's good for now." He didn't mention he'd spoken to Flynn's father, and Flynn didn't ask.

"Good luck, Nick. Take care of yourself. I need you on my team."

"I plan to be back on your team as soon as possible." Despite his words, as he clicked out of the chat, he felt very far away from his life as a member of Flynn's team. It had only been a few days, but it felt like years since he'd been doing his job, being someone else, living a fake life.

The word fake reminded him that he and his great-grandfather might have that in common. But even if Tomas had cut corners in life, he knew his grandfather, Marcus, had not. And he believed now more than ever that Marcus had been killed because he was trying to right a wrong from the past that probably had to do with Tomas and Lucinda, because he'd had the info on Juliette in his file. Or he was just trying to get to the truth.

A truth that might kill him and Isabella, too, if they weren't careful...maybe even if they were careful.

———

The food arrived just after Isabella left the bathroom, looking much less pale. He needed a shower, too, but he was more interested in eating.

They sat down at the table and instead of each picking a dish, they shared everything. He tried a salmon filet first while Isabella went for the pasta. But they didn't stay with their first choices, sometimes laughing, as they both went for the same dish or the same bite, and he was feeling better by the minute.

When they'd finished eating, Isabella got up and stretched out on the nearest bed. "Now I'm full and exhausted. Is it okay if I take this bed?"

"Of course," he said, wishing he could share it with her. He'd enjoyed having her fall asleep on his shoulder when they were on the train. He liked keeping her close.

"I finally feel more relaxed," she said. "We're safe here, right?"

"I believe so."

"You could have just given me an emphatic yes."

"You would have seen right through that. You know what the odds are—same as me. In this case, I think the odds are good."

"I never thought I'd feel this comfortable with you, Nick. I never thought I'd like you so much, or that I'd ever trust you. After you were such a jerk that first night, I never wanted to see you again."

"You could have stopped at you never thought you'd like me so much."

She laughed. "I could have."

"I like you, too, Isabella, even though sometimes you're like a long-stemmed rose with a lot of thorns. Beautiful, but if you get too close or put your hand on the wrong part of the stem, you could get hurt."

Her expression darkened. "Is that how you see me?"

"You're a woman with a lot of sharp edges, finely honed to guard her heart. But you also have a big heart, and the courage of a lion."

"How can I be a rose and a lion at the same time?"

"I don't know, but somehow you are." He paused as his computer dinged with an incoming text. He grabbed it from the dresser where he'd put it when they'd sat down to eat.

"It's Captain Lavezzo," he said in surprise. "He wants to know if I can come in tomorrow and talk to him."

"About what?"

"It doesn't say."

Another text from Lavezzo came in: *Tomorrow morning at nine would be good. Please confirm that you can be there. It's important that we speak in person.*"

"He wants to meet in person tomorrow at nine."

"What are you going to say? We'd have to leave tonight to get there in time, unless there's a really early train in the morning."

He considered his options. Lavezzo had been at the party last night, arguing with Catherine. He might have even killed her. Despite his presence at the party, he'd been surprisingly absent from the follow-up investigation. Now Lavezzo wanted to talk to him. And he didn't like it.

If Lavezzo had killed Catherine, maybe he'd sent the two men who had come after them. If he texted back, Lavezzo would know they were alive. If he said he wasn't in town, that would also raise the question of where he was, and he didn't want to give that information, either.

"I'm not going to answer him now," he said. "I'll text him tomorrow after we talk to your mom and try to find Leoni's family. I don't want to go back before we have a chance to do both things."

"Could you just make the appointment with Lavezzo later in the day?"

He closed his computer and set it on the chair. Then he sat down on the bed next to her. "I don't want him to know we're alive and not in Rome."

"Oh." Realization entered her eyes. "Good point. After I saw him and Catherine together right before she died, I have to wonder if he's on the right side of the law or not."

"I agree, and he can do whatever he needs to do without us. Not showing up in his office doesn't prevent him from doing his job."

"Okay. I trust you, Nick."

Her words touched him in a surprising way. He'd wanted her trust. And he'd certainly thought he had it. But hearing her say it felt very different.

She cocked her head as their gazes held together for a long minute. "You're staring at me."

"You're staring back."

"I have trouble not looking at you," she admitted. "Especially now that you're banged up in a really sexy way."

He laughed. "I didn't know it was possible to be banged up in a sexy way."

"It definitely is."

As she ran her tongue across her lips, his body tightened.

"Nick," she continued.

"Yes?"

"I want to kiss you."

His stomach flipped over, and he had to clench his fists to stop himself from immediately reaching for her. "You're hurt and you need to rest. You don't need a kiss."

Disappointment ran through her eyes. "You said it was my decision."

"This isn't the right time. You've been through a lot, probably feeling a little buzz from the adrenaline. You're grateful to be alive. Kissing me seems like a good idea, but you're not thinking straight. You have a concussion."

"Wow, are you done yet?" she asked.

"I might be," he said, seeing the humor dancing in her eyes now. "Too much?"

"You always try to do the right thing, don't you?"

"Not always."

"Oh, I think so. You have to pretend to be a lot of things you're not: dangerous, evil, uncaring, cold, ruthless...but you're none of those things. You're a good guy, Nick. It's okay to be that."

He sucked in a breath. "To be honest, Isabella, I've lost track of who I really am. I've had to walk a lot of fine lines, and sometimes I don't know if I'm going too far into the dark side."

"I don't know who you are on the job, maybe more like the guy I first met. But the man I've gotten to know the past few days is impressive. And I really want to kiss him...if he'll let me."

"You're killing me."

"Not yet."

"Here's the thing, Isabella. I don't know if I want to stop with a kiss."

She met his gaze. "Who said anything about stopping? I know what I want, Nick, and you're not taking advantage of me. If anything, I'm taking advantage of you. And it doesn't have to mean more than it is."

"What is it?"

She shrugged. "Do you want to find out?"

He slid down the side of the bed and cupped her beautiful, slightly battered face with his hands. And then he lowered his head and kissed her. He wanted to go slow, to savor every second, but her mouth was too hot, too needy, too welcoming, and he couldn't get enough.

He pressed her back against the pillows as he ran his fingers through her hair, trapping her head for another kiss before sliding his lips down the beautiful curve of her neck. It was only the red, raised scratches that gave him pause. He lifted his head to look into her eyes.

"Please tell me you're not stopping," she said.

His body hardened at the urgent need in her voice. "I don't want to hurt you. You're pretty scratched up."

"You're not going to hurt me, and I'm not going to hurt you. We'll make each other feel better."

Her words made it all sound so simple and when she took off her top, he completely lost all sense of reason. Her breasts were soft and full, and when she pulled him down on top of her, he went willingly.

He would make her feel good and make himself feel good. He just hoped she was right about them not hurting each other. Maybe it could just stay as simple as she'd made it sound. But he really didn't think so.

Fortunately, he was done thinking.

CHAPTER TWENTY-THREE

The worst day had been followed by the best night, Isabella thought, as she woke up Tuesday morning, with Nick's arms wrapped around her, his breath lifting the hair by her ear. She felt deliciously warm, and she didn't want to move. She wanted more of Nick, more kisses, more touches, more of everything. She wanted to stay in this bed forever, because she couldn't remember feeling this good, even though she knew there were plenty of dark shadows dancing just outside this happy bubble.

As the sun streamed brighter through the windows of their hotel room, she also knew it would soon be time to move on, to do what they'd come to Florence to do, which certainly hadn't been sleeping together.

But she didn't have any regrets, at least not yet. Frowning at that thought, she pushed away the feeling of foreboding. It didn't matter what came next. She wouldn't trade making love with Nick for anything. He'd been impatient and urgent at times, but also slow and savoring in a way that drove her crazy. He'd thrown her off-balance and kept her there, which was a rare experience for her. She liked to control the pace of sex, the way things were happening, but sometimes her brain got in the way of just being in the moment. That hadn't happened last night.

Nick had taken the lead, and she'd let him, because his lead was really, really good.

As his arms tightened around her, he murmured, "Morning, beautiful."

She turned over to face him, dislodging his arms around her, but he immediately put them back as he gave her a smile.

"How's the head?"

"A lot better. You cured me."

He laughed. "You cured me, too. Just what the doctor ordered."

She smiled back at him. "Somehow, I don't think that's what the doctor ordered when he told us both to get to bed early and rest."

"We followed part of that order," he said as he gave her a long, slow kiss.

She loved the feel of his mouth on hers, the way his fingers ran down her bare back, evoking all sorts of hot memories from the night before. But her brain was starting to kick in. "You have to stop doing that, or we're never going to get out of bed."

"I can think of worse things."

"Like going to see my mother."

"What will that be like?" he asked, giving her a thoughtful look. "Will there be screaming? Or will it be cold, quiet, awkward, uncomfortable tension?"

"Maybe all the above." She paused, searching for the right words. "I don't hate her, Nick. I just had to stop loving her so much because it was too difficult."

He propped himself up on one elbow as his gaze narrowed. "Because she trusted the wrong man and ended up in jail?"

"That was the biggest mistake. Or maybe the second biggest mistake."

"What would have been the first?"

"Having unprotected sex with a man who didn't want to be a father and having a baby when she was twenty-one, with no money, no family support."

"That must have been rough."

"She tried to be a good mom. She was fun when I was little. She was so young herself that she would play games with me all the time. But she had to work, too, and that meant that I was on my own. Still, that time in my life was better than when she got married. We moved into a nicer house, and I had a bigger bedroom. But she was around even less, and it wasn't because she was working, it was because of Gary. She wanted to be the perfect wife. She completely changed everything about herself to do that. She wasn't fun anymore. She wasn't spontaneous. She didn't pick me up from school and say let's go have an adventure like she did when I was little. It was all about entertaining, exercising and looking good for Gary, dressing right, and making sure I wasn't causing any problems."

"You—cause problems?" he teased.

She made a face at him. "I wasn't that bad. I just hated watching her fade away. But she wouldn't listen to me. She did not want to hear what I had to say, and then her fairytale completely unraveled. She was shamed and dropped by her friends when the truth came out about Gary and the fraud she was helping him perpetuate. It was awful and got worse when she went to prison while I was trying to finish high school."

"What about after she got out? What happened then? Did you move back in together in Chicago?"

"I was at NYU when she was released. I'd gotten a partial scholarship and was working, too. My grandmother helped us both. She sent my mother money so she could rent a studio apartment in Chicago. There wasn't room for me there, and, honestly, I didn't want to see her. I was angry."

"That's understandable."

"One year turned into the next, and we'd text occasionally. She'd call every now and then. On school vacations, I'd go to a friend's house or just stay in New York. I didn't see her for several years, not until my college graduation. She was supposed to come with my grandmother. But she brought a date, a man who talked a lot about AA, how he'd gotten sober six months earlier, and how he'd spent time in jail after a DUI. I guess they had that in common. He was trying to change his life, but all I saw was another loser. After that, I told myself I just didn't have to care about her anymore. But it kept bothering me. His history —her history. She was going down another bad road, this time with someone who seemed unstable."

"What did you do?"

"Nothing right away. I waited too long. It was almost two years after that graduation party before I made it back to Chicago to see them. I got in a day early, and I found them both drunk. I had to get him into rehab and my mother back on her feet. By the time I returned to New York, I'd lost my job. I had to start over. All because of her bad choices. After that, I was done. I couldn't be a part of her drama. I'd occasionally text her back if she said hello, but I didn't want to know anything else. That probably sounds selfish."

"You needed to protect yourself. I can see why loving her is hard."

"I feel bad that I don't do more for her sometimes," she confessed. "I am her daughter. And I want her to be okay. I hope the move here is a good one. When I heard about it, I didn't know what to think. Maybe my grandmother is right. Coming back to Italy will remind my mother of who she was, who she once wanted to be. Hopefully, it's not too late for her to be happy."

"I don't think it's too late for her to be happy or for you to reconnect with her."

"Well, we're doing that today, so we'll see. You don't have to worry about what you're walking into. She's not horrible. She's just...I don't know how to describe her, because she's been a lot of different people. I'm not sure who she is now, who she is on her own. But she might not be on her own. She mentioned something about a man in her life again, so there's that." She blew out a breath. "I'm sorry. I'm rambling on, and I don't usually do this. I don't talk about her. I don't bring my friends to meet her."

A smile played across his lips. "So, we're friends now?"

"I think we became more than friends last night." She didn't want to think about how much more, because her feelings for Nick were a little too strong. "We should move on with the day, get showered, dressed."

"Hang on," he said as she started to get up. "Don't flip the switch that fast."

"We have a lot to do."

"And we'll do it. But don't jump out of bed because you suddenly remembered how good last night was."

"I wasn't thinking that at all," she lied. "I just need to use the bathroom. Why don't you order breakfast?" She slid out of bed and hurried into the bathroom, very aware of Nick's eyes following her every step of the way.

———

After breakfast, they left their hotel room just after ten. As Nick escorted Isabella downstairs, he could feel her tension. She'd been unusually quiet since she'd gotten dressed, and he wasn't sure what was going on in her head. Maybe she was nervous about seeing her mother again, or she regretted last night, or perhaps she was worried someone would try to kill them again.

Just going through all that in his head made him tense, too. Not about her mother or their night together, but the real possibility that someone would try to hurt them and that he wouldn't be able to protect her. He needed to make sure that didn't happen.

He felt better today. The pain in his head had settled into a dull ache, and he'd had a shower and a good breakfast, so he was ready to face whatever was coming.

An electronics store two blocks from the hotel was their first stop. He took Isabella's hand when they left the hotel, acutely aware of everyone in their immediate vicinity. Their destination was located on a side street under the shadow of the Duomo, Florence's magnificent cathedral. There were no customers in the shop, only one older guy working the counter.

On the way to that counter, he picked up two prepaid phones. "Ciao," he said. "I'll take these, and I'm picking up a package for Bill Jamison."

The guy gave him a sharp look and then went into the back room, returning with an unmarked cardboard box. Nick paid with his alias credit card. The man said absolutely nothing as he handed him a receipt.

After leaving the shop, he led Isabella around the corner and into the shadow of an alley where there were no people and no cameras. He opened the box and took out the gun and ammunition provided. He loaded the weapon and tucked it between his lower back and the waistband of his jeans, pulling his shirt down over it. He put the rest of the ammunition and one phone in his backpack. The other phone he handed to Isabella.

She'd gone a little pale at the sight of the gun. "You think we're going to need a weapon?" she asked.

"I hope not."

"The danger seems very real again."

"It is real. You can't forget that. Let's find a cab."

They returned to the main street and flagged down a taxi. Several minutes later, they pulled up in front of the art gallery owned by Dario Micheli. The gallery was one large room with dividers set up to steer visitors into different time periods.

As they looked around, a man came out of a back room. He was short and stocky, with a receding hairline and thick glasses.

He gave them a friendly smile. "*Buon Giorno.*"

"Are you the manager?" Nick asked.

"*Sí*. I am Elio Barone. How can I help you? Are you looking for a particular artist or style of art?"

"I'm interested in art by David Leoni. I understand you

showed one of his paintings several months ago, but it was stolen," he said.

Elio's smile faded. "Unfortunately, that is correct, and we have no others by Signor Leoni."

"My name is Nick Caruso. This is Isabella Rossi. Each of our families donated paintings to the Museo dei Capolavori, and they were also stolen. It came to our attention that the robbery here was similar, and that David Leoni was a friend of the painters in our family, Tomas Caruso and Lucinda Rossi. Have you heard of them?"

"I haven't. I'm sorry to learn of your loss, but I don't know how I can help you."

"Could you put us in touch with the owner of that painting? We'd like to see if we can find a connection between the artists and their paintings."

Elio hesitated. "I'm sorry, but I cannot give out that information."

He'd had a feeling that would be Elio's response.

"Do you have a photo of the painting that was stolen?" Isabella asked.

"That I can help you with." Elio opened a drawer and looked through some papers, pulling out a brochure that listed several paintings with details about the artist and the price of the painting. He turned to one of the last pages and handed it to Isabella. "This is it."

"Can we take this with us?" she asked.

"*Sí*. I don't need it anymore."

"*Grazie*," she said.

As a group of customers entered the gallery, Elio moved away to help them, and they left the gallery.

Isabella paused on the sidewalk to look at the brochure. "Leoni's painting has a similarly narrow point of view, Nick. It's a picture of stones, weathered by water or wind. The background around the stones is blurry, out of focus. It feels very much like the ones by Tomas and Lucinda." She handed him the flyer.

"Tomas's painting was a bird in a tree, the branches of which faded into a blur of colors." Her brows drew together as she thought. "And Lucinda's painting was of steps that went to nowhere and the edges were blurred. That's kind of weird, don't you think?"

"Frankly, I think most art is strange."

"But don't you see that each painting is featuring a specific thing?"

"That's true," he muttered as he handed her the brochure.

"I wonder if they go together in some way. If there's a reason you need all the paintings to see the full picture."

His pulse sped up at her words. "You might be on to something."

"It has been known to happen," she said, a smug smile on her lips.

As she put the brochure in her bag, he pulled out his phone and flipped to the photos he'd gotten from his grandmother. "Here's Frederico's painting. It's a little different, just shapes and geometric tiles, but the edges are blurred, which matches the others."

She looked at the picture on his phone. "It feels very much the same, but I don't know what the shapes represent. However, I still think I'm on to something."

"I think so, too, but how many more paintings are there?" he asked.

"At least one—the gift from Tomas to the mysterious *J*. If *J* was Juliette Sabatini, then she either had the painting and her descendant has it now, or the *J* is someone else."

He went over that scenario in his mind. "If we agree Catherine is Juliette's daughter, then I don't think she had the fifth painting, because after the museum robbery, there was a break-in at our house. That wouldn't have happened if all the paintings were together. There has to be at least one that is missing. And maybe you're right. *J* could be someone else."

"I think if we could put all the paintings together, we'd be able to see the full picture, and then we'd know what is going on."

"That's true. But—"

"No buts, Nick. It's too early to rip my brilliant theory apart. At least let me have a minute of satisfaction."

He smiled. "I was just going to say that if the paintings form some sort of picture, that's great, but why would anyone need to steal the actual canvas if they could just take a picture and put it together, the way we're doing?"

"Damn. That's a good question."

"There has to be something else about the paintings."

"Something on the back of the canvas," she suggested. "That you can't see unless you physically have it in your hands."

"Or, as Sam suggested, the paintings could be covering another canvas, maybe a priceless original or a counterfeit."

"Okay. You might be on to something now, too."

"Thank you. I'm still giving you credit for tying them together. We're just not all the way there. But there might be someone who can help us get there."

Isabella let out a long sigh. "Yes. It's time to see my mother."

CHAPTER TWENTY-FOUR

Isabella grew increasingly more tense as they got in a taxi and headed for her mother's apartment. Nick had helped her access her texts on his encrypted computer before leaving the hotel, so she had her mom's address, and she had decided against calling her mother first. She was just going to drop in and see what happened.

Nick put his hand over one of hers, and it was only then she realized she was tapping a relentless beat on her thighs.

"I want to say it will be okay," he began. "But I don't know if it will."

"Me, either. And I appreciate you acknowledging that." She drew in a breath and let it out. "But I'm not going to see her so we can suddenly repair a relationship that broke a long time ago. This is about the paintings, and I want to make that clear to her. I don't want her to think I have another reason for visiting."

"Isabella, don't do that."

"Don't do what?"

"Put up barriers before you need them."

"That's when you put barriers up—to prepare for disaster," she said.

"Or...you can see how things go without trying to control or define everything in advance."

"You really don't know me, because I always prepare." She didn't like the gleam of amusement in his eyes. "It's not a bad thing. It saves me from being surprised."

"Or it prevents you from being in the moment."

"Well, it's my mother. I get to do what I want. I'm not telling you to go to your parents' vow renewal and try to rebuild that relationship. So, I'm not sure you should give advice."

He put up a hand. "Fair point. I just have one more thing to say."

"Am I going to want to hear it?"

"Probably not. Let's find out."

"What?"

"I'm not telling you to keep an open mind for your mom. I want you to do it for yourself. You feel conflicted about her. You have good memories and bad memories. You don't really know who she is anymore, and until you let her show you who she is, you're always going to be confused."

His words made sense, even though she didn't enjoy hearing them. "You're not completely wrong. It's just messy and complicated. And I don't like messy and complicated. I don't think you do, either. That's why you're trying to solve big problems and clean up the dirt in the world."

"One thing I've learned from going undercover is that I can't control what's happening around me. All I can do is adapt. I have to be flexible and trust in myself."

"That doesn't sound easy."

"It's easier when I stay focused on the goal. Our goal today is not to fight with your mom, but to get her to help us."

"I can't make any promises."

"You really have a thing about not making promises," he said dryly.

"It's better than promising things I can't deliver."

"I suppose."

She saw the disappointment in his eyes and knew she had to say something else. "I heard you, Nick. I'll try."

He met her gaze. "Good."

A few minutes later, the cab pulled up in front of a building in the Murate art district, a mixed-use neighborhood with apartment buildings interspersed with cafés, boutiques, and artisan shops.

After exiting the taxi, they walked through an iron gate to the front door of a three-story building. There appeared to be three units, and her mother was renting the bottom floor from the owner of the art gallery where she worked.

She took a breath, squared her shoulders, and rang the bell. The door opened a second later, and she stared into a face very much like her own. Her mother had the same dark-brown hair, down to the wild waves that were hard to tame. Her eyes were also brown with flecks of gold, but her mom was shorter than she was by about four inches.

Shock ran across her mother's face as they gazed at each other. There were other emotions, too, but she couldn't get caught up in them.

"Isabella," her mother finally said. "I was not expecting to see you."

"Can we come in?"

At her question, her mother's gaze moved to Nick, then back to her. "Are you going to introduce me to your friend?"

"This is Nick Caruso, Anna's grandson." She didn't know why she felt compelled to label him in a way that didn't make it seem like he was her friend, but it was too late to take it back.

Nick shot her a sharp look and then turned to her mother. "It's nice to meet you, Sylvie. I've heard a lot about you."

"I've heard a few things about you as well. What are you both doing here? Is something wrong? Is my mother all right?" She paused, her gaze narrowing. "What happened to your face, Isabella?"

"It's nothing. I'm fine."

"It doesn't look like nothing."

"Why don't we talk inside?" Nick suggested.

Sylvie's lips tightened. "Come in." She stepped back and waved them into the apartment.

Isabella's first impression of her mother's living space was of bright colors, warm sunlight, and greenery everywhere, not only indoor plants, but a beautiful garden patio accessed by French doors in the small living room. There was art on the walls, a mix of eclectic paintings, and at least six different mirrors with mosaic inlays and other decorative notes.

Seeing her mother's space now reminded her of the first apartment she could remember living in with her mom. They hadn't had a yard, but her mother had made a little garden on the balcony with both real and fake plants that could survive the brutal cold of a Chicago winter, making her feel like they were surrounded by plants even though they were in the middle of a city.

"What's going on?" her mother asked as they stood in the living room. "Do you want to sit down? Do you want something to drink? What's happening? Is something wrong with your grandmother?"

"Grandma is fine," she said, instinctively wanting to ease the worry in her mother's eyes.

"Okay, good." Her mother let out a breath of relief.

"But there was a robbery at the museum where she and Anna volunteer," she continued. "They weren't hurt, but the paintings they donated to an exhibition were stolen—one by Tomas and one by Lucinda."

"Are you serious? I can't believe Lucinda's painting is gone, although, to be honest, I thought I lost it a long time ago."

"Why would you think that?"

"After I moved to Chicago for school, I went looking for it and couldn't find it. I thought I might have accidentally thrown it away with my boxes. But then your grandmother told me last week that she'd found it and put it in a show at her museum and hoped I didn't mind. Which I didn't. But—it was stolen? I don't understand. Why didn't my mother tell me?"

"She didn't want to worry you while you were getting settled into your new life."

"But she told you."

"Yes. And I jumped on a plane."

"Always eager to help your grandmother."

There was an edge to her mom's voice that she could not tolerate. "Why wouldn't I be? She saved me from foster care. And she saved you, too, more than once."

"You're right. Why are you both here now?"

"Well, a couple of reasons." She tried to sound focused and businesslike. "Grandma and Anna went to the States. We got them out of Italy just in time. There was a break-in at their house after they left, and since then, well, it appears that someone may be trying to stop me and Nick from asking questions."

"Your face," her mother said again. "What exactly happened?"

"Someone ran our car off the road. We were in an accident, but we're okay."

Her mother turned to Nick. "Is she okay?"

She didn't like that her mom needed Nick to confirm what she'd already told her.

"She's good," Nick said shortly. "But she was lucky, and so was I. We need to find out who's after us. And we believe you might be able to help."

"I don't see how. I didn't even know about the robbery."

"But you know Lucinda's work, her painting," Nick said. "And what's happening is tied to that."

"I studied Lucinda's work when I was young. She was my inspiration to be an artist. I was fascinated by her. I even went to the school where she used to teach. I wanted to be exactly like her, but I was never as talented as she was." Her mother paused. "The painting that was stolen wasn't nearly as good as some of the sketches in her book, so it didn't mean that much to me. I was sad that the rest of her work had been destroyed in the fire that took her life, so I clung to what she had left." She paused. "I still can't believe someone stole that painting. It was lying around in my closet when I was a teenager. I never thought it was that important."

"We need to figure out why it was valuable," she said, feeling her headache returning, which probably had more to do with this uncomfortable situation than the car accident.

Her mother gave her a sharp look. "You look pale. You need to sit down. I'm going to get us some lemonade."

As her mother moved into the small kitchen, she and Nick sat down on the sofa. It felt better to be off her feet. While her mother was getting the drinks, she looked around the apartment once more, her gaze coming to rest on three small, framed photographs on the side table. They were all of her and her mother, two taken when she was under five, the third from her twelfth birthday, right before her mother married Gary.

She was stunned to see them displayed on her mother's table. When her mother and Gary had gotten married, the only photographs in the house had been of the three of them or her mom and Gary alone. Her mother had told her she didn't want Gary to feel like he wasn't part of their family.

So why bring these photos back now?

Her stomach twisted with tension. She didn't want to do this. She didn't want to think her mother missed those days, because those days were long gone.

Nick followed her gaze and picked up the photo nearest to him. "You were a cute kid."

"I don't know why she has those out," she said tightly.

He gave her a compassionate look and put the photo down. "Because she wants to remember the good times. Maybe you do, too."

She felt too choked up to argue with him.

"I'm going to help your mom." He gave her leg a squeeze before getting to his feet.

She didn't want him to help her mother or to like her mother, but she couldn't tell him that. It would make her sound childish, and maybe that's what she was being. She wasn't a kid anymore; she was an adult, and she needed to act like one.

Nick and her mother returned a moment later, and she put her game face on. He handed her a lemonade and sat down as her mom took the chair across from them.

A long sip of the sugary drink almost immediately gave her more energy. "So, we need to figure out what Lucinda and Tomas's work had to do with paintings by Frederico Germain and David Leoni," she said. "All four artists had their paintings stolen this year, and we know they painted together at Tomas's studio."

"That's true," her mother said. "Frederico was about ten years younger than Lucinda and David was probably twenty-five years younger."

She was surprised her mother knew that much. "How do you know that?"

"I read Lucinda's diary. She talked a lot about the people she painted with at Tomas's studio."

"Lucinda had a diary? Do you have it?"

"No. I got rid of it years ago."

"How could you do that?"

"I asked my mother, and she didn't want it. You cared nothing about art, Isabella. I didn't think it would matter to you."

"It would matter now that we're trying to figure out if she and Tomas were killed."

Her mother's jaw dropped. "The fire wasn't an accident?"

"It's looking less likely. Someone also suggested to us that Lucinda was a forger, that she was copying, not creating. What do you know about that?"

"I know she copied a lot when she was learning her craft. Her sketches recreating famous paintings were very good. But if you're asking me if she said that's what she was doing in her diary, she did not."

"Okay. So, you're an artist—"

"I'm trying to be again, but I haven't been in a long time."

She ignored that as she reached into her bag and pulled out the brochure from the gallery. "Here's the painting by David Leoni that was stolen six months ago." She handed it across the table. "Nick, can I have your phone? Is it okay if I turn it on for a moment?"

"I think so." He nodded, turned on his phone, and handed it to her."

"I want you to look at the painting in the brochure and then look at these," she told her mom. "Each one features a narrow focus with shadows or blurs at the edges."

"The stone wall is very well done," her mother murmured.

She got up and moved around the table to sit in the chair next to her mother. She held up the first photo by Tomas. "This is Tomas's bird in a tree." She flipped to the next picture. "Lucinda's stairway to nowhere." She gave her mother a chance to see each painting and then moved to the last one. "Frederico's patterned tiles. Am I crazy, or does it feel like they're all part of a bigger picture?"

Her mother took the phone from her hand and looked through the photos once more. "I think you might be right, Isabella. But how do they go together?"

"That's what I'm hoping you can tell me. Why would they pick these particular scenes to paint?"

"I can't read their minds. What do you think?"

She was shocked her mom wanted to know what she thought. "Well, someone stole all their paintings, so they have to go together. It's possible that the pictures form a bigger scene when put together, or the canvases are covering up stolen art or forgeries and this actual picture we're seeing means nothing."

"Those are two different ideas," her mom muttered.

"But there's another thing. We believe there is one more painting that they're looking for. Tomas exchanged letters with someone he only called *J*. It sounded like he'd given her a painting to keep safe. It also appeared that he had strong romantic feelings for her. I thought maybe Lucinda and Tomas were involved—"

"No, they weren't together that way," her mother said. "Lucinda wrote about Tomas in her diary. She wasn't in love with him. He was her best friend in the world. And she wanted him to be happy." Her mother paused. "She wanted him to stop running away from love that was complicated. He had feelings for her close friend, but her friend was married, and he said he couldn't pursue it."

"Who was the friend? Was it Juliette Sabatini?"

Her mother gave her a confused look. "No. I don't remember seeing that name in the diary. Her friend's name was Jasmine."

"Jasmine," she echoed, shooting Nick a quick look. "That starts with a *J*."

"Do you know her last name?" Nick asked.

"It was Pariso. I remember because Jasmine Pariso sounded so exotic and beautiful. It stuck with me. Lucinda and Jasmine inspired me. They were chasing their artistic dreams. And that's what I wanted to do. But I didn't want to be exactly like them, because they were weighed down by husbands, children, and responsibilities."

She frowned. "I don't get it, Mom. You say you were inspired by them, and you went to the States to have a life, to chase your dreams—what happened?"

"You know what happened. I had a baby. I couldn't be selfish and be an artist. I had to take care of you, Isabella."

"I know I was the dream killer, but what about when you met Gary? You could have painted then, but you didn't. You gave up every part of yourself to be his wife. You devoted yourself to him, to entertaining his friends, dressing the way he wanted you to, following him blindly." She hadn't meant to get started down this road, but now she couldn't stop. "Even after you got out of jail, what did you do? You fell for some other guy with a million problems that you had to take care of. What happened to the girl who traveled across the world to have her own life? You can't blame me for all the other bad choices."

Her mother stared back at her, moisture gathering in her eyes. "I don't blame you, Isabella, not for any of it. I made decisions, and a lot of them were bad. But that's why I'm here. I want to find myself again. I want to be someone you can be proud of."

She could feel herself weakening and feeling sorry for her mother, and she hated that. "You said a few weeks ago that you were talking to a man here. How long will it be before you become a part of his life and give up your own?"

Her mother flinched at her sharp words, and she felt a rush of regret, but she couldn't bring herself to apologize.

"You don't pull punches, Isabella. You are a strong woman, much stronger than I ever was. You won't lose yourself, and I'm glad about that. The man I was talking to is an old friend. His name is Stefano. A mutual friend told Stefano I was here, and he called me. We're planning to have dinner together this weekend. But it's not a date. It's just a catch up."

"It sounds like a date. He's single, isn't he?"

"He's divorced," her mother confirmed.

"So there's a chance dinner could be the beginning of a relationship."

"I don't believe so. He lives in Rome, and I live here. It's also been thirty years since we were together. And we were kids then. We're nothing like we used to be. I'm also not looking to get involved with anyone. I need to be on my own for a while. I know that."

"I hope that's true." She blew out a breath. "And I'm sorry. I didn't intend to say all that."

"You've been wanting to say it for a while. Frankly, I'm relieved you finally did. I'd rather have you yelling at me than freezing me out, like your grandfather used to do to me. The silence is always worse." Her mother paused. "I know I hurt you, Isabella. I will make it up to you some day. I don't know how, but I hope the first step is by living a life that won't make you ashamed of me."

She didn't know what to say to that, and her own eyes grew suspiciously moist. "We should get back to why we're here. Jasmine Pariso might be Tomas's secret letter recipient. How do we find her?" She looked at Nick, who had remained silent during the passionate exchange she'd just had with her mother. "It will be the middle of the night in California. You probably can't reach your team. Should we call Stefano?"

"Wait," her mother said in confusion. "You know Stefano?"

"We've met twice. He came by the house after the robbery to check on Grandma."

"That was considerate of him. Do you want me to call him?"

"No," Nick answered for her. "I don't think we should involve Stefano. I'm going to wake up someone on my team. I'll make my call from the patio."

Silence followed his departure. She folded, then unfolded her hands, then said, "I like the way you've decorated. It feels like how we used to live."

"It feels more like me," her mother agreed. "How are you, Isabella? How is your job? Your move to LA? Do you like it there?"

"The job is good. The weather is warmer."

"And Nick—is he your boyfriend?"

"No," she said quickly. "He's just..." She couldn't think of the right word.

Her mother gave her a knowing smile.

"Don't do that," she warned. "Don't start thinking there's anything happening with Nick. I'm not interested in a relation-ship. I have a career and a life." Although, she had to admit, her life had gotten better with Nick in it. However, that seemed like an ironic statement, considering they'd almost died together yesterday.

"You don't want to be like me, and I understand that. I didn't want to be like my mother, either. But I turned out to be more like her than I thought, afraid to be myself, to live my own life. I did care for Gary, foolishly, I know. I thought he loved me and you. I believed you deserved a father figure and a family. That's what attracted me to him."

"Gary didn't care about me, Mom. He just tolerated me. He had a hidden agenda the whole time he was with us."

"I can see that now; I didn't see it at the time. I haven't done well when it comes to choosing men. I get taken in by charm and flattery or their need for me. My therapist told me I've probably spent most of my adult life desperate to have a man's love because I didn't get that from my father."

"You have a therapist?" she asked in surprise.

"I started talking to someone a few years ago after my last bad decision. I sometimes wonder if you have chosen not to have a relationship because you don't know what a good relationship looks like."

"Maybe there's no such thing."

"There is such a thing, and I want you to find it. Break the cycle of Rossi women who choose the wrong men. I think you're the one to do it."

"I doubt that," she said as Nick returned.

"We finally got lucky," he said, a gleam of excitement in his eyes. "Jasmine Pariso is alive and lives in Cortona, about an hour and a half from here."

"Seriously?"

"She's ninety-two years old and lives with her granddaughter's family."

She jumped to her feet. "We'll have to take the train or rent a car."

"You can take my car," her mother offered as she stood up.

"We might not get it back right away."

"I don't need it."

She hesitated, not really wanting to owe her mother anything.

Her mom read her mind. "Don't think of it as a favor from me, Isabella, just a lure to get you back for another visit."

"I guess—"

"No." Nick shook his head. "We'll rent a car. We shouldn't be in a vehicle tied to your mother. Is there a rental car agency nearby?"

"Two blocks over," her mom said. "On Via Corso. I used it when I first arrived."

"Good." He paused. "Sylvie, do you have somewhere else you could stay? Or perhaps I could put you up in a hotel for a few days, maybe in a different city."

"You think I'm in danger?" she asked in surprise.

"I honestly don't know," he replied. "But until this is over, it might be wise to stay elsewhere, just in case it occurs to someone else that you might know something."

"I haven't made many friends here yet. But I was thinking about going to Milan before I start full time at the gallery next week. I haven't been there in a long time."

"Then go there," he said. "Go as soon as we leave."

"I suppose I could."

"He's right, Mom. You should go somewhere else for a few days. I don't want you to get hurt."

"I don't want you to get hurt either," her mom said worriedly.

"I can take care of myself, and I have Nick. He's a trained FBI agent. We'll be okay."

"Okay, but you're going to need to text me later and tell me what's happening. I know you probably don't believe this, but I do worry about you."

She wanted to believe it, but she wasn't sure she did. "I'll text you." A tense moment passed between them as they gave each other a long look. A part of her wanted to hug her mom, but she couldn't quite get there. "We should go."

"Take care of my daughter, Nick," her mom said.

"I will," he promised.

As they left the house to go to the rental agency, she said, "You shouldn't have made my mother a promise you can't keep."

He gave her a determined look. "I will keep it. I'm not going to let anything happen to you, Isabella. A lot of other people have let you down in your life; I won't be one of them."

She felt a rush of emotion at his words. "I don't want you to feel responsible for me."

"Too bad, because I do. I care about you, and you're just going to have to deal with that. Now, let's go get a car."

CHAPTER TWENTY-FIVE

It took over an hour to get a rental car as the agency had only one vehicle left and it was still being cleaned, so they weren't able to get on the road until after one o'clock. But Nick was happy with their ride, a sporty SUV with plenty of power and maneuverability. He stayed on the main highway, changing lanes often to see if a car was sticking with them, but the trip had been unremarkable. Now it was half-past two and Cortona was only a few miles away. He was hoping this would not be a wasted trip and that Jasmine Pariso would have the answers they'd been searching for.

Isabella had been unusually quiet since they'd left her mom's house and gotten in the car. She always had plenty to say, questions to ask, or theories to float. But she seemed distracted as she looked out the window at the passing scenery. He suspected she was thinking about her conversation with her mother. He felt like they'd had a small breakthrough in their relationship, but he didn't know for sure.

Sylvie had owned up to her mistakes, and she seemed determined to start over and have the life she'd once envisioned. She wanted to make Isabella proud of her. He thought there was hope for them. If Isabella was willing to give her mother a chance. That wouldn't be easy, and he couldn't judge her for how she was feeling. He had enough of his own baggage to deal with. He might have to address his stubborn determination to keep a distance from his parents, too. Being so caught up in the past the last several days had reminded him that his family, as dysfunctional as it might be, was still his family.

"Did you believe her?" Isabella suddenly asked.

He glanced at her, seeing the troubled question in her brown eyes. She never wanted validation for her thoughts, so the question surprised him. "Are you talking about your mother?"

"Yes. What did you think of what she said? I need an objective opinion."

"I believe her desire to change is real. She looked at her life and saw a need to make a big change. What did you think?"

"She said all the right things. Things I wish she'd said ten years ago or even before that. But it's hard not to think she'll end up back in another bad situation."

"Maybe she's learned from her experiences. But her life isn't your life. Not anymore. You're both adults. You can have distance between you but still love her."

"Seeing her in that apartment reminded me of who she used to be, a warm, bright, colorful, and happy person. I didn't expect to feel so confused by her, Nick." She shot him a pointed look. "And it's your fault. You told me to keep an open mind, to not prejudge, or put up walls before I knew if I needed any. Look what happened, no guard walls up, and she got back in."

He smiled at her disgruntled expression. "You let her in because you wanted to. You needed to. There's love between you two, Isabella. If there wasn't, she wouldn't be able to hurt you so much."

"I don't want to feel hurt anymore. I don't even want to be angry with her. Oh, I don't know what I want."

"I think you do."

She gave another heavy sigh. "You're right. I know what I want. I want to see her again after all this is over. When I have a clear head. When I'm not thinking about anything else. Then, we'll see."

"Sounds like a plan."

"Two miles to go," she said as they passed a sign. "I need to get my head back in the game. This trip went fast. And so far, no one is shooting at us, so that's a good sign."

"I hope so," he said as he took the next exit. "I also hope we're going to get some good luck. If Jasmine doesn't have the painting, I don't know what we should do next."

"Now who's looking too far down the road?" she chided. "Jasmine might give us exactly what we need."

"I hope you're right. Do you still have the letters?"

"Yes, they're in my bag. Why?"

"I'm thinking we might use them to get in to see her."

"Good idea, Nick."

"We'll see."

As he got off the highway and drove through the rolling hills of Tuscany, he was once more struck by the beauty of the landscape, especially when they drove into the enclosed city of Cortona, with its cobblestone streets and historic charm.

Jasmine's house was located slightly past the main part of the city in an area with more space between homes and sat under a trio of lemon trees thriving in the Mediterranean sun.

After parking the car, they walked up to the two-story house with its vine-covered walls and used an old brass ring to knock on the door.

Several minutes later, a young tired-looking woman carrying a toddler on her hip opened the door with a weary, questioning, "*Pronto? Come posso aiutarti?*"

"Is Jasmine home?" he asked, hoping she spoke English.

"You want to see my grandmother?" she asked in surprise, her accent thick.

"Yes. My name is Nick Caruso. She knew my great-grandfather, Tomas, a long time ago. I have something to give her that he meant to send her a long time ago."

She stared at him in wary confusion. "My grandmother barely remembers who I am. I don't think she'll remember some man from her youth."

"Would it be possible to ask her? I speak some Italian if that's an issue."

"She speaks English...sometimes. She doesn't speak very much at all anymore. She's ninety-two years old."

As another baby screamed somewhere in the house, the woman shifted the toddler on her hip, and then shrugged. "*Va bene. Entra.*" She took them down the hall and knocked on a door, then pushed it open. "Noni," she said. "There's someone here to see you."

He stepped into the room with Isabella close behind him. A white-haired lady sat in a chair by the window overlooking the valley. She was thin, and her arms and face were freckled and weathered by age. She slowly turned her head. Her green eyes were dull at first, then took on a new light as she looked at him.

"Tomas?" she questioned, as if she were seeing a ghost.

His gut clenched. She thought he was his great-grandfather.

A baby screamed louder in the hallway.

"I'll let you talk," Jasmine's granddaughter said. "Seems like she remembers Tomas after all."

He moved further into the room, sitting down on the side of the bed across from Jasmine while Isabella hovered nearby.

"Hello, Jasmine," he said.

"I never thought I would see you again," she said in a distant voice. "I look out the window every day, wondering if you might come. I was told you were dead. But you're not dead, are you?"

He wasn't sure how to answer that question. He looked to Isabella. She handed him the letter Tomas had written to *J*. "Why don't you read that to her?"

"You look familiar," Jasmine said, her gaze moving to Isabella. "Is that you, Lucinda?"

"I'm her great-granddaughter," she said. "And you were her best friend, weren't you?"

"I was. A long time ago. She helped me achieve my dream of being an artist. My husband didn't want me to paint. He wanted me to stay home with my children, but they were older; they didn't need me anymore. I would go down to the square and paint, and that's where I met Lucinda. She told me to come to the studio. She and Tomas would teach me. So I went, and they didn't just teach me about art, they showed me another world. But it wasn't a world I could have." She turned back to him. "I'm sorry, Tomas. Sorry I couldn't leave him or my children."

"I understand," he said, not sure how to handle the complexity of this moment. She seemed to accept that Isabella was Lucinda's great-granddaughter, but still thought he was Tomas. "This was a letter that came back undeliverable." He handed it to her.

Her hand shook as she pulled the paper out of the envelope. "I didn't think you wrote me back. I waited for a long time, but then we moved. My husband suspected something was going on, so he took me and the kids out of the country. We moved to Washington DC, and we lived there for many years. When he died, I finally came back to Italy, but the studio was gone, and so was your shop, your home. I was told you and Lucinda were dead. My heart broke again. I wished I hadn't waited so long."

As Jasmine read the note that Tomas had penned her a long time ago, his gaze met Isabella's. She sent him silent encouragement to keep going.

"You figured out David was going to betray you," Jasmine said, looking up at him. "I wasn't sure if it was true, but I wanted to warn you. You had such big dreams of saving art for Italy, slyly replacing originals that were targeted to be stolen by *La Mano Nera* with the copies we all created in the studio late at night. And then you would hide the originals away for safekeeping. You thought everyone was with you, but David was working with *La Mano Nera*. He was playing both sides to make money. I was afraid to put his name down in my notes to you, but you figured it out."

"Yes," he said, shocked to hear exactly what had happened. Jasmine had just confirmed they were counterfeiters, but she'd also stated the reason why.

"David ruined it all," she continued. "He told Juliette what we were doing. I knew we couldn't trust her. Juliette was too submissive to her husband and her brothers. We all wanted to believe that she didn't like what they were doing, that she was turning on them and was loyal to us. But it was she who turned David into a traitor. What happened to David?"

"He's dead now."

"Is it wrong to say I am happy about that?"

"No, it's not." He paused as he heard Isabella gasp.

She was standing by the dresser, and she had a silver ring in her hand. She brought it over to them. "Is this your ring, Jasmine?"

"Yes. I usually have it on, but it's gotten so big now, it slips off my finger." She took the ring from Isabella and traced the *P* with her finger. "It was so long ago that we were the *Protettori*."

"*Protettori*?" Isabella echoed. "What does that mean?"

"Protectors," he said, answering for Jasmine.

"We were protecting our national art from thieves. It was the most important thing I ever did in my life." Jasmine closed her eyes for a moment.

He looked at Isabella. She made a gesture for him to keep Jasmine talking while she looked around the bedroom. As she closed the closet door, she paused, and then her gaze flew to his. On the wall behind the door was a painting.

His heart skipped a beat. This painting looked very much like the others, the focus on one single object, this time a castle on a distant hill, the edges blurred with colors. "Jasmine," he said. "Is that my painting?"

She opened her eyes and looked from him to the art on the wall. "I hid it away for a long time, Tomas, just as you asked. But then I missed you so much I took it out so I could feel closer to you. You inspired me so much."

He barely heard her words. They'd found the missing painting. They had the final clue. "Can I have the painting back? Can Isabella take it off the wall?"

She hesitated, then nodded. "Yes. It is yours, after all. Is it time now? Time to bring them all together? I didn't know where the others were after all these years. I didn't know how to use the paintings to get the others."

"Get the others?" he echoed.

"The originals. You remember, don't you? Or is your mind going, too?"

"I remember," he lied. "What did I tell you about the paintings?"

"That when they were put together, the location would be clear. And it would be time to retrieve the originals, the ones that we stole and replaced with copies. Then we would give them back to their rightful owners. We couldn't move too soon, or the thieves would be on to us, and we wouldn't be able to keep going. So, we would wait until the time was right to retrieve the paintings and then the world could still enjoy them, not just the thieves who were stealing Italy's most precious art."

Another piece of the puzzle clicked into place. The location of the stolen paintings would be revealed when they were all put together.

Isabella took the painting off the wall and handed it to him, a gleam in her eyes. He had a feeling she had already figured it out.

"Thank you for this," he told Jasmine. "For keeping it safe all these years."

"I hope you knew I loved you, Tomas, even though I couldn't be with you. I had to honor my vows."

"I knew." He took her hand and gave it a gentle squeeze. "Read my letter again, and you'll always know how I felt."

Her eyes watered with tears as she gave him a smile. "You're leaving now, aren't you?"

"I have to get the paintings."

She nodded as he got to his feet. "We won't see each other again."

It wasn't a question, so he didn't give her an answer. He just leaned over and kissed her on the cheek and then he followed Isabella out of the room. They could hear Jasmine's granddaughter dealing with her children down the hall, so they hurried out of the house before she could stop them and ask why they had her grandmother's painting.

They jumped into the car, and he quickly drove away, not stopping until they were several blocks away. Then he pulled over by a park and looked at the painting Isabella had on her lap. "You know where the paintings are, don't you?"

"It's the school," she said with excitement in her eyes. "The school Frederico started. The one with the courtyard, the artists painting in the open air. Don't you remember what we saw when we stood there?"

"The trees, the rock wall, the river..."

"And the castle on the hill in the distance."

"Damn! You're right, Isabella. But..."

She groaned. "Why is there always a but?"

"If the paintings were hidden in the school, why wouldn't Frederico have done something with them? Why didn't he burn them when he burned his own?"

"Louisa and Victoria said he went mad with alcohol and mental illness."

"There's something we're missing."

"Lucinda," she said. "She taught at the school. Maybe Frederico never knew the paintings were there. She might have hidden them there without his knowledge."

"Okay. That's making more sense. If they are at the school, where would they be?"

She thought for a second. "Oh, my God!" She shot him a

triumphant smile. "I think they're in plain sight, Nick. Remember all the paintings in the hallways?"

"I thought that was student art."

"Maybe it was a combination of copies of the masters mixed in with student projects. Remember Lucinda's sketchbook—the picture I showed you a few days ago. It was a copy of a famous painting. My mother said they would study the work of master artists to help them understand technique."

"Are you suggesting that priceless paintings have been hanging in an art school and no one knew? What about the teachers? Wouldn't they recognize an original over a copy?"

"Maybe the original is behind the copy. Either way, we have to go to the school. I think the other two paintings, the stairs and the patterned tiles probably reflect the interior of the school. We didn't go up the stairs, so we didn't see what they looked like, and I didn't notice the floor, but maybe the tiles will lead us where we need to go."

He started the car and pulled away as she put the painting in the back seat.

The idea of the paintings being at the school was wild, but it also made sense. He pressed down on the gas, eager to get back to the highway. It would take them at least another hour to get to Rome, which was frustrating. They were so close. He didn't want anyone else to find the paintings before they did.

"Did you feel bad lying to Jasmine?" Isabella asked a few moments later. "Pretending to be her lost love?"

"A little. But it was less complicated for her to think I was Tomas than to have to explain it all."

"And it made it easier to get the painting. She might not have let you walk out with it if she didn't think it was yours."

"Probably not."

"You shouldn't feel bad, Nick. You made her happy. You gave her a letter that expressed Tomas's love. She has that now, too."

"That's true. I'm okay with what I did. It's certainly not the first time I've lied, and this lie was for a good reason. It's sad they never got together. I could hear the love in her voice. It was real." So real he'd actually felt shaken when Jasmine had told him how much she loved him. It had made him wonder what it would be like to have someone feel that way about him. Or to love someone the way his great-grandfather had loved this woman.

But Tomas and Jasmine had stayed apart because they didn't want to hurt other people. He didn't know if that was kind and generous or remarkably stupid and shortsighted. But it was what it was. Right now, he was more interested in the other part of their story—the saving of priceless original art.

"They formed a group called the *Prottetori*," he said. "They copied paintings and somehow replaced the originals before they could be stolen."

"How would they know which ones would be stolen?"

"Probably from Juliette."

"But then they would still have to switch the paintings out before the theft. That would be tricky."

"Sam told us that some people at the studio worked for museums and galleries. That would have given them access to switching the paintings."

"They still had to know which ones and when. Jasmine said Juliette couldn't be trusted. She had to have been working both sides."

"Maybe Juliette wasn't cool with what her brothers were doing, so she told her artist friends what paintings were being targeted. Then the *Protettori* copied the art and swapped it with the originals. The Falconeri crew thinks they stole originals, but they didn't."

"The originals were hidden away, so that when things cooled down, they could be sent to their rightful owners," Isabella finished.

"But David betrayed them in some way."

"Maybe both David and Juliette betrayed them, and that's why Tomas and Lucinda were killed. I think that's it, Nick."

"Me, too," he said, meeting her gaze. "But who has restarted *La Mano Nera*? It wasn't David or Juliette."

She sighed. "You always ask the tough questions." She thought for a moment. "Catherine would have been a good bet since she's a Falconeri, but she's dead."

"And someone killed her. Why? Was she going to talk? Was she having an attack of conscience herself?"

"What if Lavezzo is the one running this?" she asked. "What if he and Catherine had a personal relationship? He asked her to lure the paintings out of their hiding places with an exhibition. She turned off the alarms. And he acts like he's going to investigate the robbery but never finds anything."

"Maybe you should be a detective instead of a reporter," he said, impressed by her logic. "If that theory is true, then the argument you witnessed between them might have been Catherine telling Lavezzo she wanted out."

"She was upset about the security guard getting hurt when she came to the house. She might have felt guilty that he almost died during the robbery. Perhaps she didn't know the thieves would go that far."

"But she knew too much, and Lavezzo, or someone else, killed her." He paused. "There is another person who I wonder about—the unnamed boy that Juliette delivered after leaving her husband. He would have been a Falconeri, too. Catherine was in her sixties, I believe. We'd have to check her date of birth, but her brother was born when she was about eight, so he'd probably be in his fifties. That doesn't narrow it down much, but it gives us somewhere to start."

"It seems more likely that someone like Lavezzo would kill Catherine rather than her brother, whoever he is. Unless..." She gave him an excited look. "What if Lavezzo is her brother? Do we know his family history?"

"I asked Flynn to look into them, but I never followed up. I got sidetracked by Juliette."

"Lavezzo is about the right age. But if he was her brother, would he kill her over stolen art?"

"People kill family members all the time," he said heavily. "Sometimes for no reason at all. But we can figure out who Catherine's brother is later on. All we need to do right now is get to the school and find the paintings. Nothing will be resolved, and no one will be safe until we do that."

CHAPTER TWENTY-SIX

As Nick drove back to Rome, Isabella's mind raced with what they should do when they got to the school. But then they hit a traffic accident outside of Rome, and the jam of barely moving cars made her nervous for another reason. Was this accident another setup?

Even if it wasn't, the sky was darkening, and the clock was ticking toward six o'clock. The school might be closed by the time they arrived. And she did not want to wait until tomorrow.

But if it was open, and they could get in, then what? They'd have to look at each painting, and with their very unexpert eyes determine if something was original or not. That seemed like an enormous challenge. Maybe they could get some help from Louisa and Victoria. Or maybe they shouldn't involve them at all, because who knew what role Frederico had played in the group. On the other hand, they ran the school. It probably wouldn't be possible to do anything there without their knowledge.

She just wished the paintings gave a bigger clue than just a general place to go. Why weren't there more specific directions? They'd gone to the trouble of creating a set of paintings that would lead to a location. Why stop there?

On impulse, she grabbed the painting from the back seat and

turned it over. The canvas had been attached to the frame by small tacks. There was nothing written on the back of the canvas. But there was a loose edge between the canvas and the frame.

"What are you doing?" Nick asked.

"I want to take this apart."

"Why?"

"To see if there's anything hidden on the wood frame beneath the canvas. I need something to pull up the tacks."

Nick shifted is his seat and then took a small compact tool kit out of his pocket. "You should be able to find something in this."

"Wow. You're quite the Boy Scout."

He laughed. "I was never a Boy Scout, but I often find myself in situations where I need the right tool."

She found a flathead screwdriver and pushed it under the first tack. With some maneuvering, she pulled the tack out and then continued along until she had released two sides of the canvas. Pulling up those sides, she saw nothing written on the frame or the wood, but she'd gone this far. She might as well keep going. She finished taking the painting apart and as she turned the wood around, her pulse jumped.

"There are numbers," she said. "One-five. I wonder what that means."

"No idea," he muttered. "Could it be the fifth painting?"

"Possibly. But what does the one mean? Maybe it will make more sense when we get to the school. I wish I knew if the other paintings also had numbers on the frame. This could mean absolutely nothing."

"Wasn't there a number in Lucinda's sketchbook that we couldn't figure out?"

"Yes," she said, remembering the number two that had been placed on one of the stairs in the sketch but then taken out. She looked at the actual painting again, but there weren't any numbers on the art itself. "There's no number on the canvas, just the frame."

"Those numbers have to mean something. We just have to figure out what."

She handed him back the tool. "I wish this traffic would speed up," she said with a groan as they came to another complete stop. "I'm afraid the school will be closed when we get there."

"Well, we'll soon find out."

Unfortunately, soon was almost an hour later. It was after seven when they finally arrived. The school was dark, with not a single car in the parking lot next to it.

"It's closed," she said with intense disappointment. "What should we do? I hate the idea of waiting until tomorrow."

"Let's see if there's an open door," Nick replied.

"That seems unlikely."

"You never know. But wait one second. I want to park further away. No reason to announce that anyone is here."

He moved the car a block away, and then they walked back to the school. She had the now deconstructed piece of wood with the numbers on it in one hand with the canvas rolled up in the other, just in case they needed them for some reason.

They walked around the back of the school and paused in the courtyard. Even in the twilight, she could see the castle on the hill in the distance, the tree by the rock wall and the river. What she didn't see were stairs or patterned tiles. Maybe those were inside the school. But just being here and seeing the same scenes that had been painted by five idealistic artists over fifty years ago strengthened her conviction that they were in the right place.

Nick walked around the interior perimeter of the school, checking doors and windows.

"There are no cameras and no obvious alarm system," he said when he returned to her. "After what Victoria said about their crumbling infrastructure and financial issues, I'm guessing security is the least of their concerns." He took out the tool kit she'd returned to him and headed toward the back door.

"We're just going to break in?" she asked, feeling a little breathless at the thought.

"Yes." He paused, giving her a sharp look. "Unless you're not up for it? We can wait until tomorrow."

"We'd have to go through Louisa and Victoria then, and we don't know if we can trust them. We're here. Let's do this."

Nick worked quickly and efficiently, opening the door in less than three minutes.

"Nice," she said. "If the agent career doesn't work out, you can go to the dark side."

"I've seen too much of the dark side already. I'm not switching over." He opened the door for her. "Let's not turn on any lights. We'll use the flashlights from our phones."

She took out the prepaid phone he'd given her and turned on the light as Nick did the same. Then they started down the hall.

"You take one side, I'll take the other," she said. "There are so many paintings here. We should make one quick pass down the hall and see if anything jumps out at us."

"All right, but I'm not sure what I'm looking for."

"Anything that looks really well executed."

"I'll give it a shot. A priceless painting has to be better than some of this junk, right?"

She wasn't sure what he considered junk. Art was definitely subjective.

As she passed a classroom door, she saw the number six on the door, and that made her wonder if the number on the frame was related to the number on the door. The frame in her hand read one-five. She moved further down the hall to the next classroom with the number five on the door, while Nick moved in the opposite direction. She put her light on the paintings next to the door, and then she saw one that looked incredibly familiar.

It was the same painting she'd seen in Lucinda's sketchbook. Her heart raced. As she pulled the painting off the wall, she heard footsteps and then a grunt. She whirled around to see Nick lying unconscious on the floor with a man dressed completely in black standing over him. The gun in his hand was pointed straight at her.

He said something in Italian, but she couldn't understand him. She hugged the painting close to her chest, almost like a shield. The canvas wouldn't protect her from a bullet, but she didn't know what else to do.

How had he found them? And was there more than one person in the building? It seemed quiet. She couldn't hear anyone else.

He uttered a sharp, louder order in Italian, motioning his gun toward the painting.

She swallowed hard. He would probably kill them both as soon as she gave him the painting. She had to stall. Nick wasn't dead. He'd just been knocked out. If she could slow things down, maybe he'd wake up and they could get away.

"There are four other paintings," she said. "I know where they are. You can't kill me, or you'll never get them." She didn't know if he spoke English, but a second later it didn't matter, because a rocketing blast came from behind her.

She instinctively ducked down to the ground, waiting for the pain to rip through her or to see blood coming from Nick's head. But it was the man with the gun who fell to the ground.

She turned around in shock to see Stefano striding down the corridor, weapon in hand. "Oh, my God," she gasped.

"Are you all right, Isabella?" Stefano asked as he put his gun away.

"I—I think so," she stuttered. "How did you know we were here?"

"I spoke to your mother earlier. She was worried about you. She thought you might be headed here. It looks like she was right to be concerned. What are you doing here?"

"We found another one of Tomas's paintings, and we realized that if the stolen paintings were put together, they provided a picture of the view from the courtyard of this school."

"Why would that be important?"

"Because Tomas and Lucinda were in a group of people who were trying to protect art from thieves by stealing it themselves and putting up fakes to be stolen." She stumbled over her words, her gut telling her that things weren't adding up. Why was Stefano here alone? Where were the other police officers? Why had he just shot the other guy and not even tried to take him into custody?

More importantly, her mother hadn't known they were going to the school. She'd thought they were going to find Jasmine.

"Is that one of the paintings?" Stefano asked.

"I think so."

"Where are the others?"

"I'm not sure. I believe they're scattered along these walls. There's a number on the back of the frames of the pictures that were stolen that say what floor and what room number, but I don't have the other paintings; I only have this one."

"What was the number?"

"One-Five," she said. "And this classroom is number five."

"I read the report on the painting stolen from the gallery in Firenze."

"David Leoni's painting?"

"There was a number two-twelve on the frame."

"That has to be the second floor, classroom twelve."

"Let's find out," he said. "After you."

"What about that guy? Shouldn't you call for an ambulance?"

"The man I shot is dead, and Nick is unconscious. I assume the assailant knocked him out."

"I guess. I didn't see what happened. Maybe I should check on him."

"You can do that later. I don't want to leave you here in case that man has a partner."

Despite his words, there was an iciness in his voice and in his eyes. He wasn't going to take no for an answer. She was afraid he'd pull out the gun and shoot her if she didn't comply, and as they moved toward the stairs, she was terribly afraid that she and Nick weren't going to get out of this alive.

———

Nick had come back to life at the sound of the gunshot, his brain clearing as he heard voices through the sharp, throbbing pain in his head. It took every ounce of strength he had not to move, not to give away the fact that he was conscious.

Isabella was talking to Stefano. Apparently, Stefano had shot the man who had knocked him out. That man was dressed in black, a pool of blood spreading around him and sliding down the hallway. Stefano had shot him in the head. It had been a kill shot. Maybe he'd been unconscious when Stefano told the gunman to put his weapon down, but he didn't like the fact that Stefano was alone.

Stefano wasn't at all concerned about the man he'd shot or about him. Stefano wanted the paintings. He was part of this. He was either in charge or working with someone else. Hell, maybe it was Lavezzo.

As Stefano and Isabella moved down the hall, he opened his eyes, seeing their flashlight beams bounce off the stairwell walls. He remembered hearing Isabella say she'd found the painting. She must think the other ones were upstairs, or she was trying to stall and save him by getting Stefano to go to another floor.

He rolled over and pulled his gun out from under his shirt. He should have had it in his hand when he'd entered the building. He'd made a costly mistake allowing himself to get jumped, but it wouldn't be a fatal mistake. He would save Isabella if it was the last thing he did.

He grabbed his phone from the floor so he would have some light and stumbled to his feet. The pain was so overwhelming, darkness threatened to descend back over him. He leaned against the wall as he caught his breath and tried to get his balance. That's when he heard another pad of soft footsteps coming from the doorway that led to the courtyard.

He raised his gun, ready to take out whoever was coming inside, but a gunshot would mean giving away the fact that he was conscious and had a weapon. So, he waited...

His breath caught in his throat as he saw the woman creeping down the hallway, keeping to the shadows. He flashed the light on her, and she froze.

"Sylvie," he murmured in shock.

When she realized it was him, she hurried down the hall, stopping again when she saw the dead body on the floor.

"*Oh, God!*" she breathed, putting a hand to her heart.

He moved down the hallway, taking her hand, pulling her away from the body and into a small, recessed area by the restroom. "What are you doing here, Sylvie?"

"I figured out the paintings were from the courtyard at the school. I didn't have a way to get in touch with Isabella, so I came on my own."

"Did you tell Stefano we were coming here?"

She looked at him in confusion. "No. He called me and said Isabella was in trouble. I remembered what you said about not trusting him, so I told him I didn't know where she was. But he made me worry even more. Where is she?"

"Upstairs," he said as he heard Stefano order Isabella to keep moving.

"She's with Stefano?" Sylvie asked in shock. "How did he know she was here?"

"I'm guessing he had us followed. Or maybe you."

"This is my fault? Oh, God!"

"You need to leave. Call the police. Tell them what's happening."

"What if I call the wrong person? Stefano is with the Polizia."

She made a good point, but not every cop would be dirty, and Stefano was here on his own. "Just go. Make the call."

"No. You do it." She shook her head with the same stubborn glint in her eye that Isabella often had. "My daughter is in trouble, and Stefano—I can reason with him. I can make him let her go."

"You can't make him do anything. He just killed that man on the floor."

"I can't believe he did that."

"He did. And if you don't leave, you'll end up getting hurt, too. That would destroy Isabella."

"At least she'd be alive, and that's what matters. I have to try. And you can't stop me."

He silently cursed as she moved away. He wanted to tackle her to the ground, but that wasn't going to get him anywhere and would only make Stefano aware of their presence. Maybe her presence would benefit him.

Sylvie headed up the stairway that Stefano and Isabella had used. He'd go up the back. If she could distract Stefano, then he might have a better chance of taking him down.

He thought about calling the police himself, but if the police arrived and saw Stefano in trouble, they might shoot him instead. He moved toward the back stairs, taking them as fast as he could, each step shooting a dagger of pain through his head. But that didn't matter. He had to save Isabella and her mother.

CHAPTER TWENTY-SEVEN

Isabella had found the third painting when her mother's voice rang out, shocking them both. Stefano whirled around.

"Sylvie," he said, shocked to see her. "What are you doing here?"

"I was going to ask you that. Did you have me followed?"

"You need to leave," he said, ignoring her question.

"Not without my daughter." Her mother moved determinedly down the hall. "What are you doing, Stefano? Did you kill that man downstairs? Did you knock Nick out? What has happened to you? When did you become a killer?"

Isabella could feel Stefano's tension grow with each question.

"*Silenzio*," he said, waving his gun in the air. "I don't answer to you. We are nothing to each other, Sylvie."

"We were once friends and then more than that. You loved me, and I loved you."

"You loved yourself. You never cared about me," he said bitterly. "You never looked back. You didn't think I was worthy of you."

"That wasn't it at all. And if I had looked back, what would I have seen? A police officer sworn to protect the public threatening my daughter?"

"She got in the way. I told her to leave Rome many times. But she is like you, determined to get what she wants."

"You have the paintings you want. Let her go."

"I don't have them all—yet. I can't let her go."

Stefano's evil smile twisted Isabella's stomach. And she could see her mother's face pale through the light Stefano had trained on her.

"She knows too much," Stefano continued. "So do you."

At his words, she tried to quietly slink down the hall, putting a few feet between them as she debated the odds of being able to take him out by hitting him over the head with the painting in her hand. He was taller than her, and the old frame would probably just split apart without slowing him down. She needed something else. As she turned her head, she saw a shadow at the opposite end of the hall.

There was someone there. She didn't know if it was Nick or another man in black.

The shadow wasn't moving now. If the person was tied to Stefano, he would have declared himself. He would have come to help. It had to be Nick. And she knew what he wanted to do. They'd spent so much time together she could read his mind. He needed space to take out Stefano without hurting her or her mother, but Stefano was between her and her mother, and she needed to get him to move so Nick would have a shot.

"I think this is another painting," she said, bringing his attention back to her. She pointed to the painting on the wall a few feet away from her. "That will make four. You can find the other one on your own. We won't tell anyone, Stefano. You can let us go. I'll return to the US and my mother will pretend she was never here."

Stefano ignored her pleas. "Which one is the painting?"

"That one." She pointed to what might be one of the priceless paintings, but she had no idea if it was or not.

Stefano moved past her to take a look. Then he froze at the sound of footsteps coming up the front stairs. He lifted his weapon once more as another man rounded the corner and strode down the hall, a light on the scope of a gun aimed at all three of them.

"What—" Stefano began, his words cut off by the blast of that gun.

She grabbed her mom and pulled her back against the wall, shocked that once again the target was not her, but Stefano. He collapsed on the ground, clutching his side with bloodied hands as he screamed in pain and then cursed at the gunman in Italian.

As the shooter moved closer, her mother pushed her behind her. She would be no defense against bullets, but the man didn't seem in a hurry to take them out. Instead, he stopped in front of them and gave them a long look. That's when she saw that there were no gloves on his hands. But there was a glint of silver. A silver ring with the letter *P*.

He had a hood over his head and dark glasses over his eyes, but when he pulled down the hood and shoved his glasses on top of his head, she recognized him immediately. It was Matthew Pierre, Dario's associate.

"You," she gasped in surprise, stepping around her mother. "You're involved with this? Why? Where did you get that ring?"

"From my mother—Juliette. You know who she is, don't you?"

Everything clicked into place. "Juliette is a Falconeri. And you must be her unnamed son."

"That's the perfect way to say it," he replied, a hard edge to his voice. "Unnamed. Unimportant, until now. I see you found some of the paintings."

"Why did you shoot Stefano?" she asked, noting that Stefano was still writhing in pain on the floor. "Aren't you working together?"

"He was going to cut me out," Matthew said harshly. "That won't happen. The paintings are mine. They belong to my family. And they've been gone a long time."

Another terrible fact presented itself. "If they belong to your family, why did you kill your sister? Didn't Catherine deserve to have the paintings, too?"

"She was too soft, just like my mother," he said, without a hint of care in his voice.

"I don't think your mother was soft. She was a criminal like her brothers, like her husband, and I guess like her son and daughter, too. Why did she even have that ring? She wasn't one of them."

"She pretended to be. Until she had second thoughts about betraying her friends."

She licked her lips, needing to keep him talking. "Why did you wait so long to find the paintings?"

"I didn't know about them until year and a half ago when my mother confessed her sins as she lay dying. That's when she told my sister and I the truth about who we were and where we came from."

"What exactly did she tell you?"

"Everything," he said. "She told us about her brothers, my father, *La Mano Nera,* and the *Protettori*, the artists who were determined to ruin my family. She was sent to find out what they were up to, and she provided valuable information after joining their group. She even drugged Tomas and Lucinda so her brother could get into the house and find the counterfeits."

"Juliette drugged them?" she echoed in astonishment. "She was part of their murder?"

"She didn't know Roberto was going to kill them and burn the studio down. At least, that's what she told us. She said my father was in on it, too, and that terrified her. She was surrounded by evil. After that, she took my sister and ran away. I was born five months later. We lived a life of poverty. I had nothing, no money, no father, no history."

"She was trying to get you a better life."

"She wasn't succeeding," he said bitterly. "But even without the Falconeri lineage in my head, I was following in their foot-steps by stealing what we needed, and sometimes more. When she told me who I really was, I finally felt like I belonged in my family. I knew what I needed to do. I needed to finish the job my uncles had started. I needed to get the paintings back. Because they're mine, and I will have everything I deserve."

She could hear the obsessive madness in his voice. "I still don't understand why you killed Catherine. Didn't she help your men get into the museum?"

"Yes, but then she wanted to call everything else off. She got squeamish when her security guard was hurt. I knew she would betray me. I couldn't give her that chance."

He was completely without remorse. He would kill them, too. They were only alive now because he needed two more paintings. She looked at Stefano, whose breath was more labored now, and his eyes had closed. "How did you get involved with Stefano?"

"My mother told me Stefano's father worked for her broth-ers. He was their inside man in the police department. When I learned Stefano was his son and was someone eager to make more money, it seemed only fitting that both of us should continue a relationship begun a very long time."

She'd had no idea Stefano's father had been involved in *La Mano Nera*, too, but it made sense why he and Matthew were working together. They should go to jail together, too. She had to make that happen. "Stefano was about to get the next paint-ing," she said. "It's there. On the wall over his head."

As Matthew stepped over Stefano, he kept the gun trained on them. But as he reached the wall, he turned to look at the painting.

In that split second, another shot rang out.

Her mother screamed and pulled her down to the floor.

She looked down the hall and saw Matthew on the ground, his eyes shocked and wide open, blood coming from the back of his head. She put her arms around her sobbing mother as Nick came running down the hall.

"It's okay, Mom. It's Nick. We're safe now."

"Are we? Is it really over?" her mom gasped. "What if someone else comes?"

"I don't think there's anyone left, but we have Nick, so we'll be okay." She bit down on her lip to stop herself from bursting into tears along with her mother.

———

"Are you all right?" Nick asked when he reached them. He wanted to throw his arms around Isabella, but she was hugging her mother.

"We're okay," she told him. "I knew you were there."

"I thought you did. Especially when you got Stefano to move down the hall."

"I wanted to give you a shot at Stefano, but Matthew took it first."

"I was stunned when I saw him come down the hallway," he admitted. "I didn't think he would shoot Stefano that fast. I was going to take Matthew out after that, but he was too close to you. I couldn't risk it. But dammit, Isabella. You could have lost your life."

She met his gaze with water-filled eyes. "I'm still alive. So is my mom. And so are you. That's all that matters."

"I should have done better."

"No. Don't blame yourself. You're the reason we're all still breathing. I'm just worried that there's more to come. We should get out of here."

"I agree," he said as they got to their feet.

The sound of sirens froze them in place. While he wanted to appreciate the arrival of the police, after what had gone down with Stefano, he knew this would get messy. He used his sleeve to wipe his prints off the gun he'd used and kicked it down the hall. It might still be traced to him, but it would buy him time. This was going to be a complicated situation, and having a gun in his hands would make it worse.

"You need to put your hands up," he told them.

"Why?" Isabella asked.

"Because a police officer has been shot, and they'll think we shot him," he said tersely.

Her gaze swung to Stefano, whose eyes were closed, but he was still breathing. "He's the criminal, not us."

"It may take some time to prove what happened. When the police see two dead men and an injured officer with the three of us unscathed, they're going to take us into custody. When that happens, don't say anything. Whenever they ask you a question, tell them to call Captain Lavezzo and ask for a lawyer."

"Will Lavezzo help us? Or is he part of this?" she challenged. "He was with Matthew and Dario the night Catherine was killed."

"Matthew said he killed his sister."

"But Catherine was arguing with Captain Lavezzo. He might still be involved."

"My gut says Catherine wanted out, and she was hoping Lavezzo would help her. Anyway, just keep asking for a lawyer."

"Can't we stay together?"

"They won't let that happen," he said, hearing officers running into the building. "Hands up."

Sylvie and Isabella raised their hands in the air as the police descended on them with orders to get on the ground. There was new terror on Sylvie and Isabella's faces, and he wanted to comfort them through the chaos, but as he'd predicted, they were instantly separated, taken downstairs, and put into separate police cars. The only good thing was that they weren't shot in the process.

The officer who threw him into the car did so with a ruthless, angry line to his mouth.

"Call Captain Lavezzo with the Carabinieri T.P.C.," he told him. "He'll tell you what this is all about."

The door was slammed in his face. He had no idea if anyone would make that call. And he hoped he was right about Lavezzo. If he wasn't, they might not be out of danger yet.

CHAPTER TWENTY-EIGHT

Two inspectors, followed by a man who introduced himself as Commissario Toran questioned Isabella off and on for what felt like hours. She kept repeating what Nick had told her—that she needed them to call Captain Lavezzo with the Carabinieri T.P.C. and that she wanted a lawyer.

Finally, after midnight, she was pushed into a holding cell with one other woman sitting on a hard, narrow bench. Her heart swelled with relief when she realized it was her mother.

Her mom jumped to her feet, and they embraced for several long minutes. She held onto her mother like she'd held on to her when she was a kid, when she was scared, and her mom's tight hug was instantly reassuring and calming.

"My darling girl," her mother whispered as she stroked her back. "You're all right."

"I am." She pulled away so she could look into her mom's eyes. "How about you?"

"I'm no stranger to a cell," she said grimly. "But I never wanted to see you in a place like this."

"I never wanted to see you in a place like this, either."

The years fell away as they both remembered her one and

only visit to her mom in jail. She'd never returned, and her mother had never asked to see her again.

"I wish you hadn't seen me there," her mom said. "The look on your face was worse than anything I had to endure. It broke my heart." She drew in a breath and let it out. "I'm sorry if I made another mistake tonight. I didn't tell Stefano that you had gone to see Jasmine, but I did say you were looking for the stolen paintings. That was probably too much."

"He already knew that."

"But perhaps I gave away more than I thought. Obviously, he knew I'd seen you. I don't know if that helped him find you, or if he had someone follow me."

"He couldn't have followed you. He got to the school before you."

"No. I actually got to the school before you, but it was locked up, and you weren't there, so I went to a café to get a coffee. I waited about thirty minutes and thought I'd try the school again. That's when I saw the back door open, and lights jumping around the school. Stefano could have followed me to the school."

"Maybe. But I'm surprised you beat us there. The traffic was so bad."

"I drove to Rome about an hour after you left my house, and I didn't stop in Cortona."

"That makes sense. We had to wait for the rental car and then we were with Jasmine for a while. She had Tomas's final painting. That put it together for me. But you guessed the school even without it."

"I spent a lot of time in the courtyard painting those scenes, and it suddenly hit me. What better place to hide paintings than in an art school? It's strange to think I looked at those paintings dozens of times when I was a teenager, but I never imagined they were originals, just excellent copies. And they were hung on the walls for over fifty years. I guess we're lucky the school never repainted. They just covered the cracks with art."

"You should have gone to Milan like we planned."

Her mother gazed into her eyes. "I came here because I didn't want you to be hurt, and I had no way to reach you because your phone was off. I also thought maybe I could help. When I walked into the school and saw Nick next to a dead body, my heart stopped."

"You're lucky Nick didn't shoot you."

"He quickly realized it was me. He wanted me to leave, but I heard you and Stefano upstairs, and I thought I could talk Stefano out of hurting you. That was stupid. He'd already killed one man. He wasn't going to stop for me. I just didn't think he was that evil. I mean, I always knew he had a darker side. Even when we were kids, he'd go a little too far in a fight or with drinking. That was one reason I left him behind. I couldn't see a life with him, but I had no idea he was capable of murder." She let out a hopeless sigh. "I really don't judge people very well, especially men."

"This isn't on you, Mom. Stefano covered his tracks well. And you did help me. You distracted Stefano so he didn't see Nick. Before that, you helped when you remembered Lucinda's best friend was Jasmine. She answered a lot of questions about Tomas and Lucinda, the group they ran. They called themselves the *Protettori*. They were forging paintings and replacing originals with counterfeit pieces in museums and galleries across Rome. They had insider intelligence on where the thieves might strike. But when they did, they stole fakes, not originals, and the real art was saved for future generations. To be honest, I think Lucinda and Tomas were obsessively idealistic and also a little crazy. I guess that runs in the family."

Her mother gave her a faint smile. "Let's sit down. We could be here a long time."

They sat on the bench together, and she was glad they were alone, that they had this time to talk. "I met Louisa and Victoria when Nick and I went to the school a few days ago," she continued. "I wonder if they had any idea there were valuable paintings on the walls of the school."

"I doubt it. If they did, they probably would have tried to sell them. The school has always been a passion project for Frederico's family. There was never a lot of money to run it, but no one wanted to let it go."

"They mentioned the money problems when we spoke. They also remembered you as being beautiful, wild, and very passionate."

"I don't know about the beautiful part, but I was wild and reckless. I felt so restricted in my father's house. I wanted to be free. I felt very rebellious in my later teenage years."

"I can understand that. The summer I spent with Grandpa and Grandma was the coldest summer of my life. She tried to make it okay, but he didn't want me around."

"He hurt you and I'm sorry for that."

"You can apologize for the things you did, but not the things he did." She paused. "Thanks for trying to save me tonight. You didn't have to come up those stairs. I'm sure Nick told you not to."

"He ordered me to leave, but unless he was going to shoot me, I was going to get to you. I would rather die than watch you be hurt, Isabella. I know you probably don't believe that. You think I abandoned you a long time ago. I made some huge mistakes and got caught up in Gary's life, and it was bad for you...all of it."

"Thanks for acknowledging that."

"I want you to be happy. I want you to have your dreams. These last few years, I thought it would be better for you if I stayed away. But I've missed you a lot. I've read everything you've ever written."

"You have?" she asked in amazement.

"You're a good writer and so smart. You didn't get that from me."

"I might have gotten some of it. You did figure out where the paintings were."

"Well, art might be my one strength." She paused. "What did you tell the police?"

"Nothing. I said the word over and over and over again. It was so difficult. I wanted to tell them everything Stefano did, but Nick's voice was ringing in my head."

"And you trust him?"

"More than I've ever trusted anyone."

"I think he's in love with you, Isabella."

She shook her head. "I don't know. I don't think so. It's too fast. Too soon. There's a lot going on."

Her mother smiled. "And by that very long denial, I think maybe you're falling for him, too."

"Maybe a little," she reluctantly admitted.

A female officer suddenly appeared at the door. "*Venga con me*," she said as she waved them out of the cell.

They were escorted into a conference room bigger than the interrogation room she'd left a short time earlier, but now Nick and Captain Lavezzo were seated at the table along with Commissario Toran.

Nick gave her a reassuring smile as they sat down.

"We have a lot to talk about," Captain Lavezzo said, taking the lead, his face determined and purposeful.

She shot Nick a questioning look. "Are we talking?"

"Yes," he replied. "I filled Captain Lavezzo in on everything we know."

"Everything? Was that wise?"

"It was," Lavezzo interjected. "I learned that Catherine Vigonas was involved in the museum robbery on Sunday. She wanted to barter information for protection. She wouldn't name the person in charge unless we came to an agreement. Unfortunately, before that could happen, she was killed."

"Is that what you were talking about at the party? I saw you in the garden, but I couldn't understand what you were saying."

"Yes," he said. "I didn't realize anyone had seen us."

"It felt like you had a personal relationship with Catherine. She was upset, and you were trying to calm her down." She gave him a challenging look. "Am I wrong?"

He gazed back at her, his dark eyes unreadable, but then he said, "I met Catherine about eight years ago. She was working at another museum then, and there was a robbery. She helped me find the thieves. They were not related to this case," he added quickly. "We became friends. That's all, just friends."

She didn't know if she believed him, but it didn't matter. "You must have been shocked and saddened by her death."

"I was furious and angry with myself for not getting more information and not making sure she was protected. After I spoke to her in the garden, I left the party. I suspected Catherine's brother, Matthew, might be involved, even though she hadn't confirmed that. But she had told me in previous conversations that her brother was prone to violence, and she tried not to have anything to do with him. That was easy when he was living in Paris, but after his mother died, he moved to Rome. I wanted to see if I could get evidence on Matthew. Since he was at the party, I went to search his home. I didn't hear about what happened until much later."

"What did you find at his house?"

"Nothing in the house, but as I investigated further, I found phone calls between Matthew and Inspector Gangi. That's why I left you and Nick a message yesterday. I wanted you to come in so that I could tell you not to trust the inspector, even though he was a friend of the family."

"We were in Firenze."

"I understand that now. Nick filled me in on what happened in the school. I had no idea that Catherine and Matthew were descendants of the Falconeri family. That was the piece I didn't have. I thought Matthew had just talked her into smuggling out the art, but she never told me why."

"Matthew was obsessed with recreating *La Mano Nera*,

getting back what he thought was his." She paused. "Do you think Dario Micheli was involved? He worked with Matthew."

"I don't believe he was, but we will continue working to make sure that assumption is correct. I did speak to Signor Micheli, and he told me that Matthew and the manager of the gallery in Firenze had been handling that robbery, so I'm sure that was orchestrated by Matthew."

"Why didn't Matthew just take David Leoni's painting?" she asked. "Why didn't Catherine take the three paintings from the museum? Why hire a crew to break in?"

"Because the owners of the paintings would have demanded to know where they went. Catherine and Matthew had to cover the disappearance with a robbery. But Catherine was disturbed that her security guard was almost killed. That's when she decided to talk to me, to see if I could help her. I don't yet know how or when Inspector Gangi got involved with Matthew Pierre."

"Matthew told me that Stefano's father worked for the Falconeri's when they were running La Mano Nera, so Matthew approached him about continuing the tradition," she said. "But I didn't get any more information than that."

Captain Lavezzo nodded. "We'll find out the details of the inspector's involvement after he comes out of surgery."

"I think my grandfather was on to Stefano," Nick said heavily. "Juliette must have talked to my grandfather when she decided to unburden all of her sins. That's why he had her ID. That's why he went to the school. And I'm guessing he talked to Stefano about Juliette as well." He drew in a breath and let it out. "I'm fairly certain Stefano was responsible for my grandfather's car accident." He looked to the commissario. "What do you think about that?"

The older man gave him a regretful nod. "I believe that may have been what happened. We are still trying to piece everything together, but one of my officers just told me that Stefano had made sure to take over that investigation. At the time, no one questioned it because Stefano was distraught. Marcus had been one of his mentors." He paused. "Your grandfather's death was a tragedy. I respected Marcus greatly. I wish I could change what happened."

"So do I," Nick said.

"What will happen to Stefano?" her mother asked.

She shot her mother a quick look at her question, wondering what answer she was hoping to get.

"He will go to prison for the rest of his life," Lavezzo said.

"You can be assured of that," the commissario added. "He will face many charges. It may take time to get enough proof to convict him of Marcus's death, but I will do everything I can to make that happen."

"Good," Nick said.

"Good," her mother echoed, a steel glint in her eyes.

"So what now?" she asked. "What happens to the paintings? Did you find the fifth one?"

"We did not," Captain Lavezzo replied, surprising her with his words. "But we found an empty spot on the wall where we thought it should be. After bringing in the owners of the school, who were completely shocked by this, they informed me that there had been a painting hanging in that space for years. It was a copy of a painting by Caravaggio."

"But it wasn't a copy; it was probably the real thing."

"I believe so. I've examined records for all art stolen during that time period and that painting was taken in a robbery attributed to *La Mano Nera*."

"Someone got to that one first," she murmured. "I wonder how."

"I don't know, but we'll continue to investigate," Lavezzo said. "That's enough for tonight. The three of you are free to go. Thank you for helping us resolve this case."

"Your vehicles are downstairs in the lot." The commissario added, putting their keys on the table. Then both men got up and left the room.

"It's over," she said. "It's almost hard to believe."

"You can believe it," Nick said. "Let's get out of here."

It was almost two o'clock in the morning when they got to their cars. The night was still, a brilliant array of stars above them, making her feel like there were brighter days ahead.

"Do you want to follow us to the house, Mom?" she asked.

Her mother hesitated. "No. I'm going to drive back to Florence."

"Now? It's so late," she said, not liking that idea at all.

"I need to get started on my life, Isabella, and being in Rome will bring back memories I don't need in my head right now."

"We're not in Grandfather's house. We're at Anna's house."

"It still feels too much the same. I'm sure some of my mother's furniture is there."

"Then we'll all go to a hotel. You don't want to drive now."

"The weather is beautiful. There won't be any traffic. I'll be home by dawn. And then I can sleep in my place. I'll be fine, Isabella. I can take care of myself, too."

She frowned. "I don't like it."

Her mother smiled. "It's not a bad decision; it's a good one. I'll text you when I get there if you'll have your phone on."

"I will. But I'm not quite ready to say goodbye to you," she admitted.

"Then just say goodnight and come visit me when the time is right." Her mother turned to Nick. "Thank you for saving my daughter."

"You helped, Sylvie," he said. "I couldn't have done it without you."

"I'm sure you could have. You are very resourceful. So is my daughter. Perhaps the two of you should spend some time figuring out what else you have in common."

"Mom," she said warningly.

Her mother laughed. "That's all I'm going to say. Except one more thing. Can I have a hug?"

Isabella wrapped her arms around her mother once more and

they clung together for a long minute. She finally let go and stepped back, watching as her mom got into her car and drove away.

"It feels weird," she told Nick. "I didn't want to see her, and now I don't want her to leave."

"You'll see her again." He wrapped his arms around her. "I've been wanting to do this all night."

"Me, too. But let's do it somewhere else."

"Do you want to go to the house or to a hotel?"

"The house would be easier..."

"But?" he questioned.

"A hotel sounds nice, too. Maybe a room with a king bed and a big jacuzzi tub."

"They're not so common in Rome."

"True. But as my mother said, you're very resourceful, so let's see what you've got."

CHAPTER TWENTY-NINE

They checked into a luxury hotel in Trevi where, thanks to Nick's resourcefulness, they had a king room with a beautiful spa tub in the bathroom, big enough for two.

"This is beautiful," she said, walking to the window to look out over the city.

"So, bath or bed?" Nick asked, coming up behind her.

He slid his arms around her waist, and she leaned back against his chest, feeling like she didn't want to choose either, because she didn't want to move away from Nick. "I like this," she murmured.

"Me, too," he said, his breath warming her cheek.

She turned in his embrace because she suddenly wanted more. "I think we should go to bed. And then later, we'll take a bath—together. What do you think?"

"Your wish is my command."

She laughed. "How long is that going to last?"

"As long as we both want the same thing."

She'd given him a teasing question, and he'd given her a teasing answer, but it made her wonder how long they would want the same thing. Was this sizzling heat between them temporary, just part of the crazy experience they'd lived through?

"Isabella, you're getting too serious," he warned.

She agreed, but she wouldn't tell him that. "I am getting serious." She reached for the hem of his shirt. "Serious about getting you out of these clothes."

He stripped off his shirt at her words, and she ran her hands down his taut, muscled chest with a sigh of pleasure. But he didn't give her time to savor that feeling. Instead, he impatiently helped her off her with her sweater. And then his mouth came down on hers, and every other thought fled from her mind.

She didn't want to think anymore. She just wanted to taste and touch and be with this incredible man for as long as she could. They kissed their way to the bed, taking off the rest of their clothes on the way.

Nick paused long enough to grab a condom out of his backpack before they tumbled down on the soft, luxurious mattress.

And then it was just the two of them, nothing in between, no clothes, no questions, no doubts—just absolute certainty that they were exactly where they wanted to be.

———

Nick was shocked to see it was almost noon on Wednesday when he opened his eyes. The sun was streaming through the windows, casting a warm glow over the beautiful woman lying next to him. Isabella was sprawled on her stomach, her dark hair falling halfway down her back, her skin tan and smooth, just a few sexy freckles on her shoulders that he immediately wanted to kiss again. His body hardened. He couldn't get enough of this woman. They'd made love twice before the sun came up and then had finally fallen asleep close to dawn.

He should let her sleep. She'd been through a terrifying ordeal, and that reminder turned his thoughts dark as he thought about how close he'd come to losing her.

Stefano could have shot her while he was unconscious or before he'd gotten upstairs. Matthew Pierre could have killed her before he'd gotten a clean shot on him. So many things could have gone wrong, and it would have been his fault.

He'd promised her mother he'd protect her. He'd promised himself he would do the same thing. But he'd almost lost her, and that was hard to live with.

She would hate the idea of him taking responsibility for her, but he couldn't help it. He cared about her, more than he would have ever imagined. She suddenly stretched like a beautiful cat. Then she opened her eyes, giving him such a radiant smile that his heart flipped over in his chest.

"What are you doing?" she asked drowsily.

"Watching you sleep."

"Was I snoring?"

He grinned. "Not that I heard, but I was out until just a few minutes ago."

"Me, too. That's the best sleep I've had since I arrived in Rome."

"I would agree. Are you hungry?"

"Maybe," she said as she turned onto her side, pulling up the sheet to cover her sweet breasts. She gave him a shy smile. "You're staring again."

"It's your fault. You look too damn good."

"So do you." She paused. "How are you feeling this morning, Nick?"

"Do you need to ask after the night we had?"

"Well, I wasn't asking about that," she said pointedly. "I saw your face last night when the commissario confirmed that Stefano had taken over the investigation into your grandfather's car crash, and it was likely he had something to do with it."

"I knew that was coming. As soon as Victoria told me my grandfather had been at the school asking questions, I was certain his crash was not an accident."

"But it was Stefano, someone who knew your grandfather, who had been mentored by him. It was a horrible betrayal."

"Stefano was an evil person. We saw that last night. He could kill with no remorse."

Her lips tightened with that reminder. "Thank God my mother didn't stay with him when she was young. She probably would have had an even worse life. But she knew deep down that he wasn't right for her. She told me when we were in the cell together that she'd always had a feeling that Stefano could go too far with drinking and getting into fights. That made her nervous. But she never thought he would turn out to be a killer."

"He obviously fooled an entire police department for years, maybe even my grandfather."

"Or not your grandfather. Stefano told you that your grandfather came to see him, but maybe it wasn't just to ask questions. Maybe Marcus confronted Stefano about his father, about his own criminality. If Stefano survives as expected, you could ask him."

"I could, but no answer will change what happened. I just have to make peace with it." He gave her a smile. "And you don't have to work so hard to cheer me up."

"I feel bad for you, Nick. I want to make it better."

"You already did that."

She flushed. "I'm not talking about physically."

He could see how much she wanted him to be okay, and he felt a little humbled by that desire. "I'm okay. It was a shock to hear the actual truth, and I know it will be difficult to share that truth with my grandmother."

"Do you have to?"

"She has a right to know how her husband died."

"True. It will be upsetting to your grandmother and to mine. She'll be shocked that Stefano tried to kill us. I think she thought of him as a son."

"We'll help them get through it, and they will. I have a feeling our grandmothers are the reason we're both so strong. We get it from them."

A smile lifted her lips. "Maybe so. We should call them."

"It's still early there. We'll do it tonight."

"We should also try to put their house back together, maybe get a new front door. Oh, and there's your grandmother's car. We need to replace that."

"We'll do all that, but I'm hoping they'll stay in LA for another week."

"Why?" she asked curiously.

"Because I think we should take the vacation we were both ordered to take."

"A vacation, huh? I'm not very good at doing nothing."

"Neither am I. Maybe we'll be better if we do nothing together," he suggested.

"That is an interesting idea. What would we do?"

"Whatever we want. Let's start with this." He gave her a long kiss.

"And then what?" she asked breathlessly as he lifted his head.

He slid his hand down her body as he kissed her again, and the sigh she let out was all the encouragement he needed.

———

After a relaxing day in bed enjoying each other, they had more fun in the spa tub. Then they ordered ridiculously expensive room service and finally got dressed around six p.m. and went home. While Nick had reserved another night at the hotel if they wanted it, Isabella thought they should check on the house before they called their grandmothers. She was a little sorry to leave the hotel, but Nick was determined to spend the rest of the week vacationing, so she was eager to see what would come next.

It felt like a hundred years had passed since they'd been in the house, but everything was as they'd left it. It was too late to worry about the door now, so they set up Nick's computer on the kitchen table and called Anna on video chat.

But it wasn't Anna who answered the call. It was a good-looking blond guy.

"Ciao," he said.

"Flynn," Nick said with a smile. "This is Isabella."

"I was hoping I'd get to meet you, Isabella," Flynn said.

"Likewise. Thanks for your help. The information you gave us on Juliette Sabatini came in handy."

"Happy to hear that. I got your text, Nick. Now that everything is resolved, I hope you'll take that vacation I suggested."

"Actually, I'm going to do just that," Nick said.

"Good. I've got your grandmothers here, and they're all set up to chat. I have to warn you, though, that you might see some new pictures in the background. They've been doing some decorating."

"Great," he muttered.

Isabella laughed at his expression. "It sounds like your apartment needed some décor."

"It did," Anna said as her face popped up behind Flynn. "Oh, my, I can see you so well, Nick."

Nick laughed. "You look good, Nonna."

"Flynn has been taking great care of us, and Andi, too. She's a sweetheart. We also met Beck and Caitlyn." She paused, turning to Gloria, who was crowding in behind her. "Who else, Gloria?"

"Damon and Sophie, and their beautiful little girls," Gloria replied.

"Sounds like you two have been partying," Nick teased.

"They have," Flynn said. "I'm going to let you all talk."

As Flynn disappeared from the frame, their grandmothers sat down in front of the screen, and Isabella was happy to see them looking so well. "It's good to see you, Grandma."

"You both look wonderful," her grandmother replied. "Flynn told us some of what happened. I'm sure he didn't give us the entire story, but he said you found the paintings, and we're not in danger."

"And I don't have to feel guilty anymore about losing Tomas's painting," Anna added.

She suddenly realized that their grandmothers weren't talking about the valuable stolen paintings they'd discovered at the school, but the ones by Tomas and Lucinda, and she didn't know where those were.

Nick's hand came down on her thigh, giving it a squeeze. He didn't want her to say anything, and she wasn't going to. Maybe Captain Lavezzo would find those paintings and get them back. They were probably in Stefano's or Matthew's possession.

"How are you enjoying LA?" Nick asked.

"We've had so much fun," Anna replied. "Your team has been so sweet to us. They've taken us sightseeing, made sure we had food, and even took us shopping. We found some great things for your apartment, Nick."

"I appreciate that, Nonna. I think you and Gloria should stay a few more days."

"Really? Are you and Isabella heading back here soon?"

"Actually, Isabella and I are going to spend a few more days here in Italy, maybe take a drive through Tuscany."

Their grandmothers exchanged a quick look and then tried to pretend they didn't care at all.

"Well, that sounds nice," her grandmother said. "I guess you two are getting along."

"We need a few more days to see just how well we're getting along," she interjected.

"Then maybe we'll stay here a while longer," Gloria said.

"Oh, wait," Anna interrupted. "I have to go to your father's vow renewal ceremony on Sunday, Nick. I'll have to come back by Friday."

"Why don't you skip it, Nonna?"

Doubt ran through her eyes. "I can't do that. Your father would be so disappointed if I didn't show up. I don't think anyone else from the family will be coming. I have to represent."

She waited to see how Nick would respond to that.

He hesitated and then said, "I'll go. I'll represent the family, Nonna."

Anna appeared shocked by his answer, and Isabella was surprised, too.

"Well, all right then," Anna said. "I guess we'll stay longer. Flynn is going to take us to his wife's restaurant tonight. We can't wait."

"And Andi told us there's an art show going on in Laguna Beach she would take us to on Friday if we're still here," her grandmother said.

"It sounds like you'll be busy," she said, pleased that they were enjoying a vacation, too.

"Do you want to tell us more about what happened?" her grandmother asked.

"Well, one thing that happened is that I saw Mom, and I'm going to visit her again in a few days," she said.

Gloria put a hand to her heart. "That is the best news."

She wanted to leave them with only good news. The rest they could dribble out in small pieces. Since they weren't asking a lot of questions, she had a feeling they were okay with not knowing everything.

"We should go," she said. "We love you both."

"And we love you," they chorused together.

They said goodbye, and then Nick ended the chat.

She turned to him. "We forgot to ask Captain Lavezzo where Tomas and Lucinda's paintings are."

"I realized that when they were talking. I'll send him a text."

"I was thinking about the fifth painting, the one that was missing from the school wall, the one that Victoria and Louisa were sure was there a few days ago."

He met her gaze. "What about it?"

"Do you think Sam might have stolen it?"

"It crossed my mind," he admitted.

"But why would he steal just one?" she asked.

"He helped us to a point, but then he took advantage of the

situation. He's a thief. He always has been, always will be. Do you want to say something to someone about Sam?"

She shook her head. "No. Flynn is your boss and your friend, and he's been incredibly kind to our grandmothers. I wouldn't want to cause him trouble. And to his credit, Sam did help us." She paused. "I am surprised we never heard from Francesca again. That was odd, wasn't it?"

"I forgot about her. There was a lot happening fast. I don't think she was involved in any of this, but if she was, Lavezzo will figure it out."

"You have a lot more faith in him now."

"I do."

"Maybe he can also check in on that guy Joelle is seeing, Colin Devonshire. He works for Dario, and while it doesn't appear that Dario was part of this, we should make sure there aren't any red flags Joelle should know about."

"I have a feeling Joelle blows by any red flags," he said with a laugh.

"True. But I can still throw one, and I want to, because she's my family."

"You're getting more family by the minute."

"I know, and I kind of love it. So, our grandmothers are pretty happy we're going to spend time together. They think their plan worked."

He grinned. "I know. We can let them have that."

"I agree." She gave him a speculative look. "Did you just decide two seconds ago that you were going to your parents' vow renewal?"

"Actually, I started thinking about it when I watched you and your mom reconnecting. You were both trying to accept each other as you are, and I thought maybe I should stop acting like my parents don't exist and support their choice to renew their vows."

"That sounds very adult."

"It's about time, right?" he said with a grin. "Any chance

you'd go with me? There will be great food and drinks. I can't promise anything else."

"I don't need anything else."

That wasn't actually true, because she did need him, but she wasn't quite ready to say that.

———

Four days later, in a beautiful hotel in Milan, Nick put on the suit and tie he'd bought for the charity event almost a week ago. Isabella had opted to purchase a new dress, one that wouldn't remind her of murder, and was wearing a beautiful dark-red gown that set off her hair and her eyes and made him catch his breath every time he saw her.

They'd had an incredible week together. They'd driven through Tuscany, gone wine tasting, and had ridden bikes through the countryside. They'd had the picnic he'd promised her, with local wine and savory cheeses. Then they'd stopped in Florence to spend a day with her mother. They'd gone to the gallery where she worked and watched her paint on her patio with so much joy on her face that it had made Isabella cry.

After the Florence stop, they'd gone out to the coast, to the Cinque Terra and hiked along the water, explored the five villages, eaten more pasta and gelato than he had in years, laughed until their sides hurt, talked until they were hoarse, and made love as often as possible.

They'd checked in a few times with Captain Lavezzo, who had finally located their family paintings and would keep them safe until they returned to pick them up. So, they'd accomplished what they'd initially set out to do, and hopefully their grandmothers would be happy to end this chapter of their lives.

They just had one more thing to do before they went back to LA.

"Are you ready?" Isabella asked as she walked over to him and gave his tie a tweak. "That's better. It was slightly crooked."

"I'm glad you fixed it. My father probably would have noticed and been horrified. As a conductor, he likes to orchestrate everything around him."

"I can't wait to meet your parents. Have you told them we're here?"

"No. I haven't spoken to them, but I did officially RSVP, so I'm sure they're aware I'm coming."

"Did you say who you were bringing?"

"I did not." He smiled at the look of concern in her eyes. "Don't worry, Isabella. There won't be any drama. We'll probably be lucky if they even acknowledge we're there. Actually, we might be luckier if they don't. Then we can just enjoy the party."

"You want to talk to them. That's why we're here."

"Honestly, I'm not sure why we're here."

"Because you want to try. So, let's go try."

He let out a breath and followed her out of the room. When they got down to the patio of the hotel, most of the seats were already taken, so they headed for a row in the back. But then his father's long-time assistant, Jeff Gordon, spotted them and came over.

"Good to see you, Nick," he said. "There are seats for you in the front row."

"Really?" he asked, not super thrilled about that.

"Come with me."

"Go," Isabella urged, giving him a little push in the back.

They followed Jeff to the front row and sat down. He saw his mother's sister and two daughters in the front row on the other side. His aunt gave him a small wave, which he acknowledged with a tip of his head.

"Who are they?" Isabella asked.

"Aunt and cousins on my mother's side. I've probably seen them five times in my life." He paused as his father walked up to the front wearing a black tuxedo.

"He looks a lot like you," Isabella murmured.

He supposed they looked somewhat alike, both tall, with

dark hair and eyes, although his father's hair now showed signs of silver at his temples. His expression was cool and sophisticated, a little intimidating, but that's who he'd always been.

A moment later, the music started, and his mother came down the aisle in a cream-colored silk dress. She looked pretty, with her light-brown hair streaked with blonde highlights. She saw him and paused by his chair. She seemed to be waiting for something.

Isabella nudged him, and he hurriedly got to his feet, not sure what he should do. But looking into his mother's eyes, he realized what she wanted.

He gave her his arm and walked her up to his father. She smiled and gave him a kiss on the cheek as she let go of his arm. His father extended his hand, and he shook it. It was a shocking feeling to stand with them at their vow renewal, to feel a part of it. It hit him harder than he'd expected.

As they turned to face each other, he moved back and sat down.

Isabella took his hand, and he felt like everything in his life had suddenly shifted into the right place. He barely heard their vows. He was caught up in memories of their life together. There had been happy times. A lot of bad, too, but maybe he just hadn't wanted to remember the good, because he'd always been on the outside looking in. But today, they'd made a point of making him a part of it. He had no idea why, but he was happy about it.

When the brief service ended, his parents ran down the aisle like a couple of giddy teenagers as their friends surrounded them with hugs and congratulations.

He and Isabella stood up, watching the crowd make their way into the reception area.

Then he turned to her and said, "Thanks for coming with me."

"Thanks for inviting me. That was sweet what you did, giving your mom to your dad."

"I wasn't sure what I was supposed to do, but it felt right."

"And good?" she queried.

"Better than I thought it would. I know there won't be a magic fix to our relationship. I'm not expecting that. But maybe I don't have to be so angry about it."

"I came to the same conclusion, and I'm happier for it. I think you will be, too." She paused. "So, our vacation is almost over. I had the best time, Nick. It was...I don't even have words," she said, blinking back a tear. "And I swear I am not going to cry. It must be my allergies or something."

"Something like...love?" he asked, daring to finally say the word.

She sucked in a breath as she stared back at him. "Are we going there?"

"I think I already went. Tell me I'm not alone."

"You're not alone."

"So, maybe the vacation ends, but we don't," he said. "We do live in the same city, after all."

"That is convenient," she said with a happy smile. "Do you think our love will cross borders?"

"I think it's going to last forever and that kind of scares the hell out of me."

She laughed. "We really are a lot alike. Every time you kiss me, I want more. And every time you touch me, I want more. And every time you talk to me, I want more. And that's terrifying."

"That's also a lot of *more*."

"Is it too much?" A worried look entered her beautiful eyes.

"It's perfect, because I want more, too. And when we get back, I'm going to tell Flynn that I'm done with undercover work, unless it's a very short assignment. I want to prioritize our relationship."

"I don't want to hold you back. But I must admit it's nice to hear you say you want to make me a priority."

"I do. And you're not holding me back. You're pushing me forward. I wouldn't be here without you, Isabella."

"And I wouldn't have reconnected with my mom without you. We're good for each other, Nick."

"We are." He gave her a tender, loving kiss, only to be interrupted by the sound of someone clearing their throat.

He lifted his head to see his parents giving him an inquiring look. For the first time, he felt like they were the ones on the outside looking in. But he didn't care who was in or who was out as long as he had Isabella by his side.

"Mom, Dad...This is Isabella." He looked at Isabella's flushed cheeks and bright eyes and added with a loving smile, "The woman I love."

WHAT TO READ NEXT...

Want more thrilling romantic suspense?

Don't miss LETHAL GAME, the next book in the OFF THE
GRID: FBI Series.

Have you missed any of the books in this series?

OFF THE GRID: FBI SERIES
PERILOUS TRUST
RECKLESS WHISPER
DESPERATE PLAY
ELUSIVE PROMISE
DANGEROUS CHOICE
RUTHLESS CROSS
CRITICAL DOUBT
FEARLESS PURSUIT
DARING DECEPTION
RISKY BARGAIN
PERFECT TARGET
FATAL BETRAYAL
DEADLY TRAP
LETHAL TRAP

ABOUT THE AUTHOR

Barbara Freethy is a #1 New York Times Bestselling Author of 85 novels ranging from mystery thrillers to romantic suspense, contemporary romance, and women's fiction. With over 15 million copies sold, twenty-eight of Barbara's books have appeared on the New York Times and USA Today Bestseller Lists.

Barbara is known for her twisty thrillers and emotionally riveting romance where ordinary people end up having extraordinary adventures.

For further information, visit www.barbarafreethy.com

Made in United States
Orlando, FL
02 March 2024

44304589R00203